11th of Av

David R. Semmel

To my mother, Sally Dorothy (as in "Solidarity") Semmel and her parents from Przemyśl, Fannie (Metzger) and Emanuel Silberman.

Przemyśl

Pronounced "p-shem-ish-ul" in Polish

An ancient town straddling the San River, nestled in the Carpathian foothills of south-eastern Poland. On the eve of The Great War, a total of fifty-thousand Jews, Poles, and Ruthians (Ukrainians) lived there joined by at least eighty-thousand Austro-Hungarian Soldiers manning the forty-three forts that formed the perimeter of Fort Przemyśl, the largest citadel in the East.

Ukrainian:	Перемишль Peremyshl
German:	Prömsel
Yiddish:	פשעמישל Pshemishl
Russian:	Peremishl

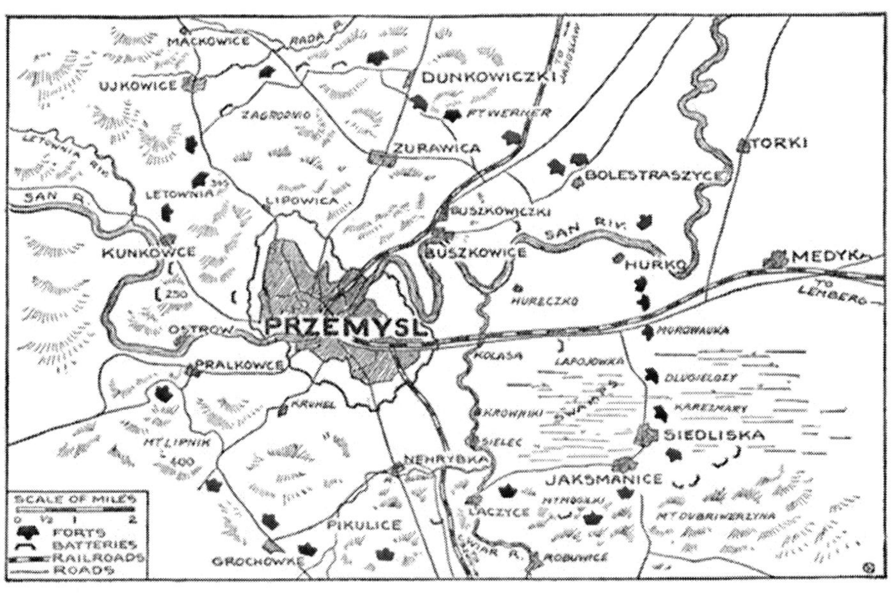

Berlin
Lodz
Germany
Prague
Munich
Vienna
Gyor
Budapest
Alps
Graz
Kobarid
Milan
Austria
Italy
Venice
Trieste
Apennine Mountains
Sarajevo
Eastern Europe - 1914

Warsaw
Russia
Nowy Korczyn
Kiev
Lemberg/Lvov
Cracow
Przemyśl
Sanok
Hungary
Odessa
Carpathian Mountains
Belgrade
Bucharest
Roumania
Bulgaria
Sophia
Servia
Balkan Mountains
Map created by
Martin Bordovsky

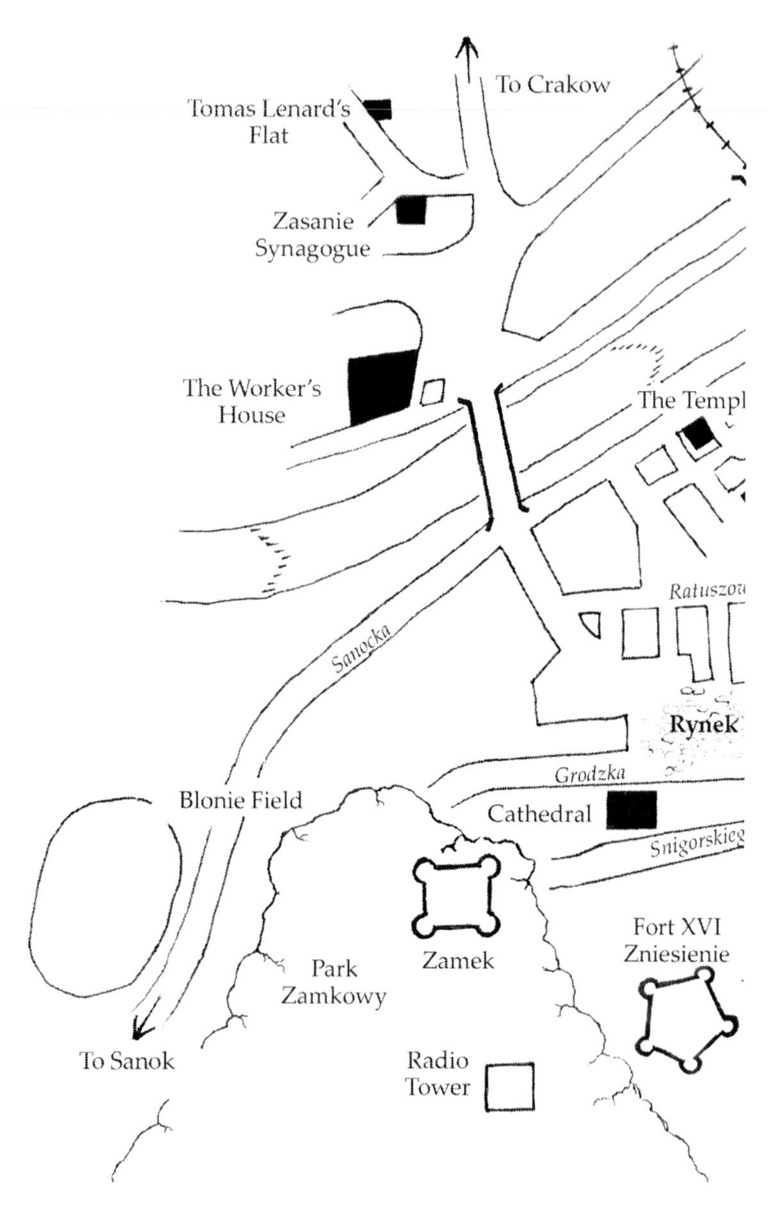
To Crakow
Tomas Lenard's
Flat
Zasanie
Synagogue
The Worker's
House
The Templ
Ratuszow
Sanocka
Rynek
Grodzka
Blonie Field
Cathedral
Snigorskieg
Fort XVI
Zniesienie
Zamek
Park
Zamkowy
To Sanok
Radio
Tower

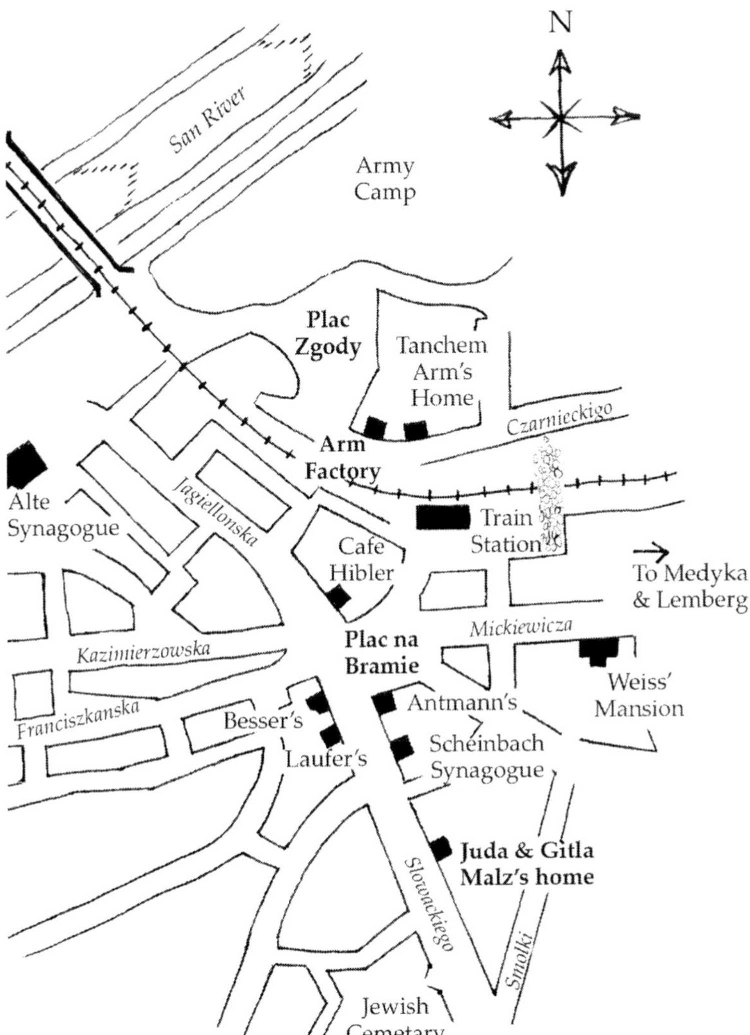

Elia's Przemyśl c. 1914

One

Przemyśl • 18th of Cheshvan, 5673 – Tuesday, October 29, 1912

A SPOTTED EAGLE kept watch over the reed beds that lined the Zasanie shoreline from its five-story perch atop the Worker's House, while across the river in Przemyśl proper vendors roasted nuts and arranged fall flowers to be sold from a fleet of pushcarts. As a cold wind blew in over the Carpathians, pedestrians clad in dark overcoats or military tunics scurried about town like ants, seemingly oblivious to the ancient fault lines of language, culture, and religion that cleaved the city into Jewish, Catholic, and Orthodox fragments.

Elia Reifer lived with his aunt and uncle, Gitla and Juda Malz, on the first-floor of a three story flat halfway up the hill between Plac na Bramie and the Jewish cemetery. The eighteen months of cutting, sanding, and hauling wood added bulk to Elia's physique and maturity to the boy's features. From the waist down, he'd become his father: a stallion's thighs and piano-stool calves. Like most of his fellow woodworkers, his hands, always slightly oversized for his stature, had become rough and strong. His hair was dark and thick, brushed back and piled high, revealing a long forehead that accentuated his deep-set hazel eyes centered on an oval face. Stubble and scabs peppered his cheek and chin after Juda introduced him to the straight razor and the styptic pencil.

A year and a half earlier Gitla and Juda had travelled to the nearby village of Medyka to bury Elia's mother, taken quickly from her prime to the grave by a fever. As *the* Jewish midwife in Przemyśl, Gitla welcomed countless babies into this world and eased more than her share of hemorrhaging mothers and choleric fathers into the next. Death was no stranger to her; she loathed but grudgingly accepted it. A month later, still mourning the death of her sister, a telegraph boy had again delivered bad news: disease had taken her brother-in-law. Contemplating the fate of Jette and Elia, her newly orphaned niece and nephew, Gitla sobbed openly, which she almost never did.

Once again, Juda had manned the cart's reigns, swerving around Hussar formations, trying to avoid pedestrians milling about the shops and cafés that lined the grand boulevard heading east. From the edge of town, where the cobblestones gave way to frozen, deeply-rutted dirt, they rode in silence, passing stand after stand of marsh marigolds budding in the drainage culvert by the side of the road, their somber quiet interrupted only by the familiar thunder of mortar fire from one of the scores of Austrian forts within earshot of the road.

At the small brick synagogue in Medyka Rabbi Sporn celebrated the life of Izrel Reifer in prayer and song before leading the procession to the cemetery, a modest square of farmland enclosed by a stone knee-wall at the edge of town. Taking her place in the wide arc of friends and family around the hole dug next to her sister's freshly-covered grave, Gitla glared at the Rabbi as he intoned the mourner's Kaddish: *He's read Torah, how dare you try to keep Elia here! He'll work for cousin Tanchem; he'll learn a craft; I'll find him a wife. Here, what? This shtetl be damned. Your black hat be damned. He's coming with us to the city; he's mine now. And Jette, look at her: me at twenty! But she's not me, just an orphan with no prospects. And the crooked foot? What about it? It was not of birth. An accident—a cart; it means nothing. Nothing! So, mister Rabbi, you match her with your nephew, the merchant junkman, like the farmer breeds a cow. He's got money, a lot I hear, and no wife. Oh, Jette, I tried, but what could I do? I am so sorry...*

Soon thereafter, Elia was in the back of Juda's cart on the road to Przemyśl. Jette had been placed in the temporary care of Rabbi Sporn.

The Malz's apartment was a typical merchant-class Jewish-quarter dwelling. The sooty façade was poured cement over brick and featured a private front entrance to the family home as well as a shared side door leading to first and second floor rental apartments. The interior was modest but well appointed with rugs from the Caucusus covering the floors, and Polish and Jewish folk art hanging on the walls. The sitting and dining room, once a flower shop, was unusually large but lacked natural light as the storefront's window had long since been boarded over and now functioned, on the street side, as a hanging spot for posters and notices. Straight back, just past the door to the root cellar, was the kitchen, flanked on one side by Gitla and Juda's bedroom and on the other by a large storage closet, now Elia's room. A door led out of the kitchen to the stable on the alley.

Six days a week, as rooster crows echoed off the city's masonry facades and medieval ramparts, Elia Reifer washed, dressed, ate breakfast, brushed his hair, and bolted out the door for work.

"WHICH ONE?" ELIA pondered as he walked briskly down Słowackiego past the Scheinbach Synagogue. At first he had guilty pangs every time he passed it by, half expecting Rabbi Sporn to drag him inside by his ear to study. But memories of the little brick building in Medyka quickly faded, replaced by the furniture factory as the center of his universe.

Three doors down from the synagogue was the Zemel grocery, and across the street, Besser's bakery, where a packed lunch—an apple, a hard roll, and some sausage—could be bought for a few Heller. As interested in as food as he was, it paled in importance to the young ladies working the counters of the two stores. A second glance from either would send him off with a smile; a "hello" was enough to keep it there for the entire day.

Eliza Zemel was a quiet, fair-skinned beauty with reddish hair and freckles. She was always impeccably dressed, usually sporting a tight vest that accentuated her ample cleavage, a feature Elia had committed to memory with great fidelity. Unquestionably beautiful and obviously unspoken for, it disappointed Elia that their conversations rarely wandered off the transaction at hand, try as he might to engage her.

Then there was the baker's assistant, Rivka Arm, who was also his boss's daughter, and some kind of cousin. While lacking Eliza's classical European beauty, her wide-set almond eyes, aquiline nose, and sepia skin gave Rivka a regal, exotic, almost biblical air; a Yemenite princess in Elia's mind. Add to that a razor-sharp tongue and the mystery of her many moods and Elia was smitten. She always had something interesting to say, and it was never about bread. Day after day, Elia would watch as Rivka's expression changed from smile to frown, without a clue as to why. Even so, when he thought about her, he couldn't help but to think about the buttery-sweet aroma of the bakery, the flecks of flour in her raven hair, and the way she seemed to linger a moment too long when they looked at each other.

Lunch secured, Elia dashed by Antmann's Café and

across the always-busy Plac na Bramie, past the Grand Café Hibler, slowing to a trot to avoid the army officers and well-heeled businessmen who congregated each morning at its entrance. Five buildings later, with the serrated roofline of the Old Synagogue visible on the near horizon, he turned sharply, skipping over the railroad tracks just as they split to enter the station. Crossing the road brought him to the four removable swing-doors in front of Tanchem Arm's furniture factory at number 25 Czarnieckiego.

Medyka • 18th of Adar, 5673 – Tuesday, February 25, 1913

IN THE BRIEF moments when she was able to sleep, Jette never lived the awful month that had shattered her life. In those blissful moments of forgetfulness she slept again in a room with Elia in the house across from the synagogue with her parents. She dreamt of kneading bread in the kitchen, her senses infused with the savory smell of her mama's barley and *schmaltz* boiling furiously on the stove. There was just her family. There never was that fetid stench of cholera death, and most of all, she was never forced to become the wife of Jacob the junkman.

"Woman! Now!"

Jette sat up in bed, pulled rudely back to reality by the sound of fists pounding on the front door. She climbed off the bed, knotting the tie of her robe. As she made for the door, a slurred, slightly flat folk song serenaded her from the door stoop. Jette tried not to listen, focusing instead on how the creaking floorboards recalled her grandmother's warning of the slow and painful death that would certainly follow from walking around the house barefooted.

I gave away my youngest daughter tonight. Tonight you are the queen and I the king. Indeed I myself have seen with my own eyes—

Jette slid the barrel bolt and opened the door just as Jacob delivered the crescendo.

How God has favored me!

Jacob playfully lunged for her. She sidestepped him, slamming the door.

The smile drained from his face. "Would it kill you to welcome me into your bed with enthusiasm on just one Shabbos?"

Jacob was tall and gaunt with a thin, deeply lined face and a scraggly beard flecked with grey. His eyes were shallow-set and bloodshot, and looked like they could fall out of his skull at any moment.

"You're drunk," Jette mumbled, crossing the anteroom on her way to the bedroom.

"It is your duty to please me!" he grunted, making for the kitchen.

Back in bed, Jette closed her eyes, focusing hard on deciphering the curious collection of sounds that came from the kitchen almost every time Jacob came home from a trip.

"Wife!"

She sat up in the bed. Cane sandwiched in his armpit, Jacob was propped up in the doorway, a half-empty bottle in one hand and a skillet in the other.

"But my lamb, I brought you a gift."

Jette stood-up as he approached. "I'm sick. Leave me in peace to sleep," she said, adding as tenderly as she could, "Please?"

The skillet dropped to the floor, barely missing her toes.

"Husband, with a night's rest, I will be in full health and able to fulfill my wifely obligations."

Jacob took a swig then shook the bottle it in her face hard enough to spill some liquid. "Drink!" he demanded.

A few drops found her forehead and rolled down the bridge of her nose before finding her mouth. Spitting it out as if it were poison, she seized the bottle, twisting it from his grasp with surprising ease. As Jette cocked her arm, she began to cry.

The bottle hit the doorframe and exploded into a thousand shards that came to rest like snowflakes on a newly frozen pond. Momentarily drawn to the eerie dance of lamplight reflected off the heavily grained wood, Jette never saw the metal ornament at the head of Jacob's cane as it plowed into her temple. A bolt of lightning arced across her vision like a photographer's powder flash just before her head hit the floor with a hollow thump.

He jumped on her, one hand thrust inside her robe, finding a breast, the other ripping at her nightgown. Jette came to and screamed, hitting him weakly in the side with her fists, trying to bring her knee up toward his groin.

Having ripped her undergarments enough for his needs, Jacob tried to push himself into her with little success. Releasing her breast, he repeatedly backhanded her across the face before gripping to her neck. Desperate as her windpipe closed, Jette signaled submission by reaching between her legs to ease his entry. She tensed as he entered her, and Jacob again went for her throat.

Jette flailed at him until a punch bounced off his shoulder and hit the floor. Only it wasn't the floor, it was metal; the skillet.

He bore down on her, red-rimmed eyes riveted on her spittle and blood-covered face.

Her hand closed tightly around the iron handle. He never saw it coming.

AFTER TYING JACOB to the bed and pulling the larger slivers of glass from her arms and legs, Jette turned her attention to the butcher-block table in the kitchen. Cursory inspection revealed nothing so with great effort she wedged herself between the table and the wall for a closer look at the hidden side. The door was barely noticeable, even with a lamp on it.

A firm tug on the wad of lightly oiled rags stuffed into the opening had several shiny metal disks jumping free. Jette pegged them as Wilhelms—German 20 Mark gold coins—before the first one hit the floor.

Handfuls of gold and silver coins and a large roll of what everyone called green ladies—Austrian 100 Kronen notes—tied neatly with a length of brown ribbon followed. All in all, an unimaginable fortune.

Exhausted, Jette collapsed in tears into a chair at the kitchen table. After a good cry, she wiped her eyes dry. "No more crying." She picked up a gold coin. "Not now, not ever."

Jette went to her sewing box for a needle and carpet thread then to the closet for her winter wrap. After ripping open the bottom hem of the cape, she wrapped notes around each coin and stitched them into the lining.

Jacob's cane in hand, treasure-cape over her shoulders, Jette Reifer left home through the back door and limped to the east. By the time the morning's first light painted the wisps of clouds on the horizon in shades of pink and crimson, she had put Medyka forever behind her.

Przemyśl • 30th of Sa'vat, 5674 – Thursday, February 26, 1914

AFTER THE BELL in the tower finished ringing, Tanchem Arm addressed his employees. "Two finished armoires," he barked to the bored stares of his eleven men, "If Mister Meyer Weiss wants two armoires by sundown Friday, then there'll be hell to pay if we don't deliver him two armoires by sundown Friday." He removed his top hat. "Push back the Army order if you have to; I make nothing from the bastards."

Clad in a fine, full-length wool coat over a silk vest and

a floral ascot, Tanchem Arm was often overdressed, and today was no exception. His hair, expertly cut and oiled, and increasingly gray about the temples, stood in contrast to his mustache, which retained all of the rich, ebony hues of his youth.

"Don't worry, we can handle both," Izac, Tanchem's son and shop foreman, said. "One armoire's already with Zsiga, fully sanded, just a couple of coats from finished. Manes is pegging the other one this morning. Everything's already been cut and grooved." Izac turned to his fellow workers, each dressed in collarless, sweat-soaked white shirts, rough, turpentine-stained leather aprons, and brown trousers. "Any problem with delivery?" he asked, rolling his eyes.

"Not problem," Zsiga, the shop's head finisher said through a heavy Hungarian accent, smoke from his cigarette spiraling up from the corners of his mouth.

"No problem, boss, we'll work like dogs," Manes said, arms folded and sleeves rolled to the elbows. Tall and impressively muscled with a wide, chiseled face, straw-colored hair, and steely, blue-gray eyes, Manes could have easily passed for a newly commissioned lieutenant fresh out of the Austrian War College, were it not for his workingman's clothes.

"Weevils," Tanchem growled. "When I was twenty I could've done a chest by myself in time for afternoon prayers."

"Really?" Manes retorted. "I guess that means that when you were Elia's age you could have finished the whole run by lunch?"

Tanchem used the cover of laughter to leave via the front door. Cigarettes extinguished, the men headed for the wood.

"HOLD IT HERE while I drive the peg." It took all of Elia's might to hold the two planks of wood steady at a right angle. Working like a surgical nurse, he followed Manes around the work table, supplying his mentor with whatever he demanded as they secured the second and third corners of what would become the base of the last armoire. At the fourth corner, Manes stepped back. "Your turn."

Assuming grips on the relevant wood pieces, Elia issued his first workshop order, "Mallet!"

No movement.

"Manes, mallet."

Silence.

"Please?"

Still nothing.

He released his grip and the planks fell out of true. "What?"

Manes grinned. "Time for the real lesson." He put his hand on Elia's shoulder, "Elia, you're a thinking man. So think."

"Think what?"

"Think about who is really building this armoire." Manes brushed sawdust off his forearm. "You or the mallet?"

"Me?"

"Yes; tools don't create, people create."

"All right."

"No, not all right." Manes picked up the mallet and handed it at Elia. "He who owns the mallet controls the production, not the one with the skill and know-how. If I want to produce goods with my worthless life, I must sell my labor to an owner of the mallet at the price he wants to pay."

Elia was drawn back to the years he'd spent dissecting Torah with Rabbi Sporn back in Medyka. "But isn't that just what work is, Manes?"

"No. I become the hammer-owner's slave."

"But he pays us. Slaves are not paid."

"Elia! Wake up! All of us here are just whores to the capitalists."

"Oh, come on. He's not that bad."

"Yes, Tanchem is a good man with a good soul. But make no mistake, when a slave is given food or even money for his toils, even by a loving master, he's still a slave."

Elia shrugged. "But it makes no sense for each of us here to own a mallet when but two or three will suffice for the entire factory."

"Why must any one man," Manes emphasized the count by raising his finger, "own anything? What if all we owned were our hands, our legs and our minds? Then imagine that not only the mallets, but all the tools, the saws, the planes, even the mills and the varnish factory belonged to no one person but to every man." Manes set the mallet on the workbench. "Think, Elia. Think it through. Socialism is not afraid of intelligent scrutiny. It's a science, the science of rebuilding a just society for each and every person on earth."

"That's a lot to ponder."

"Come to our meeting."

"I don't think I know, well..."

"If not tomorrow, then perhaps later. We meet every other Thursday at the Worker's House."

Manes reached into his leather satchel and pulled out a thin, well-worn, black leather-bound book with a red ribbon page marker and a small metal clasp keeping the covers held securely shut. "Take this and read it, then come when you're ready."

"Now take the mallet," Manes said as he gripped the planks, tying up both of his hands, forcing Elia to reach across the workbench for the tool. "And as you drive the pegs, imagine a world where a tool is just an inanimate object owned by all and owned by none. Envision that we, the workers, are the masters of production."

That night, Elia read *The Manifesto of the Communist Party* from cover to cover.

After breakfast the next morning Gitla dropped a postcard onto the table, "It's Jette. She's in New York."

An electric current bolted up Elia's spine.

"How, she doesn't say."

Przemyśl • 1st of Adar, 5674 – Friday, February 27, 1914

AS HE WAITED for a General Staff car to pass before crossing the cobbled street, Tanchem could see him drinking coffee at a table in the window, his balding head just below the lettering that read Grand Café Hibler.

"Meyer," Tanchem said warmly, shaking his hand. "Don't get up." He hung his coat on the hook attached to the booth and sat. "So how is your little girl?"

"All I work for since Esther's passing," Meyer said. Revered as the richest Jew between Lemberg and Cracow, his receding hairline revealed a skull with throbbing varicose veins that most people assumed pulsed in proportion to the sheer genius of the ideas emanating from his brain.

Tanchem shook his head. "It's gypsies that bring the typhus. Bastards."

"More likely it's the army. In any case, it was God's will."

"Amen."

The waiter approached, tipping his head slightly. "Herr Weiss?" Meyer gestured toward his guest.

The waiter turned to Tanchem, "Sir?"

"Tea."

The waiter scurried away.

"Business?" Meyer asked.

"We get by. I've managed to secure some small government orders. Cheap stuff. The men hate it, but it pays the bills. The crew is a pain in my behind, as usual."

"I can only imagine."

"I have Karl Marx, Theo Herzl, and the King of Hungry cutting wood for me."

Meyer laughed. "You keep famous company. Be careful what you complain about."

"Your orders help, my friend." Tanchem squeezed Meyer's shoulder affectionately.

The waiter delivered a cup, a sugar bowl, silverware and a teapot. He poured a cup of steaming black tea and was off. Tanchem spooned sugar into his cup and stirred.

"And by you?"

"Never better. The army brings the soldiers who spend money with the merchant so the tax collector can take it back and give it to the Duke who can pay his army. One giant circle of profit." Meyer paused to finish his coffee. "I'm worried though."

"Here?"

"Yes, here."

"Why?"

"Because we live in the most densely defended stretches of land in all the Empire, that's why. Right in the center of a vast array of fortifications, each a unique, barbed-wire, concrete, and earthworks masterpiece of Austrian military engineering."

"But the Fort protects us," Tanchem said, tracing out imaginary fortifications on the table top around his teacup.

"Does it? Personally, I'd feel safer if we were surrounded only with ploughed rectangles of black dirt and farm buildings."

"How so?"

Meyer leaned in toward Tanchem, "When we were children, if someone said there was a tree you couldn't climb or a chess puzzle you couldn't solve, what's the first thing you'd do?"

Tanchem exhaled then smiled. "I see your point."

"The peace won't last. I'm not sure where or when, but the whole continent's a tinder box, just waiting for a spark. Take a ride around the fort sometime and look at the men. Look closely. You can see it in their faces; everyone's getting ready for war."

"Oy."

"And when there's a massive emplacement, the war's bound to find it."

"Check mate. But for now, business must go on." Meyer

winked.

"Then it's set? We're on?" Tanchem winked back.

Meyer looked across the table, his expression gave away nothing. "Sunday morning. We miss work, Polacks miss Church."

"Seems fair to me," Tanchem shot back, enthusiastically.

"Let's hope that's all that's fair," Meyer said, fighting back a knowing grin. "Styfi's offering three to one straight up. We win draws."

"What about the spread? I know my Hungarian's going to score," Tanchem offered.

Meyer leaned back into his chair, "Tell me again about the wonder-kid."

"My head finisher is from Budapest. Good man. His cousin, just a kid, fifteen I think, is here for a time. But he's not just any boy. He's a magician with the ball, a dead-eye shooter with legs like a racehorse; cannons on both feet. I've never seen anything like him. No one's ever seen anything like him, at least not around here."

Meyer gave a disinterested shrug.

"Everyone else becomes a little girl when he steps on the pitch," Tanchem said, his disappointment at Meyer's lack of enthusiasm obvious.

"I'll come see for myself tonight."

"Meyer, won't the Polacks cry foul? His speech is a dead giveaway. I mean he's not even a Galician."

Meyer snorted. "It's just another pogrom, my friend, this time on a football field. To them, a Jew is a Jew is a Jew. If you're not a Christian you're a foreigner, end of story."

"They could refuse to pay."

"Those idiots wouldn't complain if we fielded the eleven Englishmen from Wolverhampton." After signaling for the bill, Meyer leaned over the table and whispered to Tanchem. "For God's sake keep him hidden. I'll get Styfi to give us three to one on two goals."

"GATHER ROUND BOYS, listen," Tanchem barked to the disorganized group in short blue striped pants and white shirts. "This is Guttmann, from Budapest."

Dismissive grunts came from the back ranks of the assembled squad.

"Hey! He may look like a lad, but trust me." He grabbed Béla around the neck and squeezed. "Tell us about this modern football they play in the big city, like we talked about yesterday."

At the factory, Béla deferred to his elders, rarely joining in the discussions. But on the football pitch, the boy addressed the team as a man; clear and concise, with a measure of confidence born of complete faith in his physical gifts. His entire look changed; his nose became sharper, chin squarer, and ears more pinned back, as if somehow he had streamlined his face for speed. Deep parentheses of flesh bracketed Béla's mouth as he carefully annunciated key terms to the group of woodworkers, bakers, laborers and mill workers in accented but readily understandable Yiddish.

"It's all about space, covering space. Forget about lines: no defense, no midfield and no forward; it leaves too much uncovered. We play as two diamonds." He knelt down and smoothed a square of dirt. "Only two are fixed: the sweeper is the rear point in the back diamond and the striker is the front of the other. Everyone else is free to flow to the action." He drew two boxes with the corners pointing to each goal then added two pebbles between them. "You see? Control the whole field and bring extra troops to bear at the point of attack."

"So—" someone asked, "the opposite sides of the diamonds can be extra mid-fielders, defenders or strikers, all depending on the need of the moment?"

"Exactly. There are no lines of defense. The opposing strikers will forever find themselves—"

"—off sides, controlled by the sweeper, moving up and

back," Béla's teammate said, triumphantly.

"As long as we can get the fucking Polack linesmen to blow his whistle," Tanchem added, bringing snorts of agreement and some choice expletives from the men.

Ninety minutes later, as the last strands of sunlight ducked behind the horizon, the exhausted players, managers and hangers-on followed young Béla Guttmann off the field.

Many muttered in amazement what not one would dare say out loud, "Maybe we really can win."

"ANTMANN'S IS PACKED," Elia remarked to Hirsch as they reached the Plac na Bramie just as dusk fell. It had been an unseasonably warm week, and tonight even the overflow tables were completely filled, spilling their guests out past the cobblestone patio into the no man's zone inhabited by carts, pedestrians and the occasional motor car.

"Yea, it is," Hirsch said quickly, anxious to return to his lecture. "Anyway, so it looks like Shackleton flatly refuses to cooperate with Koenig. Can you imagine? An entire continent of nothing but ice and snow and the English decide to make camp at the exact place the Austrians chose as their base. I wonder what's at the pole anyway. When I was a boy, I used to think there must be a real pole coming from the ice and that if you took hold of it you could spin around with the earth. What do you think of the..."

Hirsch's commentary went unheard by Elia who was busy scanning the outside tables and peering through the glass at the patrons seated in the window booths. He skipped over dozens of familiar faces before alighting on Rivka Arm's kerchief-covered head, in profile. Once there, nothing else mattered. He imagined running his fingers through the thick, black rope of hair flaring from beneath her floral scarf as it exploded into an alluvial delta of textured furrows down the back of the chair. He tried to envision the exact hue of brown at the center of her deep, wide eyes as he marveled at how their slightly down-turned edges seemed to imply confidence rather than sadness. He could almost taste her endless neck, undulating ever so slightly as she spoke.

"Elia, schmuck," Hirsch whispered before elbowing his friend in the gut. "Stop staring."

"Yea," Elia said, peering through the window just below the "Antmann's" stenciled onto the glass at a table where four girls were seated. Before he could react, Rivka turned her head and her eyes locked with his. Her gaze lingered just long enough to cross the chasm between simple recognition and intimacy. A moment later, he turned back to Hirsch, embarrassed for having been caught looking, but far more interested in the faint but distinct smile he was sure he saw on Rivka's face.

• • •

11 March '914
Julia Harmon
Ridge 111
New York

Most Precious Sister,

I can't begin to tell you how relieved I was when Gitla showed me your card from America. After what people said, I never expected to hear from you again.

At first, the junk man said that robbers tied him up, took his money and kidnapped his wife. He even went so far as to offer a reward and tried to get the police to look for you. Of course, no one believed a word he said. And while no one would say it, everybody thought he had it coming.

But enough about the past, let me tell you about

Przemyśl. When I'm not kicking the football or finishing wood, we are at the cafés, talking and drinking like old women after a wedding. But what a wedding it must have been; boys, girls, men, women, Jews, Polacks, Ruthians, common soldiers, Hungarian hussars, traders, merchants—the whole zoo. We cover a thousand topics—sports, arts, politics, oh yes, politics! Socialism, Zionism, and Anarchism—so many isms to keep track of.

Every morning I walk to Arm's furniture factory where I haul a lot of wood and sweep a lot of floors. There are eleven of us, different as night and day—but all brothers. I work as an apprentice to the most skilled of them, Manes, a socialist who talks constantly of the coming war. He says that to forestall the workers from taking over, the bourgeois are conspiring to have the workers kill each other. He's usually right; let's hope he's not this time.

Sunday is a big football game against the Polacks. We have a secret weapon and I think we can really win. I will tell you all about it in my next post.

Please write me and tell me of your life in New York.

Love,
Elia

Two

Pzemyśl • 17th of Adar, 5674 – Sunday, March 15, 1914

"SEVENTEEN FINE PIECES of kosher meat, eh sister?" Malka said, knowing that it would embarrass her sister to no end. "All lined up for the camera, dressed to play ball in their blue and whites, nine unspoken for, each ripe for the plucking."

"You dirty tart!" Rivka spat back, wagging her finger and sporting a playful grin.

"Manes, the mighty Oak. Oh, to be wrestled in those arms. Is all of him is so tree-like? What do you think, sister?" She tossed her reddish blonde hair off her face and raised her eyebrow twice.

"If daddy hears you, he'll—"

"Then there's Elia with those beautiful legs. He's just a bit green for me but oh, so tender and yummy for you. Didn't you say that you fancy him? I hope so, because every time he looks at you, he drools like a baby. And then there's Hirsch, a face like a—"

"Enough, coquette! You're incorrigible. Jump in the river before you combust. Besides, when I marry, it will be for love, not legs."

Malka nodded in acknowledgment.

Rivka mimicked her older sister's previous move, tossing a black tress from her face as dramatically as she could, "But I must admit that Soli does have quit a fine rear."

The sisters giggled as the powder flashed and the negative was exposed, capturing the Hebrew Hashacha Football Club of 1914 on the glass plate in the camera.

THERE WERE NO grazing animals and no shepherds to chase the footballers off Blonie Field, just west of town on the road to Sanok. While church bells echoed on the breezy morning it seemed like the town's people were being sucked from their homes toward a drain at the center of the chalked-off rectangle in the middle of the one flat pasture in the valley. The chatter from the throngs coming from the old town was mostly Polish with a smattering of Ruthian, while those on Jagiellońska and coming across the bridge from Zasanie were evenly split between Polish and Yiddish. A fair number of uniformed soldiers came as well, adding German, Hungarian and even a little Czech to the mix. As fans made it to the field, they segregated themselves roughly by the two main languages, Polish on the west, Yiddish to the east of the pitch. Not that there wasn't some mixing, particularly at the ends of the field where Meyer Weiss and Jurek Styfi were busy taking bets and laying off risk, conversing in the universal language of money.

"Quite a turn out, Jurek."

"One goal, Meyer. Polonia minus one. Two to one. Nine hundred total."

"Done."

"We'll talk again at the interval."

Almost everyone sang along as the army band struck up Haydn's stirring old melody, now the Austrian anthem, *Gott erhalte Franz den Kaiser.*

MEYER WAS BEAMING, holding court at a centrally positioned table at Antmann's. "Schnapps, bring us Schnapps!" he ordered to the hovering waiter, pounding his finger on the cardboard coaster on the table. "Mister Arm!" he called as Tanchem approached. As they shook hands, Meyer slipped a wad of green banknotes into his palm. "You should have seen Styfi's face!"

"Any troubles?"

"Business is business."

Tanchem stuffed the money into his trouser pocket before taking a seat. "What'd he say when the *wunderkind* hit the pitch?"

"Nothing. Absolutely nothing. For forty years I've waited for Jurek to have nothing to say. "Well, he did say one thing, right before Guttmann entered. Just one little word."

Tanchem raise his palms to the sky, "What?"

"He said 'Yes'. One little word. He said 'Yes, double the bet.'"

"Doubled?"

"Yes, as in twice as much."

"What a priceless Polack!"

"Well, not exactly *priceless*."

They snorted coarsely as the schnapps was delivered.

Meyer lifted his glass. "Well played my friend. Very well played. Brilliancy prize, in fact."

"*L'Chaim*, Meyer."

"*L'Chaim*, Tanchem."

MANES, HIRSCH, ELIA and half a dozen fellow footballers sat at a large table inside the café, nursing drinks along with a variety of cuts and bruises.

Manes reached out and poked at Zsiga whose head was resting on the tabletop, then pointed to the window table where Tanchem and Meyer were toasting. The triumph was obvious on both men's faces even from a distance. "Look at them. All of you look at them."

Zsiga lifted his head and looked as requested, then looked over at Manes, back to Tanchem, and finally back to Manes. "I need another beer."

"They think they can buy us off with free beer," Manes said before emptying his glass. Reaching out into the aisle, he managed to snag the apron of the waiter, reeling him in like a fish on a line. "Another round. Bring us another round. Dov, you need schnapps?"

Dov Zemel, who had been mumbling to himself at the end of the table, turned to display the plum-colored shiner below his right eye. "I'm going to find that rat-bastard Polack and split his head open."

"It appears we *can* be bought with beer, comrade," Elia said, just loud enough to be heard.

Manes frowned at Elia and then turned away to more receptive ears. "They bet us like horses. It's always the same, comrades."

"We played a friendly and we came up short. There is no shame in this. The fact that some people made a wager on our fun had no bearing on the outcome," Elia said, "None at all."

Manes turned and jabbed a finger at Elia's chest. "You're either naïve or you're a fool. And I know you are no fool."

Izac set his beer stein down with a thud. "Get off the kid's back and give it a rest for once? It's just a game. We played out of our minds and just barely lost. Even so, we scared the shit out of those Polacks."

Manes's eyes tightened as he leaned toward Izac. "We could have won. They held him out for the first half only to make more profit!" He stood, kicking the chair backwards. It fell against the back wall, deformed, but not broken. "Are you all idiots? Are you?"

Zsiga filled the brief conversational gap with a deeply

reverberating belch, setting all of the men at the table to laughter.

The noise level at Antmann's stayed at near deafening levels for the rest of the night, questions about motivations quickly replaced by socializing and celebrating. Heavier than usual drinking commenced as the word spread that Weiss would be picking up the night's tab not only for the footballers, but for everyone else as well.

Elia was talking to Béla with his back to the door. He turned in time to see the Arm girls taking seats only two tables away. Malka was already flirting with a troika of pie-eyed boys, while Rivka, in an animated debate with Manes, turned her head slowly, letting her eyes alight on Elia. She smiled, stopping his heart in mid-beat. Someone blocked his view of her and by the time they'd moved, she had reengaged with Manes, her back to Elia. Heart restarted and pounding hard, Elia maneuvered his way over to their table as quickly as social decorum would allow.

"No!" Manes said loudly, trying to be heard over the din of the café. "It makes no difference what you are to the Bund. You are not a man or a woman; you are a seamstress, a worker, and a Jew. Class matters, not gender, not religion. Besides, many of our leaders are women."

Rivka nodded vigorously at Manes. "The Zionists want me to milk cows or something in the desert while some bloated bourgeois rabbi makes me recite in Hebrew and then sells me into marriage like a piece of meat to some money grubbing capitalist! Here I can read seven journals a week in Yiddish, Polish, German and Hebrew. Here, I have an extraordinary world of opportunity at every turn."

"Working-class equality for race, religion, and gender," Manes added.

"Manes, Rivka," Elia said, "mind if I join you?"

Manes pulled a chair out from the table and patted the seat. Elia set his stein on the table and sat, inching the chair forward.

"Yes, please, join us." Rivka smiled, "We were just discussing the equality inherent in socialism."

"And the inequality inherent in the synagogue," Manes added.

"What do you think Elia?" She asked.

"I don't think there's anything inherently unequal or unjust with the synagogue, per se. It all comes down to people, to the individuals who are in control, the bosses, the rabbis in this case. If they are tolerant, if they are open minded, then the systems they run will be likewise."

"But they never are. Besides, under true socialism, there will be no bosses to corrupt the system," Manes asserted.

"I agree with you on a small scale. At the interpersonal level up to, perhaps, the size of a small factory, bosses aren't necessary. I believe this to be true of synagogue also. Do Jews really need rabbis to practice being Jews? No. My aunt Gitla is a prime example; the finest Jew I've ever met hasn't set foot in a synagogue in thirty years."

"So Elia, where do you disagree with Manes?"

"In the larger picture, some kind of boss is inevitable because the need for adaptation to the times is ever-present. Jews survive because we adapt our laws through Talmud. Rabbis are the ones who lead this."

The rest of Antmann's was loudly toasting a footballer so Manes leaned over in his chair to be closer to Elia and Rivka and make his point heard, "Marx says that after a brief organizational period, the vanguard melts away, leaving the proletariat to run their own affairs."

"Well, isn't that convenient!" Rivka said with little laugh and a toss of her hair.

"I am beginning to see the advantages of a socialist state. And God knows I have seen how the rabbis can treat women," Elia said. "But let me tell you one thing; socialist, zionist or tsar, there will always be a boss. Always. And if that boss is a good man—"

"Or woman," Manes interrupted.

"Or woman, the system will be inherently fair. Austria has been good for the Jews not because Austria is fair, but because Franz Joseph is a righteous man."

"I couldn't agree more with Elia. People, more than systems. Not all rabbis are unjust. Not all socialists are honorable and not all capitalists aim to enslave the workers," Rivka said animatedly.

"Tanchem is a capitalist, but a fair one," Elia blurted out.

Rivka put her hand on the arm of Elia's chair.

"So you don't think there can be a true, worker-led socialist state?" Manes asked, "So you think there are fair capitalists? So I think you're both dreaming."

"And I think you're wrong," Elia shot back.

"And the world continues to spin," Rivka said in a sing-song voice.

Manes reached for his beer stein and finished it. "You're both clever thinkers. The true socialist doesn't shy from intelligent debate. Why don't you come hear one of our Russian comrades speak next month?"

"About what?" Elia asked.

"Very topical. Vladimir Medem on why zionism is inherently contrary to socialism."

"I'll be there," Elia said without hesitation. He looked over at Rivka, thinking her even more beautiful up close than across the room, hoping she'd take her time before saying yes, prolonging the interval where it was socially acceptable for him to explore her features with his eyes.

"And so will I," Rivka said.

Elia thanked God before taking his eyes off her.

Przemyśl • 14th of Nisan, 5674, – Friday, April 10, 1914

"WHAT'S THE MATTER, Elia?" Gitla asked.

He lifted the end of the sofa and positioned it back up against the wall. "Nothing. I'm fine."

"Don't bullshit a bullshitter. All day we've emptied the house to the street, scrubbed every nook and crack, then moved our worldly goods back in, and not even a caw from my little crow."

Elia exhaled audibly then slumped back into the couch. "I'm torn."

"We're all torn, Elia. Talk, let it out."

"I have declared my solidarity with my fellow workers, with the working class."

"And..."

"And I'm still a Yid, a Jew."

"A duck is a duck is a duck."

"In my heart, I can't believe in both Zion and in Przemyśl. So I made my choice to stay, to fight for my class, and to retain our Yiddish way of life."

"I'm proud of you for taking a stand," Gitla said. "Any stand. But why the long face? Everyone is many things. It's only sad if you're only one thing."

Elia looked up studying Gitla's features. While these were clearly not the steely-grey eyes of his mother he could easily see his mother's soft, wide mouth on her. "Can I be a good Jew without the Synagogue? He asked. "Without a Rabbi?"

"That's it? That's all?" She let out what sounded like a tire going flat then continued, "Tonight we join with a thousand other households in this valley and rid our homes of all traces of leavened bread. Most will do so for one reason and one only: the rabbi told them to. They will use a candle to illuminate, a feather to sweep the cracks, and a tin to collect the offending crumbs because that is what they were told to do: eat only matzo rid the house of leaven. But what of the Malz home? Why are we doing it? I'll tell you why: because it's good to clean your house to the cracks every spring. Some holidays we clean our souls; for Passover, our homes. And do you really think God gives a rat's behind about a crumb of bread behind the stove? God is busy; she has much better things to watch. For the Malz, this whole crazy holiday comes down to the story of the matzo."

"How so?"

"Take flour, fold in water then stop time."

Elia looked puzzled.

"Up to now, Matzo and bread are one. Put the preparation in the oven, *pfft*, matzo for Passover. But take a walk before baking and *pfft*, bread—sell the lousy loaf to the Poles. What's the difference Elia?"

With the skill of a Vienna lawyer and the confidence of a Berlin surgeon Elia answered. "The difference is... time. Time."

She reached out to knock her knuckle on the crown of his skull while Elia continued, "There is a moment, an instant in time, when good becomes bad, when white becomes black. The course of things changes in the beat of a heart. The matzo, made so quickly, reminds us that time is precious."

"That's my boy. Time is our most precious gift from God. That's why the Malz house eats matzo. Not because a rabbi told us to, but so once a year we can burn the value of time into our souls. Some men, good men, need to be led, to be shown the path. Children too need to be led. In fact, I would say that most people need to be led to the inner truths. But not all. Remember always, God sees directly into each and every living heart. And to Her, an act that comes from your heart is much more meaningful than an act that comes from mindless obedience."

They sat silently for a moment. "You would have made such a wonderful rabbi, Aunt Gitla, if such a thing were possible."

"Why you little bastard!" she snorted. "I'd rather drink digitalis tea."

Przemyśl • 28th of Nisan, 5674 – Friday, April 24, 1914

ELIA LEFT THE factory at six-thirty sharp. He crossed the rail tracks and bought some chestnuts from a street roaster before fording Jagiellońska, a veritable river of humanity flowing to the Old Synagogue a few minutes before sundown and the start of Shabbat.

Crossing the bridge to the Zasanie side, his eyes were drawn to the Worker's House, abuzz with activity. As he approached the crowd, the gas lamps lining Kościuszki ignited, projecting a hundred dancing shadows on the five story brick and limestone structure, the largest building between Lemberg and Cracow.

An elderly man with a limp swung the two wooden gatefold doors leading to the meeting hall open before securing them to the brick wall with oversized hook-and-eyes.

"Sit! Move in, closer. Everyone sit!" Manes's voice commanded over the chatter of the hall, his hand gestures encouraging the assemblage to order. He paced back and forth on the dais, dressed in his woodworking uniform of flannel pants with leather strap suspenders, and black leather boots. He wore a slightly dirty white shirt, soaked at the armpits, with his sleeves rolled up over sinewy biceps.

As he perused the room, self-consciously raising his fist to the many familiar faces he saw along the way, her voice jarred him like a sucker punch. "Elia, come, I've saved you a chair."

A pleasant shiver ran up his spine. "Rivka! Be right there. Thank you."

Elia quickly turned toward Manes, yelling at the top of his lungs while thrusting his fist toward the ceiling, "Sterner!" Manes was engaged in a shouting match with a bearded man in the third row but acknowledged his apprentice by raising his forefinger into the air, signaling his intent to return the address.

As Elia turned and walked toward Rivka, Manes yelled back at him, "Reifer!" The room hushed. "The working class rises up!"

The room erupted in a cacophony of encouragement, "Yes!"

"Fight and win brothers!"

"No bourgeois war!"

Elia sat next to Rivka, keeping strictly focused on the front of the hall. A man in a white smock, a baker, stood no more than two feet from Manes and yelled directly to his face, "When?" Then he turned to the crowd and repeated, sweat mingling with flour on his red, pudgy face, "When, comrades? When?"

"May Day!" Rivka yelled.

Elia turned, looking at her with a equal parts pride, animal attraction and intimidation. He leapt to his feet, pumping his fist in the air, bellowing, "May-Day! May-Day!" Rivka rose beside him, soon joined by the entire row, then the next one, then the entire hall.

For several minutes, bakers, tailors, and woodworkers chanted "May!" in unison while the fists of shopkeepers, accountants and lawyers pushed skyward following each iteration of "Day!"

Though the evening nearly brought frost, it felt like mid-summer in the hall. His shirt unbuttoned to the solar plexus and soaked to translucence, Manes caught Elia's eye and winked.

"Sit, Comrades!" Manes yelled. "Quiet!" he implored several more times before a modicum of order was restored. As the crowd eased back into their seats, Manes prowled the stage hunched over, visibly mouthing words, occasionally licking the tips of his fingers, silently practicing his coming oratory.

Without warning, the glorious warmth of Rivka's palm spread across the back of Elia's hand as Manes mounted the podium step and began speaking.

"Comrades, friends, fellow workers," he paused, wiping his brow with a handkerchief as the house finally came to a hush. "While most of us are Yids, you must turn to the person at your side and greet him not as a Jew, but as a comrade, a fellow working man. We meet tonight as brothers and sisters, our daily toil the bond that holds us fast. Yes, do it now, turn and embrace your class, your people, your destiny!"

"Brother! Unite! Destiny!"

"But what of the bourgeoisie and their capitalist masters? What are they doing to prepare for May Day?"

"What?" The question came from a soot-covered worker in the back.

"Do you believe that they are idle?"

"No!"

Manes lowered his voice, forcing the listeners to concentrate in order to hear his words. "Do they sit idle as we organize, as we move toward our rightful place? No. The capitalists are scared, comrades. Every day they move more cannons to the fort. Dig more ditches, encamp more soldiers. And not just at Przemyśl, not just on the San. The Tsar masses his pawns to the east, the Kaiser to the west; there is no end. Everywhere, the ruling class readies to set worker on worker. No, friends, the capitalists are scared of us, and they have but one card left to play to stop us from upsetting their world order." Manes left the podium in dead silence. From the far edge of the stage, palms open and facing the audience, he answered his own question, "War."

Immediately shouts of "No capitalist war!" were heard from several seats. Soon the phrase was being rhythmically chanted by the assemblage.

Manes returned to the dais and resumed speaking well before the chants ebbed. "There is one and only path to our salvation, comrades. One road, one strategy: solidarity."

"Fight!"

"Revolution!"

"As a lone carpenter, I am nothing. But as part of the great body of workers, we are strong. Show them we are one. Come to the rally on May Day." He thrust a clenched fist into the air as he continued, "Bring your fellow workers." Bringing his fist down hard on the wooden podium, he shouted, "Tell the bastards that we are not afraid!"

The Hall exploded with shouts. "No fear!"

"May Day!"

"Bastards!"

Manes waited for relative quiet before continuing. "Friends, I have spoken enough. Now it is my honor to bring you a friend, a scholar, and a hero to the working class. He comes to us from Russia and brings with him the hope, wishes and desires of working people who suffer capitalist oppression far worse than any of us here can imagine. They are true fighters on the front line of the class war. But tonight, our distinguished guest is not going to talk about the war between the capitalist entities. He is not going to address the Tsars, the Kaisers or any other bourgeois interlopers. No, tonight our Russian comrade will tackle a much more insidious foe of the working masses. An enemy not from without, but rather from within. A wolf in sheep's clothes.

"In a rabbis clothes," someone shouted.

"Comrades, I give you Vladimir Medem!"

The room erupted in rhythmic clapping as everyone stood. From the side of the front row of chairs a short man in a dark suit stood and walked toward the dais, stepping up onto the stage in a fluid, catlike move. He had several pages of notes rolled in one hand which he set on the podium, never altering his serious expression. Medem waited impatiently for the crowd to calm to a low mumble before reading from his prepared text.

"Two streams, two factions, two enemies fighting each other to the death, the Bund and Zionism. Two factions: one proletarian, the other bourgeois. A class party and an all-Jewish movement. Different in social make-up and basis, different in their aims, different in their ways and means, different in their entire world view, and—perhaps most of all—their view of Jewish life..."

Medem spoke for almost an hour, interrupted every few minutes by standing ovations, and revolutionary chants. At one point, after delivering a particularly barbed attack aimed at the bourgeois rabbis of Galicia, a heckler questioned Medem's faith before he was shouted down and escorted out the door by a trio of burley Bundists. He finished with a flourish as his monotone finally gave way to sing-song, fist-pounding crescendo. "In all areas Zionism is a deterrent, a brake, an obstacle!"[1]

Brisk night air hit each worker in turn as they filed out into the cool, starless night, fanning out, walking toward their homes alone or in pairs. "May I see you home?" Elia casually asked Rivka, his outward demeanor belying the agonizing mental preparation and detailed choreography that lead up to his simple query. He brought an arm to his waist, elbow out.

"I'd be delighted," she said, entwining her arm in his.

They crossed the bridge and then made for the quay, strolling silently along the river until they were no longer within eyeshot of the Worker's House. Rivka navigated as they walked, while Elia's gaze alternated between the path directly ahead and quick glimpses of her face, her hair and the gentle arch of her neck.

"Do you buy it?" Rivka asked. "Medem is good, but I don't buy his drivel about Yiddish and Hebrew."

"What do you mean?"

"He seems to say that if we speak two languages, we will lose both to a third. But I fail to see his logic. I speak Hebrew, Yiddish, German and Polish. There are always many languages. Hebrew goes back to the prophets, Yiddish perhaps five hundred years. I just don't see the problem unless he's talking about language metaphorically, on another level."

Just beyond the railroad bridge a clump of trees on the crest of the levee eclipsed the lights of Przemyśl, sending a shadow down the embankment and half-way across the San. As they reached the darkness they stopped and turned to be face-to-face. Rivka's free hand found his and their fingers met, briefly touched, and then intertwined tightly.

A fragment of speech came from Elia's mouth before being smothered by a Rivka's lips. Eons passed as each of his senses took a turn re-defining his soul, recasting his life.

Their eyes met; they exchanged immodest smiles. Rivka stretched, catlike, relaxing her neck, hair cascading down her back, an ear softly alighting on her shoulder, exposing to him the most fertile strip of land the universe had to offer. With eyes wide open, Elia fell on her. From clavicle to earlobe to forehead to face, his lips and tongue lingered at every ridge, plateau and valley.

That night, Elia dreamed like he had never dreamed before.

Several days earlier he had seen a reproduction of a portrait of a woman at an exhibition at the Worker's House. The painting, by a young Spaniard, both intrigued and disturbed him with a distorted, yet curiously meaningful sense of space and order. Somehow, the artist had captured the woman from every dimensional and emotional perspective simultaneously. A part of his brain had spent the past several days trying to make sense of it, trying to apply it to his everyday experience.

He saw Rivka from a hundred angles concurrently; he saw

her face painted not only in length, height and width, but in a dozen other dimensions, and he saw himself as being in all of the spaces, places and sensations at the same time. His dream had no plot, no beginning and no end—just shadows of and suggestions of relationships far too complex to fully understand, far too intriguing to ignore.

A rooster's crow floated in the open window, waking him at sunrise.

Przemyśl • 10th of Iyyar, 5674 – Wednesday, May 6, 1914

"SIT, ELIA. TEA?" Tanchem asked.

"Well… I guess. Yes, thank you." Elia admonished himself for his awkwardness and resolved to be more forceful. They sat silently as the waiter delivered a steeping pot of herbs in hot water and a small white sugar boat with a protruding silver spoon to the center of the table before placing two white cups and saucers onto two wooden coasters. The entire set-up took no more than five seconds.

"I wanted—" Tanchem and Elia began simultaneously.

Tanchem reached for the tea pot. "That was quite the stunt you pulled off at my factory Mister Reifer," Tanchem said in a low monotone while pouring. "May I assume you are here to apologize?"

Elia's mouth was dry but he dared not take the first sip of tea. "You must know that I have nothing but respect and admiration for you, Mister Arm. The strike had nothing to do with you or your factory. It was about May Day, about worker's solidarity. When Manes and I spoke to the workers—"

"We're not talking about Mister Sterner; we're talking about you, Mister Reifer."

Elia nodded.

"Now are you or are you not going to apologize?"

Elia squirmed in his chair. "I will work next Shabbat to make up the time lost. And I will get the others to do the same. And I—"

Tanchem leaned in across the table toward Elia, "Will you answer me? Are you going to apologize?"

Elia took a long, deep breath, "No. No sir."

"I give you a job and you lead my workers out on strike against me and refuse to apologize. Is there some other reason you're here? Have I missed anything?"

"Um, well, yes. There is."

"Out with it!"

Tanchem loaded sugar into his cup as Elia spoke. "Mister Arm, I wanted to talk to you with regards to your daughter. Rivka and I have talked on several occasions and I believe that we have many interests in common." He thought about the skin that ran from her ear to the back of her neck. "We both enjoy the theater." He could feel her thick black hair as it flared out from the knot below her kerchief. "So, I would like your permission to accompany her to the theater to see your very talented elder daughter as she performs in the Aleichem play." He paused. No response. "Of course, my intentions are completely honorable." He tried not to think about her lips, her breasts.

"You have some nerve, Mister Reifer," Tanchem growled.

Elia's pulse sped. "Sir, I..."

Tanchem spun the spoon around the cup more times than was strictly necessary to dissolve the sugar before abruptly smiling at Elia. "Good thing that I like nerve, Elia. There's far too little nerve in today's youth."

Elia dropped his head and sipped his tea, stunned.

"And I appreciate resolve and conviction. While I can forgive you for striking my factory, I would never have forgiven you if you had jettisoned all of your beliefs just to please me. A man, a real man, does not apologize for acting on his principals."

"Mister Arm, I can't thank you enough for you—"

"Mister Arm? Only the priest calls me that. You will call me as Tanchem."

"Thank you, Tanchem."

"Now, about my Rivka." Tanchem set the spoon down and spoke, looking down at his tea. "Elia, you're a good boy growing into a good man. Coming to me like this takes much courage and even more heart." He sipped his tea. "Rivka may be my youngest, but ever since Lea passed on, it is she holds the Arm's together. She is the rock of the family, the rock to Malka, and my rock." He again took a sip, then for the first time looked up at Elia. "You have my blessing to take my daughter to the theater." Elia let the words roll over him like a warm bath. "But if you ever do anything to dishonor my precious, I will kill you with my own hands. Understand?"

"Yes, sir. Your trust in me touches me to my soul," Elia said. "Of course I must now ask Rivka."

Both men smiled and sipped tea before Tanchem added, offhandedly, "Of course, I will be attending as chaperone."

Elia daubed his mouth with a napkin. "But of course."

Sarajevo • 4th of Tamuz – Sunday, June 28, 1914

IT WAS A typically humid, scorching Bosnian summer day. Archduke Ferdinand's convertible *Graf und Stift Rois De Blougne* coasted down the Appel Quay, taking the route and the speed suggested in the strongest possible manner by Governor General Potiorek, host of the military reception that had just concluded at City Hall. In spite of the anarchist bomb that blew up the car behind them on their way from the train station to town, Ferdinand and his wife, Sofia, showed not a hint of fear as they chatted in the backseat with the giddy ease of expectant parents. Being a commoner, Sofia was forbidden to ride in the same carriage as her husband while in Austria proper, but here in the provinces no such rules were enforced. Being together on their anniversary was a present that delighted the couple to no end; they were as in love this day as they were on the day they married, fourteen years previously.

The royal couple ignored the tug of deceleration as the roadster slowed, following the mayor's car as it turned onto Franz Joseph Street, away from the River Milgacka. Sitting forward in the front passenger seat, Potiorek immediately protested to the driver, loudly declaring this to be the wrong route while poking the hapless wheelman with his crop. The driver slammed on the brakes, bringing the *Graf und Stift* of the heir to the Austrian Empire to an abrupt stop directly in front of a nondescript food store with "Schiller's" painted on the window glass.

Unseen, a thin, tubercular man crept from the building's shadows, a Belgian made semi-automatic Browning pistol in hand. The first bullet sailed effortlessly through the car's door, hitting Sofia in the stomach, killing her unborn child instantly and rupturing her abdominal aorta, sealing her fate. The assassin leapt off the curb to the open-air automobile, taking aim at the speechless Archduke from point blank range. The projectile found its mark, slicing open the pale white skin on his Excellency's neck, tumbling through sinew and viscera before exiting just to the side of his third vertebra before coming to rest in stuffing of the car's seat-back cushion. The sound of blood spurting from Ferdinand's carotid artery mingled with the rev of the V8 as the royal driver stomped on the gas, U-turned, and squealed away across the Lateiner Bridge, toward the governor's home.

Sophie tried several times to speak but could muster no wind. A trickle of red formed at the corner of her mouth, ran down her chest and merged with the growing tangle of shredded silk and blackening gore where her stomach had been. As they cleared the bridge she summoned all of the remaining life from within her and managed to push out a faint whisper, "For heaven's sake, what's happened to you?"

Meanwhile, Ferdinand was frantically using both hands to try to stop his blood from leaking out through the two holes in his neck. Choking on his own fluids, he vomited violently down the front of his uniform, clearing his throat just long enough for him to utter his last words, "Sophie dear! Sophie dear! Don't die! Stay alive for our children!"[2]

Both were dead before noon.

ENTERING THE THEATER, Tanchem led them to a block of empty seats in the fourth row where they sat: boy, girl, father.

Once seated, Elia and Rivka turned to assess the patrons in the theater. A group of ardent Zionists was sitting next to a small klatch of devoted socialists, lit cigarettes the only common ground between them. Meyer Weiss and daughter Zipre, as close to royalty as there was in Jewish Przemyśl, sat talking in the front row. Morrie the waiter sat chatting with Flamenbaum the newsman. Woodworkers Max, Moe, and Hirsch were there, smoking while scanning the crowd for friends and young ladies of their fancy.

Rivka read aloud from the program that was handed to theater goers at the door. Elia ignored the program in his hand, shifting to read over Rivka's shoulder:

<u>SCATTERED AND DISPERSED</u>

Scenes from Jewish Life, in Three Acts

By Sholem Aleichem

THE LIGHTS WERE cut and as the heavy red curtain closed the audiences' silence gave way to claps and cheers. Within seconds the theater was alive with a chorus of appreciation that organized itself into rhythmic clapping and foot stomping. As the curtain reopened and the lights came up, the reception lost its cohesion, though not it's volume.

Elia, Rivka and Tanchem joined the other theater goers on their feet and began alternating chants of "Malka!" and "Bravo!" as the players took turns stepping forward and bowing, each smiling broadly as they squinted, trying to spot parents, siblings, and loved ones in the dimly lit theater.

Moments later the theatergoers headed out onto Jagiellońska and fresh air. The crowd formed a crush just past the door and Elia, shuffling slowly just behind Tanchem, took Rivka's hand. Through a forest of heads, Elia was finally able to make out the cause of the bottleneck; a young boy was taking coins and handing out newspaper extras as fast as he could. Tanchem dove into the crowd and emerged seconds later with a sheet of freshly printed newsprint before the threesome made a beeline for a streetlamp on the quay for detailed reading.

They saw the oversized type at the same time.

Przemyśl • 22nd of Tamuz, 5674 – Thursday, July 16, 1914

AFTER SEVERAL PULLS on the Havana, Meyer was convinced that the cigar was fully ignited. He reached toward the table and casually slid one of his white ivory pieces forward two squares, adjusting its position so that its circular base was fully inscribed within the white square. "Pawn to King's four," he said absentmindedly in Polish.

Jurek, who had just moved to a sitting position fully square with the table immediately lifted a red pawn by its bulbous head and, angling the base toward Meyer, sailed the piece in a short arc to its resting place, dead in the center of a red square. "Pawn to Queen's Bishop four."

"*Putz*," Meyer said under his breath, picking up a Knight. "Knight to King's Bishop three."

"Knight to Queen's Bishop three," Jurek said, planting his red knight behind his pawn, adding, with a grin, "Kiss my Polish rump."

"Hooligan. Pawn to Queen Four," Meyer said in a faux-angry tone. "You haven't played the damn Sicilian in two years!"

Picking up his pawn, Jurek exchanged it for Meyer's with the sleight of hand of a magician. Holding the captured piece aloft, he deadpanned, "Pawn takes pawn," then added in Yiddish, "Resign?"

Meyer smiled broadly, leaned back in his chair and attended to his cigar. "If I wouldn't tip my King to Lasker as a boy, what makes you think I'd resign to a *goy*?" He moved a piece before he removed another piece, "Night takes pawn."

Both had been exceptional young players. They had met back in '93 when they were among thirty Galicians of all ages and origins chosen to play a simultaneous exhibition against Emanuel Lasker, the great international grand master. On the train to the match in Lemberg, their fathers ignored each other while the two boys honed their skills by calling out moves while manipulating imaginary pieces. Over the years, as each amassed their own fortunes, they developed a close working relationship that occasionally bordered, but rarely actually crossed over into, friendship. While neither had ever seen the inside of the other's home, they had met for lunch, cigars, and chess at Hibler on the third Thursday of each month for nearly a decade now, continuing their old habit of calling out moves in homage to their chess pedigree. Like a bridge across a great river, they connected two of the three great constituencies that made up Przemyśl, the Poles and the Jews. This flow of information helped the shopkeeper, the priest, the Colonel of the Fort, and even the police. But most of all, it conferred a huge financial edge upon the two chess players.

"Just because you went a few more moves than me doesn't mean you hadn't lost at the same time as me, and the other twenty eight—after Lasker's first move. Knight to bishop's three."

Meyer lowered his voice as he leaned out over the table, "My people in Vienna tell me to not be fooled by the demands. There is no answer Serbia can give that will be accepted. It has already been decided. Knight to bishop's three."

"I know, I know," answered the Pole. "My men in Berlin are sure that Germany will support Austria if they mobilize against Serbia. The Kaiser says Russia is in no way ready for war."

"Nonsense! The Tsar is bound to Serbia by treaty. I can guarantee you that Russia will not stand by idly and allow Austria to violate the Serbs."

"Makes sense."

"I know it for fact. My agent in Saint Petersburg is the brother-in-law of the Russian minister to Serbia. Or I should say, was. He dropped dead last week in Belgrade. Bad timing!"

Both men chuckled nervously before pulling on their cigars in unison.

"And don't forget the French," Jurek added. "Poincaré is in Russia this weekend."

"*Tsurus*. Nothing but *tsurus* ahead." Meyer considered the chess board. "Like our game, you can survey the pieces, run the possibilities, and predict the future. Austria is a Rook to Germany's Queen. Serbia is a bishop. A fienchettoed bishop, lurking, dangerous.

"And Poland is a pawn," Jurek said. "A passed pawn."

"Passed pawns ignored in the middle game come back to

haunt in the end."

"Is Europe playing the middle game?" Jurek asked.

Meyer shook his head. "The middle game doesn't start until major pieces are exchanged. Everyone's still playing the opening."

"Could be, old friend. Could be. Still, we can think ahead, play out the game in our heads."

Both men paused, contemplating. "Brilliant," Meyer said. "War means a free Poland which means—".

"Trouble."

"Solve the puzzle, Jurek. It's mate in four."

The Pole sat back in his chair. "Austria mobilizes against Serbia."

"Attack"

"This forces Russia to mobilize, forcing Germany to mobilize, forcing France to mobilize, and forcing Britain to mobilize."

"Check."

"Once nations begin mobilizing, conscripting infantry, co-opting industry, and confiscating railways, nothing stops it."

"Checkmate."

Three

Przemyśl • 10th of Av, 5674 – Sunday, August 2, 1914

GITLA WOKE BEFORE sunrise, dressed without bathing, packed a bag, and left home without waking Juda. She walked barefoot west out of town on Mickiewicza past the shuttered café row: the Edison, the Grand, the Boulevard, and the Elite. As she passed the Weisses' manse, she began reciting a series of *Kinna*, each one passed to her by her mother, each one commemorating a tragedy that had historically befallen the Jewish people on this day. As the sun began casting shadows on the road behind her, she finished the last lament, the story of the fall of Batar, the last fort to hold out against the Romans.

With the first traces of dawn, freshly printed posters nailed to every tree, wall, and post emerged, announcing universal conscription and the formation of a dozen new Austro-Hungarian regiments to be composed of the boys and men of Galicia. General Kusmanek himself had signed the orders and had used the occasion to stir up patriotism and boast of the invincibility of Fort Przemyśl. All of Galicia, it seemed, would awaken to news that the Cossacks were riding west and that the Austrians were heading east; all across the continent enemies had been named, industry had been mobilized, and conscriptions had been ordered. The war was on.

Just past Kolasa junction the cityscape dissolved into fields and swamps, albeit punctuated with an occasional farmhouse or barn. The Lemberg road was a mess, with wheel ruts cut deeply into the dirt and piles of horse manure dotting the spaces between. Gitla walked on the side of the road, her babushka pulled tight over her face against the onslaught of black flies. On any other August morning this far from town, she would almost certainly walk alone and in silence, save the occasional farmer heading for the fields accompanied only by a symphony of birdcalls. But today was different. Directly ahead of Gitla was yet another detachment of Austrians leading a long train of horses, each straining against an oversized cannon or a wagon filled beyond capacity with artillery shells. The air was thick with guttural, military German that disturbed Gitla in a way that odor never could.

"To Lemberg, to Kiev, to Moscow!" was all Gitla heard, repeated endlessly with vexing Teutonic enthusiasm.

The density of human, horse and steel increased as she passed Fort Ten, marking the inner ring of Przemyśl's defenses. Her city had always been an armed camp and there had never been a time in her life when the military wasn't working on the massive arc of forts, batteries, and trenches.

Gitla allowed herself a brief smile as she recalled a hearthside discussion between her father, recently returned from reserve duty, and her brother, many years before.

"Cossacks always come west, Germans always march east. To the north are the vast, impassable swamps of the Pripet Marsh, and to our south rise the mighty Carpathians. So what do you think lies at the very center? Between armies,

swamps and mountains?"

"Przemyśl?" Moses asked in a crystal-clear, ten year-old alto.

"Fort Przemyśl, son. The strategic value of our position didn't go unnoticed by the generals, the Tsars and the Kaisers; they built here the most formidable fortress in Galicia, in all of Austria, perhaps in the entire world."

"The world?"

"To defend the city and the place it occupies, the armies built a system of forty-three forts in several rings, the outermost at a forty-five kilometer circumference. Connecting the forts are kilometer after kilometer of earthworks, barbed wire, trenches, and fortified pillboxes, all spelling certain doom for anyone foolish enough to attempt a frontal assault. Prodigious amounts of concrete and steel, up to three meters thick in some emplacements renders siege impossible, even with the highest caliber of cannon. The forts are equipped with the latest guns, howitzers and cannons. More than one thousand in total and manned by a hundred-thousand of the finest troops the empire had to offer: the Tenth, the Forty-Fifth, Forty-Sixth, Austrians, Galicians, the Hungarian Twenty-Third..."

Gitla stubbed her toe hard on a rock hidden in the mud, propelling her back to the twentieth century, where she sat on the ground massaging her sore foot, just outside the village of Hureczko, within eyeshot of the airfield.

"Try shoes," a fat, red-faced soldier yelled to her.

Gitla looked down at her toe and noticed it was bleeding before spitting on the side of the road while muttering something in Yiddish.

About a kilometer from the last fort, Gitla turned hard right off the road through a small but dense stand of evergreens, into a field of spear thistles before coming to what seemed to be an impenetrable wall of flowering greenery at the bank of a wide but dry creek. For as long as anyone could remember, women of the Arm family had come to this particular stand on this day each year to collect the thorny stems of the sweet briar.

Spreading a canvas tarp, she pulled a small machete from her satchel and began hacking away at the sprawling vines, inured to both the rumble of the earth beneath and the buzz of flying machines above her. After cutting off all the flowers, Gitla wound the canes into necklaces and bracelets. Twenty minutes later, a carpet of dainty yellow roses strewn about her feet, she tied off the bundle, hoisted it over her head and set off for town, blood oozing from a hundred tiny cuts on her hands and feet.

Gitla made it back to the city by noon and took up a spot on the Plac na Bramie where she handed out the barbed wire jewelry in silence. Friend and stranger alike wore the briar thorns until sundown as a reminder of the pain and suffering her people had endured down through the millennia. Many cried; almost everyone who took a wreath had a son or a father or a husband who would be in uniform by Shabbat.

Tomorrow, everyone's world would be different; tomorrow, nothing would ever be the same. It was the saddest Tish B'Av of Gitla's life.

Przemyśl • 11th of Av, 5674 – Monday, August 3, 1914

"NEXT!" ROARED THE impeccably uniformed major in the general direction of Elia, his eyes cast down toward the desk. "Name, birthplace, date and race!" he barked.

"Elizar Reifer, sir," Elia said, wondering what his older brother would have looked like today had he survived childhood. "Medyka, eighteen ninety-six. Yiddish."

The officer looked perturbed. "Medyka?" He scanned a pile of leather binders piled on the side of the desk and eventually lifted half the stack to a new pile, leaving the one he sought on the top. He opened it and scanned several pages before stopping on one, his finger stuck to the entry in question.

"The Tenth, Gustav the Fifth, König von Schweden Regiment, attached to the Forty-Eighth Brigade under the Twenty-Forth Infantry Division, Tenth Corps, First Army," he barked in machine-gun German without raising his head. "Will you swear to defend the…" he glanced up at Elia, losing his focus. "What year were you born, son?"

Elia stood at attention, avoiding the Austrian's eyes, "Ninety-six," he said, quickly adding, "January thirteen."

"Who was your father?"

"Izrel Reifer."

The Austrian dropped his pen and reached up to take his field officer's cap off. Scratching his balding head he set the pike-gray hat on the table such that it rocked back and forth on its stiff leather brim. The Austrian moved his finger across the page, noting that the hand written birth record seemed to match what the boy had said. He looked up, suspiciously. "Really? And your papers?"

"Destroyed in a fire." It was neither the first nor last lie told at the castle that day.

The impeccably uniformed Major look at Elia, back at the ledger then to Elia again before shaking his head and snorting, "*Juden.*" He put his cap back on and inked his stamp, prepared to slam it down on the papers before him.

Just as the Austrian's hand reached its apogee, Manes stepped out of the line and blurted in German, "My most esteemed major."

Still holding the seal aloft, the army officer glanced in the general direction of Manes, asking dryly, "And who would you be?"

"Manfred Sterner, Sir," he replied. "I can vouch for this boy. We have worked in the same factory for the past year. The finest sixteen-year-old I have ever known."

The major glared at Elia, "Sixteen?"

Elia turned to Manes then back to the major, who sported a thin smirk, "But I... um..."

"The army is for men," the major picked up the sheets of paper in front of him and dramatically ripped them in two. "Leave before I have you throttled," he said coldly, pulling his tunic tight beneath his belt.

"But I want—"

"Next," he said, eyes cast down toward the desk.

Elia walked slowly to the door as the recruits broke into laughter. As soon as he was out of the hall, he broke into a run. Hirsch fell out of the queue, catching up with Elia at the bottom of the castle hill.

"Manes is a traitor. I should shoot him," Elia said.

"Shoot? Have you ever even fired a gun?" Hirsch asked.

Like the kinetoscope machines that lined the walk on the south side of the Castle, dozens of scenes from his life whirled through his mind before stopping at one featuring his father. "When I was seven or eight, on my way back from study some dog went mad and came at me. Foaming mouth and all. I froze like a statue. Out of nowhere I hear a roar and see the dog crumple on the ground, then twist in place trying in vain to get to its feet. I turned around and saw my dad holding his Mannlicher. He ran right by me to the dog. I'll never forget it. He loaded a shell, cocked it into the chamber, pointed the barrel toward the dog at point blank range and pulled on the trigger. The dog's head exploded like a melon dropped from a tower. I never really wanted to shoot the gun after that. You?"

"My uncle Mur in Dynów, he takes me hunting when we visit. I've shot my share of deer."

They walked in silence past the Blonie Field, then along the river past the bridge, these days thick with a steady stream of men, horses, carts and cannons. As they passed a kiosk with an onion-shaped top plastered with a mosaic of posters, Hirsch stopped to read aloud a large and obviously new message lettered in both Polish and Yiddish. Elia retraced his steps and joined his friend, who was staring transfixed at the poster of a mustached soldier mounted on a rearing white steed, imploring all brave sons of Poland to come to the defense of freedom and fight the Tsar; to join the Legions.

The two boys reversed course, crossed the bridge, and found their way to the Worker's House.

Two hours and many lies later, Elia and Hirsch joined the men sporting newly fitted uniforms streaming from the castle and the Worker's House. All were headed home to explain to their loved ones that they were to report to the train station at six the next morning for deployment to the front.

ELIA PAUSED AT the door stoop, catching pieces of conversation along with the aroma of his aunt's latest culinary abomination. "How can such a wise woman of the earth, a magician with a rainbow of herbs at her command, be such an awful cook?" He smiled, recalling last year's Seder when he had shamelessly pandered to Gitla's unexplainable ego, spewing out course after course of effusive praise as he choked down bite after bite of tasteless, shoe-leather-tough, boiled *flanken*. He straightened his uniform and pushed the door open, marching through the house and into the kitchen. Juda, Gitla, and Rivka were gathered around the stove in close quarters, and seemingly all talking at once. As Elia came through the kitchen door, they turned their heads in unison, still jabbering.

"What the hell kind of uniform is that?" Juda asked.

"Legion," Elia answered, "Polish Legion." Gitla shook her head.

"Legion?" Juda's agitation increased. "Legion? What do you think this is, the Scouts? Learn some knots, go on a hiking expedition? The Cossacks are animals. Animals! You'll end up in Siberia, if you're lucky."

"Enough." Gitla said brusquely, still prodding the long since over-cooked meat with a slender two tined fork.

"They cut the beards off the old Yids. They—"

"That's enough, Juda. He's not a boy and he's made his decision, however wise or foolish." She took her husband by the arm and headed for the swinging door. "He has nothing to answer to us..." Gitla looked at Rivka, "to *us* for. Now let's give the *basherte* some privacy."

Elia studied Rivka's face for a clue, a hint of feelings, but found it impossible to stay focused, losing his thoughts in the complex black ringlets of hair cascading down her neck, contrasting with the ivory triangle of skin exposed above her blouse. As she breathed, his heart kept time with each gentle swelling of her breast. "Rivka, you look beautiful tonight," he said, confidently.

"Elia," Rivka said. He moved closer, his heart racing in anticipation. "You clueless oaf."

"But why?"

"You idiot! You blind idiot!" she said, raising her voice. "Why? You ask me why?"

"We've talked about revolution forever. We've debated the process by which the workers would gain control over the Capitalists. Theory. Talk. Concept. Talk." He raised his voice, trying to match her volume and tone. "Now the capitalists have forced the issue on the working class."

"Enough with the working class, all right? For once, for just tonight can we not be part of a class? Can't we look beyond that?"

"What are you saying? Are you renouncing your—"

"You are so clueless!"

"I'm stopping all the talk and putting my life on the line for the working class."

"This is not about the precious working class!"

"For our rights here in our Przemyśl–"

"And it sure as hell isn't about Przemyśl!" They were now

squared up, face to face.

"And for our Poland!"

She dropped her head and lowered her voice, "Elia, Elia, please."

"I don't understand. I thought you'd be happy."

Head still down, she raised both arms, grabbing onto the epaulets poorly sewn onto the shoulders of his tunic. Slowly, Rivka lifted her head up until her misted, earth-toned eyes were locked on his. "Goddamn it, Elia, I love you." Her evocation of the Almighty was as shocking to her as to him.

She pulled his head into her chest. His hands found her waist. "Rivka, I love you too," he said into the black cloud of her hair that seemed to envelop his head, curled by the late summer humidity. He breathed a premature sigh of relief.

"But I see you in this costume, fake silver buttons, the poorly scalloped pocket flaps, that silly beret, going off to kill and be killed," she said, pushing him away from her but keeping both hands anchored on his shoulders. "I can see my gallant Socialist hero coming home in a pine box. I can imagine visiting a stone with your name on it up on Słowackiego. Yes, Elia, I love you. But at this moment..." She welled up.

"What, sweetheart?"

"Right now, I hate you more than I've ever hated anyone in my life."

She dropped her head and cried as he pulled her toward him in embrace. "Shhh, it's all right. I'm no hero. I don't want to die. I am now and have always been a..." He stuttered, searching for words, "...a coward. I'm a coward, Rivka." He pushed her back so they could see each other. "Your beautiful eyes, your hair, your chin," he moved his hand from her waist to her face, gently wiping aside the tear beading just below her right eye, "I love the freckles across your cheeks."

"But Elia..."

"I'll be back for you, my Rivka. I won't die, I promise." He moved his hand from her cheekbone to the back of her head and pulled her close. Elia's fingers danced along the hairline on the back of her neck as their mouths opened and their lips touched, then refused to part. Rivka's arms met at the small of his back and pulled him into her as Elia's free hand found its way up her frock to her breast, caressing it in the palm of his hand.

Rivka finally broke the embrace, pushing Elia's head back. "That, Mister Reifer, was not the act of a coward."

Przemyśl • 12th of Av, 5674 – Tuesday, August 4, 1914

"WHAT IS THIS?" the old man said as he put his arms around Rivka, leaving a palm shaped flour print on the shoulder of her blouse. She continued to weep and knead. "Don't cry, sweetheart." He gently squeezed her, to no effect. He released his grip on her shoulders and grabbed her hands, stopping the kneading. "I am Isidore Besser!" He spoke in mock grandeur. "I am the master bread maker. I order you to stop crying."

A tear streaked down Rivka's cheek, clearing a path through the dusting of light brown flour that clung to her skin.

"Sweetheart, sweetheart. You simply have to stop crying. I must insist."

"Why?"

"My pumpernickel recipe does not call for salt water."

Rivka smiled as she continued to cry.

"What's this?" Isidore pointed a finger at her chin. "Don't look down." As she looked down, he gently grabbed her nose. "Gotcha!"

Rivka threw her arms around the old man, a good half foot shorter than she, pulling his head tight to her neck. "Talk,

talk" he whispered into her ear.

"My Elia joined the army. He's going to war today; this morning, by train." Her tears dried as she continued, "I'm scared for him. I'm scared for me, and I'm scared for all of us."

"Sugar plum," Besser's tone became serious, "it's all right to worry. War is never good for anyone. And it's even worse for the Jews. Now listen carefully, young one. You can make it through anything if you use your Yiddish head, not your Yiddish heart."

"What do you mean?"

"Here's the way it is. If they say 'everything is perfect,' you worry."

"All right."

"If they say there is plenty of food, you hoard."

She nodded.

"If they say the paper money is good, you collect coins."

"I see."

"They told me to have a month of flour in reserve, so since the Archduke was shot I built up six months worth into the cellar."

"But what do you do when they send your *basherte* away?"

"You take your apron off and run like the wind to the station and give him a big kiss, so he can remember why he needs to come home in one piece."

She pecked the old man on his cheek, tossed her apron on the chair, and was out the door, running toward the station just as the sun peeked up over the horizon.

"Sweetheart," Isidore whispered as soon as the bakery door slammed shut. He finished kneading the pumpernickel and put it in a wooden bowl to rise, not realizing that some salt water had made its way from his own eyes to the dough.

"HOW'D IT GO last night, Hirsch?"

"Father yelled, mama cried. You?"

"Pretty much the same."

"Yes, and?"

"Rivka was good news and bad."

"So the good?"

"She said she loves me."

"So what could be so bad?"

"She hates me too."

Both boys scratched their heads as they walked toward the brick, limestone and concrete train station dead ahead of them on the far side of Kolejowy Square.

"Say, Hirsch, what did you bring?"

"Not much. I tried to get my father to give me his Gasser pistol but he said he needed it. You?"

"Gitla tried to make me take my jersey. It's forty degrees out and she wants me to take a wool jersey. All I have is my *Manifesto* and mama's ring."

They arrived at the station square just as the rifle sized minute hand on the clock face atop of the station clicked to 6:00. A moment later, church bells tolled in the background and a few seconds after that the boys felt the concussion of distant mortar firings deep in their lungs.

They sat for an hour on the gravel by a boxcar that, as far as Elia could tell, the Jewish recruits of the Second Polish Legion brigade would be sharing with the Jewish recruits of the fourth battalion of the 10th Austrian Infantry Regiment. Elia kept his back to the men of the 10th, listening closely, parsing every sentence he heard, hairsplitting every word uttered as if it were written in the Torah.

The new Austrian battalion was made up of former bakers, brewers, several peddlers, a few shop keepers, some random laborers, a pharmacist, and an ex-waiter or two. They were all Przemyślers, they were all either friends or at least familiar faces, and they were Zionists, Bundists, football players, and musicians. While Yiddish was their native tongue, most spoke at least some German, Hebrew, French, Russian, Ruthian, and Polish. They cursed and prayed in a dozen different ways, if they prayed at all.

"Now that's a bit of irony for you comrades!" laughed Manes. "The finest clothes any of us have ever had, courtesy of Franz Joseph! See how they dress us up like dolls as we do their bidding."

Osais, a plumber, interrupted, "You ungrateful Yid! Can't you think of how aristocratic we will look in these tunics while they say Kaddish and dump us into the earth?"

"Cigarette?" Elia turned his head, recognizing the voice.

"Go bang your head against the wall, Sterner."

Manes stuck the cigarette into his mouth. "I do you a favor and this is how you repay me?"

"It was not your decision," Elia snapped back. "And you embarrassed me in front of my comrades."

Manes lit his cigarette, exhaled toward the ground then looked directly at Elia, "I humbly apologize. It was not my intention to humiliate my favorite comrade. As to the authority to make the decision, well, all I can say is anytime I have the clear option to live or die and I opt for the decision to die, I invite you to intercede on my behalf with or without my assent."

Elia sat silently, eventually letting out an audible sigh, "How about that cigarette?"

"I take it you accept my apology."

Elia lit up and both smoked for several minutes. "Taken correctly."

"Good," Manes said. "So we're square?"

"Not quite. Promise me that from here on, you'll treat me like a man."

"Yes."

"Not like a child."

"All right."

"No, I want your word."

"Comrade to comrade, man to man, you have my word." They shook. Manes smiled broadly out of one side of his mouth, the other side busily clamped onto the cigarette. Reaching down, he grasped Elia around one of his triceps and hoisted him to a standing position with the ease of a housekeeper lifting a broom from the floor. For the next hour, they mingled with the men of the Polish, Hungarian and Austrian battalions. To his great relief, Elia noted several boys who appeared to be even younger than he was.

They were all laughter and smoke until an officer called the soldiers to attention in terse, authoritarian German.

The men found seats on rough wooden benches as a roar of released steam followed by the lurch of boxcars and the squeal of steel wheels on rusty tracks announced the army's departure.

"Elia! Elia Reifer!" Someone seated by the car door yelled. "Where is Elia Reifer?"

He recognized Dov's voice from football. "What? I'm here!"

"There's some young lovely looking for you. She's walking with the train. Come quickly."

Elia was on his way to the car door before Dov finished his sentence. Grabbing a metal rail just over the door lintel, he swung himself out of the car, one foot on the train, the other hanging free.

"Elia!"

"Rivka!"

She accelerated gracefully from walk to a slow trot, crossing the chasm that separated them in the blink of her misted eye. Elia leaned further and further out of the boxcar while Rivka struggled to keep her arm steady through a slowly increasing pace. Finally, their hands joined and fingers entwined. Eyes met. Each mouthed to the other, "I love you." The bridge just a few dozen meters ahead, he let go of her hand. Rivka lost her battle against the tears but continued jogging alongside the train, empty hand extended.

Elia fished his mother's ring out of the breast pocket of his uniform and tossed it toward her, just missing her outstretched hand. "After the war, marry me?"

"Yes, *basherte*. Yes!" Rivka stopped to pick the ring up from the sooty gravel surrounding the tracks. After finding it too loose on her forefinger she found a snug fit on her middle digit.

"Still hate me?" Elia yelled to her, the distance between them now growing rapidly.

"Not if you come back to me."

Elia touched his hand to his lips and then extended his arm, throwing a kiss toward Rivka. Smiling and crying, she blew a kiss back at him. Each watched until the other disappeared as the train accelerated through a wide arc, crossed the bridge over the San, passed by both rings of Fort Przemyśl, and headed north toward Jaroslaw, on its way to the front; to war.

Nowy Korczyn • 4th of Elul, 5674 – Wednesday, August 26, 1914

"NO! NO! NO! The Mauser is not your waltz partner to be flung about the dance floor; she's your unblemished virgin, to be handled gently, in need of care and understanding. Never pull or tug on her, squeeze her tenderly." Lendas grabbed Elia's rifle, loaded a seven millimeter shell, cocked, aimed, and slowly breathed, "Squeeze," as he fired.

A dark spot appeared in the center of the forehead of the crude body outline drawn on a bed sheet tacked to some bales of hay stacked at the far end of the field. A rumble of awe passed through the battalion. "Every time, Lieutenant. It must be hundred meters away. How do you do it?"

Lendas rested the rifle butt on the top of his boot. The

Legion Company fell into a semi-circle around him as he began to tell the story. "We were poor growing up. Our town was four families. In comparison, Stalowa Wola was a metropolis."

"Didn't the train stop to let us piss near there?" Someone asked.

"I pissed on Stalowa Wola!" Someone yelled from the back of the group.

Fisticuffs nearly broke out when a burly private took exception but discipline was soon restored and Lendas was able to continue. "From the day I could walk, I would stand on one side of the oak tree and scare the squirrel to the other side where my papa and uncle would pick them off. By age six, it was my little brother Georg scaring them and me putting slugs through their little heads."

"All I ever shot in Medyka was a football." Elia managed, impressed by his own rapidly improving Polish.

"We didn't deem it a clean shot unless the slug went through one of the squirrel's eyes."

A low mumble of admiration passed through the men.

"We moved to Puławy when papa died and I joined the St. Bernardine Shooting Club mostly because I knew I could drink a few liters of beer and still win all the competitions. The club eventually became part of the Rifleman's Association, then the Rifleman's Union and finally the *Strzelcy* under Pilsudski. And now I shoot for the Legions." Lendas brought his rifle to his shoulder, "As do you."

The company continued firing practice for the next hour in a gentle rain.

"Gentleman, fall in!" Lendas yelled. A staccato, "Attention!" and twenty seconds of scurry brought the recruits into four ranks of eight, each holding a stiff, upright posture, rifle butts resting on the muddy ground to the left of each man's foot.

"Patriots of a free Poland, marksmen for freedom!" A large

group of men on horseback approached. "The time to shoot at hay has ended. With the grace of our lord Jesus Christ, now is the time for us to rid our sacred land of its Tsarist oppressors. Alone, this would seem an impossible task. But we do not fight alone."

The horses came to a stop a few paces behind Lendas.

"For, today we cast our lot in with the dual monarchy of Austro-Hungary in our common quest to rid our homes of the scourge from the east."

"Psst. Elia," Hirsch whispered, keeping his head steady and trying to minimize the movement of his lips. "It's him, the castle major."

"Brothers in arms! We will swear allegiance to Emperor Franz Joseph the First and gladly fight and happily die under his auspices."

The lead horse, a white dappled stallion, lifted its front foot from the mire it was sinking in. It made a surprisingly loud squelching sound. Lendas glanced at the regally appointed mounted officer, taking in the somewhat sarcastic nod of his *feldkeppe*.

Elia studied the Austrian's face, and then took a moment to admire the perfect fit and precise stitching that framed an impressive array of medals and ribbons pinned to his tunic. "You're wrong. It's not him," he said to Hirsch.

"Left, behind the Colonel. Don't look."

Elia froze then swept his eyes to the left, taking in the faces of the Colonel's staff.

Lendas turned to his men and barked, "Company, at ready!" Elia, Hirsch and thirty others lifted their Mausers off the mud, stamped their feet, placed their rifles on their shoulders and stood still at attention, eyes fixed to the horizon.

Lendas slogged off to a position beside his men and the dappled horse advanced to center stage in front of the troops.

"At ease!" the mounted officer commanded in German.

The Legionnaires returned their rifles to the ground but remained at attention.

He's right. In the back, it's the same one. Thank God we're in the third row. No eye contact, Elia. Focus! He'll never recognize me in uniform.

"I am Colonel Felix Ritter Unschuld von Melasfeld[3]," he said while walking his steed sideways along the troop line, a masterful display of horsemanship lost on all but a few of the recruits. "I will be your commanding officer. You will fight as an intact battalion attached to the 47th brigade, but in all other manners you will be part of the Austrian Army, with similar privileges of rank, subservient to all its rules and subject to its rigorous discipline. You will, however, wear rosettes, not stars, on your regimental colors."

There were some disappointed rumblings from the legionaries.

Oh no. He's looking at Hirsch. Focus Elia!

"Now repeat after me. I swear my allegiance to Emperor..."

Lendas translated Unschuld's recitation into Polish, stanza by stanza. As soon as the oath was confirmed, Lendas's offer to demonstrate the marksmanship of his battalion was unenthusiastically accepted by the Colonel. Lendas selected three of his ablest marksmen, all Polish farm boys, for the exhibition.

Elia and Hirsch maneuvered, trying to keep the bulk of the battalion between them and the mounted officers. As each of the first two salvos found the target at the far end of the field, an increasingly immodest, nationalistic cheer rose from the recruits. Just as the third sniper lined up his sights, Elia's focus was shattered by a light but persistent metallic prick on his shoulder. He turned to investigate as the rifle's report echoed across the range.

To Elia, the well-shined, action-ready Cavalry Saber seemed like a frozen lightning bolt arcing toward his unprotected chest. Raw fear ripped through his guts. When they had first met, the Major was no more than a paper-pushing bureaucrat, capable of no more than verbal abuse. Somehow, he'd metamorphosed into a three-meter-high monster of flesh, leather and steel; a fierce, fully appointed warrior; a death machine. The horse's rippling muscles brought back his grandfather's stories of marauding Cossacks sacking Galician villages and the infinite hopelessness earthbound men face when confronted by mounted swordsmen.

"Mister..." the Major paused, searching. "Reifer, yes, Mister Reifer, the underage boy from Medyka. And his sidekick, underage as well, I presume?"

"I can—"

"Silence!" the Major ordered, sheathing his sword.

Quiet rippled through the ranks to Lendas. He handed his rifle to a recruit and ran to investigate, saluting crisply on arrival. "Sir," the Pole said in perfect military German, "is there a problem with the cadet?" Lendas took note of the guilty look on Hirsch's face and added, "Cadets?"

"They are not cadets," the Castle Major said. "Not in the Legions and certainly not in the Austrian Army. They are underage. Boys. Children. Spoiled children who need a good beating before being sent home to their mothers."

"Sir, there must be an explanation."

"Lieutenant, confiscate their weapons."

The rest of the company began gathering around the confrontation. Lendas turned to deal with the two boys when the sea of onlookers parted, clearing the way for Colonel Unschuld's horse.

"What's all this, then?"

The Major snapped to attention. "Sir!" he saluted with a gloved hand. "These boys are not of age."

Unschuld raised one of his bushy eyebrows as he maneuvered his horse to the small space between the Major and the boys. Elia and Hirsch stiffened, partially at attention, mostly from fear. "How old are you and why are you here, son?" he said to Elia in a surprisingly gentle manner.

Elia exhaled. "Seventeen, sir. To fight the Russians. To throw the Tsar out of Galicia."

"For the Emperor. For Franz Joseph" Hirsch added.

The Commander deftly backed his horse away from the crowd to a more commanding position from which to address the whole detachment. "Legionnaires! To the Emperor, you are loyal allies. To your wives and children you are brave soldiers. But to the Tsar, you are traitors. If an Austrian is captured, he ends up in Siberia. If a Legionnaire is taken, he ends up with a bullet in his temple. The son of a Russian whore, Ivanov, has said as much in writing."

A murmur passed through the battalion.

"The Tsar thinks this will scare the Legions. Does this scare you?"

Shouts of "No!"

"The Cossacks will learn to tremble before the sons of Poland!"

Cheers in German and Polish.

"But unlike the Tsarists, we Austrians are men of honor. Men of our word. I will gladly send men to whatever fate God has ordained." More cheers. "But I will not send boys to their death. You two," he aimed his riding crop at Elia and Hirsch. "You are out of the legion."

Unschuld, the Major, and a 2nd Lieutenant conferred on horseback as Lendas rallied his men and marched them off, leaving Elia and Hirsch in the mud, rifle-less. Led by the Colonel, the mounted officers, except for the 2nd Lieutenant turned and rode off.

Hirsch turned to Elia, "We're finished."

The junior officer stopped his horse in front of the boys and spoke, his facial expression neutral. "Colonel von Melasfeld was impressed with your initiative and patriotism. You are hereby assigned to the Fourth Battalion of the Gustav von Schweden Regiment, with the rank of cadet-private. Report to Sergeant-Major Silverberg immediately."

"Where?" Hirsch asked.

"Six kilometers." The 2nd Lieutenant pointed to the horseshoe-pocked path on which the mounted officers had come and gone, then turned his horse and spurred him to a gallop in the direction he had just indicated.

Przemyśl • 10th of Elul, 5674 – Tuesday, September 1, 1914

TANCHEM SAT OUTSIDE at Antmann's waiting for his tea and his daughters, contemplating the impossibly ornate double Austrian imperial eagle adorning the manila and brown pack of Memphis Cigarettes sitting on the table. A lifelong citizen of the Empire, he had been in the Army reserve for decades, retiring from the 10th Engineering Battalion at age fifty, having reached the highest non-commissioned rank possible, sergeant-lieutenant. The sight of men with guns neither disturbed nor intimidated him as he took in the scurry and confusion unfolding on the street before him.

He pulled a cigarette from the pack and lit it. Perusing the street, he began playing a game he and his mates had played long ago, before his Bar Mitzvah. *Apple-Green facings. Yellow buttons... The Clerfayt Regiment.* He took a long drag on his cigarette, exhaling from the side of his mouth as he continued to survey the scene. *Red, amaranth-red with white... the Ninetieth... no, no, that's with yellow... cherry-red, yes, that's it, cherry-red with white, the Seventy-Seventh von Wertemberg.* A detachment of men in brightly colored uniforms rode by on horseback. *What the hell are they, Dragoons? Dark-blue facings—Ulans? Ash-grey shako, of course, Hungarians. The Eleventh, what are they... yes, Ferdinand I Hussars.*

Tanchem relaxed back into his wicker chair and smoked

until his tea arrived. “Thank you, Morrie. How’s business? You look like hell.”

“I can’t complain, and you’re no Lionel Barrymore,” the proprietor said as Tanchem smiled and patted one of the empty seats he was reserving for his daughters. Morrie noted the mostly deserted tables on the cobbled sidewalk before reaching to his waist and pulling on a loose string, releasing the stained white apron straining against his ample stomach. “Just for a minute.” He glanced at the door that led to the kitchen, “My wife will crown me.”

“So business is all right?”

“In truth, it’s better than all right, almost too good. Since mobilization I sleep maybe four hours a night. You see the streets, packed with men. They’re everywhere. A few march out, more march in. And what does an army move on? What keeps it going? I’ll tell you: coffee, tea, beer, cigarettes, and schnapps.”

“I was kind of hoping you’d say armoires.”

“I’m afraid not, my friend.”

“And how’s the family?”

“Judes is forever sickly. We both work like dogs. But she’s glad that my deferment lasted through the call-ups. Mama thinks it’s because I am the only support for her, the poor old widow. Judes says it’s because I’m a little too—how did she put it—well grazed.” Morrie patted his stomach. “But we both know it’s because they understand that keeping the boys drunk is more important than keeping them in ammunition.” He glanced around at the tables, “All things being the same, too much work is better than not enough. So we get up with the sun, feed a company or two coffee, sugared tea and cakes. Later we get the whole battalion drunk until they stumble back to camp past midnight. They sleep so soundly that the Cracow train passing right through the camp can’t wake them, while Judes and mama and I wash dishes, most nights until two. Then we do it again. Even on Shabbat.”

"You really have to tip your hat to those Austrians. They sure knew what they were doing when they deferred you." Tanchem said, reaching for his tea.

"Yes and no. I don't have to fight, and God knows I don't want to, but I also can't run." The waiter took another look around before leaning half way across the table, speaking in a near whisper, "Serving soldiers, officers, you—how can I put this?" He paused, looking around again, "I hear things. I've heard things."

Tanchem moved in closer, "Like what?"

Morrie leaned in so their heads almost touched, "Like that the Tsarists are rounding up the Jewish men and shooting them. Women raped, children bayoneted. For being disloyal, like we owe a single rotten Heller to the bastard Nicholas."

"I've heard rumors too, but nothing like this."

"All the regular army boys are going one direction—out Mickiewicza or across the river and north to the front. This morning I served a group of Austrian officers, one was a...he had two silver stars on a zigzag background—"

"Lieutenant-colonel."

"Yes, a lieutenant, just back from the Lemberg salient, here for a day. I pretended to clean tables and eavesdropped."

"Morrie, if you are going to shorten a lieutenant-colonel, call him a colonel, not a lieutenant."

"The Colonel was just back from Lemberg."

"Better. And?"

"The war is not going well. We're being pushed back all across the entire front. Lemberg falls any day or has already fallen."

"The newspapers are lying?"

"Well, if I understand what they were saying—my German is far from perfect—not exactly. They talked about how our First and Fourth have pushed the Russians back to the north, near Lublin and Zamosc."

"That sounds promising."

"Well, I thought so too, but then the Lieutenant said something about how Bruddermann's Third at Lemberg is in total collapse in front of Brusilov, exposing the rear."

"So we have no problem pushing north and east. They have clear sailing south and west. Like a fucking circus carousel."

"Yes, but as it turns, it brings Nicholas to Przemyśl."

"In chess, Russians beat Austrians. Ivanov is ten times the player Conrad is. Conrad spends all his time crying to Moltke, who ignores him as if he were a bastard stepchild while drooling over the pretty girls he'll have when he gets to Paris."

"I'm not crazy about trading Galicia for Poland."

"All of the officers agreed that there is no choice but to withdraw all our armies to a more defensible line along the Vistula."

"Vistula? *Oy vey.*"

"We will have Cossacks at the doors of Przemyśl within a fortnight."

"Are they worried?"

"They weren't Jews," Morrie said as he stood up.

"No, not that, about Przemyśl?"

"No one thinks the fortress can be breached." He pulled the two strings of his apron tight across his stomach and tied them off in a bow. "But there is one more thing I overheard from another group of men that's a bit more than disconcerting."

"Uh-oh. What?"

"Of the six Colonels stationed at the Fort, five have already sent their wives west. Gone, out of Przemyśl."

"God forbid, my friend, God forbid."

"What will be, will be. What can we do? Besides, I've got soldiers to get drunk," the proprietor said, walking toward the door.

Tanchem lit up another Memphis before consulting the

hands on his Longines. "Like I have time to lounge around," he muttered to himself, noting the low rumble of a far away mortar. "This is worse trouble than I thought."

He smoked his cigarette down to a near burn of his fingers before dropping the butt on the sidewalk; its explosion of red, glowing embers in a circular pattern reminiscent of a howitzer impact. Lifting his head, he saw his two daughters sauntering across the square. He was not pleased as they joined him in the two wicker chairs across the table.

"Malka, what the hell is that orange monstrosity you're wearing?"

"It's peach, daddy. Don't you just love it?"

"I can see your arms almost all the way up to your shoulders! And your cleavage!"

"All covered by lace. I think it looks divine. Rivka? What do you think?"

"Can't you see how the men look at you?" Tanchem said.

"Men always look that way at me, daddy," she said, batting her eyes. "Eisner says the prettier I dress, the more the officers spend."

"Damn it, I'm serious! It's no joke. You need to cover up when you go out." He realized that he could easily be overheard and lowered his voice, closing in on his daughter to make up for his diminished volume, "There are tens of thousands of boys away from home. From the big cities, from Budapest, Vienna, hell, even Berlin!"

"Oh father, you worry too much," Rivka enjoined, brushing a dusting of flour from her forearm.

Tanchem caught Morrie's eye as he was delivering drinks and cakes to a group of Hungarian soldiers. "Three," he mouthed silently, briefly holding up the same number of fingers just to be sure. He turned back to his daughters, "Izac is well. I have a post from him. He's was fixing cannons behind the lines near Rzeszow a week or so ago. Said the weather was nice."

"What else does he say?" Rivka asked.

"That was pretty much it."

"My brother: short and to the point."

"Listen girls, these are dangerous times. We are not immune from war, and the fighting may soon be on our doorstep."

"The Germans crushed the Russians in the north. All of Prussia will be back in kraut hands by next week," Rivka replied with authority.

Her father leaned back in his chair, stroking his beard. "Well, well, well. My daughter the Field-Marshall."

"Father, I talked to Zipre, who heard from Meyer who—well we know who he talks to."

That grabbed Tanchem's attention. "What did he, I mean she, say?"

"Oh, I don't know. Something about a huge victory near Konigsberg or Tannenberg, some berg. So bad that the Russian General shot himself."

Morrie delivered the three teas to Tanchem and his daughters along with perfunctory smiles and nods then was gone without a word.

"Konigsberg? Do you have any idea how far away that is? It might as well be Siam."

Tanchem sipped his tea, and then addressed his daughters in the most authoritative tone he could muster, "I'm closing up the shop and we are leaving Przemyśl. I don't want any discussion on this. It is just too dangerous. Dangerous as Austrian citizens, even more dangerous as Jews. We will go west to your aunt Sheine in Oswiecim next week. We'll be safe there and we can return when the war is over."

To Rivka, Tanchem's slow, acerbic delivery coupled with the subtle bulging of his carotid artery underscored the seriousness of his declaration. In all her memories, she could count but a handful of occasions when her father had used that particular tone with her. Nevertheless, she knew he was wrong, yet she needed to consider how to explain why.

"Daddy," she spoke to him as if she was the parent and he was her young boy, "We are infinitely safer here in Przemyśl than we would be in," she paused, thinking of how bored she had been during her one visit to Oswiecim, two years ago, "in Cracow. Our fort is totally impregnable. The best troops, the best artillery. We won't even hear the guns, they are so far away."

"Rivka, you need to—"

"No, you need to—"

He poked his index finger at her, "Don't you ever interrupt me, Rivka Chana."

Rivka reached across the table and put her hand on her father's arm. "I'm sorry, father. It's just that—"

"I received a *feldpost* from Manes today." Rivka and Tanchem frowned, both a bit perturbed at the frivolousness of Malka's interruption. She produced a postcard from her shoulder bag and dropped it picture-side up onto the table, "Our sister fort, Jaroslaw."

Tanchem and Rivka glanced at the picture of Austrian gun firing off a mammoth shell, and then turned back on each other, ignoring Malka.

"Did you read the latest communiqué from Kusmanek?" Tanchem said, trying a new approach.

Inured to such snubs, Malka flipped the card and began reading, "He sends his regards to Rivka and Tanchem."

"Of course I read it. How could I avoid it? His announcements are plastered on every wall in the city!" Rivka said, pecking at the table with her forefinger, "The Czech is far more interested in what is coming for lunch than what is coming to attack."

Malka continued reading, "And he tells us to get out of Przemyśl immediately."

There was silence around the table, punctuated only by the sound of horse whinnies and army boots hitting cobblestones.

Tanchem snatched the card from the table. He read it

again and then passed it to Rivka, who did likewise before returning it to the table.

There was another moment without words, the quiet filled by the low rumble of far off mortar fire. “Like I said, we close the shop and book the Cracow train for next Monday.”

The girls nodded and finished their tea wordlessly.

Morrie walked over to pick up the bank note Tanchem had slipped under the ashtray. Glancing at the twenty Kronen note, the waiter pursed his lips and moved his chin back and forth beneath the mustache centered on his upper lip. “You know we’re not giving silver anymore. Paper only for paper. Sorry.”

“Of course, Morrie. Of course,” Tanchem said exchanging the bill for a five Kronen note, trying not to look embarrassed. He gestured to the impatient waiter that by taking the banknote their transaction would be complete.

Malka leaned over to Tanchem and kissed him on the cheek, “I’m back to the store, father. See you for supper.”

“Daddy, you know how I really feel about leaving.”

“Don’t start with me, Rivka.”

“No, no, that’s not it at all. I agree that it would be safer to leave for now.”

“Thank God you are growing up.”

Rivka noticed Elia’s mother’s ring on conspicuous display and quickly put that hand under the table so the ring was safely out of sight.

“Yes, I am. I’m nearly eighteen now.”

“If you are going to ask if I’ll let you marry Elia, it’s a bit of a moot point now, isn’t it. Austrian army or Polish Legions, men of the common rank may not marry while on active duty. And I doubt very highly that Elia has made Major in a month.”

“Oh no! Say it’s not true, father! I had no idea.” Rivka decided not to share that her boss Isidore, a retired army reservist himself, had told her as much a few days ago.

"That's so unfair!"

"I'm afraid so, sweetheart. But it will be all right. You'll see."

"I'll be a spinster my whole life!" She cried, rubbing her eyes with her palms to redden them. "Why, I didn't even get to say goodbye." She couldn't believe she was lying to her father, what bothered her just was how easy it was to do.

"This mess will be over in no time, and then you and Elia can come to me the right way."

"Daddy?"

"Yes, dumpling."

"Isidore has friends. He knows things."

"Like?"

"This cannot be repeated, but he knows someone who knows the commander of Elia's company."

"So?"

"He told me, for a fact, that Elia will be through Przemyśl, one day, on his way to the front."

"And?"

"It is the day after you—after we are to leave for Cra—, for Aunt Sheine in Oswiecim."

He leaned back into his chair and began to stroke his beard, "Go on."

"You are my father, and of course I will do whatever you want me to do. You want me to leave Przemyśl, I will leave Przemyśl as you desire. No argument. No fuss. But please, I beg you; allow me to stay two extra days, to see my Elia."

He stroked his beard a few times, thinking, "Who would see after you?"

"I have talked with Gitla. She will take me in for the two nights." She quickly added, "And chaperone us when we meet at the station."

"So you would be on the train on Thursday?"

"Yes, with Gitla and Juda. They'll be going to Cracow too."

He let out an audible sigh, blowing a lung-full of air through his pursed lips, like a bored horse. "This goes against all of my better judgment."

"But, Daddy!"

Tanchem studied his daughter's beautiful but crestfallen face, seeing in it traces of the love of his life. The profound sadness of being forced apart from the one you love flooded his soul. "I will allow it."

"Oh, Daddy!"

"If," he wagged his finger at his daughter, "you swear on your mother's grave that you'll be on that train."

She lunged across the table and threw her arms around Tanchem, kissing him three times on alternating cheeks. "Yes, yes, yes. I do, and I will. Thank you, Daddy!" She hurried back to work as Tanchem sat, imagining how Lea would have handled Rivka's request, missing his dead wife more than ever.

Puławy • 14th of Elul, 5674 – Saturday, September 5, 1914

"DON'T LOOK OUT there again when you hear incoming!" Manes grabbed Elia by the shoulder and shook him. "Are you listening to me? When you hear a whistle, you keep your head below the trench line."

"Sorry, bad habit."

Gerson, who had been reassembling his rifle, stood up, his four-foot, ten-inch height posing no risk to his head, and declared, "Goddamn it, why do we have children in the trenches anyway? One wants to get his head blown off, the other reeks of shit."

Silverberg, the company sergeant, took offense. "Leave him alone. It's no shame to be scared here. Hell, when that shell hit I would have shit my trousers too if I had anything left in my bowels." He fished into his field pack sitting at the bottom of the trench and pulled out a mud-caked pair of wool field pants and tossed them at Hirsch without comment.

"How long since the last one?' Gerson asked, oblivious.

Hirsch disappeared around the corner of the zigzag field trench. Elia looked at the watch on his wrist, realizing that it had been quiet for longer than it should have been. He made a quick calculation. "Thirty-six seconds, give or take."

Manes, in perpetual crouch, exchanged a glance with his sergeant, "Either we got the howitzer or the Russians found the vodka factory in Puławy."

Silverberg turned to Elia, "Either way, son, time for you to run."

"Ready, sir."

"Medic!" Silverberg yelled, in German, repeating it until they all heard a bored "*Ja*?" from around the corner of the trench.

"Is Wald ready to move?"

No answer.

"Is he ready to move?"

As he finished his second request, a crouching field medic came around the corner. Hirsch followed a moment later.

"Well?"

"Sir," the medic said, "the private is gone. Dead."

Eyes avoided other eyes.

"Hell."

"*Ach.*"

Yis'ga'dal v'yis'kadash sh'may ra'bbo...

After waiting for the final line of the mourner's Kaddish to be mumbled by his men, Silverberg issued orders to the boys, "Get the body back to camp." He turned to Manes, "Take the first watch." Turning back to Elia, "Find the Field Rabbi and be sure he knows that Dov was *frum*."

A large caliber mortar shell detonated nearby, quickly followed by another. Dirt cascaded down the walls of the trench.

"Go! Now!" Silverberg ordered.

Elia took the two handles of the stretcher at the front and Hirsch the ones at the rear, and carried Dov's body the three kilometers to the main encampment.

• • •

FELDPOST – Infantry Regiment X

Rivka Arm
Czarnieckiego 27
Przemyśl

Dearest Rivka,

I trust this letter finds you, Malka, and Tanchem healthy and safe. As to myself, I am well, dreaming every night about walking along the San, our hands entwined. It seems like years since we last saw one another at the station, yet it has been but a month.

On arrival, we were trained by a Polish patriot in the arts of marksmanship, orienteering, ordinance and close quarters combat. Not the usual Hashomer fare to be sure! And now for the important news: after completing training, Hirsch and I have been reassigned from the Legion to the k.u.k.[4], serving with our fellow men of Przemyśl in the Fourth Battalion of the Gustav V. König von Schweden Regiment. The censors will not allow me to tell you exactly where we are but suffice it to say we are encamped to the north, engaged with the enemy, and on the march daily.

My commander is Osher Silverberg. Do you remember him? His son Asher played football. Before the war he was a maker of talits. Quite the change!

Life in war is hard but not intolerable. I have come to appreciate the ease and comfort of peacetime. Small things we take for granted. A warm bath, sleeping in a bed, or simply private time, become lost treasures, to someday be recovered.

We see death every day, mostly in the train of wrecked bodies being ferried from the front to field hospitals in the rear. Remember Dov Wald? The barber's son? A shell fragment, no larger than a coffee bean, sliced through his neck. Dead in five minutes.

I have quickly gotten used to the gore and the blood, which scares me just a bit. What you never get used to is the constant noise of the exploding artillery. When it's near, it's like lightning hitting your house, over and over again. But even worse is when it's just a bit farther away. You don't so much hear it as feel it, vibrating every bone in your body.

I have a request, my darling. Can you please write to my sister Jette? Tell her that I'm safe. And tell her that I love her. Ask Gitla for her postal address; she'll know what to do.

Then there's you, my Rivka. Your love is my shield against bullets, my tent against rain, and my blanket against the cold. When despair is thick and trouble is at hand, I conjure up a picture of your beautiful face, and all becomes right again in the world. We'll be together soon. I promise.

With all the love in my heart,

Elia

Przemyśl • 3rd of Tishrei, 5675 – Tuesday, September 23, 1914

A GENTLE ROLL followed a sharp tremor as the train passed over a double slip switch. "Sweetheart," Juda said to Rivka, "I just can't bear to see you cry. I was in the army. Orders change. Sometimes they have you marching right for an hour, and then you go left for two. Don't worry about your boy, he'll be fine."

"But what that officer said yesterday—"

"He said it just to get you out of the station. You'd been there all day."

"Maybe he knew something?"

"If something had happened to the men of Przemyśl, don't you think we would have heard of it on the Marconi?"

Rivka smiled at him through her tears, appreciative of his heartfelt attempt to soothe her, even if she had already made up her mind to not be placated. She sat snugly next to Gitla, a pile of the Arm's valises crowding in on the bench, her head resting on Gitla's shoulder, buried in her aunt's kinky, thinning black hair. After ceding his seat to an elderly Polish couple heading toward Pozan, Juda stood, hand wrapped around the edge of the iron luggage rack suspended from the ceiling. All five were knee-deep in valises, sacks, and bags, rendering movement problematic.

"Ever seen the trains this full?" Juda asked absentmindedly in Polish to the seated man, noticing the slightest hint of wetness just under his thin, blue-grey eyes.

"No," the man said. He turned his head to the window, away from Juda, eying a line of horse-drawn artillery almost as long as the train. Flanked by mounted fighters in brightly accented uniforms, they moved along the road parallel to the train tracks. "Will any of us ever again see Przemyśl?"

Conversations quickly petered out into whispers as most of the people in the seventeen coach cars pulled by locomotive were resigned to silently contemplate their war-ready town. At irregular intervals the relative peace of this wordless reflection was shattered by the report of howitzers—a single, sharp jolt if the shell landed nearby, or a prolonged rumble for impacts at a distance.

"Fucking bastards," Gitla mumbled, her forehead pressed against the window to keep from bumping her head every time the train rolled over a warped segment of track. "Devastation before war."

A shell exploded nearby making the train car jump like it was a bale of hay kicked by a horse.

Gitla shook her head, "It's all gone; leveled; here; look.

Rivka lifted her head. "What?" she asked before blowing her nose into the handkerchief she clutched to her chest.

Three shells impacted in a row, much too close for comfort.

The train, moving no faster than a horse's gallop, let out a metallic scream and slowed. A valise dislodged from the ceiling rack and would have landed in the Polish woman's lap had Juda not intervened. As the coach came to a full stop, the train let out a mighty fart of steam in relief.

"Stumps." Gitla said, peering out the window.

"Stumps?" Juda asked, perplexed.

"Stumps. Like where trees used to be. A whole forest worth of stumps. They murdered a whole forest."

The tracks shuddered as a big cannon shell was fired from a nearby fort toward the Russian lines, eight kilometers to the north.

"To make a clean alleyway to shoot at the Russians," Juda said, gesturing with his hands.

"The whole forest, damn it all. The whole thing."

"Better trees than people."

"And the village? Dunkowiczki. There used to be houses and farms—there and there. They burned them. Burned them to the dirt! We don't even need the Russians for war; we can destroy the land all by ourselves."

Juda looked away. He'd had this discussion with his wife before and had no stomach at this particular juncture to answer to all of the complaints she had for the male elements of humanity. Once engaged, there would be no stopping her. He counted thirteen more shell impacts before the train lurched backwards towards Zasanie. "They'll never take the forts lobbing small stuff like this at us," he concluded.

The train had only begun to move when a soldier jumped onto the stair at the end of the car where he could be seen speaking to a civilian standing by the exit. The soldier jumped off, waiting for the next car, presumably to again board and spread his message. A whisper started traveling through the car. As the civilian conferred with another who had been standing next to him, many, including Juda, yelled out, "What is going on!"

"Gentleman and ladies!" the civilian called. It took a moment for the voices in the car to silence. "As you can see, we are headed back to Przemyśl. The Russians have attacked the fort." He paused, a hundred eyes riveted on him.

"Let's go anyway!" one man shouted, followed by another. "It's dangerous either way, let's get to Cracow!"

The civilian hesitated, trying to form his words. "Um, we don't really have, how can I say this, any choice."

"Why!"

"No!"

"Cannot be!"

"But it is", he continued. "Blown up. Gone. There are no tracks to Cracow anymore."

The passengers fell silent. Wheels groaned against the track as more artillery rounds fell.

"The rails and the roads have been cut. We are encircled."

"You mean..."

"The fort has been invested. Przemyśl is besieged."

Four

Przemyśl • 10th of Tishrei, 5675 – Tuesday, September 30, 1914

"WAR SERVICES LAW, pumpkin," Juda said over morning tea.

"But you served. You retired. It's not fair!"

"You want fair? I'll give you fair," Gitla said to Rivka, jabbing at the quarter loaf of dark rye on the table with her finger. "Is it fair that the boys at the forts salivate for a lousy crust of bread while the Viennese strut about like peacocks feasting daily on spätzle and schnitzel?"

Juda shrugged. "The tower on Katedralna Hill is the only link the fort has to the outside, to news. Besides, it is our fortune that I know wireless. Weiss has already tried three times to bribe me to pass messages first to him."

"Take his money next time, schmuck," Gitla said to her husband like she meant it, drumming the fingers of her left hand on the wooden table.

"I made three trips to the forts yesterday. No signs of Russians to the south though we still seem to be shooting off our cannons," Rivka said, spreading jam on a slice of bread.

"South is all right," Juda said with authority. "Most of the action is north and west. We hold all the passes and may even be in Sanok by now. We'll be linked up and relieved in a matter of days. Stay away from forts five through eight and you'll be fine this week."

"You're such a big shot at Antmann's with all your secret communiqués, Juda dear. Free beer all siege long," Gitla said, rubbing her husband's shoulder. "The bread girl and the sauerkraut lady hear things too."

"Seriously, ladies, this thing could be over next week or could go on all winter. We need to prepare for the worst."

"Izzy begs me to stay quiet about his cellar," Rivka injected. "About how much flour he has stacked away."

Juda nodded. "No use in rubbing anyone's nose in it."

"Or inviting the Viennese to just take it," Gitla added, now serious. "I've got cabbages and salt to make two, maybe three barrels of kraut. I could use some help cutting and kneading. And if we can get ten or so liters of vinegar I can lay away six month worth of beets."

"I can get the vinegar," Rivka said. "It's stocked by quartermasters as part of rations. They'll do anything for real bread."

"You would, too. I've lived on zwieback. It's like eating shoe leather."

"I'll need some Kronen." She paused. "He'll just pay me less. Izzy's such a sweetheart."

"Besser? A *mensch,*" Gitla concurred. "A good man, making a small fortune in ten and fifty Heller coins having you ferry his bread to the forts. He'd just scrape by if he only had to bake for the yids left on Franciszkańska. We should buy, or better yet, trade with Besser. A few bags of flour for some kraut."

Rivka smiled sweetly, "Don't worry; I'll take care of my little Isidore."

The three rose and left the home. Juda climbed Katedralna Hill and took his seat at one of several Marconi sets, codebook in hand, ready to decipher. Rivka headed to the bakery and picked up two sacks of *semmel* rolls while Gitla packed her canvas sack full with sauerkraut, preserves, and wild honey. The woman met just past the inner defensive ring before making their way across crater-filled fields to Fort III where they peddled their goods to soldiers longing for small reminders of better times.

Nowy Korczyn • 23rd of Tishrei, 5675 – Tuesday, October 13, 1914

"WHO'S GOT A smoke? I need a Memphis," Elia asked, leaning against bullet-pocked tree.

Manes passed an open carton to Elia.

"I could use some food that might have actually been alive sometime this century. This shit isn't fit for a dog. To hell with cigarettes," Hirsch said, tapping an empty beef stew can with his knife.

A boy dressed in black and wearing a *keppe* approached the camp from town. He kept his eyes on the dirt path, dragging a lame leg while balancing the bundle he clutched in both arms. His slight frame and large cargo cast a long, erratically moving shadow on the ground in front of the soldiers.

"Hang on, Herschel. Here comes the cavalry," someone said.

When the boy was within earshot, Hirsch called to him, "Chocolate! Dear messenger of God, please have sweet chocolate tonight."

The boy approached a makeshift table erected by the soldiers from trench boards and freshly felled timber. A dozen men drew to a tight semi-circle around the lad as he prepared to display his wares by pulling on several bow-tied knots holding his sack together. The uniformed men inched closer, some tense with anticipation, others just curious or simply bored.

"What's your name, kid?" a soldier asked.

"Shlomo," he said, the drama of the moment completely lost on him as he pulled the canvas back, revealing a few dozen 100 count boxes of cigarettes.

"Crap," Hirsch mumbled, as he and several other men left the circle.

Manes pulled a carton from the bag, displaying for all to see the cover advertisement of a rosy cheeked, red vested cigarette offering, jolly-faced man standing beneath a globe printed in Cyrillic. "The whole world smokes Russian Renta cigarettes," he read aloud, adding with his own jolly smile, "Only when the alternative is no cigarettes at all."

The remaining men laughed as Manes tossed the cigarettes back to the table.

"How much?" Max, the company carpenter asked.

Shlomo looked up at his prospective buyer. "Ten if coin, twenty if note."

"Usury! Twenty for cigarettes? Let the Russians come back here for twenty Kronen."

The boy was unmoved.

"Ten by note. But only because you're lame."

Shlomo began tying the strings back together.

Manes dropped three ten Kronen notes onto the half closed canvas. "Two for thirty."

The boy snatched up the notes and examined them before securing them in his pants pocket. Manes helped himself to a carton. "What the hell else are you going spend your weekly pay on, gentlemen?"

Standing firm on price, Shlomo sold all his Russian cigarettes to the troops before limping back toward town.

TWENTY MINUTES LATER in a cold drizzle, Silverberg, three *Hasidim*, and the limping cigarette boy, who apparently never made it home, appeared at the edge of the field, walking toward the soldiers gathered under a tarp, drinking tea and smoking Rentas.

"These things taste like shit." Manes said, spotting the approaching party. "What's the Sergeant want with the black-hats?"

"They probably need help clearing a building or defusing a shell," Elia said, drawing deeply on his new brand before flicking it into a puddle and spitting. "Shit is about right."

The Sergeant addressed his men once in earshot, "Boys, gather round."

They slowly assembled around the table.

One of the black-clad men, walking a half a step in front of the others, addressed the men in a remarkably loud and clear voice.

"Shalom, brothers, and welcome to my town. I am Chaim Frydenberg, Rabbi of Nowy Korczyn. This is Avner Feiner, synagogue *meister* and Avraham Bauman, one of our leading citizens, head of the burial society."

He took note of the Rentas, "And I see many of you've met my son, Shlomo." Chaim put his arm around the boy, who tried hard to show no emotion before breaking into a gap-toothed grin.

"The war is a terrible thing," the Rabbi continued. "Most of our sons are gone, taken by the Tsarist army. One or two we hid, a few got across the river and joined the Emperor's Army or ride with Pilsudski."

A few men mumbled their skepticism aloud.

"But today is day that transcends war, which goes beyond the bounds of all earthy concerns. Today we both finish and start anew the great cycle of Torah, the eternal and unending gift from God. While you may have to fight tomorrow, the people of Nowy Korczyn would be honored if you would come to our modest synagogue and celebrate this night with us."

Manes flicked his cigarette into the grass. "It seems to me your God and your Torah hasn't done all that much for the working class soldier lately," he said, then added with enmity, "Mister Rabbi. I don't need your moralizing, your bourgeois superstitions, or your town's naive piety. Manes would rather drink by himself."

"Listen, Sterner," Silverberg started, before being muted by a wave of the rabbi's hand.

Rabbi Frydenberg walked up to Manes and looked him in the eye. Seated at the makeshift table, Manes and the five-foot-tall rabbi ended up face to face. "I am Chaim, or Mister Rabbi, as you like. And you, I take it, are Mister Sterner or Manes. Which do you prefer?"

"I'm Manes; Comrade Sterner to you."

"Mister Comrade Manes," the rabbi began. "You seem to be strong man. A man the others respect; a man of judgment."

"I trust my own eyes and ears, if that's what you mean. No rabbi is going to tell me what to think."

The brigade slowly closed in on the two men.

"Right you are, Mister Comrade Manes. Right you are to trust your senses. No so-called expert can tell you what to think, can they."

Hirsch leaned to Elia and whispered, "It's a trap."

Manes nodded to the rabbi, "The working class can think for itself."

Elia nodded to Hirsch.

"Yes, yes it can. So true." Frydenberg began to turn away but stopped, looking lost. "But I'm a little confused. Perhaps just one little question for you, Mister Comrade Manes, all right?"

"Go ahead."

"I am an old man and my mind is not what it once was."

"Manes is dead," Elia mouthed to Hirsch.

"When did you live in Nowy Korczyn?" The rabbi's voice

grew stronger. "How is it that you know the soul of our village?"

"This is my first visit to Nowy—"

Chaim cut him off. "And when did I have the opportunity to moralize you into this state of aversion?"

"Well, I..." Manes pursed his lips, his shoulders slumping.

"I must be getting old. I can't remember doing this, though given your experience here, I must have."

"Rabbi, I didn't mean to..."

"Oh, this is your first visit to our town, isn't it? And we have only had the pleasure of meeting just this instant, yes?"

Manes laughed, shaking his head.

"Then someone told you about us, about me. Or you just don't like my ugly face. I couldn't blame a handsome young man for that. I'm just a feeble old man."

"Give up, Manes!" one of the soldiers blurted out.

"Resign!" Hirsch added.

"Just a feeble old man, the Rabbi muttered, shaking his bowed head, hiding a smirk from the howling troops.

"Tip your king, soldier!" Elia yelled.

Manes stood, towering over Chaim. "All right, I give up. Resign! I love Nowy Korczyn. The people are beautiful. I give a day's pay a week to the Temple!" Manes joined the balance of his battalion in laughter.

The rabbi held his hand up bringing a jovial silence to the clearing. "It is a truly wise man who can laugh at himself." He took a step forward and embraced Manes as best he could. Manes returned the hug, lifting Frydenberg clear off the ground.

"Simchat Torah!" Elia yelled over and over. He was soon joined by everyone else.

The rabbi turned and started walking toward town. He waved an arm and called over his shoulder, "Let's drink! To the synagogue!"

THE SYNAGOGUE WAS a two-story brick box with a clay tile roof capped by a secondary slate bonnet. A large concrete pad sat between the packed gravel street and the brick riser that led through double wooden doors into the sanctuary. The interior was dominated by a dark wooden Ark resting on a carved limestone slab protected by a wrought iron gate. Long wooden benches provided seating for worshipers in front of the velvet-covered *bimah.* White-washed walls were covered with Hebrew verses, each framed in a decorative floral border.

Bottles of schnapps and flasks of vodka circulated freely in front a fresco of the Jerusalem skyline painted across the wall holding up the women's balcony.

By the time Rabbi Frydenberg approached the Ark, most of the soldiers and townsmen were well on their way to being drunk. After opening the gate under the crown topped Ten Commandments, presented in relief and guarded by a pair of fearsome limestone etched lions, the Rabbi passed scrolls to Avner and Avraham before taking the last one himself. The three townsmen carried the scrolls to the three chairs next to the *Bimah* as the congregation sang old melodies with even older words. Two young boys and an elderly man with a cane left the benches to attend to the Torahs, removing their embroidered velvet covers, the sterling *yads* before lifting off each scroll's shield and finial.

Rabbi Chaim, Avner, and Avraham began a march in a wide arc around the *Bimah,* with more singing, more men rising, encircling one side of the gallery. As they stepped out, one by one, the seated men and boys joined the procession. The three men took a turn, lifting their scrolls overhead, held aloft only by two poles. As the liquor flowed, it became a contest: which man could spread his arms furthest, displaying the most Torah.

With each revolution, the Torahs were passed to other men and new competitions joined, fueled by ever more alcohol.

Soon, the entire main floor was up, marching and passing back and forth the three Torahs.

By the fourth circuit around the synagogue, the soldiers of Przemyśl had joined the competition and the synagogue at Nowy Korczyn was a riot of singing, dancing, drinking, and revelry.

On the sixth lap, a stocky, bald-headed butcher named Ejchler spread one of the scrolls to five full panels. The feat, apparently a local record, was celebrated with cheers and schnapps.

"Take a turn, Manes." Elia slurred.

Fifteen minutes later the exhausted Rabbi addressed his congregation, now considerably calmed. "Had I been blessed with daughters, I would die happy to have this man as my son-in-law." He wiped the sweat from his brow with a handkerchief. "For the first *aliyah*, I call to the *Bimah* the lion, the only man to ever show six panels." He pointed to the back row. "Manes Sterner: honorary son of Nowy Korczyn."

The soldiers cheered and reveled as Manes weaved toward the *Bimah*. He kissed the Rabbi, and then turned to acknowledge his audience. In a matter of seconds the synagogue came to order, the jovial became deferential, the gleeful turned reverent. He chanted, "*Bar-chu et Adonai ham vorach...*"

One by one, the Rabbi called up all of the soldiers to read the final Torah portion of the yearly cycle:

> *Never again did there arise in Israel a prophet like Moses – whom the Lord singled out, face to face, for the various signs and portents that the Lord sent him to display in the land of Egypt, against Pharaoh and all his courtiers and his whole country, and for all the great might and awesome power that Moses displayed before all Israel.*

Continuing without pause to the beginning of the cycle:

> *When God began to create heaven and earth the earth being unformed and void, with darkness over the surface of the deep and a wind from God sweeping over the water God said, "Let there be light"; and there was light. God saw that the light was good, and God separated the light from the darkness. God called the light Day, and the darkness He called Night. And there was evening and there was morning, a first day.*

An hour later the tipsy locals and drunken soldiers from Przemyśl spilled out onto the muddy dead end street where the synagogue stood. Once again taking up arms and lighting cigarettes, the men from Galicia led the inebriated celebrants in a song and hoot-filled parade punctuated by rifle shots, into the cool, starless night sky. When they reached the center of Nowy Korczyn, no further from the synagogue than the Scheinbach was from Plac na Bramie, the Rabbi declared his intention to lead the two hundred marchers for seven full circuits around the market square.

The next morning, after coffee, cigarettes and some serious retching, not a single man in the battalion could remember exactly how wide Manes had held the Torah or how many laps around the square had actually been completed.

<u>FELDPOST – Infantry regiment 10</u>

Elia Reifer

Dearest Elia,

First of all I love and miss you and I hope and pray for you daily— and you know how much I dislike prayer! But with all seriousness, I trust this letter finds you safe and healthy.

As you might know, Przemyśl was besieged by the Tsarists with contact to Crakow only reestablished the day before yesterday. What you probably did not know is that I am still in the city, living with Juda and Gitla.

I was hoping, no, dying to see my Elia, even if but for a minute, so when I heard a rumor that your Tenth was being deployed through Przemyśl, I talked daddy into allowing me to stay just for a few days after he and Malka left. But alas, Przemyśl these days is nothing but rumor; no Tenth, no Elia. Our train made it just past Zasanie before we were forced to return when the Russians blew up the tracks. That was three weeks ago.

Now, my love, the difficult part: Even as trains arrive hourly to stock the fort and bolster the city, returning nearly empty with ample space for the trip to the west, I have decided to stay in Przemyśl. Please don't be cross with me love – I have to stay.

Isidore has no one other than me to sell his breads at the forts. He's like a zayde to me and I cannot leave him to fend for himself. The Russians are fleeing and the siege will soon lift, but just in any case, we have laid away plenty of provisions. Besides, Juda has been pressed back

into service as a wireless operator so he and Gitla are here with me too.

Daddy will be fuming when he receives my post, but I am not a child and people here rely on me. And don't you worry about me. Przemyśl is safe and compared to what you must face, no real hardship.

I'll tell you what hard is – living in your room, sleeping in your bed wrapped in your blankets – surrounded by you – without you. That's cruel; nearly intolerable.

Elia sweetheart – flip this card and look at the picture of the river. I want you to know that every night I dream of warm summer nights on the quay, on a blanket next to you, watching for streaking stars in the heavens or in your eyes.

With all the love in my heart,

Rivka

Przemyśl • 28th of Sh'vat, 5675 – Friday, February 12, 1915

THE COAL-FIRED BREAD ovens vented into a narrow walkway that separated Besser's Bakery from an apothecary. On most days, the prevailing breeze pushed the heavenly aroma out onto Słowackiego, enticing local shoppers to stop in for a fresh pastry, while teasing hungry soldiers marching past the store on their way to the forts.

"Please, Rivka, please don't go. Who needs the money, anyway?" Isidore said pulling rolls off the cooling rack and putting them into the grey burlap sack on the kneading counter.

"We are not selling our breads to the Polacks for valueless paper, or worse, for lousy Viennese scrip," Rivka shot back. "And that's not really the point and you know it. If I don't bring it to the boys on the front, all the fresh bread ends up on the tables of the Generals at the Metropol and the working class eats moldy zwieback."

"Rivka, it's not safe out there anymore. And our sack or two of rolls can't feed fifty forts. Besides, we should cut back a bit, in case this thing goes on and on." He paused and put a hand on her shoulder, "*Our* bread? So exactly when did you become my partner, Miss Arm?"

"Mister Besser," she said, throwing her arms around the old man, squeezing him tightly.

"It's Isidore, precious."

"Oh, Isidore," she said playfully.

"Please?" he whispered into her ear. "A meter of snow last Shabbat, and now minus ten at midday and minus twenty-five by night. Who needs it? Stay here with me."

"All right, I'll deliver these today then we're done with the forts. We'll sell our—I mean your—breads to the Poles and be happy. No, not happy. War is so full of choices between bad and worse, between feeling awful and getting killed."

"That's my little sheep with the Yiddish head."

The sound of boots being kicked against the stone foundation of the building to rid them of snow followed by the ring of bells hung across the door jamb alerted them to the arrival of soldiers, sending Besser scurrying from the back room, past the main counter, and towards the door, standing ajar.

"Tomas, come in, my son. And don't worry about the snow."

"All right if the men wait inside today?"

Tomas was a thin and pale, just like every soldier that manned the forts over the winter siege. His features were smooth and angular; a scab on his badly chapped lower lip was the only splash of color to be found on his entire face.

"Of course. Yet another day in our crummy paradise."

"Thank you, Mister Besser." Tomas nodded toward the door as two more Hungarian soldiers came in out of the snow, the last one closing the door again to the sound of bells. Each propped his rifle up by the coat rack then stood to the side in the bakery customer queuing area, rubbing their hands together for warmth. Tomas's glasses, nestled deeply in his eye sockets, instantly fogged.

"No, thank *you* Mister First Lieutenant Lenard," the baker quickly corrected. "And for heaven's sake, call me Isidore. Or, Izzy."

The soldier shrugged, "The army needs for your rolls to make it to the fort and I don't want Miss Arm robbed again."

"Hungry?" Isidore asked the Magyars.

All three soldiers looked at the baker, inhaled, feasting on the nearly edible aroma of freshly baked bread that wafted through the store, and then looked down at the floor.

"Of course, I'm an idiot." Besser addressed one of the privates, "You, what's your name?"

He looked up, "Imre."

"So young." He patted the boy on the cheek. "When did you last eat?"

"Fourteen hundred yesterday, sir. Soup."

"To call it soup is a stretch. More like warm water with a few specks of sinew of highly questionable origin," Thomas added.

Isidore counted out three squares of honey-nut roll from the large collection in the wicker basket resting on the wooden countertop and set them on a china plate. "Eat! Eat my boys," he said to the soldiers, waving with both hands.

As the Magyars descended on the plate, Rivka appeared from the back room with a large canvas sack slung over her shoulder. Each man consumed his square in a slightly different manner; one devoured his in two bites; another savored a hundred tiny nibbles.

"Drink some hot tea before you brave the snow," Isidore said, guiding a small glass tumbler under the spigot before flipping the brass stopcock on the samovar.

Each of the soldiers licked his fingers clean of the last hint of honey before joining Rivka and Isidore for tea.

A PRIVATE NAMED Laszlo walked in front, rifle cocked and ready, while Imre followed closely behind him, carrying the burlap sack filled with bread rolls over his shoulder. A few paces behind, Tomas escorted Rivka, carrying Imre's rifle as well as his own. On particularly frigid days like this, Rivka wore Juda's old army coat with a wool blanket draped around her shoulders. Her head was covered by a babushka and further wrapped in a long scarf, treated by Gitla with a concoction of herbs said to repel the myriad diseases constantly circulating within the confines of the besieged forts.

They chatted as they slogged through the snow to the east toward the outer ring.

"As for me, before being conscripted, I was teaching at the University of Szeged after taking degrees in both physics and mathematics from the Budapest University," Tomas told her, stealing a glance at the uncovered parts of her face.

"I don't want to sound too naïve, but I find this science, these invisible waves, to be almost spiritual. I see nothing in science that contradicts the existence of God. I really appreciate the opportunity to discuss this—" They ducked as the party was sprayed with slush by the wheels of the passing flat-bed supply truck.

"Bastards did it on purpose," Tomas said, under his breath.

"So these X-rays are like light but we can't see them? And they can pass through anything?" Rivka asked, oblivious to the supposed insult.

The rumble of a shell hitting closer than usual briefly upset the group's gait.

Tomas continued, "Not lead, but most everything else. And the important point is that they act in very specific ways when they pass through crystals of pure element. And because they are so small, we can use them to probe the very structure of matter itself."

"So it's sort of like identifying where the glass in a kaleidoscope came from just by the pattern you see in the eyehole?"

"Exactly. You're brilliant, Rivka. After the war you should come to Szeged and take a degree."

For a brief moment this marvelous dream seemed to be within Rivka's reach before reality came crashing down in the form of two horse-drawn wagons. The first, loaded with broken, bleeding, and moaning men, the last stacked with neatly arranged corpses, each covered with a rough field blanket.

Rivka fought back a flood of horrible images of war and joined the Magyars in staring at the ground as the wagons passed.

"Tell me about you, Tomas," Rivka said as the wagon passed behind them and they resumed walking. "You wear a cross yet I've heard you use Hebrew. Are you—, did you, is there a family back in Szeged?"

Tomas exhaled, his breath looking like cigarette smoke in the frigid air.

"I was born, raised, and became a Bar Mitzvah in Gyor, but in fact, I do not believe in God any more than I believe that the moon is made of cheese. At age seventeen I fell in love, or so I thought, with a Catholic girl. We were both young, stupid. As these stories usually go, she soon was with child. Her father was a powerful man, not one to be made a fool of, so we ran off to Budapest. I took the sacrament to wed Vilma, for our Jonas, and, I suppose, because I thought it would ease my way to University."

Rivka turned to see Tomas looking at her.

"She died of a breast tumor soon after I received my degree. After burying her I contacted her father, as a good Catholic should. Within a month he had the marriage annulled and bribed the courts to award Jonas to his custody."

"I'm so sorry," Rivka said, turning her head back to the road.

"Life has a way of just going on." The wind gusted. A tear from the corner of Tomas's eye rolled down his cheek before freezing in a ridge on his chin.

They turned off the Lemberg highway onto a smaller road. Just past the junction they came to two three-gun tripods set up in a wind-blown clearing at the top of a small rise. Boot prints pointed the way to the field where six soldiers were on their knees, clearing snow, hacking away at the frozen dirt with their bayonets.

"Digging for beets," Laszlo said as he passed by.

Rivka stopped in her tracks, glanced at Tomas, then at Imre's bread bundle, then back at the field.

"Rivka, please don't do this. You can't save everyone," Tomas said, raising his voice as she stormed by him.

"Put it down!" she yelled at the soldier. "Give me my bread!"

"Rivka," Tomas said, now softer, as if pleading, "It's not legal to feed the troops."

As Imre set the sack down in the snow, Rivka spun and looked at Tomas, with mouth pursed and daggers in her eyes. "This is my bread, not yours. You may think that there is no greater power watching as we walk by these boys, no right or wrong as they catch a whiff of my bread. You may be able to ignore the screaming from their empty stomachs, but I can't."

Tomas leaned against his rifle while Rivka took six rolls from the sack and forded the snow to the men. After a brief discussion, Rivka waived off the payment one of the starving men offered at her. One by one the six took a roll then dropped to their knees, snow to their waists, furiously crossing themselves before devouring the bread. As she retraced her steps through the snow back to Tomas, he called out, "I won't tell anyone," and then whispered to himself,

"Because you are so good; because I desperately want to make love to you, Rivka."

They headed for Fort XV, now faintly visible through the light snow and smoke. Eventually, the mood calmed, and Tomas and Rivka restarted their conversation.

"And you? What of your life, Rivka Arm."

"I've lived in Przemyśl all my life".

"Lovely little hamlet."

"Sarcasm is not wit."

"Sorry, I..."

"I'm just pulling your leg. I know it's hard to imagine, but it actually was quite lovely before all this."

"And what of religion. Of God?" Tomas asked. "Seems you were alluding to the subject back there."

"God, hmm..." Rivka's voice trailed off as she contemplated the question and tried to formulate a response, looking for the words that would be both accurate and convey the impression that she was an erudite, modern thinker.

"I do believe in God, but not in a corporeal sense, more as a summation of human morality."

"Then there is absolute right and wrong?"

"No, but people like to group with other people who share their moralities. As Jews, we have an elaborate set of stories, metaphors really, that define our common moralities. Catholics have the New Testament. Ottomans have the Koran."

"If they have all the rules, then why do they all need a God?"

A barrage of mortar fire, three loud reports in a row, came from the fort off in the distance, followed by an explosion from an incoming round.

"We had better not be walking into another shell fight, Rivka."

She continued, "Remember, there are no absolutes. If you boil it all down, distill it to the essence, all religions are based on just a few basics. Dictums such as 'thou shall not kill.' If it all depends on just a few of these, you really need people to not question them."

"God as an axiom. Excellent."

Rivka smiled.

Tomas was even more pleased. He thought that never, not once in a decade, had he had an exchange at that intellectual level with his petite, vacuous wife, Vilma. He snuck a glance at Rivka, trying to imagine what her face and body would look like stripped of all the layers that covered her against the cold.

THE EARTH SHOOK, then shook again.

"Artillery barrage. Looks like tens or twelve's," Tomas said, huddled behind a stand of boulders a few hundred meters from the entrance to Fort XV.

"What's the count of the hits behind us?"

"Twelve then thirty between salvos, I think," Laszlo said.

"Two guns at forty two seconds between shells," Tomas concluded, adding, "And timing ahead?"

"Forty-two also. Must only be one cannon," the private said, looking up from his watch.

Tomas addressed the privates, "One gun aimed forward versus two behind us. We go forward to the fort."

"Looks like about a minute in this snow to cross the field," Imre said.

"Agreed. Single file, following me," Tomas commanded. "Laszlo will keep track of time. At thirty five seconds he yells 'ready'. At forty seconds he yells 'cover' and we all hit the snow and cover our heads."

"And pray," Imre added, crossing himself.

"As soon as it hits, count to three, then get up and follow me into the Fort."

Laszlo peeled his leather glove back and looked at his

watch.

"Got it?" Tomas asked.

Four heads nodded.

"Count it down."

"Twenty."

"Ten"

"Five, four, three..."

A high pitched whistling noise was followed by a flash and an immediate concussion as the space between the rocks and the Fort became a mélange of snow, dirt, shrapnel, and smoke.

"Now!" Tomas shouted, dashing from behind the rocks into the open.

They rushed through the field as fast as they could, trying not to make fresh tracks and staying between the sticks that had been placed in the snow to show the safe route around the mines. Sometimes this meant sliding down the rim of a bomb crater and climbing back out a few meters later.

"Ready!" Rivka heard from just behind her. She sped up, placing her foot in the snow just as Tomas's foot vacated it.

"Cover!" Laszlo yelled, diving into a drift with Imre.

Rivka hit the snow, covered heavily a moment later by Tomas, like a woolen comforter pressed fast to her back along the entire length of her body, from head to back to buttocks to legs. A split second later, as a shell's impact concussion shook them, a pleasant shiver radiated out from the soft wisps of hair on the back of Rivka's neck. She tilted her head, exposing more skin as his warm, wet lips alit on her.

Laszlo's, "Three!" separated Tomas from her and brought both to their feet, running.

Soon, Rivka and the Magyars were safe underneath the twenty meters of dirt, steel and concrete – Fort XV, otherwise known as Fort Borek.

"RIVKA, TAKE THE bread and stay close behind us. Imre, Laszlo, in front with me."

A mob grew at the fortified entry portico as rumors of the bread's arrival spread through the Fort.

"Form a line! There's enough, no need to push!" Tomas yelled.

The artillery men ignored him, pushing closer. Rivka didn't need to understand a word of Hungarian to be concerned as they all backed up toward the side wall of the entrance.

"They've only brought enough for the officers!"

"I'll pay twice for each roll!"

"A silver Krone for one! Silver for a lousy roll!"

"I beg you!"

"Let's just take the bread!"

Tomas cocked his rifle, "I'll shoot the first one who grabs for the bread." Imre and Laszlo cocked their rifles too. "You should set a higher price." He said, turning to Rivka.

"Let's just give it to them. Who can blame them, they're starved."

As her back touched the dirty concrete wall, the end of the barrel of Tomas's rifle rested on a corporal's chest. Like all of the men, he looked thin and gaunt, with bloodshot eyes and a radiating bodily stench. He was hatless, with numerous scars on his scalp. Like about half the men in the mob, he had recently had his head shaved, likely to rid him of the ubiquitous lice that plagued every fort, camp and trench from the Urals to the English Channel.

"Magyar brother, either you shoot me or I'm getting some food," the corporal said, grabbing the rifle barrel and guiding it to a spot on his tunic that was over his heart.

Tomas had just pushed him back into the crowd with his rifle, when a gunshot reverberated in the enclosed concrete, silencing all but the artillery rounds.

"Attention!" the officer barked, holstering his pistol.

"Lieutenant Colonel Kaszás, sector commander," Tomas

whispered to Rivka, bringing his gun to his side, standing straight up and leaning his head back a few degrees toward her.

"Fall in!" Kaszás commanded, pointing at the far wall.

The men quickly lifted their siege of the bread party and formed two lines a dozen or so meters away as the Lieutenant Colonel approached the three soldiers who were guarding the woman.

After saluting crisply, Tomas was dismissed with a perfunctory half wave, half salute. Kaszás then addressed Rivka, "Do you speak German?"

"Yes, Colonel," she said, noting that other than an impressive saber and a nice collection of stars on his facings, he looked like all the other men: tired, dirty and hungry.

He bowed to her, "Lieutenant Colonel Georg Kaszás, at your service."

She nodded, "Rivka Arm, baker."

"Please accept my humble apologies on behalf of the Twenty-Third Artillery Brigade. Our behavior has been quite unbecoming of Magyar soldiers."

"That is not necessary, sir. The starving should never be asked to apologize to the well fed."

He briefly contemplated before speaking. "You have my undying gratitude for risking life and limb to bring food to the men at the front. If we are ever—when we are relieved, I am going to see to it that you receive *Die Zivilverdienstmedaille*, or whatever medal they are giving to civilians."

"I'm not giving you bread, I'm selling it to starving men. A medal? I should be shot as a capitalist, a gouger."

Kaszás leaned in toward Rivka and smiled broadly, displaying a nasty array of crooked, yellow teeth, with his back to his men, so only she could see, and whispered, "Our time will come soon, Comrade, our time will come soon."

Turning to the men, he spoke forcefully, "There will be no bread bought today."

Moans and sighs.

"It is not fair that men now manning the cannons can get no bread. That men without silver are denied."

More moans and sighs.

"Fort Borek will buy all the bread and divide it evenly amongst all the men."

Rivka accepted Kaszás' first offer for the sack of rolls and each of the men manning Fort XV feasted that afternoon on quarter rations of canned pork stew accompanied by half of a freshly baked, hard crusted *semmel* roll from Besser's bakery.

THE ARTILLERY PETERED out after noon. Rivka and Tomas left the fort for town at 14:00, after an hour without incoming fire.

"Will I ever see you again?" Tomas asked as they retraced their steps through a crater.

"It's not like you're going anywhere any time soon, Mister Lenard. Come in the morning, I'll save a honey roll for you. We'll have tea," she said as they approached the rocks at the far end of the field.

As soon as the pair disappeared behind the first large boulder, Tomas sped up and put his hand on Rivka's shoulder. "Rivka, please."

She stopped walking and turned to him. Tomas put his free hand on her waist. Their eyes met. He pulled her to him. Their lips met. She instinctively pushed back for a moment before relenting; now using her arms around his waist to pull him tight to her. Eyes closed, mouths opened, and tongues entwined.

She broke the kiss and pushed back. They each took a small step back from the other. "I'm sorry, Rivka.'

"Don't be sorry, Tomas. I liked it and I... I'm fond of you. Very fond. But we can't do this. I have a, a boy in the army.

This can't lead anywhere."

"You intrigue me, Rivka. Time here moves when we're together. And it's not like I want to marry you. And I can't even begin to say what the provost would say if a proper Catholic professor married a Jewess." He moved a step closer and put a hand on her waist, "But tell me, why does it have to lead anywhere?"

She turned and started walking, "Because it is wrong. It's breaking faith."

"Rivka, we're both stuck in this hellhole, surrounded by people who want to kill us, with men killing each other for two thousand miles in every direction, each of our hearts heavy. If we can find some calm, some peace, some pleasure in each other's arms, it's not wrong and it's not any real breach of faith."

"I don't think so," Rivka said as they reached the main road.

"As long as we don't fall in love, it's no different than taking a bath or having a massage or any other pleasure. Just more so."

"That's just rubbish, and you know it."

"Why does it have to be so? Open your mind."

She stopped and turned. After waiting for a group of soldiers to pass, she spoke, "Trust, fidelity, love, these are feelings that you do not, no, cannot have all to yourself. They are, by definition, the feelings of a pair, where both must agree or all is lost. You may not think that kissing me, not that we would stop there, is a breach of faith but what you think is irrelevant. What would Elia think, that's what matters, how would *he* feel?"

"He wouldn't feel because he wouldn't know."

"A crime is a crime even if the police don't know it happened. Besides, how can you put yourself in a position where you have to either lie or hurt someone you love?"

For the first time in their short relationship he was at a loss for words. “Of course you’re right... I was just rationalizing. I just wanted...”

“Sex. You wanted sex. Stop the presses! Issue an extra! A soldier far from home wants sex.”

He smiled broadly, glancing around to be sure no one could hear them talking. “Yes I do.”

“Know what? I do too. But I want a lot of things. Like hot tea at Antmann’s.”

As they walked into town, she thought about Elia, determined to lose her virginity to him at the earliest possible opportunity.

“MORRIE, TOMAS LENARD. Tomas, Morrie Antmann, the owner,” Rivka said. “How are you holding up? Can you sit?”

Morrie glanced over the empty bar and the thinly populated tables lining the windows looking out at the square. “Sorry, no time, Riv.” He glanced at the door that led to the kitchen, “Since Judes passed, no time at all.” He shuffled away, mumbling.

“Typhus,” Rivka said, “She died on New Year’s Day.

“A million tragedies, all around us.”

“Indeed,” Rivka concurred, thoughts drifting.

They drank hot tea with honey in silence. While Rivka stared out the frosted window at the mass of horses on the Plac na Bramie, Tomas stared down at his tea, watching the vortex created by his nervous stirring.

“What?” Rivka exclaimed, breaking a long silence. Leaning toward the window, she used her glove to scrape clean the frost obscuring her view.

“What is it?” Lenard asked, looking up.

Rivka pressed her forehead to the icy pane, struggling to make out the scene unfolding on the Plac through the smeared, streaked glass. Trembling, she kicked back her chair and wiped her brow with her hand before bolting for the door, leaving her hat, gloves and shawl behind.

Civilian and soldier alike referred to Kusmanek's entourage and their majestic white and dappled grey mounts as "the herd." Today, the herd's seventy horses were tied to the black iron railings in front of the Café Metropol where the supreme commander of the fortress and his general staff were taking their lunch.

By the time Tomas reached her, Rivka was on her knees, thigh deep in snow, straw and horse urine, sobbing uncontrollably.

He took his attention off her for a second to look at the horses. "Oh my God," he said while his hands stroked her head.

"Bastards! Bastards!" she managed to squeeze out between sobs and gasps for air.

Tomas knelt in the fetid slush, crying with Rivka, while dozens of porters streamed out from the Café laden with silver platters overflowing with beets, carrots and greens, offered to the seventy horses by a cadre of junior officers until the beasts could eat no more. Long after Tomas was back in his quarters and Rivka had returned to the bakery, the General Staff finished their marathon lunch. Many of the officers fed handfuls of sugar cubes taken from the coffee service to their mounts before riding off en masse to inspect the front lines.

New York • 29th of Sh'vat, 5675 – Saturday, February 13, 1915

THREE SOLID KNOCKS had Marta tossing the *New York Times* on the coffee table and heading toward the door. Julia didn't look up, focused on Hans and Fritz Katzenjammer, recent additions to the *New York World*'s comic page. She would read, then repeat aloud: "*Vun ting is sure, if vee find a island mit cannibals on I send you ashore, you little skallywaggers.*" The colloquial English mixed with the occasional German word was good practice for the sort of patois often spoken on the Lower East side of Manhattan.

Marta slid open the iron plate, creating a two by four inch gap through which she could safely communicate with anyone who came to the door of the house at 111 Ridge Street. "Whadda ya want?"

"I'm looking for Sophie," a man's voice said. "She here?"

"No one here by that name. Good day." Marta slammed the iron plate shut and headed back to the couch. As she was reaching for the paper, the man at the door knocked again. Marta returned to the door and reopened the slot.

"What?"

"I'm here for Sophie. Big redhead. Joey King over on Spring sent me."

"Wait," Marta said, shutting the speaking hole and turning to Julia who had put the *World* down and was now looking at the *Times*. "King? Do we know a Joey King from over by Spring Street?"

"Przemyśl. Here," she pointed at the words on the news print. "It's talking about Przemyśl."

"Right, but this guy's got the name of one of the girls. Do we let him in?"

"Przemyśl, Przemyśl. King? Hmm... no."

Marta opened the slot, "Go away."

"But the King ..."

"You need a fat lip buster? You wanna fuck with us?"

"The King," Julia said with a smile. "Marta, come sit and read this to me."

She slammed the iron plate closed, "Coming, Julia."

As Marta finished reading, Julia's consciousness was flooded by voices and images from a family visit to Przemyśl, pulled from fragments of memories that lingered in the deep recesses of her memory.

She recalled a small but brilliant sliver of red-orange

peeking out from between piles of dark clouds hung over a denuded grain field under the twilight sky. Julia remembered that it rained all that day in Medyka and that the horse cart wheels had cut fresh grooves in the mud.

"The King!" she could hear little Elia saying, over and over again, becoming more animated with each poster that he pointed at.

"The Emperor Franz Joseph," her father had corrected.

"For sixty years the Jew's savior," her mama had droned.

She could see the breath coming from Elia's mouth as he pointed and called out, "Fort Hurko!" Julia heard her father lecturing from the driver's bench, voice deep and sure, pretending he was a rabbi. "A Skoda mortar can lob a cannonball all the way Mościska. And those round turrets, they swivel so we can point the cannons anywhere. Some are even with electric motors that retract the mortar after each firing. Przemyśl cannot be taken by any mortal force of arms." Again and again he said it. "Przemyśl cannot be taken by any mortal force of arms."

Julia saw every café and beer hall filled to capacity, overflowing onto the street. She could feel Elia's head on her shoulder, staring up at the new electric lamps connected by slender threads wrapped around glass insulators at the top of each pole. She could practically reach out and touch the banner held by a pair of brightly colored Hussars trumpeting 2 December 1908 as the Night of Light in Przemyśl, in honor of the diamond jubilee of the reign of Emperor Franz Joseph.

She breathed deeply after feeling the concussion of mortars lifting fireworks skyward from the station, echoing off the Zasanie hillside.

Julia mouthed along with every man, woman and child in Przemyśl, "drei! zwei! einz!" before gasping as lamps bathed the town in warm, yellow light for the first time…

Another knock on the door brought Julia back to the lower East Side of New York City.

Przemyśl • 3rd of Nisan, 5675 – Thursday, March 18, 1915

MAJOR GENERAL STEPHAN Ljubičić, commander of the 45th Brigade of Magyars, nervously brought his men to attention as General Kusmanek and his entourage marched into the hushed mess hall and mounted the hastily erected platform. In the tense silence Ljubičić's beaten down, starving men radiated a palpable homicidal air, and he found himself fondling the polished wooden grip of his service revolver and mumbling a plea to his savior. "Please, Jesus, they've given enough. Don't make me shoot them. Not for that bastard." Oblivious, Kusmanek stepped forward to address Ljubičić's troops.

"Soldiers, half a year has passed while we children of almost all nationalities of our beloved country have incessantly stood shoulder to shoulder against the enemy. Thanks to God's help and your bravery, I have succeeded, despite the enemy's attacks, despite the cold and privations, in defending the fortress against the enemy. You have already done much to win the acknowledgements of the Commander-in-Chief, the gratitude of the country, and even the respect of the enemy.

Yonder in our beloved country, thousands and thousands of hearts are beating for us. Millions are waiting with held breath for news of us.

Heroes, I am about to make my last demand of you. The honor of the Army and country requires it. I am going to lead you out, a steel wedge, to break through the iron ring of the foe, and then, with unflagging efforts, move farther and farther till we rejoin our Army, which, at the price of stubborn battles, has already approached quite near us. We are on the eve of a big fight, for the enemy will not willingly allow the booty to slip through his fingers. But, remember, gallant defenders of Przemyśl, each one of you must be possessed of a single idea, 'Forward, ever forward!' All that stands in our way must be crushed."

Ljubičić's aide leaned over and whispered in his ear, "He's fucking joking. Thin tea and moldy zwieback all winter and he expects us to break through and defeat a million well-fed, dug in Russians?" Ljubičić scanned his men for signs of aggression.

The general continued, "Soldiers, we have distributed our last stores, and the honor of our country, and of every one of us, forbids that after such a hard fought, glorious, and victorious struggle we should fall into the power of the enemy like a helpless crowd." Kusmanek moved out from behind the makeshift rostrum, perspiration beading on his forehead as he shook his fist wildly. "Hero-soldiers, we must break through, and we shall!"[5]

Ljubičić pawed his revolver as Kusmanek waited on stage for cheers that would never come. After a nervous pause, he dismissed the men. As Kusmanek and his officers rode the herd back to town, Ljubičić sat at his desk and thought about not being there to kick the football with his twin ten-year-olds, Petar and Janka, and about never seeing how beautiful his daughter Magda would look at her first communion in the white, flower-patterned dress that his wife Ana had sewn. Eyes moist, he composed a long farewell letter to his wife and children in Zagreb.

Przemyśl • 5th of Nisan, 5675 – Saturday, March 20, 1915

"SIR, THE SORTIE was not successful. They were—"

"They were what?" Kusmanek yelled at the colonel.

"They were driven back. Artillery fire. Perhaps five thousand casualties."

"And what of the other Honveds?"

"They didn't make it. Not even to the Russian line."

"How many fought?"

"Well, our regiments aren't at full complement because—"

"Tell me how many," Kusmanek screamed.

"Four."

"Twenty goddamn thousand Hungarians was all we could muster?"

"Sir, the men... they're—"

"Blast! Incompetents!"

"Sir," General Tamassy, chief of the Honved and Kusmanek's second in command, interrupted, "The Russian food dump in Mościska is twenty-five kilometers to the east. East, away from the main body of Austrian forces and into the heart of the enemy. Four or forty regiments could not be expected to defeat a million Russians." He paused briefly, "Sir."

Kusmanek was a formidable man with a square chin and intense eyes. His uniform, even in these worst of times, was always perfectly tailored, expertly pressed and adorned with a full complement of ribbons, medals and lanyards. His face was dominated by a bushy moustache resembling two whisk brooms, each growing out of a nostril at a 45 degree angle.

"Get out, get out!" He screamed at the colonel. "I am the Lion of Przemyśl! I am not going to spend the balance of this war freezing in Siberia!"

The room cleared, leaving the two Generals alone.

"I will not have history remember me as another General Mack," Kusmanek said, slamming his fist down on the Fort map spread across the large table.

"Ivanov is no Napoleon and unlike Mack, we have fought bravely for months."

"Perhaps another sortie, this time..."

"It's over sir."

"But if—"

"It's over."

Kusmanek stared at the Hungarian, trying to calibrate the challenge in his tone. For the first time in his career, he chose to ignore the challenge.

"They've taken hill four-o-three."

Kusmanek raised one eyebrow, "Really?"

"From those heights, they can rain shells down on Przemyśl. It is just a matter of time before—"

"Before we are forced to capitulate," he interrupted. "I can see that. I'm no War College cadet."

"Of course not, Sir."

Kusmanek turned his back to Tamassy, dropped his chin into his palm, and fell deep into thought. Eventually, his head rose and the Czech turned to the Hungarian and issued an order: "Get Dankl on the wireless."

"Sir, we still don't have contact with Nowy Sącz. The Russians are still broadcasting over our frequencies."

"We'll send our surrender plan by airplane tonight."

"What plan?" Tamassy asked. "Sir."

"We will destroy it all. Leave not a single gun, bullet or bayonet. Not a scrap of food or an animal that isn't a rat or a louse."

"Surely you don't intend to blow the bridges?"

"I said everything. Bridges, too," Kusmanek said, sliding his hands into tight leather gloves.

"Sir, the town's civilians, specifically the Jews, are in a state of utter panic ahead of the Russians. Thousands are fleeing across the San. Besides, if we—"

"To hell with the Jews! They can suffer and cope with surrender as we all must."

"Blowing the bridge will only delay the arrival of foodstuffs for the civilians."

"Do I need to remind you who the commander of this citadel, Herr General?"

"We will leave nothing, sir," he said, saluting briskly and snapping the heels of his shiny knee-high boots before leaving the map room to coordinate the destruction of Fort Przemyśl and any items of value it contained.

Przemyśl • 6th of Nisan, 5675 – Sunday, March 21, 1915

"WE HAVE HAD a slight change in orders," the commander of the Fort's administrative facility, Lieutenant-Colonel-Engineer Deuter, told the jammed mess hall. "Those of you living here, the civilians, you may not leave until all our work is completed and I have released you from duty."

Almost all the men in the room, paymasters, engineers, advocates, and technicians, were way ahead of the common soldier with current information and knew what was coming. Juda had known for three days, having been the one to receive and decode the General Staff's final instructions to Kusmanek. The night before, at his insistence, he had buried the remaining silver coins in a hole at the back of the cellar while Gitla hid a large cache of preserved fruits and vegetables in crawlspaces under floorboards in three separate rooms of the house, each covered by old runners.

Deuter continued, "We are surrendering the Fort at dawn tomorrow."

Vacant stares covered the faces of fifty non-commissioned officers.

"Wireless men will take all papers, and I mean *all* papers, including worksheets and scraps, outside for burning. We will use the latrine behind the tall mast. Use as much petrol as required. The Paymaster-Major, assisted by his four divisional paymasters, will remove all bank notes from the vaults and burn them in the same fire. Sappers will wire the radio rooms and we will blow the entire facility at precisely o-five hours."

The proposed burning of millions of Kronen caught the attention of many of the otherwise resigned men. Noticing this, the Lieutenant-Colonel-Engineer added, "Oh yes, one more item. Anyone caught absconding with as much as a Heller of the Emperor's money will be summarily shot." He then looked at the Paymaster-Major and his four helpers and added, "along with the five paymasters."

Vacant stares returned to the faces of the fifty non-commissioned officers.

Deuter stepped out from behind the small rostrum and tugged at his tunic from the bottom, flattening the folds over his stomach as best he could. He stamped his right heel hard on the concrete floor, the metal heel-piece producing a revolver-like report that echoed loudly down the length of the semi-circular ceiling.

"I will now read an order from our commander, General Kusmanek."

He cleared his throat and produced a small slip of paper. "His Excellency, Emperor Franz Joseph, appreciates his subjects' loyalty and their continued commitment to Austria's noble cause. The defense of Fort Przemyśl by his brave and heroic subjects against overwhelming numbers shall forever be remembered as one of Austria's finest and proudest military endeavors. As of twelve-hundred on twenty-two March, all uniformed soldiers of the realm are to peacefully surrender to the forces of Tsar Nicholas of Russia. Prior to surrender, all items of value whatsoever are to be destroyed."

At 22:30 sharp Deuter dismissed Juda along with the nine other War Act civilians working at the administrative center. By then, all of the papers in the wireless room had been mixed with 10, 20, 50, and 100 Kronen notes, doused in petrol and burned in the pit behind the tall radio tower. The banknotes were being incinerated in small batches and would require most of the evening and early morning hours to assure complete destruction of the lot.

Juda was down the hill like a shot, anxious to get back to Gitla and Rivka, desperate to burn his Austrian Army issued green work fatigues before the Russians arrived. Breathing hard and relieved to be back on a city street, he headed toward home, glad that he wouldn't be climbing the Katedralna Hill again anytime soon. There were fires and explosions coming from all directions now. Not Skoda firings or incoming shells, but purposeful arson, wanton destruction of everything from radios, to guns, to forges.

As Juda merged onto Grodzka he became aware of a stream of soldiers, seemingly attracted from every compass point, moving across his path toward the *Rynek*, ahead on his left. The current quickly became a tide, then a torrent of soldiers, running, acting as if possessed, yelling unintelligibly.

The second siege had been a desperate few months for everyone within the Fort. Owing largely to inept and often corrupt leadership, it had fallen especially hard on the lowly infantry soldiers. Juda, Gitla, Rivka, and most townsfolk, in contrast, had been prudent, organized, and well prepared. They had thought of safety and security. They had cached ample food. Juda had prepared for every possible eventuality. But he wasn't the least bit prepared for what he witnessed at midnight at the *Rynek*, on his way home, on the day that Przemyśl finally fell.

"JUDA, THANK GOD you're home," Rivka said as he walked past the table to the hutch at the far end of the kitchen. "We spent the day putting the shutters up." Hearing the pop of a cork and the gurgle of pouring liquid, she walked up behind him and embraced him around his waist.

"You all right?" She asked. He was shaking. "Juda, are you all right?"

"No."

She hugged him gently. He emptied the Kiddush cup in a single tilt, then set the metal chalice on the table, swallowing with a slight tremor that caused Rivka to briefly tighten her hold. "What happened?"

The sound of booted feet on wooden treads came from the stairwell behind them. Rivka let go of Juda and took a step backward as Gitla's head popped through the threshold. She stopped momentarily on the top stair, "Juda, you look like death. What's wrong?"

He turned and Rivka moved to the side. "I... I... you wouldn't... I..." His eyes closed and he covered his face with his hands, weeping. Gitla walked over to her husband and put a hand on his shoulder. "Sit, sweetheart. Talk. Don't hold it in. Let it out." She guided him to the chair where Rivka had been sitting. Keeping her hand on his shoulder, Gitla moved around the chair and sat gingerly on his lap.

Juda looked up at his wife, his eyes red and misty, letting out a long sigh as he shook his head. "There are no words..."

"Talk, talk sweetheart. Get it out. You'll feel better."

"You're probably right."

Under normal circumstances Gitla would have said, "I usually am." But today she simply touched Juda's cheek.

After a nod and a long exhale, Juda began his story. "'Leave 'em nothing but cinders,' the major said. So we destroyed it all—papers, money, everything. I was in charge of the radios. When were released, I ran down the hill. Explosions were still coming from all over—it seemed they were blowing up every single building in town. And not just the forts - the bridges, the army camp, the stables, everything. Just past the church, I noticed that a lot of foot soldiers were running wildly toward the square. Even given everything going on today, this breakdown in order seemed so odd to me, so I decided to have a look. By the time I came to the *Rynek*, the entire square was packed with horses carrying men who looked to be dressed for Purim." Gitla moved off Juda to a chair as he continued, but she kept her hand resting lightly on his arm. "You need to understand; the entire garrison was there, from Kusmanek on down, a thousand officers on a thousand steeds. Every good horse left in Przemyśl."

Rivka sat, then inched her chair closer to Juda.

"Kusmanek came to the head and dismounted. The men on

horseback came forward in waves, a hundred or more across and ten or twenty deep. On command, they dismounted as one. Kusmanek drew his sword and yelled a command. The men stamped their boots on the cobbles while he sheathed his saber. With all the commotion, it seemed like not a horse in the square moved a hair."

"Noble beasts, accustomed to the noise of war," Gitla offered.

"Meanwhile, foot soldiers had begun assembling—no, assemble is the wrong word—more like they just appeared out of thin air at every intersection surrounding the square. Something was odd. At first I couldn't put my finger on it, but soon it became clear. They ignored each other and they couldn't have cared less about the officers in the *Rynek*."

"What, then," Gitla asked.

"They were dirty and they smelled, they were about to be marched off to Russian prison camps, yet all they cared about - all they could do - was to drool at the horses like hungry wolves."

"Oh no..."

"It was getting crowded on the street by this time so I moved back up the hill, out of harm's way, just as Kusmanek yelled another command and every officer drew his service revolver. The *Rynek* went silent for an instant as the General grabbed his horse's bridle and put the revolver to the poor beast's temple before shouting '*Vorbereiten sie.*' A moment later all the men joined him yelling '*ziel*' in unison. It sounded like a football game cheer or a chant at a political rally. I never did hear them say '*feuer*' over the noise that followed. Such a noise I will never forget." Juda buried his head in his hands.

"Bastards," Gitla seethed.

The corners of Rivka's mouth sagged as she fought back tears.

Juda looked up and wiped the dampness off his face with the back of his hand. "I need to finish, all right?"

“Of course my love,” Gitla said, reaching for her husband’s hand.

Juda met Gitla halfway across the table for a brief kiss before he continued, “You can’t imagine what a sickening sound it was. No one can because such a devilish noise there has never been. It was not a single noise, like a shell—that would have been infinitely preferable—they fell in waves, like a row of dominoes. Some of the horses didn’t die right away and screamed out before being silenced by another gunshot. I even heard the muffled cries of a few officers who were trapped when their horses fell on them.”

“It serves them right, the heartless curs,” Gitla snorted. “Go on, dear.”

“Kusmanek called the men to attention then marched them out of the square, right by me. The General was stone-faced and I saw that some of his men were crying. But many more were smiling. Smiling! Why? Why on heaven or earth would they be happy?”

“Because they lost whatever humanity they had,” Rivka said shaking her head. Gitla nodded in agreement.

“I’m sorry, but it’s not the worst of it.”

“Oh?” Gitla and Rivka said in unison.

“By the time the Viennese marched off, there were hundreds, if not thousands of conscripts converging on the *Rynek*.” He signaled Rivka to fetch the vodka. “Battalions of angry, starving men who had survived on nothing but zwieback and lard face-to-face with a hectare of freshly slaughtered meat.”

Juda uncorked the bottle and nervously fondled the cork. “It started with just a small group of men, four or five soldiers descending on a stallion, hacking at it with their field knives. One of the privates managed to cut a thick slab of meat from a thigh and held it up in the air for all to see before tearing into it with his teeth. Other soldiers joined them. More knives. Everyone was covered in blood.”

He poured himself another cup of vodka.

"The scene that followed was..."

He closed his eyes, which did not stop the tears from flowing.

"Hell. It was hell. Not the one from books, and not the one in your imagination, a real place, right here in our *Rynek*. Good men, reduced to the level of rats. Just imagine, Gitla." Turning to Rivka he asked, "Can you? Can you just imagine?"

Both women shook their heads. He drank and swallowed with a slight shiver. "I've just been there. I've seen it. I've seen hell." There was a long silence.

"Yes you have, husband, my dear husband."

"Can you blame the men, the conscripts?" Juda asked Gitla. "Can you?"

"No," she answered.

"Of course not," Rivka added.

"I don't look down on the horse-eaters. We boast of being something higher, of being human. But deprived of the necessities of life, we all revert to animal. There's not a Jew or a Viennese officer in Przemyśl who wouldn't have ripped the meat off a horse's bones today if they too were starving." Juda reached out for the women's wrists and held them tightly, "No, the well-fed can never judge the starving. Never."

"Never." Gitla and Rivka echoed.

"Come here, sweetheart," Gitla said, standing. Rivka joined her and the three held each other close for a long time, long enough for Juda's trembling to end.

Five

Sanok • 23rd of Iyyar, 5675 – Friday, May 7, 1915

ELIA AND HIRSCH ferried bodies from the front to the makeshift morgue next to the command center for the next six hours without a break, glad for the relatively cool, overcast day. By mid-afternoon most of Sanok had been taken, although a detachment of Russians remained holed up in the castle by the river. While exhausted soldiers rested at the front line, a battalion sergeant argued with a German 2nd Lieutenant over the use of artillery on the last of the holdouts. All such arguments, framed to try and spare Sanok's few remaining historical buildings, fell on utterly deaf ears.

As the task of razing what was left of Sanok was handled by German gunners using a trio of howitzers at nearly point-blank range, a hefty soldier came running up to the command center. Winded, he bent over with his hands on his dirt-covered knees, barely able to keep his balance, gulping for air. "Medic. I need a medic. Now!" He struggled for air, "We have a wounded man on Chopina Street, on the other side of Park Miejski, at Zacisze. My, my..." he coughed, "My brother."

A sergeant who had been studying a map, turned, "Gevral,

what the fuck were you doing on Chopina anyway?"

Gevral was still breathing hard.

"What would happen if every goddamned corporal decided to attend to family in the middle of a battle?" He turned to a medic, "Go get him," then he turned back to Gevral, "I'll deal with you and, God willing, with Mendel later. Go get him. Now!"

"Sir," the medic said with a vague salute, leading Gevral, Elia and Hirsch toward town.

When they were almost a block away, the Sergeant yelled, "Move it!" Elia broke into a trot as another yell came. "He's my nephew!"

They made their way to Chopina Street the long way in order to avoid the mopping-up operations. "Before the war I was a tailor. Had a shop of my own, just off the *Rynek*, in a building that seems to be gone," Gevral explained, shifting his Mannlicher rifle from shoulder to shoulder. "I was called up early from the reserves. Sent Rose and our four children to stay with my uncle's family in Opole."

"Where'd your brother get it?" the medic asked Gevral.

"Leg. I think it shattered his femur."

"We'll get him out of here. Not to worry."

"There's our home." Gevral pointed to an untouched three-story brick apartment block. "Mendel is in the alley, just around back." They crossed the street and walked quickly past the home. After Gevral cautiously peeked around the corner, they ducked into the shadow of the alley.

"Mendel, thank God you're all right," Gevral said, propping his gun up against the sooty brick before falling to his knees to embrace his brother.

"Thank God you've come," Mendel replied with surprising vigor.

Gevral turned to the doctor, "Morphine, now! Please."

Elia propped the rolled up stretcher while Hirsch lifted the rifle off Mendel's lap and stowed it next to Gevral's gun as the medic rifled through his bag of field dressings.

Mendel was clearly the younger brother, and notwithstanding his blood-drenched pants, appeared to be the fitter one as well. He was slumped against the wall about three meters in from the road, his rifle, bayonet fixed, lying across his lap, his boots nearly touching the neighboring building across the narrow passageway.

"Take these," the medic said handing the wounded man two pills. "Under the tongue."

Mendel eagerly did as instructed while the medic examined his wounds, calling out his findings like a coroner during an autopsy. "Shattered left femur, mid thigh, femoral artery intact, major quadriceps trauma, right fibula abrasion, clean exit." Turning to Gevral, he spoke with tenderness none of them thought him capable of, "He'll make it; he'll be fine." He looked at Hirsch and Elia, "Move him."

Elia gestured to the street. "Corporal, Herr Doctor." As they exited the alley, the medic reached into his jacket for his cigarettes and offered one to Gevral.

Elia and unfurled the dark green canvas sling and laid it next to the patient like they'd done a thousand times before, when the crack of a gunshot shrieked down Chopina and echoed sharply off the tight walls of the alley.

Elia instinctively glanced toward the source of the noise. In the street the doctor was calmly pressing on his neck with his hand, cigarette still smoldering between his fingers, trying to stop the geyser of blood draining from his brain.

Another shot echoed.

Hirsch hit the ground as Gevral dove into the alley, landing on him.

"Gun!" Gevral screamed at Elia, scrambling to his feet, his back to the street.

The medic collapsed in the dirt, eyes fixed, dead.

A shadow crept along the wall as Elia frantically groped for a weapon. Securing a Mannlicher, he thrust it out over

Mendel and Hirsch towards Gevral, who locked onto the rifle with his hand.

In the thin sliver between Gevral and the wall, Elia saw the soldier. He wore black boots, an olive field jacket with crossed supply straps, and brown pants, cropped at the calf, billowing over his thighs. His face was angular and ghostlike, with high cheek bones, a straw-colored moustache, and wispy matching eyebrows. A stream of blood, flowed freely down his chin to his neck, and onto his field tunic from an open wound on his left cheek. In a brief and awful moment, their eyes met. Elia could swear they'd met in Przemyśl, perhaps on Blonie field during a football match or at Antmann's for beer and politics. But as the adrenalin flowed, whatever humanity had bubbled to the surface evaporated as visions of broken comrades obscured any possible compassion and a voice in Elia's head began screaming for vengeance, growing louder with each pulse of his heart.

Elia reached for the second gun as a distinctive metallic click came from the street; a miss-fire or an empty magazine, followed by a sickening gasp from Gevral. The two Austrian soldiers, stared with remarkably casual disbelief at the tip of the bayonet that had just gone through Gevral's back, severed his renal artery, skewered his intestines and emerged between the bottom two buttons of his tunic.

Gevral's rifle fell to the dirt as the silver blade disappeared back into his body.

Elia cocked his rifle.

Gevral's body tensed briefly, and then collapsed in a heap.

The Russian tried to cock his rifle but the bolt was jammed.

Hearts racing and hands trembling, the Russian and the Galician leveled their stares at one and other, simultaneously realizing that the prospects for their lives from this moment forward revolved around a single germane fact; one rifle had a bullet in its chamber; the other did not.

The Russian dropped his rifle and ran.

By the time Elia had leapt over the bodies and made it to the street, the assassin was no more than twenty paces away. He brought the slowly bobbing head into the crosshairs of his rifle and, as instructed, gently squeezed the trigger. The runner stumbled, and then fell like a sack of potatoes tossed from a cart. A burgundy stain oozed from a hole in the back of what was once the Russian's skull and wicked its way through his dirty blond hair.

Elia dropped the rifle, his stomach in knots as if he'd told his mother a lie.

WHILE MENDEL RECOUNTED to a gathering of field medics the story of the gun-battle on the streets of Sanok, Elia and Hirsch made two trips back to the alley to collect the remains of Gevral, the medic and the assassin. By the time the boys returned with the last corpse, the tale of the heroic stretcher carriers had spread from the hospital to the First Battalion, to the Army headquarters outside of town, with added embellishment at each stop.

"Thank God it's Silverberg," Hirsch said, sitting on an empty cartridge crate, looking down the street. Elia lit a cigarette and pulled the sweet, harsh smoke deeply into his lungs. Looking to the rapidly dimming sky, he exhaled a series of smoke rings.

"You all right, Elia?" Hirsch asked.

"No."

Silverberg, Manes and an Austrian officer flanked by several aides approached the boys. Elia rubbed the glowing tip off of his smoke using the edge of a wooden cross brace on the crate, then pinched the remaining embers out between his thumb and forefinger, saving the butt in his shirt pocket for later. Both he and Hirsch came to attention.

"The whole battalion has heard about what happened today. You've brought great honor to the men of the Tenth,"

Silverberg said, excitedly.

Elia bowed his head, unable to look at him.

"This is Captain Malczewski. He has something for you two."

Elia stared at his boots as the desiccated Malczewski stepped forward. "For bravery in the field befitting a soldier of the realm, and by the authority invested in me by the Emperor Franz Joseph, I hereby promote both of you to the rank of private, with all the responsibility and privilege befitting of the rank." He snapped his fingers. An aide came forward with two pike-gray field uniforms, complete with metallic white buttons and parrot-green facings under the collars. They were exactly like those the rest of the battalion wore, only cleaner.

"And for private Reifer, our expert marksman," Silverberg added, "a red lanyard."

The Captain curtly dismissed the assembly.

Five minutes later, Elia was walking out of Sanok in his new uniform. After crossing the San on a hastily assembled pontoon bridge, Manes came up beside him, weighing him down with an arm around his shoulder.

When they had been passed by the bulk of the platoon, Elia stopped.

"What?" Manes asked, "What's wrong, comrade?" Streaks appeared on Elia's dusty, sun-burned face.

Elia wept.

"It's kill or be killed. Kill or be killed."

Elia compose himself. "But I shot him, Manes."

"You did what you had to do."

"No. You don't understand."

"What?"

"I...I...

"Tell me, Elia."

"I shot him in the back, Manes. In the back."

Przemyśl • 26th of Iyyar, 5675 – Monday, May 10, 1915

ZIPRE WALKED WITH her father as far as the portico of Przemyśl's Old Synagogue. Like many modern young women, Zipre refused to enter the majestic old limestone synagogue, in protest of the gender segregation practiced there. Her deceased mother, her aunts, and countless other female relatives had entered this building with their husbands, uncles, and brothers only to part ways just past the door: men continuing into the great hall and women climbing two flights of stone stairs to the balcony. One group performed the time-honored rituals, the other observed from afar.

"I'll do Kaddish at the cemetery," Zipre said with measured spite.

"I love you," Meyer said as he turned and walked into the synagogue.

"I love you too, father," Zipre whispered as she pulled her scarf over her hair and walked briskly up Jagiellońska toward the cemetery.

Two months after the Russian takeover, food had returned to the market stalls and a relative calm had descended on Przemyśl. The absence of artillery din was a divine pleasure that Zipre would never have imagined a few months ago. Yet it was all wrong. These men sat at the café just like the other ones. They drank tea or schnapps like the others. Yes, the uniforms were different. Yes, the language was foreign. But most of all, the faces were unfamiliar. "Avoid eye contact," she could hear Rivka telling her as she ducked into Laufer's Apothecary, a few doors up Słowackiego, next to Besser's Bakery.

"Good morning, Feiga," she said to the elderly woman behind the counter.

Feiga Laufer was perpetually hunched over making her seem even shorter than she was. Her deep hazel eyes were framed by grey hair and bushy, black eyebrows. For the better part of half a century she had sold medicines, lotions, and untold knickknacks to the people of Przemyśl, privy to each family's particular needs, wants, and desires, recording them in her head with the fidelity of a scribe and the recall of a learned rabbi.

"Candle?"

"Yes, please," Zipre said, dropping some copper on the counter.

"Will the Austrians return?" Feiga asked in hushed tones, leaning toward Zipre as she picked up the coins. "What does your father say?"

Zipre glanced around the empty shop. "Father's agent in Cracow said the Kaiser's assembled a million men under Mackensen, and that the Russian lines had already buckled. Within a fortnight the Germans will be in Przemyśl."

Feiga mumbled under her breath in Yiddish.

"What do you hear, Feiga?"

"Me? I'm just an old woman. I know who has problems with smelly feet; I remember at what age each Jewish girl began her menstruation. War? What do I know of such things? Your father knows, not me. What else does he say?"

Zipre smiled thinly. "Father says the same thing always: armies come and go; governors come and go; only gold remains." She paused. "But I am not as sanguine as my father. Things will never be as they were, not for any of us."

"Things are never as they were, sweetheart," Feiga said, bringing the full weight of her stare to bear on Zipre as she handed her a brown paper sack with a candle and a small box of matches.

Other than the occasional swerve to avoid a pile of horse manure, Zipre walked straight uphill on Słowackiego with deliberate speed, keeping her head down and her gaze on the cobblestones just ahead of her. The brilliant sun of the early morning had turned overcast; she left no shadow on the stone pavers beneath her.

The size of a small farm, it was called the New Cemetery, but to most, it was just *the* cemetery. It was on the fringe of town, on the road that leads to Dobromyl, just past a small Roman Catholic chapel and *goyish* burial grounds. There was a rubble stone wall enclosing two sides of the sacred place, running along the road, separating the plots from the chapel. The balance of the grounds were defined by a line of stately larches toward the top of the gentle slope that followed the contour of the road and a knot of smaller trees and bushes at the crest of a steeper ridge a few hundred meters away. The wall was broken by a large iron gate, wide enough to drive a horse cart through, which was padlocked shut, along with a smaller, unlocked, pedestrian gate.

Passing into the cemetery, Zipre pictured her mother's face and began to weep, gently at first then with increased emotion, as she walked by a number of familiar monuments. She only stopped once, to pick up a small, smooth rock by a rusted fence post.

Situated halfway up the hill, the Weiss/Hecht burial plot was among the finest in the cemetery. Save for a chest-high stone entrance, the full perimeter of the ten by ten meter square was enclosed by a well crafted iron knee wall, replete with clusters of metal leaves, spires, and stars of David, with an inner hedge of neatly trimmed boxwoods. All of the nine limestone markers were elegantly engraved and had slate roofs that made them look like an irregular row of dollhouses. While most of the stones were etched in Hebrew, the one in front, obviously one of the most recent, was rendered in western script:

Esther Weiss
1871–1905
Beloved Wife and Mother

Kneeling before her mother's grave, Zipre struck a match and lit the wick of the *Yartzeit* candle. Standing, she placed the stone she had picked up on a small ledge under the slate cap and began saying Kaddish: *Yis'ga'dal v'yis'kadash sh'may ra'bbo...* By the second verse she was deeply in her own spiritual world, completely oblivious to the sound of crunching twigs and leaves beneath boots, growing louder. *Oseh sholom bimromov, hu ya'aseh sholom olaynu, v'al kol yisroel; vimru Omein.* As soon as she finished, her senses returned and she saw them out of the corner of her eye. Her brain screamed trouble; flight reflex took over. She wheeled around and raced down the path, retracing her earlier steps. "How many? Two? Three? Blue pants, yellow stripe—Cossacks—rapists and murderers. Can I make the gate?"

Her practical thoughts were interrupted by the man furthest up the hill yelling, "Halt!" Zipre turned her head briefly to survey the situation. There were three: two men, or boys, running down the outside paths and one, slightly older and fatter, walking and yelling well behind her on one of the interior routes. A quick assessment of the geometry of her situation told her that she was not going to make it to the grass field, not to mention the gate or the road, before the two runners would intercept her. She stopped by an unfamiliar grave and was immediately surrounded by three soldiers. Frozen with fear, she dropped her head, staring at their black knee-high boots.

"Papers!" the fat soldier shouted in accented Ukrainian.

A shiver ran up Zipre's spine, as she recalled how Don Cossacks were always the perpetrators of the worst pogroms in all of the stories her grandmother had told her growing up.

As she extended her arm to present the document to the red faced Slav, he seized her by both wrists. Twisting her so that her palms were facing up, he laughed as the papers fell silently on the dirt path. "Look at these hands." He spoke toward his comrades, smiling evilly.

"The hands of a spy! A Jew spy!"

"The hands of a whore!"

"Let me be! Please, let me go!" were the last words Zipre spoke that day. She never saw the fist coming at her and later couldn't recall which of the trio had first thrown the punch. In all her years, she had never been hit, and from the first blow she receded into a state of semi-consciousness, experiencing the pain and degradation of the next minutes as if they were hours. She felt as though she were out of her body, like she was watching a nightmare from above.

Zipre remembered hitting the ground. She remembered her blouse being ripped and her skirt bunched up around her waist. Her underpants ripped by filthy fingers. The taste of blood in her mouth. Dirty, coarse hands latching onto her skin like leeches. Nervous laughter. Shouted words: "Whore! Bitch! Christ killer!" The slobber and stink of one; abrasion from the rough face of another. Deep dull pain of forced entry from all three.

She remembered the arrival of men on horses. Arguing. Shouting. She might have been taken back to town by cart.

Zipre woke in her bed the next morning, scared at first and then relieved to see her father from the eye that wasn't swollen shut. As she drifted in and out of consciousness, memories of the past day slowly started coming into focus. At first, she allowed herself to feel fortunate to be alive, but these thoughts were quickly washed away by a flood of unrelenting pain.

New York • 5th of Sivan, 5675 – Tuesday May 18, 1915

"MILTON, HERE'S A buck. Go to Saperstein's and ask him for the magazine. The one for Harmon."

"Um, OK, boss."

Holding the black wooden shaft, she thumped his chest menacingly with the large brass head of her cane, "*The Illustrated War News*. Should be fifty cents."

"OK, boss."

"Be sure it's the April issue, not March," Julia shouted at Milton's back as he crossed Spring Street. "And pick me up today's *World!*"

"OK, boss."

"Then meet us at the Spring Street station. And hurry!" Marta yelled to Milton.

"OK, hurry," Milton said, without turning.

Marta turned to Julia. "Ma'am, with all due respect. He is such an idiot. How can you?"

"He's a dear. And he's muscle. Every army needs artillery; every business needs muscle."

"Enough with the General Julia shtick, already."

As they walked, Julia reached up to put a hand on Marta's shoulder, "Seriously, Milty is like a brother to me."

"I've always wondered about him."

"We met on the Kronprinz, two days out of Bremen. Bad weather had set in and the boat heaved all night long. Now for most people in steerage, this was the first time on a boat and the waves sent many to the gunwales, puking out what food they managed to carry onboard. But not Julia, no siree! For me it was like being rocked to sleep."

"I suppose it was nothing after what you went through getting to Germany, obtaining the papers, with the gypsies and all."

"They were theater people, Russians."

"Whatever. Go on."

"I wasn't tired so I took a walk on the part of the deck they let me walk on. I'm leaning against the railing, looking out at the mighty black nothing and what do I hear? Crying. I turn and see this huge boy, Milton, so I come up to him and ask him if he's all right. He says he's scared and alone, his sister didn't make it, shit her life out in the infirmary. He doesn't know what to do, where to go. I cuddle him and tell him it will be all right, that I'll be his new sister; take care of him. At Ellis, I'm Mrs. Harmon going to my husband, Alan Harmon, on Spring Street. Gave them his name and some of my coins, and they let us in."

"That's lucky."

"That's America."

"There's Milton, by the IRT."

"I'll tell you the rest of the story later."

Milton handed her a newspaper and a brown bag with the magazine sticking out of the top. Reaching into his trouser pocket, he produced a handful of change and gave it to Julia. Passing the magazine off to Marta, she eyed the pile of coins in her palm, picked up some coins and handed them to Milton. "For Cracker Jack," Julia said, heading down the stairs.

"Three," Julia said.

"Fifteen," the fare man responded.

They spun themselves through the turnstile before wading into the multitudes crowding the platform. Marta eavesdropped on the conversations around her while Julia kept her nose buried in the *World's* sports page, studying the Aqueduct race charts.

"See?" Marta said with pride. "I told you it would be all women. It's a big day for us."

Julia put her finger on a line on the page before looking up, first at the crowd, then at Marta. "I still can't see what a baseball game has to do with suffrage, but what the hell; it's a nice day for a ballgame."

"You of all people should understand. Take the fight into the heart of enemy territory. What better battlefield than the Polo Grounds? At the game today we'll be five thousand strong."

A small group of women approached, handing out sashes taken from a canvas sack one of them had slung over her shoulder. Marta took two. "Here, wear this, Julia. It's high time you got serious about politics."

"I prefer to dispense equal rights with Ole' Jake here." She tapped the brass tip of her cane on the wooden platform.

"That's fine for you and me, but what about the rest of the world? Do you really want men, and only men, deciding things? Like the war in Europe?"

Julia stared menacingly at Marta before reaching for the sash and exhaling loudly. "Bitch."

Marta smiled as the platform began to shake and as the racket of metal on metal grew louder.

"ONE FIFTY-EIGHTH, POLO Grounds! All passengers must exit."

The two women and Milton sat in a sea of Suffragettes nine rows up, just past third base.

"I love the double steal," Julia said. "You take bases on guile, on confusion, and on speed. See the Cub at the back of the steal, the one on second?"

"Yeah."

"Heinie Zimmerman. Max's cousin."

"No chance! Does Max have coin on this game?"

"Max has coin on every game, but not like that. Heinie's clean."

The crack of ball meeting bat filled the stadium.

"Damn, behind again."

"Ah, now we know who's got book on the Giants. You know the Suffragettes are giving Schulte and every other man who scores today five bucks?"

"You invade the enemy, and then pay them? I thought this was war?"

As soon as Julia said the word "war," her demeanor changed: her eyes tightened and her brow wrinkled. "Gimme the magazine," she ordered Milton. "And go get yourself something to eat."

The cover featured a red line drawing of the distinguished Minister of Munitions, a Mister N. Chamberlain. She ran down the table of contents, her forefinger under each entry as she tried to recognize the mostly foreign words. "Marne, Gallipoli, Ypres, Łodz, Przemyśl. What's this say, here?" Julia said, pounding the page with her finger.

Marta scanned the words before reading out loud, "The Fall of Przemyśl. Failure of Russia's First Attempt—Settling Down to a Long Siege—Austria's Desperate Efforts at Relief—What the Fall of the Fortress Means to Russia's Campaign."

Julia rifled through the first section, looking for photos of places she might recognize. Turning a page she came on a black and white picture of a fort, not one of those near Medyka, but almost identical, completely reduced to rubble.

"Anything in there about the boat the Kraut submarine sank?" Marta asked.

"Fuck the Lusitania. And fuck the Russians. And the Germans too," Julia replied, without looking up.

Again stamping her finger, this time at the text, she looked up at Marta, "Read. Read it out loud."

"The fall of Przemyśl was a great blow to Germany. For months strenuous efforts had been made to relieve the fortress."

"Hold on a sec, Doyle's batting," Marta said.

The crowd groaned as the umpire yelled, "Strike three, yeeeer out!"

"Best man on the team, my ass. Swing the fucking bat!"

"Keep reading," Julia demanded.

"And if the men created and helped to retain this feeling of confidence, how much more so did the attitude of the Austrian officer! The Austrian is a fop and a great patron of English tailoring. His well-fitting uniform, his spotless gloves, his polished patent boots, have formed never-failing subjects for the caricaturist's satire. And here he was in his element, with his frogged jacket, his speckless coat and his jingling silvered scabbard. He filled the cafés, made himself and his kind an excellent circle, took his coffee and rolls in the great dining room of the Café Sieber, and the tatterdemalion children of Przemyśl could watch him through the big plate-glass windows, open-mouthed and a little awe-stricken, and receive to their shrunken frames a reflection of the luxury and glory of that far away capital of which they had heard – Vienna.

Through the streets by day the officers rode and walked. Such as were mounted were astride those thoroughbred horses which it was Austria's pride to contribute to the world. The war held no more gallant or wonderful sight than Przemyśl presented, even in its darkest days. General Kusmanek, commanding the garrison, represented the culminating point of military magnificence. Riding through the streets with his 70 staff officers, a brilliant cavalcade with flashing accoutrements and flawless uniforms, he brought back to war something of its departed glories."[6]

"Here, boss," Milton said, handing Julia change first, then a hot dog in a bun with onions and mustard wrapped in wax paper. Next, he presented a bag of salted in-the-shell peanuts to Marta. She lobbed a perfunctory "thanks" his way before setting on the bag, neatly cracking open the shells, allowing the empty husks to fall on the picture of General Mackensen, the victor of Przemyśl, standing in front of a hotel, flanked by his staff.

Balancing the hot dog on her thigh, Julia picked a nickel from the pile of change in her hand and presented it Milton.

"Wud I miss?" he asked.

"Nut'in. All quiet on the baseball front," Julia said, sweeping the small pile of shells off the magazine onto Marta's lap.

"Get ready," Marta said as Cy Williams's fly out to shallow center ended the Cub's half of the seventh. She reached into her canvas bag and produced two American flags, each stapled to a wooden dowel. "Here, take it."

"For what?

"Now."

Marta stood, followed by Julia and each raised her flag overhead, whooping loudly, joining about 5,000 other women, clustered on the third base side but sprinkled throughout the Polo Grounds.

"Suffrage now, votes for women!" the women chanted, drawing an occasional male heckle.

Banners began to replace the American flags.

"Lunatics and convicts can't vote! Are women to be grouped with them?" Marta read from a sign about ten rows up.

"What's that one say?" Julia asked, pointing.

"Kaiser Wilson, remember your sympathy for people of Europe not self-governed? Twenty-million American women are not self-governed. Take the beam out of your own eye!"

Milton ate Cracker Jack as the demonstration died down and the Giants came up to bat in the bottom of the inning. Marta continued reading.

After the Giants made their first out, a group of women a few rows down began chanting suffragette slogans.

"Go back to the kitchen," an older man yelled from directly behind Marta. "Or back to the bedroom," the man next to him yelled, his diction slightly slurred. "I ought to teach you some respect, ya' stupid bitches."

"Respect?" Julia said to herself several times. Normally she would have let such drunken ravings pass. After all, this was a ball park, not the parlor of her house. But not this time, not those particular words. She stood and turned, cane in hand. "I'm sorry, were you addressing me?"

Milton and Marta turned without standing.

"I'm thinking that you'll want to apologize to the lady," Marta said.

"Like, now," Milton added.

The two men stood and looked down contemptuously at the two women and the man-boy holding a box of Cracker Jack. The men's height and the number of beers each had drunk imbued them with overabundant self-confidence.

"I got a better idea. Why don't you kike quiffs just shut the fuck up."

Milton set his box down. Julia moved the brass knob at the end of her cane to his chest, "Easy, Milty, easy. They called us Jew whores, not you." In a flash, Julia gripped the shaft of the cane and with all the strength in both arms, swung the club, deftly guiding the metal knob into the groin of one of the men standing above her. As he doubled over in pain, the other man reached for Julia's arm only to be intercepted by Milton. A quick twist and a pull accompanied a sickening snap, and the other man was on his knees, wailing over his dislocated forefinger. He collapsed onto the sticky wooden plank in front of his seat.

As Julia raised her weapon, preparing to club the prostrate hecklers, Marta tugged on her sleeve. "Cops. Let's beat it."

Other than the run the Cubs scored in the top of the first following the double steal, no other runners crossed home plate that day.

Przemyśl • 6th of Sivan, 5675 – Wednesday, May 19, 1915

"I KNOW THAT working on Shavuot is strictly forbidden but I have been up all night praying and I know you are fair and that you will understand and forgive me given these particular circumstances," was the last prayer Meyer Weiss said before walking over to his meeting at the Café Elite.

Meyer had no trouble arranging the meeting with General Artamonoff, the Russian commander of what was now called Peremishl, as each man's reputation as an erudite and prosperous capitalist effortlessly spanned the battle lines.

"Bring us schnapps and canapés," Weiss ordered, in German, "and a coffee for me." Meyer turned to the Russian. "Forgive me, General. I was up all night. Business, you know."

Artamonoff nodded.

The lunch became a pleasant affair once the two men discovered their mutual obsessions with billiards and modern science and their common fluency in German.

"Our Third will easily fend off the Austrian Third in the Dunajec salient," the Russian said, selecting a mushroom pâté canapé from the waiter's assortment. "Frankly, I'm more worried about the German Fourth breaking out to the north." He ate the small pastry puff whole. "But the one thing we can count on is the krauts not having a clue as to what the blintzes are doing!"

Meyer joined the Russian in hearty laughter. "Then the Tsar's victory is assured," he said with convincing enthusiasm as he raised his opulent schnapps glass in toast to the Tsar.

Artamonoff had previously been the head of the Russian Army's cartographic service in St. Petersburg, and was as at ease with merchants and intellectuals as he was with the finer accoutrements of privileged living. Meyer spared no expense on his new friend, serving a multi-course epicurean feast of trout, pheasant and scalloped potatoes followed by the oldest French cognac and finishing with the finest Cuban cigars. Their discussion wandered from politics to sport then settled on science, a topic both men were well versed in and with which Artamonoff seemed most at ease.

"It is a pleasure to be able to keep, how shall I put this,

cultured company." Meyer glanced around, and then lowered his voice, "The Austrians can be so provincial."

"Perhaps at our next lunch you will allow me to relate my experience with the Budapest Professor Baron Eötvös and his work with torsion balance surveys."

"I've heard of his work," Meyer said. "Application to underground mapping."

"Think petroleum, my good man. Imagine pinpointing the location of petroleum pools deep in the earth before drilling."

"I own some small tracts of land to the southeast where the occasional well yields the black ooze. Knowing where to drill, the profit implications are staggering."

"To Eötvös," the Russian said, lifting his glass. "To profit!" They both emptied their glasses.

"General, I hate to see the governor of our little village, a man of the world, a cultured man, living in a Hotel like a common merchant. It simply does not befit your stature."

As Meyer poured, Artamonoff looked at his schnapps glass. "Ludmilla gives me no peace with her complaints about the barn we reside at in the village she thinks is in the center of nowhere."

"I am a widower with but one daughter, living in one of the finest residences in all of Galicia. Will you and your lovely wife do me the honor of making my house the residence of the governor of Peremishl?"

The General looked up at Meyer and sighed. "It would be an honor, a true honor."

"Then you accept?"

"I would be in your debt."

"Yes..." Meyer bit his tongue. "Then it is settled, my friend. You move to my house and we have lunch every Monday."

"Settled." They shook hands and drank.

"About the decree..."

"The decree does not apply to obvious friends of the Tsar, like you. I shall have a word with Kiriakov immediately."

"How very, very kind of you, Governor." Meyer reached into his vest pocket and removed a piece of paper. Sandwiched between two fingers, he passed it discreetly to his new friend. "I have taken the liberty of listing for you a few more Jewish friends of the Tsar."

"Why, thank you, Mister Weiss."

"Meyer. Please, call me Meyer."

They concluded lunch over coffee, exchanging details of the lives of their children. Right after Meyer signed for the meal, Artamonoff raced off to the City Hotel, anxious to inform his wife of this most fortuitous development.

Meyer walked back to the synagogue and spent the balance of the afternoon reading about the great-grandparents of King David, the lord's anointed one, the beloved king of the Jews.

Two days later, at dawn, in the name of army discipline, three Ukrainian enlisted men from a small town outside of Kiev were hanged from a makeshift gallows hastily erected on the Rynek.

Dangling from nooses, the bodies were left to putrefy in the unseasonably hot Galician sunshine, an example to soldier and civilian alike.

Przemyśl • 21st of Sivan, 5675 – Thursday, June 3, 1915

A CROWD HAD been gathering at the temporary fence separating Plac Zgody from the military encampment near the quay ever since the 10th had marched through town.

Save a few young boys who tried to enter the camp only to be shooed away by baton-wielding military police, most of the townspeople were content to watch the building of the vast army camp from afar, hoping only for a glimpse of a loved one. Many had brought flowers, fruits, and cakes, both for their returning soldier and to give to the police in exchange for confirmation that their loved one had made it home alive.

"Finally, here's Zineman," Elia said, pulling a rope tight between a stake and a tent pole. "Maybe we can get out of this swamp now."

"If he holds us here one more minute, I'm going to shoot him in the back," Manes said, pounding a tent stake into the sandy soil.

"Liberty at sixteen-hundred, assembly here at midnight, zero hundred hours, sharp," the battalion commander said to men.

Elia stood and let out a deeply held breath. He stared at the ground, hand on his forehead.

Manes looked up at Elia and dropped the sledgehammer. "I am so..." He stood. "I can't believe I said... in the back."

"It's all right. Really, it is."

"Thanks, Elia." Manes reached out and bear-hugged Elia.

"Thank you, Manes for being my comrade; for being my friend."

"Thank you, Elia."

"Manes?"

"Yeah?"

"No offense, but you're not who I want to hold right now."

Manes laughed. "Same for me, brother. Same for me!"

Elia turned serious, "Why didn't I see her? Something's wrong."

"She's fine, Romeo. Probably baking. Lots of Polacks and Krauts to feed tonight."

"Did you hear what Juda was yelling at us? I couldn't make it out."

"No, but he didn't look sad or anything. No black on Gitla. She's fine, trust me, Elia, just fine."

"But..."

"She's fine."

The bells of the Cathedral tolled, soon joined by a cheer that rose from the camp, passed the rail trestle, and landed in the waiting ears of parents, siblings and lovers waiting on Plac Zgody.

By the fourth and final bell, all tools had hit the ground and every one of the sons of the city was in full flight. Soon the barricade separating the soldiers from their loved ones ceased to be a factor, as part of it was moved by the police, the rest trampled by the mob. Two masses of humanity ran at each other.

Elia dove into the front line, looking from side to side, occasionally jumping for a better view. He searched, ignoring dozens of vaguely familiar faces, oblivious to the many frantic requests as to the whereabouts of a townsperson or soldier.

"Have you seen Silverberg? Shimon Silverberg? Why isn't he your sergeant?" A hysterical woman screamed at the wave of soldiers.

The fortunate ones paired off quickly, evidenced by hugs, kisses and even small displays of dancing. The others stood around empty handed, sobbing at the fresh realization of a loss, or congregated around a bereaved mother or a heartbroken widow.

He heard hundred of voices at once, all meaningless, until a single word wafted gently across the Plac and into his ear.

"Elia!"

Suddenly the din of joy and sorrow fell silent, even though everyone was still talking. Elia heard only her, as if she were whispering in his ear as they lay on the grassy slope of the Josef quay, watched only by the stars.

"Elia!"

He saw her through a gap in the humanity as colors drained to gray, even though soldiers still wore ribbons and families were dressed in their finest clothes. Rivka's hair was a reflective, shimmering black, flecked with a dusting of flour, like a cup of coffee reflecting moonlight.

"Rivka!" He ran at her.

"Elia!" She ran at him.

They fell into each other, arms wrapping tightly, her head alighting on his chest and neck, his lips buried in her hair. He was desperate to kiss her, but each time he tried to push back from the clinch, she tightened her grip, burrowing her face deeper into his neck, pressing her breasts more firmly into his chest, and flattening her thigh against the front of his trouser.

Elia whispered to her ear, "Rivka, I love how you sound when you breathe. I love how you feel against me. I love how you care." He took a deep breath, "I love how you smell."

They held each other for another silent moment before Rivka loosened her grip and both pushed back to arm's length, face to face. "Elia, I love everything about you." Their lips fell together and opened and their tongues danced, heads pressed firmly together by fingers nestled in the hair of the other.

Rivka pushed back and spoke, "I love how you smell too. But you really could use a bath."

Elia laughed as the color and sound returned to the Plac.

"Let's continue this later, where we can be alone," Rivka whispered to him as they strolled arm-in-arm toward the Malz home.

"IT WASN'T LIKE that," Rivka protested. "He was, he is, a Jew, just like us. And not even from Russia, from Vilna."

"Weren't you worried that the Germans would suspect you of harboring the enemy?"

Juda put his arm on Elia's shoulder, "The whole Russian Army moved into homes, or at least all the officers. It was a posted proclamation. There was no choice. We were lucky. They cleaned Rothman out, all his silver, gone. Bethauer had to watch his daughter like a hawk. She's what, fourteen? Even Meyer had to give up his house, even if it was to the Governor. By any measure, Pytor was a saint of a man. Rivka fed him and Gitla did his washing, and he always brought more than he ate; he kept us safe from the Cossacks."

They took a break from the conversation to allow Elia to eat. After chewing several mouthfuls, he dropped his fork, piquing everyone's attention. He looked at Gitla, "I've always said it, but tonight, for the first time, I actually mean it."

She set her fork down and looked up at him, smiling. "Huh?"

"Your *flanken* is delicious."

Everyone laughed. Gitla rose from her seat and came around the table behind Elia and put her arms around him, squeezing tightly, saying over and over again, "Little *momzer*."

"I hear Silverberg didn't make it," Juda said.

"No, and so close to home. Got typhus or something in Sanok and was gone in two days. The bravest Jew I ever met. After all the shells and bullets they fired at him, he died by, well, in the latrine. So unfair."

"Dead is dead," Rivka offered.

"No, dead is not dead," Elia said, his face tightening.

Gitla watched her nephew push a slice of pickled beet around in circles. It left red streaks on the china. "What?" she asked.

"Nothing, I just feel a bit queasy in the stomach, that's all."

"Queasy?"

"After army rations, I guess I'm not used to such richness."

Gitla set her silverware on the plate, "Don't bullshit a bullshitter, mister Reifer."

"Gitla, I just—"

"Elia…"

He took a sip of lukewarm tea. "I killed a man."

"It's war, Elia, everyone kills in war," Juda offered, tenderly.

"I shot him as he ran. I shot him in the back."

Elia spent the next few minutes relating the story of the two stretcher carriers, the rescue gone wrong, the Russian murderer and his demise, the brief celebrity and the promotion.

"It's war, Elia, everyone kills in war," Juda offered, again.

Elia nodded, unconvincingly.

"Elia, my sweetheart," Rivka interjected. "In times like these we are forced, not once, but over and over, to make the decision between the unholy and the unforgivable. In exactly the same way that the well-fed have no right of moral judgment over the starving, the civilian has no right of moral -judgment over the fighting soldier.

She extended her hand across the tabletop and took Elia's.

"What matters is not which you choose because both are unspeakable, Elia. What matters is that you feel and you know, in your head and in your heart that it is a fork in a lane with no righteous path to travel on. Feeling guilty means you feel. The real tragedy of war is not when people kill. It is when people cease to feel bad about killing."

"I love you all so much." Elia said, barely audible.

Gitla rose with dishes in each hand. "Juda, a hand in the kitchen?"

A fast learner, he loaded up on dishes and headed toward the kitchen.

SŁOWACKIEGO AT NIGHTFALL was bustling with an even split of Austrian and German soldiers, some marching on duty, others enjoying their first taste of city liberty in months.

Elia steered Rivka up the hill as soon as they left the house, their handhold turning into arms around waists after a few paces. As soon as they were out of eyeshot, they stopped and turned toward each other. "Where…" One word was all she got out before her lips were smothered by his. For the next few minutes they were lost to the world of here and now.

Though the sight of couples kissing and pawing each other in public was not unusual, Elia and Rivka received their fair share of hoots, catcalls, and obscene words of encouragement.

They broke the kiss but kept the embrace. "I don't want to go to the cemetery, Elia."

"Sweetheart, we don't have to do anything you aren't comfortable with."

"No, it's not that. It's awful. It's a secret, sort of, though everyone knows.

"What?"

"Zipre was attacked in the cemetery. By the Cossacks."

"Bastards."

"She's going to be all right. For a moneyed girl, she's pretty tough. Meyer had the perpetrators hanged."

"Too good for them."

Rivka pulled him in, burying her face in his neck. whispering, "No more sad talk. Not tonight. Tonight I want you and only you." She pushed back just enough to bring them face to face, and then whispered, "Do you want me?"

"The world can go to hell. The world is going to hell. You are my world. Yes. Yes now. Yes tomorrow. And yes forever. I love you."

"I longed for you, every day you were away."

They held each other as a group of four half-drunk German infantrymen loudly suggested, in a most congenial manner, that perhaps the couple should hire a room at a hotel of their choosing.

"Castle Park?" Elia suggested.

"No. It's not like before. The trees are gone. First Hungarians then Russians camped there. Nothing now but a sea of mud."

"Damn."

"We can go to my house. No one's there."

"Tanchem's?"

"Father and Malka's train isn't in until the morning and Izac's company is still up at Jaroslaw."

"Could you be comfortable in your own home, your own bed?"

"I could with you."

"We'll be seen, Rivka. Reputations matter."

"To hell with reputation, Elia, there's a war on. Besides, no one will see us. I have a plan."

"A plan, sweetheart?"

"Ancient family secret."

"What kind of—"

Rivka put her finger on his lips. "Trust me." She pulled her finger off and kissed him. "Now, let's walk." They strolled down the hill, hand in hand, following Elia's old route to work.

"There's a trap door in the back of the shop, on the floor, under the rug by daddy's drafting table. It leads down to an old coal cellar shared by three buildings."

"Czarnieckiego twenty-five, six and seven?"

"Exactly. Here's the key to the shop."

A few minutes later they kissed and pretended to go their separate ways. Rivka went through the front door of her father's home, bolted the door behind her, lit a candle, disrobed, and slipped into her bed. Elia walked in circles before making his way into the Arm factory, to Tanchem's drafting table, to the coal cellar, up the ladder, and into his lover's bedroom. He peeled his clothes off before diving into Rivka's open arms.

For the first time they embraced, skin to skin. Their lips met, their mouths opened, their hands explored new realms. The war never happened and there never was a siege. Only two people had ever lived in Galicia, on earth or in the heavens.

"Oh, Elia. My lover, Elia. "

"Rivka, my beautiful Rivka."

The moment overwhelmed Elia, silencing his voice yet elevating his senses in ways that before this night were inconceivable. Sheer force of passion, generated by a constant stream of new discoveries—the feel of her breast, the caress of her thigh, the mutual exploration to the very core of intimacy—seemed to nullify feelings of horror, loneliness and even guilt he had brought back from the war. It was a religious awakening, a long-desired affirmation of the true plenty of life after a bitter winter of dearth and death; the quenching of thirst after giving up on the hope that water really exists.

God had finally delivered on a weapon capable of defeating the endless malevolence that encircled their lives and Elia and Rivka were determined to deploy it. They made love twice that evening; the first time furiously and to a quick resolution, the second time slower and more mutually fulfilling, ending with dreams in each other's arms.

Elia made it back to the camp with only minutes to spare. He stretched out on his field blanket in his tent and smoked a cigarette before rolling over, trying to find a comfortable sleeping position on the uneven ground.

That night he had another dream about the painting of the woman by the Spanish artist. She was the woman he had just made love to, only now seen from a hundred angles simultaneously. Rivka's body was a complex form, possessing not only length, height, and width, but dozens of other dimensions, most measured with sensation, not a rule. Liberated from spatial constraints, she leapt off the canvas, freed to explore indescribable worlds of warm, sweaty skin and pure emotion.

His dream had no plot, no beginning and no end, yet it finally made everything he had ever known, felt, or believed in make sense.

Przemyśl • 26th of Sivan, 5675 – Tuesday, June 8, 1915

"OF COURSE I know what happened to your daughter, Meyer," Gitla said.

They sat in the corner booth of the woman's salon on the well-cushioned, high-backed, wicker banquette, Meyer with his back to the wall, Gitla facing him.

He positioned his pipe, a box of matches, and a tin of tobacco on the table and began his preparations to smoke while Gitla's eyes wandered first to the rococo silver sugar boat centered on the table, then to a painting of a heavily armed, smirking royal on a beautiful palomino horse. In the middle of his ritual, Meyer looked up at his guest and asked, "Mind if I smoke?"

She shrugged, "Mind if I fart?"

"Gitla, Gitla, Gitla," he said, shaking his head, smiling.

"You know how much I hate this place, Meyer."

"I'm sorry, but I really did need to talk in confidence."

"So we couldn't meet in the woods? Any place but the Hibler."

"Look, Meyer Weiss, taking a meeting anywhere other than this Café is so out of the ordinary as to guarantee suspicion."

A waiter in formal attire delivered tea and sweets. Gitla waited until he was gone before speaking, barely above a whisper, "A wolf loses his hair but not his nature."

Meyer said nothing, knowing that as in chess, no direct response—a tempo move—was usually the best response to an unfocused attack.

Gitla focused on the barroom, off limits to women. "So I suppose these are your new friends?" The room was packed with German officers playing billiards and drinking in a fog of cigar smoke. "Eight months to find Przemyśl, a day to find billiards and booze."

Meyer chuckled, playing with his teaspoon.

Gitla leaned over the table, "Cut the crap. I wouldn't play your little game when we were young and I'm not about to start now."

Meyer stared at her without blinking. "I've asked you to tea to seek your—"

"I know why you asked to see me."

He leaned in toward her, lowering his voice. "I will pay you handsomely."

"That's so like you, Meyer."

"And be forever in your debt."

"Now that's a fart in a tub."

"If you could help me."

"Help the mighty Herr Weiss?"

"I believe that my Zipre may be, be..." The most powerful Jew in Eastern Galicia put his palms on the table and focused on the geometric pattern embossed on the zinc ceiling. A few tears pooled in the depressions his eyes sat in. Gitla reached out and covered Meyer's hands with hers.

"Pregnant," she said, barely above a whisper, squeezing. He leveled his head. "How did you know?"

"When the banker buys soapwort, he's both constipated and playing doctor or he's a worried father pretending to be an herbalist encouraging his daughter's womanly flow." She let go of his hands and sat back in her chair. "I'm betting on the latter."

Meyer smiled thinly, "You haven't changed a bit, Gitla. You would have made a formidable merchant had fate pushed you down that path."

"Perhaps," she said, "but for today, your daughter is in need of an abortionist, not a merchant."

"I often think about what would have happened if we had—"

"This you have to say now? Sometimes I forget just what a bastard you can be, Meyer Weiss."

They sipped tea and nibbled at cakes and cookies for the next few minutes.

"Can we continue, Gitla?"

"By all means."

"All right. How much shall this all be?"

"Money, always with money." Gitla looked up at the ceiling. "This is so much more serious than your precious banknotes. Zipre could bleed to death. It may not work and she may end up with a mongrel or worse."

"I understand risk," Meyer said.

"This isn't like business."

"I understand the risks to my daughter."

"Good. First, I will need four Kronen for medicine, and not a Heller more. Less than the price of a box of cigarettes. The rest I shall find in the woods."

"Four?"

"Four. Second, leave town. Go to your flat in Cracow. This will not be pretty and the last thing I need is a squeamish father kibitzing over my shoulder. Rivka and I will take care of your daughter."

"And?"

"Third, if it does not take, or if for any reason Zipporah decides to keep it, you will promise to love and care for both her and her child forever after, regardless of the circumstances."

"I agree," he said. "She has no reservations about ending this."

"What makes you so sure?"

Meyer shrugged.

"Fourth, look me in the eye and tell me that you will not have me hanged if your daughter doesn't make it."

He looked at her and said, "Whatever happens, I am forever in your debt."

"Yes, and speaking of debt, allow me to add a final term."

"How can I object, dear Gitla?"

"I want your word, before God, that if we are successful, you will owe me one very large favor. I have no idea what it might be or even if I will ever use it. I just want you—"

"I will never, repeat, never forget this Gitla. You have my word."

Meyer signaled the waiter with a quick movement of his thumb and forefinger then pulled a roll of banknotes from his pants pocket. Once the bill arrived he peeled off a purple ten Kronen note and tossed it on top of the handwritten tabulation resting on the small silver tray. He could not help but notice how much the Princess Rohan, framed on the right side of the banknote, resembled his Zipporah. A deep sadness came over him as the waiter took her from the table in exchange for a small pile of silver coins.

He left one coin for the waiter and pushed the other four across the table toward Gitla, feeling uncomfortable that the payment for such an important transaction should be so small.

Przemyśl • 28th of Sivan, 5675 – Thursday, June 10, 1915

GITLA WALKED UP Mickiewicza toward the Weisses' house, oblivious to the guttural laughter emanating from the two tables of German officers lounging on the terrace of the Metropol. A block later she arrived at the Weiss manse, where Rivka met her at the door, relieving her of the bundle of greens she was carrying on her shoulder.

Rivka brought Zipre into the kitchen where Gitla was drying her hands on a white linen cloth. "Sit, my child," the older woman said, patting a chair next to her. Faded plum-colored bruises on her forearms and under her eyes were the only sign of Zipre's beating. She appeared hale and recovered as she sashayed across the room, planting a kiss on Gitla's cheek. "Sit, sit," she said, gently pushing her toward the chair. Seated, Zipre's eyes locked onto Gitla's face and she spoke forcefully, "You are so sweet to come take care of me. I want, no, need for this nightmare to end. I want to love my children. I, I, um, cannot, um, I." She stuttered and began to weep, but only briefly before straightening her sitting posture and regaining her self-control. Zipre patted her stomach, "I cannot have this baby."

"So how do you feel? When was your last period?" Gitla asked. Rivka served tea which Gitla ignored. Without the slightest hint of modesty she leaned forward and reached into Zipre's blouse, palpating both of her breasts.

"I was due two weeks ago. My last menstruation was mid-April. It's been four weeks since I was... twenty eight days since Mama's *Yartzeit.*"

Gitla nodded several times before pushing her patient's torso backwards until she was splayed across two chairs and her head rested on Rivka's lap. In one swift motion, Gitla knelt before her, pulling her dress up and her undergarments down, positioning Zipre's legs and hips to expose her genitals for examination.

"Esther and I were best friends growing up," she said, keenly eyeing the telltale bluish tinge of her vagina. After a rapid but skillful probe of Zipre's insides, she added, "You're pregnant. There is no doubt about it."

"Well, that much I knew. I've been throwing up for the past week. So how did you know Mother?"

"Before she met your father we were in gymnasium together. She taught me how to wear lip rouge; I taught her how to smoke cigarettes."

"Impossible!" Zipre snapped.

Rivka playfully covered Zipre's mouth with her hand. "I can't decide which is more incredible, your mother strolling to the synagogue while smoking a cigarette or Gitla collecting flowers wearing lip rouge?"

Gitla helped herself to a biscuit, allowing time for the light mood to slip away. "Listen girls, it's time to be serious." She pulled Zipre back to a seated position. "You are certainly a month pregnant. The seed in your belly is smaller than a grape. More like a raisin. And it is not," she shook a finger at Zipre, "a baby. So let us not call it one. Babies live and breathe. This thing cannot live outside of you. It is not a baby." She paused to sip tea and let it sink in. "From here on, we shall call it," she stared up at the dark oak crown molding girding the ceiling, "a raisin." The girls chuckled nervously.

"How exactly do we get the raisin out of Zipre's belly?" Rivka asked.

Pointing to the bundle of plants on the table Gitla began to lecture, "They grow everywhere. You've trod on them all your life, never knowing their power."

The girls leaned in closer.

"First, we weaken the strings between the raisin and the stomach; the bloodlines that nourish the thing. Make your womb inhospitable. You'll drink a half liter of cotton root bark tea every three hours, day and night, fresh herbs daily. On day two, I'll make an oil infusion using two stronger abortificants: rue and wild carrot." She lifted a specimen of each as she spoke. "I'll soak a wad of cotton in the oil and you will apply it vaginally. You should begin bleeding within hours."

She paused to finish her tea. Rivka reached out for Zipre's hand. "On day three you drink a strong tea made from tansy. One liter, all at once, followed an hour later by another liter. This will cause the stomach walls to contract and if we are lucky, you will expel the thing."

Zipre looked at the table of herbs, "And what if I am not so lucky?"

Gitla reached into her cloak and pulled out a small amber vial. "Oil of pennyroyal," she said. "It is poison and will make you sick. But it will expel the raisin."

Zipre straightened her posture and lifted her head, "Very good then. Let's get started."

The cramps began almost immediately. Bleeding commenced during the first night. By the second day she was convulsing, vomiting bile, and bleeding clotted blood. On the morning of the third day, Gitla again poured a sample of Zipre's menstrual blood, caught in a small rubber cup inserted against her cervix, into a large clear glass jar. Taking out a large, rectangular magnifying glass, she scanned the chaotic swirls of the merging liquids. Unlike the past four times she had checked, thin yellow filaments were obvious and abundant, proof positive of pregnancy termination. She let out an audible sigh, glad to have only used two drops of the lethal oil.

Six

Przemyśl • 1st of Tishrei, 5678 – Monday, September 17, 1917

THOUSANDS GATHERED ON the banks of the San a few minutes before noon on a hot, overcast day. They came from every corner of town and represented the full spectrum of the town's Jews: Orthodox, Hassidic, Progressive, Secular Atheist, and *Shabbos* Jews. Coalescing into clusters of friends and extended family, they milled about, trading vignettes—a post from a son at the front, theories about the war, or simply the latest gossip sweeping the town. Solidifying their boundaries as they engulfed stragglers from the periphery, distinct groups formed and moved toward the riverbank. After reciting the *Tachlich*, the assemblage disbanded and each member stepped to the river's edge. Following a period of silent contemplation—seconds for some, minutes for others—individuals emptied their pockets, casting the breadcrumbs, scrap paper, and lint into the eddies and currents of the San. Pockets turned inside out, flotsam washing down the stream, their souls were purged of the past year's sorrow.

Having visited the water, Rivka and her clan climbed to the top of the treeless quay, extending New Year's greeting with all who happened by. As the haze began to lift the temperature spiked, the conversations ebbed. Alone at the edge of the gathering, Rivka watched the parade of people, considering what sorrows might have been purged from their souls as well as what crumbs remained in their pockets.

Two years on and Malka still pines for the synagogue wedding she never had—as if Manes would ever have set foot in a synagogue, even for her. Only a Feldrabiner's blessing, a night of consummation, and Lea to rear alone. Mister Weiss has everything yet is terribly lonely. How he desperately wants to be liked. Daddy too is lonely—he wants Izac and the workers back: you can't be king without subjects. He wants Manes back too, but to hug him or kill him? We all long for Mama. Mama. I miss you so much... Zipporah's not hard to divine: she wants to find a caller who wants to be her husband—not Meyer's son-in-law—and tries each day to forget the unspeakable. Gitla: the faster she delivers babies the faster the pine boxes come—she carries everyone's pain—always sad for others, never for herself. Petra: no matter what she casts to the San she'll never get over losing Dov. Isidore, my sweet Isidore—torn between charity and greed...

A distant rumble of thunder broke Rivka's concentration. She looked down at her hands, "And then there's Rivka." She exhaled, mouth open. "So where do I begin?"

Trieste • 1st of Tishrei, 5678 – Monday, September 17, 1917

THE 10TH WAS encamped along the hundred-meter-wide rise—little more than a scrub-covered sand dune—that ran parallel to the shoreline and kept the vast coastal swamp from draining into the Adriatic.

The men from Przemyśl were exhausted from another day of hard labor in sweltering heat and humidity. As tiring as it was unloading crates of munitions from the endless stream of trains and boats, to a man they were glad not to be idle a few dozen kilometers north at the front lines, bored to near insanity and rotting in the trenches amid the constant din of incoming and outbound artillery fire.

Manes and Elia sat naked and cross-legged in their tent, slowly pulling on the final few draws of their cigarettes. In spite of being just past 23:00 it wasn't dark. The lights of Trieste glowed through the haze, a permanent fixture in the summer night sky, and a nearly full moon hung overhead, reflecting chaotically off muted ripples in the sea; ample light found its way through the gray canvas for the men to see each other inside the tent. As one talked, the other would puff on his cigarette, the glow briefly illuminating his chapped, dirty red leather face, one of the more obvious consequences of nearly four years of war.

"It's finally happening. The revolution is at hand," Elia said.

"Russia is the vanguard. Germany is next. Just you watch. The workers on both sides of this will stop making shells and bullets and the war will end."

"Can you believe the French army? Refuses to fight."

"I hear they shot the leaders then told the families they died in battle."

"Those behind the lines judging those in the trenches," Elia said, shaking his head. "Swine."

Manes shook his head and pursed his lips, "What the capitalists finally grasp is that the troops are the workers. If we do not fight each other, we might just turn around and march on and take back our homes, our factories. What a colossal mistake they made arming and training us."

"Not only did the capitalists sell us the rope we'll use to hang them, they were nice enough to tie it in a noose."

"You speak with great wisdom," Manes said before inhaling. "For a *shtetl yid.*" He blew smoke through a toothy smile.

"Bastard," Elia answered, smiling. "You know, Manes, at some point we—you and I and everyone else in the regiment—are going to have to make a decision as to who we are fighting in this war. Sometime soon we are going to have to cast off our uniforms and turn our guns on our real enemy."

"Like Russia. We threw the tsarists out of Przemyśl. They regrouped, changed flags and marched back to Petrograd and tossed the Tsar into the river."

They smoked in silence.

"It's hot as hell tonight. What the hell good is a sea if it makes no breeze?" Elia said, exhaling.

"It's the new year. Perhaps it will bring peace and revolution," Manes said, adding with a grin, "I mean peace or revolution."

"Amen," Elia said, pulling the netting aside then flicking his smoldering butt out of the tent and into the sand.

"Amen. Peace or revolution or a cool breeze."

"I have an idea." Elia crawled out of the tent.

He went from tent to tent, rousing the men. "Comrades! Fellow soldiers! The time has come! Join me!" In no time Elia led thirty naked men on a noisy march down the sand dune to the wet sand on the shoreline, their feet occasionally lapped by a small waves.

A ship's light was visible on the horizon as conversations wound down and ended. The men's heads bowed, arms dropped to their sides. One soldier bent over and scooped up a handful of sand. Someone else followed him, then another, and soon everyone. The first man stepped into the sea so the water nearly covered his shins, lifted his head, and began chanting:

> *Who is a God like You? You forgive sins and overlook transgressions. For the survivors of Your People; He does not retain His anger forever, for He loves Kindness.*

The rest of the detachment waded in and joined the prayer:

> *He will return and show us mercy, and overcome our sins, And You will cast into the depths of the sea all their sins; You will show kindness to Yaakov and mercy to Avraham, As You did promise to our fathers of old.*

Each man cast his handful of sand into the waters of the Adriatic.

An hour later, after a rowdy moonlight swim, Elia, Manes and the rest of the 10th were back in their tents sleeping.

Early the next morning, a female *anopheles* mosquito alit on Elia's arm. Piercing his skin with her proboscis, she injected a miniscule amount of saliva into the wound before sucking his blood into her abdomen. In addition to anticoagulation proteins, the saliva contained sporozoites of the parasite *plasmodium falciparum* which had been growing in the intestine of the mosquito for weeks and had recently been discharged into her salivary glands. Within hours the sporozoites congregated in Elia's liver and began to multiply. Three weeks later, long after the itch caused by his body's immune response to the mosquito saliva had abated; the sporozoites would metamorphose into merozoites and attack Elia's red blood cells, triggering a release of toxins causing paroxysmal chills and violent fevers.

Elia awoke the next morning and scratched the itch on his arm, hale and refreshed after the midnight swim and a good night's sleep.

New York • 1st of Tishrei, 5678 – Monday, September 17, 1917

THE ODEON THEATER
58 Clinton Street
Presents
Arbuckle and Keaton in:
~~~~~~~~~~~~~~~
"Coney Island"
Shows 10:00 am to 11:00 pm

"Been ages since the last post from Elia," Julia said, turning away from the movie toward Marta.

Fatty drops his head and cries by the turnstile as he watches his girlfriend enter the amusement park with another man. Just as he loses all hope, he notices a dustman bringing a half dozen or so recently emptied trash barrels back into the park one by one on a small hand truck.

She continued, oblivious to the multiple calls for her to "Shut the hell up!" from darkness of the audience behind them.

"Something must be wrong—what do you think?"

"I'm tryin' to watch a picture, Julia. All right. What? Don't you like 'em anymore?"

With unexpected stealth and agility, Fatty climbs into the last barrel and after a brief scratch of the head by the confused dustman, is chauffeured onto the Midway in the style to which he had become accustomed.

"I like a lot about New York—my house, my girls, the subways, Coney Island—but most of all, and you know it's the truth, I love Buster and Fatty." Julia reached for a handful of popped corn from the oil-stained brown paper bag lodged between Marta's legs.

"If something was really bad, you would have heard by now," Marta said before stuffing her mouth with her own
~~~~~~~~~~~~~~~

handful.

Arbuckle struts off triumphantly with the girl but as he passes Keaton who is swinging a mallet on the 'Test Your Strength' machine, he gets whacked in the jaw and is knocked over. Buster, sitting on the tester's platform, breaks out in laughter. Arbuckle picks up the sledge hammer and crowns Keaton so hard that the metal rabbit rises to the top of the scale and sounds the bell and the attendant awards Arbuckle a cigar.

Marta laughed so hard that she sprayed half a handful of partially chewed popcorn from her mouth. Julia took another handful.

"You all right, Julia?" Marta whispered, handing the nearly empty sack to her.

Fatty can't find a bathing suit to fit his girth and ends up in a woman's one, with a hat and wig to boot. Keaton enters, laughing hysterically at the big man in drag.

The theater rang with laughter as Julia sat plucking out the un-popped kernels from the bag, putting them into her vest pocket. "Down in front," someone yelled when she stood up.

"I've got to go. See you at home," she said to Marta as she brushed by her knees on the way to the aisle.

"But don't you want to see the end of the movie?"

The man at the end of the row began to stand but before he could get up, she had shimmied by him and was up the aisle toward the lobby.

Leaving the theater for Broome Street, cool darkness gave way to blinding sun and stifling heat as butter and corn yielded to garbage and horse-waste. She kept her eyes nearly shut, mostly to shield them from the sun, but also to try to fight back the first tears.

Reaching East River Park, Julia found a shady stretch along the heavy wrought iron fence that separated the cobblestone walk from the river. Eyes fully open and only the slightest bit damp, she chanted barely above a whisper,

Who is a God like You? You forgive sins and overlook transgressions

For the survivors of Your People; He does not retain His anger forever, for He loves Kindness; He will return and show us mercy, and overcome our sins—

"Who am I kidding?" She stared at the water. "This doesn't mean I believe in you, God. Or whatever, whoever you are." The water smelled of dead fish and sewage. "But that doesn't mean that you and I, we can't understand each other. You give me nothing and I ask for nothing for myself."

Julia reached into her vest pocket and came out with the scant handful of corn pieces that she cast onto the brown water. The kernels swirled in the turbulent water and floated out of sight, downstream, toward the ocean.

"But just in case I'm wrong about all this and you really are the God everybody talks about, please look out for my Elia. Please. Okay?"

Seven

Kobarid • 8th of Tishrei, 5678 – Monday, September 24, 1917

THE ITALIAN ARMY had fought a dozen battles against the Austrians; the line between the end of one and the start of another had long since blurred. While the Italian conscripts were content to rest, an overly enthusiastic field artillery officer from Genoa kept eying a buildup of enemy troops two ridges in the distance and was sure that they could be hit with his 4.5 inch cannon if it were properly positioned at the top of a west-facing slope. So in a scene reminiscent of Exodus, seventy-five men pulled on two ropes, painstakingly dragging the multi-ton *artiglieria da campo* up the hill. The going was slow on the rain-slicked Alpine scrub, and there was a palpable lack of enthusiasm. The troops, mostly ex-munitions workers from Turin, had recently been transferred to the frontlines—punishment for a traitorous revolt if you asked the officers—to break a strike if you polled the privates.

The gun barrel had been forged nine months earlier at Campo Tizzoro, just outside of Pistoia. It was six meters long and carefully grooved inside such that the shell would be ejected with enormous spin, adding considerably to the range and accuracy of the projectile. The barrel was mounted on a sled-like tripod base. Behind was a skid plate with a huge iron shovel brake, designed to dig into the earth and anchor the machine firmly against recoil. In front were two steel reinforced wooden wheels which had recently been retrofitted around the circumference with sixteen extra-wide pads—s*tivali* the troops called them—necessary to keep the whole contraption from sinking to the axles in the brown Paivian mud.

Once positioned on the crest, the foot soldiers retreated back down the hill, not waiting for orders from their superiors.

What happened next could never have happened without a truly multi-national effort.

The Genovese officer looked across the valley through binoculars made in Milan under license from, ironically, Carl Zeiss of Jena, in the very heart his enemy's Empire. He consulted tables calculated centuries ago in Scotland before instructing his four-man artillery detail to make minute adjustments in attitude and azimuth.

A shell, manufactured near Stoke-on-Trent, and fitted with an impact fuse, was loaded into the breach. Artillery men braced as a captain pulled the firing cord, driving a small hammer into the igniter at the base of the shell. A small charge set off a violent chemical reaction which moved through the much larger propellant charge at hyper-sonic speed. Thanks to the work of a Swedish chemist some fifty years earlier, the main fuel, a stabilized form of nitroglycerin, instantly transformed every four moles of the solid explosive into 35 moles of gas, with little or no residue. Because there was no solid carbon produced, the explosion was almost entirely "smokeless," allowing the gunner an unobstructed line of sight to his target and, far more importantly, not advertising the location of the firing battery to a potential responding enemy.

Confined within the brass casing of the shell, the

4-becomes-35 equation created an almost incomprehensible, if momentary, spike in pressure. Seeking relief, the ten-kilogram payload accelerated away from the shell with a force several thousand times that of the pull of gravity, exiting the barrel at nearly 600 meters per second.

About a foot long, encased in pressed steel, it was, in form, a large bullet. Yet unlike a bullet, the inside was of a well-articulated and devious design. The tip was a fuse, primed to go off on physical impact, and, most specifically not from the massive g-force of firing. Connected to the fuse was a cylinder, about one-sixth the diameter of the shell, filled with gunpowder, centered, and running the length of the shell to the main charge of perhaps 200 grams, in the rear. Thanks to the imagination and inventive genius of the long since departed Henry Shrapnel, a Lieutenant in the British Royal Artillery, the space between the shell casing and the internal powder cylinder was filled with upwards of 300 pieces of irregular lead shot, each weighing about 10 grams—just like every other shell launched since the beginning of the nineteenth century. Right above the main charge was a steel plate, angled to facilitate the optimal ejection vector for the lead projectiles.

Strictly obeying laws codified by Isaac Newton some four centuries earlier, the shell traced a parabola in the sky, covering over three kilometers in about five seconds. Within a fraction of a second of impact, the fuse had ignited the central charge, rupturing the steel casing and ejecting the shrapnel. Another fraction of a second later the main charge ignited, scattering the eponymous shards in a spray of lethal arcs radiating out from the point of impact.

After communicating a small change in trajectory, the officer ordered his men to fire again. Looking through his binoculars, the enthusiastic officer noticed a small, dirty-white puff rise from the hillside in the distance.

As designed, the fuse primed the cylinder charge on

impact, dislodging a coin-sized piece of casing and hurdling it through space at hypersonic speeds. Fifteen meters later, the shard effortlessly sliced through something soft and wet before coming to a rest on a tuft of dry grass, a stone's throw from the blast site.

Elia and the dozen or so other men on a cigarette break instinctively crouched low in the trench and ducked their heads upon hearing the blast. After two years, it was an oft-repeated ritual in the foothills above the Kobarid. While the men were either lying or squatting as close to the dirt as possible, many continued conversations with unseen comrades who were likewise hiding in the trench. Elia, head down, took a deep draw on his cigarette as a second shell hit a bit further away. After exhaling, Elia spoke into the ground as the smoke from his cigarette made its way up around his helmet. "Kerensky is doomed," he said with authority. "Kornilov is marching what remains of the Russian army to Petrograd and has only Lenin to turn to for defense. Russia has turned. One way or another, the war is over when they sue for peace. The real question is who is next. My guess is France. Once the Krauts are free from the lines in the east, they will overwhelm the west. The French are tired. Whole divisions have refused to fight. It's just a matter of time before some general like Kornilov turns his cannons around and marches on Paris. Or Germany. Yes, the Bolsheviks have shown the way. An army of workers that can march on a so-called enemy can just as easily turn and march on the so-called leaders."

Another explosion nearby.

"Manes?" Silence. "Then its back home to our girls."

The shelling stopped, there was only silence.

"Manes?" Elia, still crouched, turned his head. To his surprise, Manes was standing—or rather leaning—against the leading wall of the trench. Elia could see the smoke from Manes's cigarette spiraling up over his head but Manes's face was out of view.

"Manes, *dumkopf*!" Elia said, hitting him in the thigh with a clenched fist.

Nothing.

Elia stood. Manes's hand rested on a weed clinging to the clay soil at the edge of the trench. The cigarette wedged between his fore and middle fingers had burned down dangerously close to the skin.

"What did I say, old friend?" Elia asked in a sarcastic tone as he reached over and slapped Manes's cheek. "What did I say? Did I offend...?"

Elia felt eerie, wet warmth, more like a slab of bread soaking in hot soup than a man's face. He held up his hand and watched as several crimson droplets meandered their way from the pool of blood in his palm down his forearm where they were soaked up by the rolled-up sleeve of his field tunic.

He recoiled in horror before turning to his friend. Manes's head had rolled to the side and he was now staring at Elia, eyes fixed, lifeless. His mouth was open, frozen, in mid-sentence. Elia could see a small entry wound just above Manes's left cheekbone and a much larger exit wound above the right ear. Through spirals of cigarette smoke on the dirt and grass beyond the bunker he could make out a trail of what had been his best friend's brains.

"No!" Elia screamed, shaking Manes's lifeless body angrily. "Goddamn it, no!" he yelled over and over before embracing the corpse and trailing off into mournful whimpering as they rocked back and forth.

After a long cry, Elia insisted on being one of the stretcher carriers to take Manes's body to the morgue. Moments after returning to the trench, with sweat pouring down his face, stinging his eyes, he began a shiver that didn't break for days.

Przemyśl • 15th of Tishrei, 5678 – Monday, October 1, 1917

EVERYONE IN PRZEMYŚL, Pole, Ruthian or Jew, handled Monday morning differently. Some went about their daily routine as if nothing would ever change, walking to work, doing errands or picking through the stores and pushcarts for what fresh produce could be found. Others made sure to avoid the pubic posting places: *Rynek*, Plac na Bramie, the train station. But a large minority couldn't wait for news and actively sought out and confronted the newsprint as it was nailed to wooden billboards at seven every Monday morning.

Malka carried her daughter, Lea Sterner, even though at nineteen months she was an accomplished toddler. It was a constant source of humor between the Arm sisters that Eisner had encouraged Malka to work through both pregnancy and nursing. German and Austrian officers, it seemed, simply shifted their attention from her face to her swelling breasts and never tired of buying overpriced tailored clothing from Malka. Lea was a fine-looking baby. At first fat, pink and bald, but now long and trim with thin curls of light blond hair falling on her neckline. She had almost died over the winter—Gitla's concoction of boiled garlic and honey had been widely credited with saving her from the croup. She had never seen or been seen by her father, but did not want for love, having been anointed as the extended family's miracle baby, particularly by Tanchem who adored his first grandchild, the namesake of his departed wife.

Rivka and Malka were always in the group that wanted to know, and know right away. They joined the small crowd of mostly younger Jewish and Polish women milling around the billboard at the east end of the Plac na Bramie. The faces, after four years, were familiar, if aged. To Rivka, the worst were those fellow seekers who had gone missing—a mother whose son had shown up on casualty lists, a wife or lover who had broken down in tears on the previous Monday after seeing name of their man in fresh, typewritten black ink.

As the bells tolled seven, two smartly dressed Austrian officers marched toward the billboard. Rivka imagined them as some giant cuckoo clock with tin soldiers announcing the hour, parting the gathering. On the worst days they would hammer up three pages of casualties; today a single page with only a few names brought a momentary elevation to the otherwise somber mood in the square.

After nearly two hundred weeks of rehearsal, the ritual was precisely choreographed. Rivka was to wade through the crowd to the post where she'd scan the newsprint before shooting a glance at her sister. Only then could both start their day, heading off to their jobs.

Rivka waited as the more aggressive in the crowd made their way to the front to look for familiar names, then walk away only to be replaced by slightly less anxious neighbors. No one smiled. A few had tears. The worst part to Malka was that it was never clear if the tears were for themselves or because they now knew something that soon would destroy the life of someone waiting in line to read the list.

There was a gap near the front and Rivka made her move, leaving Malka and Lea behind. She read to herself, "Rancewicz, Łukasz—Redka, Myroslav—thank God." Rivka exhaled then continued, "Siebert—Siekierski—Sterner—Tarka—T..." Blood stopped flowing while she reread the entry, "Sterner, Manes – killed in action: Kobarid, IX 24." A shiver moved up her spine and exploded in her head. "No!" Rivka shrieked. "Why? Damn it all, why?"

Rivka turned, looking for her sister, oblivious to the consolations of those gathering around her. In the distance, Lea began to cry.

"Rivka!" Malka screamed, pushing toward her, the child in her arm gulping for air between wails. They embraced with all their might. "Which one" Malka whispered into her sister's ear.

"Manes." Malka's eyes closed tightly. She did not cry, but then Malka almost never cried.

The sisters held each other up as the crowd dissipated. Horses, wagons and pedestrians of all persuasions steered a wide berth around them while offers of condolence went unheard or unacknowledged as they rocked gently in front of the billboard.

Przemyśl • 20th of Adar, 5678 – Monday, March 4, 1918

MEYER LOOKED ABSENTLY at the board, working through a last gambit to see if he could force his queen's pawn to the eighth rank. "Fourteen articles in the Brest agreement, fourteen points in Wilson's speech. What is it about fourteen anyway, Jurek?"

"From this point the winner is the last to blunder," Jurek offered, the upward inflection of his voice matching the movement of his eyebrow. "Draw?"

Meyer had a pawn advantage, but it was a doubled, frozen in place by a solid phalanx of opposing pieces and no matter how he played it, the gambit ended up in stalemate. "Draw," he said, extending his hand across the board.

They shook. "I don't know about Brest, but I can tell you every Pole I know has memorized the thirteenth of Wilson's points."

"Not the Jews. Please, have a go."

Jurek set his cigar down on the ashtray and straightened up in his chair. "I think this is how Article Thirteen goes: 'An independent Polish state should be erected which should include the territories inhabited by indisputably Polish populations, which should be assured a free and secure access to the sea, and whose political and economic independence and territorial integrity should be guaranteed by international covenant.'"

"Well done, and oy vey," Meyer said, shaking his head.

Jurek puffed on his cigar as Meyer emptied his tea cup and took up the newspaper with "Armistice in the East" splashed across the masthead.

"So Lev caved," Meyer said in German, scanning the text of the article.

Jurek exhaled, trying to make rings in the air.

"Listen to this, 'The contracting parties will refrain from any agitation or propaganda against the Government or the public and military institutions of the other party.'"

"I give Lenin about two weeks on that one," Jurek commented.

"Or this, 'The territories lying to the west of the line agreed upon by the contracting parties, which formerly belonged to Russia, will no longer be subject to Russian sovereignty; the line agreed upon is traced on the map submitted as an essential part of this treaty of peace. The exact fixation of the line will be established by a Russo-German commission. No obligations whatever toward Russia shall devolve upon the territories referred to, arising from the fact that they formerly belonged to Russia. Russia refrains from all interference in the internal relations of these territories. Germany and Austria-Hungary purpose to determine the future status of these territories in agreement with their population.' So Kuhlmann wins," the Jewish banker continued.

Jurek leaned over the board and spoke in hushed tones, "Better you should start working on your Polish, my friend. The Central Powers have let the pawn pass. Brest-Litovsk is a dangerous gambit. All Germany's pieces are now flung at the west in a final attack. It's mate or resign."

"I don't see mate."

"Trotsky's no fool. If Germany wins, he has a defensible border, if they lose he takes back what he just ceded."

The Pole tapped his cigar on the dish to the side of the board. A barrel of ash broke off and came to rest, fully intact, in the glass tray. "And we both know—"

"That when Austria is done, the Poles will get a nation and when Russia recedes, the Ruthians will get one too. So where does that leave the Jews? I'll tell you where, with—" he put two fingers briefly over his lips. "I'm sorry Jurek, what were you going to say?"

"Just that the central powers are finished and Russia will be at war with itself for some time. There is a vacuum, and we both know that history, like nature, abhors a vacuum."

Meyer sat back in his wicker chair, stroking his grey goatee absentmindedly, "*Tsurus* for the Jews, and *tsurus* for me."

"Don't be such a pessimist, old man. You'll be fine. The color of the uniforms changes, the language goes from German to Polish, but otherwise, it's business as usual. Money is still money."

Meyer flagged the waiter, "Schnapps for me. Mister Styfi?"

"It's midday, I... oh why not. Schnapps for me too. Oh, hell. Schnapps for everyone!"

"Damn, you're good, Jurek," Meyer said, tipping his head, thinking, "So typical, buying a round for the house when the house is deserted."

"So are you, Meyer," Jurek said, tipping his head back, thinking, "So like you, crying over impending ruin even as you've moved all your assets to Zurich."

When the drinks arrived, a table of mid-level German officers and a handful of scattered locals acknowledged their benefactor with loud shouts and raised tumblers. Jurek raised his glass toward the officers and spoke in German, "Here's to von Kühlmann, to the treaty of Brest-Litovsk, and to the victory in the west!" He then turned to the locals and addressed them in Polish, "Here's to the treaty of Brest-Litovsk, and to foreigners out of Poland!"

Everyone in the Hibler enjoyed their schnapps.

Przemyśl • 20th of Tishrei, 5679 – Thursday, September 26, 1918

"SORRY, SILVER ONLY," Isidore said to the old woman trying to pay for a loaf of dark rye with Franz Joseph paper.

"Usury, I say, its usury. Not just the silver, the price is up every month for a year."

"Are you buying or not?"

"With paper money I buy, with coins I—"

"Next," he snapped, snatching the brown paper bag from across the counter.

The woman mumbled an epithet and turned to leave just as the next person in line, a well dressed man with his hat pulled low over his brow, tossed two silver coins on the counter. "Allow me, madam."

Icing a babka in the back room, Rivka's ears perked up. The voice was a familiar, but she couldn't quite place it.

Isidore picked up the coins, assayed them with a quick bite, and then handed the goods to the woman before tossing the coins into the till. "Pleasure, Missus Granatenstein," he said.

She took the bread. "That was a real *mitzvah* and you are a true *mensch*. Thank you," she said to the stranger before turning to the baker, "There really aren't any gentlemen left in Przemyśl." The door chimes rang as she found her way out.

"Next," Isidore said even though he was already face to face with the gentleman.

The man removed his hat. "Two sacks of *semmels* for the forts."

The corners of Isidore's mouth pushed up hard into a wide smile. "Rivka! Get out here. Bring the sacks for the forts."

"I'm busy. What is it?" came from the back, followed by an inquisitive, "Forts?"

"*Semmels*, bring out the *semmels*."

Rivka dropped the icing sack and headed toward the front counter. "Have you gone soft, Izzy?" She stopped walking as soon as she could see the back of Isidore's head. "We haven't made *semmels* since—" she moved from Isidore's bald-spot to the face of the customer he was waiting on. "Tomas?"

The baker and the baker's assistant came around to the front of the counter and embraced the Hungarian until the next customer in line complained. Isidore told her to wait while they hugged a little longer.

"PROFESSOR! OVER HERE," Rivka called, waving at Tomas as he walked across the Plac.

"Professor?" he asked. "I can't remember the last time anyone called me that."

"This is my sister, Malka."

He took her hand and kissed it. "Enchanted."

The three sat, drank, and talked. Tomas related what happened to him after the siege—the march to Mosciska—the camp outside of Lemberg—the train to Omsk—the hunger—the hope-crushing winters of Siberia. "I pretended to be a Professor of Engineering and got assigned to the factory across in town, across the river, fixing German diesels left over from the war. I've always been good with my hands and besides, the food was better there. After Brest, they set all the prisoners free. I was excited to get to home and find Jonas. Unfortunately, the train to Budapest never got out of Russia. They dumped us in Kiev and there were no other trains."

"Jonas?" Malka asked.

"Son. My first wife died and her father took him. But that's another story altogether," he said, his eyes taking in just how beautiful she was. While she was clearly Rivka's sister, he couldn't help but see that down to the smallest feature, everything about her was just slightly more feminine, more perfect. “In any case, I found work in Kiev with the Putilov Company. They were desperate for anyone who could make sense of their engines. Once I had saved up some money, I made it to L’vov and was hired on by the Fiat agent who offered me a position in Przemyśl. I figured it was a step towards Gyor and in the general direction of Palestine. Besides, I have friends in Przemyśl.” He nodded at his two companions, “Tomas Lenard, automobile mechanic. At your service.”

Malka cocked her head, “Palestine?”

Tomas glanced at Rivka before responding to her sister, “What else is left? All of Europe is coming apart at the seams. And I’ve had a lot of time to think about the larger issues these past few years.”

“What do you mean?” Rivka asked him.

Tomas took a long, slow sip of beer before continuing, “I suppose you could say it took a few Russian winters, but I managed to reconcile God with science and reason.”

“You, a rabbi?” Rivka scoffed.

“Not quite. I said I reconcile, not capitulate. Technology is all the time built on science we don’t fully comprehend—just because we do not fully understand the underlying dynamics of luminescence doesn’t mean we can’t construct searchlights. We don’t need to know the absolute truth about the nature of God to build a world around His laws. We don’t even have to believe in God. So it is in science, so it is with God and the Jews.”

“That doesn’t explain Palestine,” Rivka said, tersely.

“Well—”

“Yes it does,” Malka interrupted. “What I think Mister Lenard is saying is that building a society based on class is all well and good, but it’s doomed unless there’s some common underlying morality. And at the root of all morality is God, or at least the possibility of God, just like I’ve been telling you, sister.”

Rivka looked at Tomas with disbelief.

"That's one way to put it, Malka," Tomas said. "Quite insightful, actually, though I probably would have said that Jews have tried living under everyone else's system and in the end, it's never worked."

"I too am training to make *aliyah*," Malka said, with the Herzl Organization."

"Really?" Tomas adjusted his chair so he could lean closer to Malka.

"Yes, mostly agriculture, orchards and the like. The pruning and grafting of apples, pears, you know."

"I don't know, but it sound interesting," Tomas said.

"There is more to it than you would think. Pruning alone is as much art as science." Rivka stood up. "Rivka?"

"Sit, sister. Four comes awfully early and I need to get some sleep."

Tomas stood. "I've been so rude. All this talk must bore you to death, Rivka."

"No, it's all right. Someone like me is always going to be the third on a match with a couple of die-hard Zionists." Rivka smiled at Tomas, "It's wonderful to see you again. And I really am tired."

"Shall we walk you home?"

Rivka pecked him and Malka on their cheeks. "It's not like the town's invested anymore, Mister Lenard." She let out a small laugh before heading toward home.

Alone at a table on the Plac na Bramie, they told each other everything. Tomas explained about his wife Vilma and their son Jonas, and about how he'd lost them both. Malka told him about her husband Manes, interred somewhere in the Alps, and their daughter Lea, at home sleeping under the watchful eye of her father.

They talked until the barman turned the lights off at half past midnight. He walked her to her door-stoop and kissed her briefly on the lips. After exchanging parting words, Malka and Tomas stared at each other in utter helplessness as their bodies pulled together like two powerful magnets and their lips met again and remained locked for a very long time.

Eight

New York • 18th of Cheshvan, 5679 – Thursday, October 24, 1918

JULIA AND MARTA left Milton in charge. They dressed in their most respectable clothes, then strolled the five blocks down Delancy to the subway stop for the quick ride to City Hall.

The two women had argued for years over the best way to get to this day. Marta favored leaning on one of the judges or aldermen who frequented the house. Julia, rarely opposed to the judicious use of chits, muscle, or blackmail, and well connected at the Essex Market Court, would, in this and only this case, have none of it. Marta thought Julia insane; but Julia loved her adopted country and wanted to become a citizen fair and square. So she filled out her "Declaration of Intention," certifying to the Clerk of the Court that it was her intention to become a citizen of the United States, to reside permanently therein, and to renounce all of her allegiances to other nations. Five years and a day from her landing in New York City she petitioned the court for American citizenship, presenting affidavits vouching for her high moral character from Marta Miller, a business woman, and William Donovan, a well respected captain in the metropolitan police force. It had taken twenty-six months, but eventually the Bureau of Immigration and Naturalization completed its investigation and reported its findings and recommendations back to the court. A judge would rule based on these results at nine forty-five in the morning in Hall 1 of the courthouse. He would administer the oath to Julia and issue her an order of admission and a certificate of citizenship; or order a continuance of the investigation; or, worse, he would deny the petition outright.

The women chatted back and forth as they paid their way past the booth and through the turnstiles to the stairs that led to the train platforms. Marta talked about her journey from Riga as a child while they waited for the train. Once on board, she related how her family name was changed from something unpronounceable and Russian to the simple-to-say and ubiquitous Miller by an inspector at Ellis Island. As the train jerked to a stop and as they stepped onto the platform, she told Julia about going before the judge with her family. Leaving the station and walking down the broad sidewalk to the courthouse, she explained the almost intoxicating feeling of joy she had as the judge's gavel hit the desk, announcing that after five long years, the Muriechowski family of Riga was now the Millers of New York.

"Everything is going to be all right, Julia dear. I can feel it in my bones," Marta said, grabbing and squeezing her hand as they walked up the marble steps of the courthouse.

On the short journey from Ridge Street to the courthouse, both woman had touched innumerable surfaces, exchanging germs with the countless others who had also happened to touch them: the wrought iron door knob leaving home, a wooden banister at the train station, the conductor's hand, the metal pole in the car, the train seat, the glass window, the bumper of a Ford blocking the sidewalk, the marble wall of the courthouse. Perhaps it wasn't a surface at all, but rather something in the air. Untold numbers of people had sneezed along their route, sending out clouds of germ-laden water droplets in every direction. While the heavier drops would fall quickly to the ground, the smaller ones might remain aloft for minutes, and even hours, wafting from person to person, indistinguishable from everyday air. Even an act as innocuous as talking was enough to transmit the unseen malady, riding on the smallest bit of saliva, ejected accidentally and usually unnoticed by both speaker and listener.

Somewhere between Ridge Street and the Courthouse, a small but virulent colony of viruses found its way from the throat of an infected person onto the knuckle of Marta's right forefinger.

"Congratulations, Miss..." the judge looked down at the papers and located her name, "Miss Harmon. Now repeat after me. I hereby declare, under oath, that I absolutely and entirely renounce and abjure all allegiance and fidelity to any foreign prince, potentate, state, or sovereignty..."

Marta welled up and wiped a tear from her eye with her right forefinger. The judge signed several papers and handed two of them to Julia without looking directly at her. He glanced up at the line queued behind Julia and absently intoned, "Next."

As night fell, Marta's throat began to feel scratchy. The next morning her breathing became labored and she had spiked a fever. That evening, her lungs began to fill with phlegm. By Sunday morning American citizen Julia Harmon was making arrangements to bury her partner, best friend, and lover, Marta Miller.

Theories abounded. Some scientists believed it jumped to city dwellers from farmers who caught it from birds or swine. Many of the elderly believed it to be a return of the deadly pandemic of 1890, spread far and wide by the constant movement of army men. A vocal minority blamed nefarious foreign agents; anarchists, hell bent on destroying America, or the Bolsheviki and their ilk, all notorious foes of both decency and hygiene. But in the end, none of the reasons mattered to Julia. Her Marta was gone.

Kobarid • 19th of Cheshvan, 5679 – Friday, October 25, 1918

"YOU KNOW, *SIGNORE* Corporal, for a place housing a quarter of a million Italians, the architectural detail of this camp is awfully disappointing," Virgilio said, still shaking, trying to smile. "Is no Genoa, yes?"

"Have some more tea," Elia offered, "It helps me when I'm with the ague. Not that I'm an expert or anything, but I have lived through, what, four attacks. You have to drink warm liquids, no matter how hot you feel."

"And what about your eye, *Signore* Nightingale?"

"It was just a simple misunderstanding with some Austrians. The working class debating the issues of the day."

"With their fists?"

"Some people are less eloquent than others."

"Or just plain stupid." Virgilio sat up and forced down the lukewarm tea. "Like Cardorna's master plan. He knew the Austrian's had built camps for only fifty thousand so he brilliantly led his entire Second Army into the hills with no bullets, no shells, and no plan, knowing that the sheer number of surrendering men would overwhelm your prison system, thus bringing the Empire to its knees."

Elia chuckled and offered his prisoner a cigarette. After lighting it, Elia spoke as the Italian coughed out his first draw, "You are the funniest man I've ever known. But you're not altogether wrong—we all get to go home next week."

"God willing." Virgilio crossed himself, smoking mechanically. "I know you think the war's ending because the soldiers are tired or revolting or something in Germany. There may be something to that. Or America coming in. Or everyone's just tired. Who cares? I get to go back to Bobbio. You get to return to your unpronounceable Eden—what, *Pishmal*?—in Galicia, Austria, Russia, Poland, Germany. Say, what is it going to be anyway?"

"Yes, that is the question, isn't it?" Elia lit a cigarette. "My town is," he paused, looking at the mountains on the horizon, "simmering."

"So now that the Austrians are through, the simmering pot, it boils over?"

"The war isn't yet over and each side is here, organizing for the next one. Jews with fifty different political agendas, each organizing a militia. We're going to wear blue and white colors after Armistice Day. Poles already declared a country with flags and armies in red and white. Ruthians have the same idea, only in yellow and blue. It seems that Poland and Ruthia or Ukrainia or whatever it is overlap when drawn on a map."

"Piedmont and Lombardy they're not."

"And best of all, both think the Jews owe allegiance to their side. One particularly adamant Polish captain expressed this very opinion with his fist on the chin of a Jewish soldier, setting off the brawl in the mess."

"Thus the plum under your eye."

"I tried to argue that all of us should pull together to assure a new order directed by and for the working class. That this is an opportunity to cast off our capitalist masters, like the workers in Russia, and establish a Soviet Galicia, for the people. 'People.' That's the last word I remember saying. I woke up a few hours later, sore as hell, with this."

"It should be a wonderful train ride home."

"Home is home, no matter who's in charge."

"Not for me. Did you know I was born in America?"

Elia raised his eyebrows. "You moved from America to

Europe?"

"We moved back when I was a baby. Papa traded a store in the Promised Land for a farm in the hills. We were landed but far from rich. I was drafted and went to war. Papa went back to America. After this mess is done, I'm moving to America, to Philadelphia with the love of my life."

"Name?"

"Luisa. You?"

"Rivka."

"This is life and this is joy: an hour of embracing and then to die."

"Amen."

"And your family?"

"My sister's in New York."

"Married?"

"Uh... widowed."

Virgilio crossed himself. "I'm sorry."

"No, it's all right. She's fine, probably remarried by now."

"Still—family—nothing more important."

"Once everything's settled, Rivka and I are going to America to visit my sister."

"Then I must insist that you look us up!"

"Philadelphia, right?"

"Correct, *Signore* Corporal."

Elia smiled. "Here's a happy thought: by the time you awake, I'll no longer be *Signore* Corporal; I'll be Elia Reifer again."

"Joyful indeed. In any case, you and Rivka will be our guests. Our sons will play baseball together."

"Perhaps, my friend, perhaps. Now finish your tea and sleep. You need your strength. Tomorrow, I'm on a train home; you're walking."

Virgilio finished drinking and lay down. He closed his eyes and whispered, "*La pace è con lei*, Elia."

Elia covered him with mosquito netting. "Shalom, Virgilio."

Cracow • 27th of Cheshvan, 5679 – Saturday, November 2, 1918

FOR A TOWN already on edge, divided into three armed camps, the news of the train's imminent arrival spread through Przemyśl like yet another vicious rumor. At first, each faction saw the arrival of large numbers of loyal, battle-hardened troops as a boon, tipping the scales in its favor. But as the day wore on the kin of those lost to war perseverated on thoughts of undeserving survivors alighting from the railcars and falling joyously into the arms of their sworn enemies. Like petrol on a fire, the missing souls stoked the flames of hatred in a deep and visceral way that no speech or poster could ever hope to match.

In spite of the underlying dynamics of the coming train, the sheer sum of human desire for reunion with loved ones managed to overpower the unfocused fears of the people gathering at the station. Mothers baked pies and cakes, wives and lovers brushed hair and rouged lips, children were dressed in Sunday or Friday best. The priests and the rabbis would be there, but there would be no formal reception, no speeches, and no triumphal music welcoming the men home after four years on the march.

The train was due in at five in the afternoon. For the first time since the Legions disarmed the Austrians and took control of the town, Poles, Ruthians, and Jews congregated in one place without shooting at each other. The three peoples coalesced into distinct groups, with only a few people on the fringe of each crowd interacting with the others.The train was late and the crowds grew restless. Some of the younger children began intermingling as priests and rabbis led small groups of girls in songs.

ELIA LOOKED AT the blue and white armbands on most of his men, thinking it absurd that a unit's allegiance could be changed by tying a scarf of a particular color around one's bicep. A few hours before, just past Ostrava, there had been a bloodless coup as the German Lieutenant who was in charge was politely tossed off the train, replaced by a Polish Captain sporting a red and white armband. As the train pulled into Cracow station and disgorged the men in the rear six cars, a uniformed man sporting the blue and white sash boarded and identified himself as Wolf Blusztajn. After a long winded lecture exhorting the Jewish soldiers to fight for a Socialist Poland, he asked for volunteers.

When few were moved, Elia took up the cause, making an impromptu speech, moving about half of the Jewish men to join with him. Blusztajn conducted the initiation like a priest giving communion. Each man's Austrian cap pin was removed and replaced by the pin of the *Soldatenrat*, a small brass menorah with the word "Forward" inscribed in tiny Hebrew lettering. An armband was the final piece before the swearing of allegiance to the *Volksrat* and to Poland. A detachment of Jewish women, with blue and white kerchiefs on their heads, boarded the train, offering thick, hot bean and beef soup with black rye bread to everyone in the coach, regardless of armband. The boys of Przemyśl were finally in Galicia; to a man, it was the most delicious meal they had eaten in years.

Blusztajn made his way over to Elia, who sat on the wooden bench with a bowl in one hand, using a thick piece of bread to scrape the last few beans into his mouth. The line of men made a space for Wolf, who plopped down, straddling the bench, facing Elia.

"Thanks you, Corporal."

"It's Elia, Elia Reifer," he said, extending his hand after wiping it on his trousers. "Tell me, what's the news from Przemyśl?'

Wolf leaned in, "An agreement was signed yesterday establishing a National Council. Five Ruthian, five Polacks, and one lonely Jew."

"Who?"

"Rosenberg."

"The attorney?"

"Yes." Now that the food was gone, everyone's attention turned toward Elia and Wolf and they were soon surrounded by ex-soldiers, hungry for news of home. "Poles have the center and Zasanie. We control Franciszkańska, Jagiellońska, Słowackiego, and part of Mickiewicza. Ruthians have the rest."

Someone pulled his service revolver, yelling out, "We have only these; how can we defend our homes?" There were mumbles from the Jewish troops.

Blusztajn stood to better address the men, "It was the good wisdom of the Austrians to place the main weapons storehouse on Mickiewicza. Report to the gymnasium in the morning, we'll issue real guns then."

After two days of passing through territory with nothing but alien names, the train now rolled through familiar territory. Someone in each train car had a relative or friend in every station they passed. Bochnia, city of the salt mines, was the hometown of a Jewish soldier's grandfather. Tarnow, from where they had launched the attack to liberate Przemyśl, was a Polish lieutenant's birthplace. There was Rzeszow, the city Rivka's mother was from, and then Jaroslaw, a stone's throw from Medyka, still a pile of rubble years after the fighting was over.

Elia felt the first chills just as the train turned south, making its final run into Przemyśl. "Please, God, not now. Not today. Please."

As the train slowed into a wide turn left, crossing the San over the new steel trestle, the chatting stopped and Elia, shivering violently, passed out.

Przemyśl • 29th of Cheshvan, 5679 – Monday, November 4, 1918

RIVKA WAS KNEADING over-boiled potatoes and meal into dough destined to become several loaves of corn rye when the bakery's door flew open and Isidore came running in. He bolted the door behind him.

"What?" she asked, rolling off errant pieces of dough from between her fingers.

Her boss ignored her and pulled the roller-shades down over the windows, then peeked out at the street from the thin sliver between the shade and the window frame. "Shut the lights, now."

Isidore went to the back room and sat in his chair, his face red, his brow damp with sweat. "I was delivering to the City Hotel when I heard them. They smashed windows, carts, they, they..."

She poured him a glass of water from the pitcher on the kneading table. After a few gulps, he had calmed enough to resume.

"Riots. They're breaking down doors with their rifles, cleaning out the shops, smashing anything they couldn't carry."

"Where?"

"All up and down Franciszkańska to *Rynek* and the Plac. A few places are on fire."

"Polacks?"

He took another sip of water. "Ruthians, I think. They invaded, took over the center. I ran into Morrie. He said they're disarming the *Soldatenrat*, arresting the leaders. Even arrested the Polish General in charge, what's his name?"

"Puchalski"

"The mob's heading toward the station, looting the Jewish establishments. Everyone's hiding." Isidore gestured toward the basement door. "Come, we need to lock ourselves in the cellar."

"The station?"

"Come on, Rivka. No time to lose."

Her brow furrowed. "Oh God, Daddy and Izac," she said, heading toward the door.

He reached out and grabbed her arm, holding tightly. "Sweetheart, they'll hide too. Now let's—" He was an old man, but his grip, born of decades of kneading, was vice-like. As strong as it was, Rivka's quick glance at his hand followed by her unwavering stare into his grey eyes, rendered Isidore's grip utterly limp. "Be careful Rivka. Please be careful."

A few moments later she was out the door, heading toward her home in full run, oblivious to the rioting, swerving in wide arcs to avoid any congregations of people between her and her family. Rivka approached from the far end of the station, staying in the shadow until she could see the factory. The door was ajar and a small mob of people, Ruthians judging by armbands, had gathered in the street and were pointing into the factory, screaming with hysterical anger. She pulled her scarf over her head and face and ran across the street into her house, unnoticed in the commotion three doors down at the factory. Passing through the kitchen, she grabbed hold of the largest butcher knife at hand and headed to the basement and the passageway.

GITLA PREPARED A strong tea from the roots of wild Artemisia she had found growing in the turned earth of a shell crater up the hill from the Castle. "Get up Elia, before your rear becomes part of the bed," she said, taking his temperature with the back of her hand on his forehead. "Better."

"How long have I..."

"Two days."

Gitla propped him up with an extra pillow, "Drink, Elia."

Elia blew across the tea cup then took a sip. Realizing it

wasn't hot at all he drained the cup. When it was empty he looked up at his aunt. The lines on her face were deeper and the bags under her eyes were darker. She had aged, but not in a completely unnatural way. If anything, her face had become more angular, more defiant than ever. "Aunt Gitla, it's so good to be back." She reached out and they embraced tightly. "Aunt, I need to—"

"*Pish?*"

He chuckled. "Well, yes, now that you mention it." Gitla left the room and Elia dressed in the clothes Gitla had laid out for him. His uniform, into which he had slipped every morning for four years, was nowhere to be seen.

The front door slammed hard. Elia instinctively dashed for the entry, almost knocking Gitla over as she came from the kitchen.

"I'm all right. Get into the cellar," Juda said, sliding the iron bolt to the locked position, blood oozing from his nose. "Good morning, Elia. And welcome home." The growing blood stain on his graying beard made it sound a bit ironic. Gitla pulled out a handkerchief and applied pressure to his upper lip, stanching the flow of blood.

"What's happened?" Elia asked, using same tone he would have used in asking a returning patrol what the situation was over the next ridge.

"I'm not sure. There's a mob moving toward the Plac from *Rynek*. I was running up Franciszkańska when I saw four or five men attack Mister Hartman. He tried to fight them off with his walking stick and they shot him. A gentle old man whose worst crime was kibitzing over chess. They shot him dead right there in the middle of the street."

"Rivka," Elia said quietly, disappearing back into his room.

"To the cellar, now," Juda tried yelling.

Elia reappeared, holding his service revolver.

"Gitla, Elia—now," Juda said with finality.

Gitla took her husband's hand and lead him toward the

cellar stairs as Elia headed for the door.

The bakery was locked and the shades drawn. He hadn't seen his Rivka for what seemed like a lifetime, and wished he were bringing her flowers, not his Steyr-Pieper semi-automatic. He tapped on the side transom with his knuckle then hit the door with the butt of the pistol. The shade moved just enough to make him visible from inside. Just as Elia was ready to give up, the door cracked and a hand reached out and pulled him in. The door slammed shut behind him.

"Elia, my boy, welcome home," Isidore said, throwing his arms around him and squeezing tightly. "I tried to stop her, really I did," he said. "She's gone to look after her father. The mob was headed that way."

Elia shot out the door, covering the route he had taken to work in another epoch faster with a pistol than he ever had, with or without a football.

TANCHEM AND HIS son were working on a rocking chair in the front room of the factory when a rifle butt rapped heavily on the wooden doors.

"Go away!" Izac yelled, in Polish.

Another loud rap. Then another. "Open this door, bastard Jews! Open now or we burn your treasonous nest to the ground!"

The woodworkers looked at each other. Izac, his foot accidentally mangled two summers ago at Gorizia by the wheel of a *Schlanke Emma*—an Austrian howitzer—limped to the door and lifted the thick plank holding the double doors fast. A soldier in an Austrian uniform, denuded of rank and regiment insignias, pushed the door open with his rifle.

There were two uniformed soldiers with rifles and fixed bayonet at the door and perhaps another dozen civilians milling around in the street, most armed with clubs and cudgels. Most sported Ruthian colors.

"Where are the Jew soldiers?" one of the Ruthians asked as he and his compatriot pushed into the factory, shoving Izac aside. "In the back perhaps," the soldier said, answering his own question, moving toward Tanchem while the other one went to check out the back room. Izac limped over to his father as the second soldier came back, shaking his head. The one in front of Tanchem, the senior of the two, put his booted foot on the top of the two fluted, lathe-spun horizontal supports of the rocker they had been working on before looking at Tanchem.

For a moment, the Ruthian and the Jew studied each other, registering distant traces of recognition, their mouths fixed in contempt.

"No one here," Tanchem said.

"Really," the soldier said, bringing all his weight to his right foot, snapping the top balustrade. Izac made a move for the intruder but Tanchem reached out and halted him with an outstretched arm.

"There is no need for this."

The bottom balustrade shattered.

"I told you, there's—"

Tanchem had not finished his sentence when the quiet soldier's rifle butt found his temple. He collapsed in the doorway, drawing the laughter of the mob on the street watching the events unfolding through the open doors.

Izac had been in the artillery corps and had spent most of the war fixing the wheels on the barely mobile cannons; he had seen enough action to not freeze under pressure. Reaching into the scrap bin to his right, he found a meter-long dark oak spindle that would have ended up as a post for a fine bed had it not cracked at a knot. Bracing with his good foot, he swung with all his might at the junior soldier's head, finding it with a deep and satisfying thud. Izac had a second or two to enjoy the moment before a bayonet ripped his work shirt, entered his ribcage, and severed his aorta.

He was dead before he hit the ground.

Rivka watched in horror from the top of the ladder leading to the trap door in the back room. She had lifted the hatch only to find the carpet drawn over the secret passage and had bunched it back just in time to witness the events unfolding in the front of her father's factory. As soon as her brother hit the ground, she began to shimmy up through the carpet, the knife held so tight that her knuckles looked as white as fresh snow on coal.

The crowd called out for vengeance and formed an increasingly tight semicircle in front of the factory. The soldier pulled his rifle out of Izac and dropped it on the floor; sawdust soaked up the blood dripping from the bayonet. Bending over and pulling a trench knife from its scabbard, he grabbed Tanchem by his beard and pulled him to his knees.

Many in the mob shrieked, "Shave the yid!" as the Ruthian began cutting his whiskers.

"The Jew attacked Iwan, just as all the Jews attack our soldiers."

"An eye for an eye!"

Rivka cleared the carpet and, knife in hand, ran frantically at the back of the man holding her father by the beard.

"An eye for an eye, Jew!" the soldier yelled, sliding the blade from just under Tanchem's bearded chin to just below his ear, completely severing his carotid artery. Blood sprayed out of the wound, some reaching all the way out the door to the edge of the street, causing the mob to recoil backwards for a moment before they let out a hearty cheer.

To the mob, the expression on the face of the executioner barely changed. Several people lobbed congratulations his way, which were returned only with a blank, somewhat surprised stare. A moment later, a small trail of blood appeared at the corner of his mouth then his eyes rolled back into his skull. He collapsed forward, on top of Tanchem. Suddenly revealed, there stood Rivka, a young woman in a grey dress and shirt, wearing a well soiled apron, with dashes of flour in her dark hair, holding a bloody butcher's knife. A thundering silence filled Czarnieckiego as the mob and the woman contemplated each other.

A moment later, an old woman on the street pointed and yelled, "It's the baker's girl!"

ELIA CAME ACROSS the tracks just in time to hear a club wielding man in front of the factory yell, "Murderess! Kill the murdering Jewess!" The next few seconds elapsed as if Elia were watching a malfunctioning kinescope.

The knife Rivka held slipped from her hand. The only thing he could hear was the pounding of blood between his ears as he studied the definitive contrast before him: the sheer beauty and overpowering humanity of Rivka and the horror and gore of the pile of corpses, one of which was undoubtedly Tanchem, his benefactor, boss, and his father-in-law to be. As she disappeared from the light, back into the factory, he became furious this his first glimpse of her after the ordeal both had been through over the past several years was to be in a milieu of tragedy, not of joy.

Elia stopped and brought his Steyr to eye level, fixing the man with the club in the sights before gently squeezing the trigger. The pistol's report froze everyone except the target who dropped to the dirt clutching his shin, screaming inconsolably. Elia dashed toward the entrance just as someone threw a smoking bottle into the factory. There was a small explosion and flames shot from the woodshop.

"Rivka!" Elia screamed over and over again, slowing to a trot as he neared the threshold before coming to a complete stop as the heat from the fire became unbearable. Brandishing his weapon to keep the bloodthirsty mob at bay, he once more yelled her name into the inferno.

Half a try at a word, half uncontrolled sobbing, it came

from her vocal cords, but it wasn't really speech, yet it was indisputably Rivka. He glanced at the mob, and then turned to the fire. Taking a deep breath, Elia closed his eyes and dashed through the doorway, leaping over corpses, into the abyss. Three strides into the fire, his foot caught on a wood scrap and he fell forward, landing hard on the floor, losing the pistol. The room was rapidly filling with smoke though there was some breathable air on the ground.

On his stomach, face pressed to the floor, he frantically reached in large arcs for his weapon, calling her name as he searched. By the time he found the smooth metal of the barrel, it was becoming increasingly hard to breathe. As he tucked the pistol into the back pocket of his trousers, he got up on all fours and tried to call her name but took in too much smoke, breaking into a violent hack instead. As he rested back on the floor, there was another cough, not from him. Elia crawled toward the sound with an urgent competence, another field to cross, barbed wire to breach, murderous live fire to duck. He reached her in seconds.

She lay on the floor next to the hatch, head down. "Rivka, thank God. Come on, we need to get out of here. Down the ladder." She was shaking violently, not moving and the flames were advancing toward them. Elia picked up her head and turned it so she would see him. "Now." She went limp, crying in short, barely audible waves. He pulled the wooden hatch open and swung his legs around into the hole, finding a rung on the ladder. Grabbing Rivka like a sack of flour, he dragged her across the floor and off the edge, bracing himself as he lowered her down the ladder, sitting her on the floor of the crawlway. He scampered back up the ladder and pulled the hatch shut. It was pitch black, but at least the air was better in the cellar. Elia put Rivka over his shoulder and carried her to the ladder that led up to the Arm residence.

Two members of the mob were badly burned and the adjacent building was set ablaze when the flames in the factory found the solvents closet, igniting a huge fireball of benzene and toluene. As the rioters chanted for revenge against the treacherous, murderous Jews, a wind shift pushed black billows of smoke into the street in front of what had been the Arm Furniture Factory, dispersing the mob.

THE CAMP BY the river had been evacuated by the Germans weeks before the armistice. In their zeal to get home, they had left tents, benches, and piles and piles of garbage. Since the withdrawal, the site had become something of a transient's camp, occupied by a mixture of army deserters, the homeless, gypsies and hordes and hordes of rats.

Elia pulled Rivka close enough to wrap both arms around her. "Sweetheart, we're safe here until dark." Still, she said nothing, crying gently into his chest. In time, she fell asleep.

Elia watched Rivka sleep as the daylight waned, burying his nose into the side of her neck, her pulse shallow and her skin clammy. Still asleep, she wrapped her arms around Elia's head and pulled his face into her chest, his chin resting on her bosom.

Rivka's eyes opened a few hours after sunset. "I'm scared," she whispered. "I've nothing left." She began to tremble. "Nothing..." A tear escaped from her eye, clearing a path through soot and dirt as it raced down her cheek.

"I know, sweetheart." Elia tightened his hold on her. "You have me. And I have you." His lips easily found hers but she quickly turned away.

"This isn't exactly," she managed, fighting back tears and gulping for air, "what we had in mind for our reunion." They both managed weak smiles.

"Not exactly. I figured we'd meet at Antmann's. Embrace in front of everyone, take a walk down by the river and talk politics or arts. Then we'd make love all night long on your feather bed."

"Light a match."

"What?"

"Strike a match, Elia; I want to be sure it's you."

He dragged the head of the match across the striking side of the box, illuminating both faces in warm, yellow light. And for the first time in thousands of days, Elia and Rivka were face to face. They studied each other carefully.

"It's really you, Elia Reifer, isn't it?"

"Yes, sweetheart. And we're never going to be apart again."

"Elia," she said, voice raised. "Elia." It lowered again to a whisper, "They murdered daddy and Izac. And I—" she paused then and began to gulp for air. "I killed the soldier." She cradled her face in her hands.

Elia put his hand on her shoulder, "Rivka, now listen carefully. War is horrible for many reasons. But the worst part—"

"Shut up!" she shouted. "Shut up, shut up, shut up!"

"Rivka! Grab hold of yourself." He blew the match out and wrapped her in his arms, stroking her hair with his open palm, rocking her gently, for a short eternity.

"I'm sorry, Elia."

He squeezed her. "It's all right, sweetheart. It's horrible what war does to men. To women. It—"

"Stop." She pushed back from him and put her hand over his mouth. "Not now. No words; just hold me. Please?" They embraced, wordlessly.

"Rivka?" Elia whispered.

"Elia?"

"We need to get out of here."

"They think we're dead."

"I know. So we can't stay in Przemyśl."

Rivka sighed. "Or Galicia for that matter."

Elia nodded. "We'll need papers, and a place to hide."

"Gitla will help us."

"We can't go there, it's too dangerous"

"Lenard," Rivka said, thinking about how two days ago the prospect of Tomas and Elia meeting was the cause of almost endless concern.

"Who?"

"I'll explain later."

Sometime after midnight Elia and Rivka left the tent city. They climbed the railroad berm just before the quay and walked across the San on the railroad tracks, camouflaged on all sides by the bridge's thick steel box girders. Emerging on the Polish controlled side of the river, they were just another disheveled couple hurrying to safety after the most tumultuous day in Przemyśl since the Russians breached the fort's defenses, some five years earlier.

They reached Tomas's apartment on Kraszewskiego, next to his machine shop, a stone's throw from the Zasanie synagogue, without incident.

Zasanie • 1st of Kislev, 5679 – Tuesday, November 5, 1918

MALKA SAT AT the small wooden table, half-awake, while Lea ate oatmeal from a wooden bowl, managing to get most of the cereal into her mouth. The remainder formed a trail from the bowl, across the table, up her bib and ending in small globs on her chin. An electric hum accompanied the harsh light coming from the nouveau light fixture that was hung crookedly over an old couch and chairs. Tomas snored loudly in the sleeping nook, hidden behind floor-length burgundy drapes embroidered in floral damask. A sliver of dawn's light squeezed in a window between the back door and the coal brazier, lost in layer upon layer of varnish on the dark oak floorboards.

Lea ate and Malka daydreamed until three sharp knocks at the front door interrupted them. Startled, Lea dropped her spoon and looked at her mother. Malka stared at the door, confused. Lea began to cry.

Three more raps, this time with muffled crying.

When Malka picked her daughter up and headed for the sleeping nook she stopped crying. Pulling open the drapes, they saw Tomas, dressed from knees to elbows in a gray union suit, pulling his revolver from its hiding place under the mattress. He handed the gun to Malka, who held it over her head at arm's length, as far from Lea as was possible. Tomas headed for the door.

"Who's there?"

"Mister Lenard, let us in. Please—"

"It's five in the morning. Who's there?"

"Elia Reifer and Rivka Arm. We're in trouble. Please."

Two deadbolts clicked and the door swung open. Malka peeked out from behind the drapes, and then rushed to Tomas's side. Elia and Rivka entered and the door was bolted behind them.

Elia's face was a bloody mess and his hair was singed, with one spot burned down to a coin-sized scab on his scalp. They both reeked of smoke and garbage. Rivka was shaking, supported by Elia's arm around her waist. Blood, now dried, had wicked its way up the arm of her linen blouse and onto Elia's shirt where he held her to his chest. She lifted her head, revealing wet, swollen eyes sunk into deep, purple sockets. Covered in oily black grunge, the only visible flesh-tones to be found were in the tracks that her tears made meandering down her cheeks.

"They're gone!" Rivka cried as she was embraced by her sister with all her might. "Daddy and Izac, murdered; dead." Lea began sobbing along with the Arm sisters as they clung to each other, slowly rocking to the beat of their broken hearts.

Elia collapsed on the couch as Tomas drew a bath for Rivka. After a short soak, Rivka crawled into the bed nook and curled into a fetal position.

It was well into the afternoon when Elia woke and climbed into bed with Rivka, carefully embracing her so as not to bump a bruise or pressure a cut. "Rivka?" Elia whispered. "You awake?"

"I am now."

"Sorry, but we need to talk." He stroked her hair.

"I've got a headache," Rivka said. "About what?"

"We need to talk about our plans, our escape."

"My daddy and brother are dead, the factory is burned to the ground and I murdered someone yesterday. I'm a goddamned orphan." She rolled out of Elia's arms. Turning her head toward him, she spoke, eyes tightly focused, enunciating every syllable. "Now what was it you wanted to talk about?"

She slept until morning.

"WHEN I HEARD what was going on I took the truck and drove to find Malka and Lea. Eisner had boarded up the shop," Tomas said, pausing for a sip of tea. "I pounded on the back door until they came. They must have been hiding in the basement. On the way back, we could see the factory on fire across the tracks, from Jagiellońska. Malka was frantic to find her daddy and we were all set to leave the truck and run over when a small detachment of Ruthians intercepted us, demanding papers."

"On Jagiellońska?" Elia asked.

"Yes. Everywhere."

"So the agreement is dead."

"It would seem so. They arrested the commanders, Jewish and Polish, and took their weapons."

"How'd you pass?"

"I used my work papers, said I was on duty fixing a dynamo and started spewing out Russian technical terms from math, physics, and philosophy until their eyes rolled back into their heads and they waved me on. I asked about the fire. They said a mob of Jews had murdered an officer."

"What about the bridge?"

"Same game, in Polish this time."

Elia told Tomas what he knew about the murders. "I'm not sure what happened. All I know is that Izac, Tanchem, and two Ruthian soldiers were dead when I got there, and Rivka was standing in the doorway holding a bloodied knife, about to be charged by the mob."

"Good for her."

Elia finished his coffee, coughing after swallowing some loose grounds that had accumulated at the bottom of his mug.

"What now, Elia? If they find out you made it out alive, they'll hang the both of you."

"We're going to have to get the hell out of here. We're going to have to leave. Now."

"Without papers?"

"There's no choice."

"You won't get far."

"We can blend in with the gypsies and Czechs. I've crawled across every inch of ground between here and Tarnow. Remember?"

Tomas shrugged as Rivka emerged from behind the drapes and headed for the coffee pot. Tipping the pot over, only a few drops remained. She set it down with a metallic thud then began to cry.

Elia ran to the counter. "I'll make another pot."

Rivka wiped her face with her sleeve. "Thank you sweetheart. I'm sorry. I have a headache."

While Elia coaled the stove and percolated another pot, Rivka sat and talked quietly with Tomas. A few minutes later, mood improved, she welcomed the steaming mug and glossy sugar bowl as if they were champagne and caviar.

"It's settled then," Tomas said.

Elia poured himself another cup. "What?"

"Gitla," Rivka said, nodding her head.

Elia scratched gingerly around the scar on his scalp. "But how can—"

"It's settled, all right? I know what I'm doing."

"Rivka—"

"Trust me."

Elia turned toward Lenard. "Tomas?"

"I need to work a few hours or else the Polacks become suspicious. I'll stop at your aunt's house on my way."

Elia sipped his coffee then exhaled. "Then I guess we have a plan." Rivka and Tomas nodded. "Oh yeah, one more favor, while we're at it."

"But of course."

"Ask Gitla for my leather book. It's in my duffle."

Before he left, Tomas had his driver rummage through his shop to find the stencils and paint the word "Mechanic" onto the side of the truck in Polish and Ukrainian. It never ceased to amaze Tomas just how easily even the most bellicose men could be intimidated by science. While long lines of pedestrians waiting to cross the San were subjected to any number of questions and searches, just a few words from the man in the machine truck was enough to addle the bridge defenders and speed him on his way. Thomas noted that while racial and political animosity was one thing, no one, it seemed, wanted to take responsibility for the stifling of technology.

The whole south bank of the San was now under Ruthian control. The Jewish quarter was eerily calm, absent the usual gaggle of vendors and merchants pushing their wares on the street in front of their stores. Tomas saw several formations of troops, irregularly armed, wearing uniforms that were anything but uniform. Other than a few Hassids, the Jewish population was nowhere to be seen. From Ratuszowa all the way to Plac na Bramie, almost every window was either shattered or boarded up except for the Café Hibler, which seemed to have miraculously avoided even the most superficial of damage.

They pulled over the truck a few doors up from the Malz home as Tomas instructed.

AS TOMAS ENTERED, Elia pushed the door closed and slid the bolt to the locked position, returning his Steyr to the pocket of the suit-coat he had borrowed from Lenard. Malka went back to preparing her daughter's lunch, soaking black bread in soup, while Rivka kept Lea occupied on the couch with yet another game of peek-a-boo.

"Your aunt is quite a woman. Sharp as any tool in the shed. She's as hard as—"

"She cries inside, Tomas," Elia said, curtly.

"I didn't mean it like that. It's just close to inconceivable what she did. Juda said there was almost nothing left to collect: bones and a few scraps of charred flesh." He handed Elia a small package wrapped in brown wax paper.

Rivka approached the men, carrying Lea.

"Did you see—?"

"Yes. Told her everything."

"Thank you. When are the funerals?"

"Rivka, it's not a good idea to—" Elia started to say.

Rivka jabbed her forefinger at his lips, stopping less than a centimeter away. "Don't start with me."

"Interment is this afternoon." Tomas glanced at his watch. "Right now, actually."

Rivka set Lea down on the floor and lunged at the door hasp. Elia dropped the package and locked onto her forearm just as she began to slide the bolt open. She struggled to no avail and then gave up, glaring at Elia, "You bastard. Let go of me."

"Rivka, I'm sorry. I'm so sorry," Elia said, securing his

grip.

"How dare you!" she screamed.

The sound of Lea bawling immediately filled the room.

"They'll recognize you and then they'll kill you."

"Let me go!" She kicked Elia in the shin. He hardly flinched, deftly moving to her side, making it impossible for her to do it again. "They're burying my daddy and my brother!"

Malka dropped her ladle and raced toward the door.

With her free hand, Rivka hit Elia in the chest with a tightly clinched fist, crying out for her father and brother. She flailed at him again and again. Elia released her wrist and put his arms around her. She tried to hit him with both hands, but was too close. After a few more tries, she dissolved into tears, collapsing into him, all of her weight resting in his arms.

Holding Lea in one arm with Malka tightly clinging to the other, Tomas came to Elia and Rivka, forming a tight, grieving huddle. One by one, they stopped crying, first Elia and Malka, then Tomas, and finally Lea and Rivka. They stood in silence until Rivka began a chant which was quickly joined by the others. It was an all too familiar chant, repeated countless times over the past five years. And it was the same chant being intoned by Gitla, Juda, and a small gathering in front of two fresh holes in the cemetery on Słowackiego, across the river, just a few thousand meters away.

Nine

Przemyśl • 4th of Kislev, 5679 – Friday, November 8, 1918

GITLA WAS COLD and soaked after being caught in a cloudburst while being rowed across the river by an acquaintance. Clearing the steep riverbank, two impossibly massive piles of dirt, concrete and twisted metal loomed over the spindly pines at the far end of the field—the remains of Bolestraszyce's two forts. Just past the trees was the road connecting the two forts. Gitla made a beeline toward what looked to be the sole surviving commercial establishment in town. Strutting by a man leaning on a rifle next to a fancy automobile, she pushed the swinging shutters aside and marched into the tavern.

Meyer was the only patron there. He stood briefly as she sat down across from him.

Gitla raked the tavern with her gaze, noting the impressive collection of stuffed game and fish on the walls, thinking that their presence must have been sheer torture to the boys during the siege. The room was dark and smelled like urine. The table was wobbly, with a permanent coating of dirt and beer over yellowing shellac. Leaning on the bar was a man with a hideously mangled hand, head down, reading a Polish newspaper, moving only to turn the page with his good hand.

"My, oh my, how the mighty have fallen," she said.

Meyer smiled. "Such a pleasure to see you again, Missus Malz." He shot an order at the barman in Polish, "Lucjan, two teas, with honey," then turned back to Gitla, "I thought you'd be more comfortable in a place like this."

"Who you kidding? You must own this dump."

He shook his head, "Associates, not me."

Gitla forced a smile, "Kidding aside, Meyer, thanks for coming. I know what a schlep it is from Cracow."

"I don't hear from you for ages, and then from the blue my agent sends a telegram saying G. M. needs to see me. Well, M. Weiss never forgets his friends."

Gitla cocked her head, "Friends?"

Meyer slowly nodded his head, "Friends."

"How's your daughter doing, Mister Weiss?"

"Zipporah's doing—" he stopped as Lucjan brought a tea pot, cups, napkins, a honey pot with a wooden dripper and a plate of small cookies on a platter he balanced on his crippled hand. He left without saying a word.

"She's doing well, thank you; taking a degree in French Literature at the Jagiellońian; a marvelous student. It's not easy being a Jew there, or anywhere for that matter. But at least in the big city we can blend in easier than in Przemyśl."

"How's her head?"

"We, we never talk about it. She doesn't have many friends. I suppose her books are her friends."

"I see..."

"Enough about the Weiss family. Have I lost all manners? I'm so sorry to have missed the funerals. You must be crushed."

"Crushed is the right word. My cousin was, was..." She averted her eyes momentarily. "Two more drops in the ocean of insanity."

He leaned toward her and switched to Yiddish. "I truly am sorry. Our families go back half-a-dozen generations. Tanchem was more than just my friend. We played chess, we drank, and we argued politics. He was like a brother, and in business, he was a peer."

"Thank you, Meyer. I know you don't say that about everyone."

"But that's not why you're here, Gitla." He dropped to a whisper. "So tell me, what can I do for your nephew and his bride-to-be?"

She snorted and put her hand over her mouth.

"My agent watches the cemetery; only two graves were dug this week."

Gitla explained what had happened. She told him what Elia had told Tomas to tell her—that their lives were in the balance, and that the only place that they would be safe was with his sister in New York. She told him all about Tomas and Malka and Lea. About Tomas's son in Gyor. About their desire to make *aliyah*. She leaned toward him and lowered her voice, "They need papers and the means to get out of here."

"I took the liberty of putting those wheels in motion yesterday." Meyer leaned back into his chair, satisfied as if he had just announced "mate in four" at the tea house. "I have some pull at the Finance Ministry—I helped the Polish government secure a note."

"Jurek?"

"Senior Advisor to the Minister of Finance, if you please."

She shook her head, smiling.

"My agent will contact you."

"There is one more thing."

"There always is."

"Help Tomas. Help him get his boy back so they can go to Palestine. It's the only way for Malka and Lea to have a life."

Meyer pondered for a moment. "I don't know, Gitla.

Kidnapping is difficult business. Why don't we just—"

"Meyer," she said, staring him down. "You are going to do this."

"Really." His face became rock-hard, serious.

"Not because I took care of your daughter and you owe me, not out of the kindness in your heart, and not because you can. No sir. You are going to help us get the Lenard boy back because it's me, Gitla Arm, demanding it."

Meyer sat back in his chair, his stern gaze giving way to a wide smile. "Bravo," he said, nodding vigorously. "Brilliantly conceived and beautifully played. Check and mate."

"I'm not joking, Meyer. We've both sat on this. Two decades is a long time. You *owe* me."

"Do this and we call it even, Meyer. Everything is washed. Everything."

"No. Never," Meyer said, shaking his head.

"What? I will not take no for—"

"We'll get the child back. You have my word, Gitla. But things are not washed between us—not now, not tomorrow and not ever."

Gitla reached across the table and took Meyer's hands. Their fingers entwined as each pulled, rising out of their seats, bringing them closer until their lips met. A moment later, they were back in their chairs.

"In a different world, in some other reality..."

"I know. In a different world." It took them both a moment to regain composure. Finally, Gitla pulled a letter from her jacket. "From Cracow, post this to America, will you? It's from our boy to his sister."

"I thought you were done asking for favors."

"Goodbye, Meyer."

"Goodbye, Gitla."

She wrapped her head with a scarf, shook his hand, and headed out the door. Gitla made it to the pines before breaking down. She cried the whole way home.

When she was gone, Meyer exhaled heavily, tossed a silver coin on the table and walked out the door into the waiting Benz. He felt fortunate to have so many plans to conceive and so many schemes to hatch to occupy his mind during the long drive back to Cracow.

Zasanie • 8th of Kislev, 5679 – Tuesday, November 12, 1918

"DOES THIS SAY what I think it says?" Tomas asked Rivka, handing her the note that had been slipped under the door sometime during the night. "My Polish is pretty good, but I don't cover Cracow. And I'm never given such a specific timeframe."

Rivka read aloud, "Tomas Lenard, work roster for twelve November. Nine-ten: Ores Transport, three Plac Kolejowy, Cracow. Overhaul. Transit papers and work order attached." She looked up at Tomas, "Gitla got to Meyer."

"How can we be sure?" Elia asked.

"She did." Rivka nodded. "A reason to be on the roads and a truck to hide in."

"Still," Elia cautioned, "What if..."

Malka, who had been boiling water for oatmeal, interrupted, surprising the others who assumed she wasn't listening, "We're going. It's Meyer. Best get ready."

"How are you so sure?" Elia asked.

Stirring the porridge, she looked up. "Because three Plac Kolejowy is the address of the train station." She set the wooden bowl down in front of Lea and walked over to the adults. "And the Cracow – Vienna train departs daily at ten past nine every morning, except Sunday."

As Lea ate, everyone else made preparations to leave.

"Malka, may I have a word with you?" Elia said, barely above a whisper. He gestured toward the sleeping area. She picked up Lea, walked over to Tomas, sitting on the sofa, and deposited her on his lap, pinning him down before joining Elia behind the curtains. "I am so very sorry for you."

"That is thoughtful of you, brother, but I know you care."

"It's just, well, we don't really talk all that much and—"

"Elia, while we might not have all that much in common, I've always known that you like me. Love me. And I love you too."

He put his hand on her shoulder. "Thank you, Malka. I want to take care of you—I love you like a sister."

"Thank you, but you really need to care for Rivka. As strong as she pretends to be, she's soft. Such a vulnerable little girl inside."

"I will. And I know."

"I admire Rivka; I admire people who can sublimate their despair, their most visceral pain into anger. Anger can be shed, directed away to be absorbed by others. Not so with heartache. It never leaves. But I make no pretense. I'm not one of those who can perform such emotional alchemy. I will never recover."

"Malka." Elia reached to comfort her but she took a half step back.

"But life goes on. I have Lea to worry over and Thomas's shoulder to cry on. And yours." She moved forward and they embraced tightly.

They stepped back and Elia pulled a small book from his coat pocket. "This is difficult. I mean no disrespect; I don't want to rub salt in open wounds." He handed it to her. "But I think he would want you to have this."

She took the book with both hands.

"To remember him by."

Malka thumbed through the book, lingering on pages where Manes had written notes. She read aloud, "The workers have no country. We cannot take from them what they have not got. Since the proletariat must first of all acquire political supremacy, must rise to be the leading class of the nation, must constitute itself the nation, it is, so far, itself national, though not in the bourgeois sense of the word."[7] She looked up at Elia, "Look," she pointed. "Look what he wrote."

Elia read Manes's note, scrawled in the margin, "Galicia, not Palestine.'"

They embraced again, his arms around her shoulders, her head on his shoulder, Manes's *Manifesto* in her hands, sandwiched between them.

"Elia," she said, handing the book back to him. "Rivka is right, you are a real sweetheart."

"No, please..."

She put her forefinger to his lips. "I love you for thinking of me, for bringing a piece of Manes's life to me. He was my first true love and I will never forget him. But I know he was also more than just your friend, he was your brother. Perhaps even more, he was somewhere between your brother and your daddy. So we each need something of him to take with us. I have Lea, the ultimate memento, yes?"

Elia nodded.

"And I have Tomas. He loves Lea like his own. Do you know how many times he has mentioned that Lea is Manes's child and not his own? How many times he has thrown that in my face?"

Elia shrugged.

"Never. Not even when we fight. For this, I owe him my heart. No, you take his book; it is not the part of Manes I want to remember."

"Malka..."

"Besides, Sterner would roll over in his grave if he knew I was taking his precious Marx to Eretz Israel."

"I suppose he'd be happier knowing it was heading to New York."

"Listen, Elia," her tone again serious, "I don't really care what you do with this book. Toss it in the San for all the good it's brought us." She put her hand on his face, squeezing his flesh tenderly. "What I care about, what I want, is for you to take care of yourself." He winced as she pinched his cheek. "And what I want most of all is for you to take care of my sister."

TOMAS DROVE WITH Malka in the passenger cab and Lea between them. Rivka and Elia rode in the back of the flatbed, covered by a thick, oily tarp, lying on a cushion pushed all the way to the back of the cargo area, behind the metal lathe and drill press.

They hit the first road block before clearing the fort. Malka did the talking, her Polish flawless, her plan simple genius. "My husband is a mechanic, here are his work papers," she said, stepping out of the cab to meet the soldiers, a gauze mask covering her mouth. "I come with to talk for my man—his lungs are not so good—Spanish influenza." Her offer to allow them to inspect the vehicle was immediately rejected by the sentries who were backpedaling as fast as they could, waving the party through.

Back in the cab Lea was sleeping. As Tomas reached to release the hand brake he was intercepted by Malka. "Wait," she said, pointing out of the passenger window. "Look." Tomas and Malka stared out of the dirty window at the unfolding vista before them. The sun was just starting to clear the trees on the crest of the hill, casting a brilliant orange light that illuminated the skyline of Przemyśl—the churches, the Old Synagogue, the bell tower, the Temple, and the castle. They watched in silence as the sun fully illuminated the city.

"We'd best be moving on. Say goodbye, sweetheart."

"Goodbye, Przemyśl," she said. "And good riddance."

She successfully repeated the influenza story in Jaroslaw, Tarnow and Bochnia, before reaching Cracow.

A WOMAN WRAPPED in an ivory-hued scarf pulled the compartment's pocket door open just as the brakes were pulled from the wheels and the train lurched forward. Settling back into the plush red banquette, Rivka, Malka, Elia and Tomas exhaled long sighs of relief while the train rumbled over a series of slip switches and veered to the west.

Soon, two policemen appeared at the compartment's window. One absently tapped his nightstick in his palm while the other counted heads.

Malka smiled and Tomas tipped his cap.

Once the officer moved on, the scarf-covered woman went to the door and opened it enough to poke her head out and look up and down the hallway. She closed the door and pulled the privacy shades closed before turning and unwinding her headdress. "We have about an hour before the border. We need to get our stories straight." Everyone, other than Lea, asleep on Malka's lap, stared at her.

"I should have known," Rivka said, shaking her head, smiling as she stood to embrace her. "Zipre, of course."

"I am, it seems to be, your tour guide."

"To where?" Elia asked, bracing the hugging women as the train lurched.

"I'm going with the Lenards." She turned to Tomas. "If that's all right with you. Daddy has friends in Palestine."

"Your daddy seems to have friends everywhere," Elia said.

"Good thing, isn't it?" Rivka added.

"I suppose so. Yes, perhaps…" Zipre said as Rivka took her seat.

"Sit," Tomas said, patting the seat next to him. "It would be my honor to accompany you to Eretz Israel."

"That is much appreciated, Mister Lenard. But before, in order to get to Jaffa, we need to get to Vienna."

"Agreed. So was your father was able to make arrangements?"

"Father said it was easy, what with all the chaos, all the

unrecorded deaths. Grease a few palms, reissue a few documents." She sat, opening her valise on her lap. "Tomas, Malka and Lea," Zipre said, "You are the family Lenard, coming from Korczyn." She handed Tomas a set of papers. "Malka, you are now Missus Malka Lenard. Congratulations."

Tomas leaned over and kissed her on the lips. "Korczyn?"

"Near Cracow, on the river," Elia interjected. "I was there during the war."

"Meet any Lenards?"

"I don't remember it so good." Elia reached for Rivka's hand. "Us?"

Zipre examined the remaining documents. "It appears that Meyer choose not to marry you two. I'm afraid you are still a Reifer, and you, Rivka, remain an Arm."

"Is that safe?" Elia asked.

"They think you're dead. And the records office is a good year behind. Your passports are real, as are your exit permits."

"And who are you, Zipre?" Rivka queried.

"I asked daddy for Sarah Bernhardt but apparently it was taken. I'm afraid I have to be content to continue to be plain old Zipporah Weiss."

The train lurched around a bend.

"Oh, Tomas, one more thing."

"Zipporah?"

"A man will meet us in Vienna and will travel with you to Gyor to secure the return of ..." she paused, struggling to remember his name.

"Jonas. It's Jonas," Tomas said. He looked at Malka then back at Zipre. "God bless you and your—" He coughed hard to clear his throat, spitting up bloody phlegm into his handkerchief. "Bless your father."

They discussed their cover stories and rehearsed for the border crossing, which turned out to be nothing more than the flashing of the outside cover of each passport and the seal on the transit papers at the gendarme through the sliding glass carriage door, at least in the first class cars of the train.

After brief stops in Ostrava, Přerov and Břeclav the party was ensconced in a two room apartment on the sixth floor of the Grand Hotel in Vienna by midnight.

Malka and Lea slept between the finest sheets available anywhere on the Continent while Tomas sat up all night in a red velvet Victorian armchair, burning up, shivering, and hacking ominously. Elia and Rivka lay naked in each other's arms all night, alternately dozing, crying, talking, and making love.

Vienna • 11th of Kislev, 5679 – Friday, November 15, 1918

DOCTOR DETRICK WAS all business. Tall and well dressed, toting a black leather satchel, he said little other than that he would perform the examination in private. Donning a thick gauze mask he entered the room where Tomas lay and shook him out of shallow sleep before firing a series of questions at him, closer in tone to that of an inquisitor than a healer. "How long has there been blood in your phlegm? When did the fever start? Any vomit? What color?" Detrick took his temperature orally, revealing nothing as he read the mercury level. Thomas's pulse was gauged, lymph nodes palpated, and a stethoscope applied to listen to the passage of air through each lung. When finished, the Doctor turned and left his patient without uttering a word.

"Where is the wife?" Detrick barked.

Malka identified herself with a brisk "*Ja,*" while Rivka, Elia and Zipre milled about, eavesdropping.

"He has the Influenza. Pulse is thin and fast and he is running at forty degrees. For now, there is little lung or bronchial involvement."

"What should we do?" Malka asked.

"Liquids; keep him hydrated. He will recover or he will not."

"What do you mean?" she inquired, incredulous.

"Now I must inform the manager of his guest's," he paused, "condition."

"Certainly there is something you can recommend," Malka pleaded.

Detrick returned the equipment to his satchel then looked at Malka and shrugged, "Perhaps you should pack."

Rivka and Elia converged on the Doctor. "Now you look here, he's a paying guest," Elia said. "Are you telling me they're going to throw him out?"

"*Ja*."

"We're not going anywhere," Malka and Rivka added, speaking at the same time.

"*Herr Docktor*," Zipre called from across the room, her German impeccable and distinctly upper class. "A word in private?" she asked, making it sound more like an order than a request. Dutifully, he followed her to the anteroom.

Zipre spoke just above a whisper, "*Herr Docktor*, how shall I put this so that you can understand? My father is a close business associate of the owner of this hotel. Do you know *Herr* Haider?"

"Everyone in Austria knows Count Haider." The Doctor fidgeted with his tie. "Of course, I don't know him personally but—"

"Well, I do. And I can assure you that the last thing the Count would want is a to-do over a guest's sudden attack of the ague."

"But this is most certainly not a case—"

She grabbed his hand and a wad of bills connected their palms. "Malaria; an episode of ague."

He glanced at the bills, then at his patient, then quickly back to the money before closing his fingers tightly around the banknotes.

"Thank you for your prompt attention and your swift diagnosis," Zipre said.

The doctor turned and left, eyes glued to the floor. Zipre turned to Rivka and Elia, still giving orders, "Elia, you need to meet father's agent downstairs, for Tomas. Please explain the situation to him.

"What's his name? How will I know him?"

The question momentarily threw Zipre off her stride. "I don't know. Daddy's always referred to him as 'The Agent.' I'd guess he'll find you." He headed for the door. "Rivka, can you look after Lea? I have several appointments."

Vienna • 21st of Tevet, 5679 – Tuesday, December 24, 1918

"THERE IS A boat for Alexandria leaving on the ninth. Not much, but she'll float. It's an easy jump from there to Jaffa. I have been assured that the proper papers will be waiting at the Hotel de la Ville in Trieste. There are boats to New York, but not until April. The trains run from Trieste to Genoa to Nice to Paris and finally to Le Havre. Documents will be waiting for us at L'Hotel Terminus in Paris. So we'll need to get to Trieste right away, and we'll need to—"

"Zipre! You are amazing!" Rivka beamed. "I'm really going to miss you."

"About that, Rivka, I—"

The door opened and Elia, Meyer's agent, and a boy walked in. Rivka ran to Elia and embraced, kissed, then embraced again while the agent removed his hat.

"Jonas. Thank God you are safe," Malka said. There was no reaction from the boy. She faced him and dropped to her knees, extended both arms. He stared at the floor, speechless.

Speaking in broken Hungarian, Zipre introduced herself to the boy. He looked up briefly, but still he said nothing.

Rivka released Elia and Malka came to her feet. "Come, see your father," Zipre said, ushering them through the door into the bedroom.

Tomas's features lit up, using facial muscles he had not used in years. "My son," he said, standing, arms extended.

The boy stared blankly at his father. What Tomas thought could have been the beginning of a smile was quickly quashed.

Elia and the agent glanced at each other, then at Tomas. "He can't speak," the agent said.

Almost fully recovered, Tomas walked over to his son and hugged him. "Look at you. All grown, a man." A tear came to Tomas's eye as he held him close. He turned to the agent, "You must be Mister Weiss's representative. I can never repay you for your kindness."

The agent bowed deeply. "Elia tells me you're half Christian. So please consider this a Christmas gift."

"I was, but no longer."

The agent shrugged, "Same god."

Tomas put his hand on the agent's shoulder. "In the name of Moshe, Jesus and Mohamed, I thank you."

"It is my occupation and in this case, my pleasure. And you may trust that I have been well recompensed for my work." He grinned. "Besides, the political debates with Mister Reifer would have been payment enough." He flashed a smile of surprisingly good teeth at Elia.

"Your home, I can't precisely place it. Greece?" Tomas inquired.

"I'm from Tabriz, Persian by birth, Jewish by blood, and person-finder by trade."

"And you work for Meyer Weiss?"

"In truth, I have never before heard of your Mister Weiss. Anonymous people pay me good money to find lost people. I don't ask too many questions."

"And, Mister Agent, do you have a proper name?"

"Béla Gabor's the name I heard him use," Elia said.

He bowed grandly, "Bakek Ben Sushan Kermanian, at your service."

"I had expected you to be a huge man, a goon," Tomas said, adding quickly, "I mean no offense, of course."

"None taken. I am what I need to be—Jew, gentile, or Mohammedan, Austrian, Frenchman, or Englishman, cultured or a ruffian. Since the war, I'm sorry to say, business has been all too good. And all too often I return to my client as the bearer of terrible news. This case is anomalous; I collect my fee and everyone's happy."

Tomas addressed Elia, "Where did you find him?"

"Béla," Elia raised an eyebrow, "and I went to Gyor expecting to do battle. On arrival, we found no trace of them. The house had long since been occupied by an Austrian family who either knew nothing of Jonas or weren't going to talk to us." Tomas sat on the bed, Jonas sat beside him, a hand on his father's mid-section. Everyone else sat as Elia continued, "We went to the church and found the Father who talked to us—"

Babek interrupted, "After we crossed his palm with silver."

"He told us that Martin, the grandfather, as well as his wife, his son, and about a quarter of the town had died soon after Jonas arrived home. It was during the war while you were trapped in Przemyśl. The army men brought it. Some kind of fever."

"Quite a common tale, I'm sorry to say," Babek noted.

"The boy was taken to the church orphanage in Tatabanya. We went there without a plan. It's amazing we even recognized him. We didn't know what the orphanage knew of his Jewish father or how Jonas would react so I distracted the monks and Béla spoke to him, told him his papa was alive and that we would take him to him. He showed no emotion and when it became clear that he would not speak, I pretended to be his uncle-in-law—a *goy* from Cracow now living in Vienna. To those monks, a Polack's almost as bad as a Jew, but with a generous donation to the order, we were out the door with him in no time."

"A *goy* from Cracow?" Tomas said with a smile. "I wish I could have been there for that."

"You're lucky to be alive at all."

"I know. As bad as the years have been, today is a very good day." He turned to his son, "Jonas, welcome home. Now thank these nice men for bringing you back to your papa."

The boy sat next to his father, his mouth a horizontal line, his eyes unfocused.

"He's been through a lot. The people at the orphanage said he never spoke. Not once in three years," Elia said.

"He's a good boy," Babek added. "I've seen this before. In time, he will get comfortable living in this life rather than the one in his head."

Tomas extended his hand to Babek, who shook it with gusto.

"He is a special boy, with the makings of a grandmaster," the Persian said.

"What?"

"Chess. He may not speak, but oh does he play. Routinely destroyed your friend here and beat me like an old rug."

Tomas looked at the boy, then at Elia, then back at Babek. "He's only nine."

Elia shrugged.

Tomas went to the night table and brought back a folded cardboard slab with a checkerboard on one side along with the leather bag containing his chess pieces. He took two ivory pawns out, one red and one white then tossed the remaining pieces and the board on the bed. With his back to the boy, he quickly swapped the pieces between his hands, and then faced his son, two fists extended. Jonas tapped his right fist.

Jonas set up the board as everyone else cleared the room

Twenty-six moves later, his position hopeless, Tomas tipped his king over.

Graz • 5th of Sh'vat, 5679 – Monday, January 6, 1919

TOMAS COUGHED, BABEK and Elia smoked, Malka read, Lea slept, and Jonas stared out of the train window.

"Glöggnitz, end of the old Eisenbahn line!" said the man occupying the seat next to Babek, just a bit too loudly, gesturing toward the picturesque snow-covered village passing quickly by the window. Only Malka looked up at him, smiling, then quickly returning to Mann's *Der Untertan.* Only a few hours out of Vienna, everyone was already sick to death of the pompous Austrian's running commentary. To hear him tell it, Austria had not only won the war but was responsible for every scientific and artistic advance of the past two centuries. Nothing, it seemed, could keep him from talking. Feigning sleep just made him up his volume, while ignoring him only seemed to encourage his jingoistic crowing.

"Yes indeed, we have arrived." He paused, as if waiting for his audience to stop applauding. "The world said it could never be done. They laughed at us. Austria is a land-locked Empire. You may be able to take a train north, board for the east, or catch a locomotive to the west, but south? How dare you! Never!"

"I wish I had a bottle of ether with me," Bakek whispered to Elia. "It's forty-one kilometers from Glöggnitz to Mürzzuschlag," the man continued. "Forty-one of the hardest, most daunting mountains on God's earth, culminating at the Semmering Pass, an aerie fit only for the boldest of eagles." Darkness briefly engulfed the coach as the express passed through a tunnel. "Prepare yourself, Frau Malka, for many such interruptions to your reading. We will move through fourteen such passages." Malka resisted the urge to look up. "Fourteen tunnels in all, bored clear through nearly two kilometers of solid rock, mostly by pick-axe, all with Teutonic sweat; sixteen viaducts, some with two stories, most with hundreds of vaults. It was first conceived back in forty-one when Minister Kuebeck entrusted Carl Ritter von Ghega to link our Capitol with the sea. They started in forty-eight, took twenty-thousand men eight years."

Jonas followed a structure as it passed by the window before making the mistake of glancing at the Austrian.

"Guard houses, my son, one every seven hundred meters. Fifty-seven in all, including Semmering station." Jonas looked away. "You know, don't you, that it was the highest rail station on earth? Eight-hundred ninety-five meters." The Austrian paused to light a cigar then resumed his lecture. "In any case, from Semmering it's down grade all the way to Mürzzuschlag. Then to Graz, where I must leave you."

This caught the attention of the adults.

"Then down the Mur valley to Maribor. From there, you either head east toward Budapest at Pragersko, or stay on the mainline to Ljubljana, and finally into the deep-water harbor of Trieste."

The train pulled into Graz at twilight, about an hour late. Babek, noticing the Austrian's limp, offered to carry his rather awkward valise to the quay. He returned with a newspaper and an assortment of pastries. "No, wait!" Babek said, in a voice louder than his usual. Malka stopped in mid-bite.

"What?"

"The torte was first conceived back in twenty-seven at the Hotel Sacher in Vienna. Its dough has been rolled no less than seven times."

Everyone burst into laughter.

Meyer Weiss
3 Grodzka
Cracow, Poland

Nice, France
January 10, 1919

Dearest Father,

As you have by now surmised from the postmark, I did not get on the boat to Jaffa and I am not heading toward Palestine. I know that this will cause you no end of worry and aggravation but please know that I am safe, clearheaded and, for the first time in my life, looking toward the future with optimism and excitement.

The mitzvah you have done for dear Malka, little Lea and Tomas is beyond divine. Your agent was able to locate his boy Jonas and he is with them now. While he shows considerable emotional damage from his difficult times, what is important is that he is with his father, with his family. They will set sail in a fortnight's time.

I chose to follow Rivka and Elia for two reasons. First, while a proud Jewess, I have no particular passion for Eretz Israel. You, Malka and perhaps half of Przemyśl are Zionists. I am not and never will be. And besides, Palestine is for families. While ultimately they may need scholars, doctors, and scientists, today what they need are babies. This, at least today, is not my calling.

The other reason, and please, sweet father, do not misinterpret what I must tell you, is that I need to be, for this time in my life, truly away. Not from my dear, loving father, but away from M. Weiss & Company. In Przemyśl, Cracow, or Palestine with you, I will never be more than the spinster daughter of a wealthy man, a magnet for swindlers and cads. On my own, in New York,

I will have the chance to achieve in academic, commercial, and, yes, even romantic terms, as well as a chance to fail, knowing that whatever happens, it happens because of who I am, not who my father is.

We should be in America by May. For a time, I will reside c/o Julia Harmon, 111 Ridge Street, New York.

I know you will understand.

I love you father.

– Zipporah

Trieste • 7th of Sh'vat, 5679 – Wednesday, January 8, 1919

"CLOSED."

"But there must—" Tomas coughed coarsely into his scarf, drawing suspicious looks from the other stranded travelers.

The clerk across the counter checked the tightness of his face mask. "No matter how many times you ask, the answer will be the same: closed."

"Surely there must be a way." Tomas tried to slide a silver coin, his last, under the bars dividing them. The clerk glanced to each side, and then leaned in toward the glass transom, keeping his face to the side of the several small holes drilled through to allow him to hear his customers. Tomas leaned in too, keeping close enough to the holes to hear and be heard but, similarly, avoiding any approach that might allow for the transmission of spittle.

"Flu hit Trieste on Saturday. We hadn't had a case here in three months. A freighter pulls in from Piraeus. The crew carouses all night, the usual things." He turned and faced Tomas, separated by only two centimeters of glass. "You know, eh?"

Tomas nodded, "I know."

The clerk raised an eyebrow, "*Honved*?"

"Just barely. I was at Przemyśl, spent most of the war in Russia as a prisoner in Omsk."

"Lucky you," the Italian said it like he meant it. "Anyway, by Sunday night a *taverna* owner and two prostitutes are dead. By Monday morning, the port's closed; nothing in, nothing out."

Tomas looked the clerk in eyes, glanced down at the silver coin, then back to the clerk. "Surely, if I made this gold there would be a boat, a skiff or even a barge to get me and my family to Egypt?"

"Signor, if this was gold, and if there were a ship, and I'm not saying there is one, you'd be blown out of the water before you made a hundred fathoms from port."

"Blockade?"

"Complete marine quarantine, enforced by Italian, French, British and American guns, not just here, all up and down the Adriatic. Rumor is Piraeus to Trieste all the way to Messina. Marseilles, Toulon, and Malaga too."

"The whole Mediterranean?"

"Like I've been saying, closed." Lea cried in the background.

"Damn." Tomas slid the coin back into his trouser pocket before flashing a thumbs-down at Malka.

"There might be a way." Tomas's turned back to the clerk. "I have many friends in the shipping business." Both men returned to their position at the glass.

"Yes?"

The Italian clerk glanced down at the empty space below the bars and above the countertop, then quickly surveyed his fellow clerks, all of whom where otherwise occupied. Holding his gauze mask with one hand, he rubbed his thumb and forefinger together. Tomas glanced at Malka who was totally consumed at the moment, trying to keep Lea distracted lest she melted into tears again. He reached into his pocket and slid the silver coin to the clerk, who picked it up with a handkerchief and quickly shuttled it into his own pocket. They reassumed the position.

"There is an open port. Both free of pestilence and accommodating to people of your persuasion."

"You mean Jews?"

"Yes, many, many boats to the Holy Land."

"Where?"

"Odessa."

THE LENARD FAMILY walked down Corso Cavour toward the waterfront, looking for a cheap hotel for the night. Stopping to rest at a vacant bench at the Piazza Duca degli Abruzzi, Malka and Tomas sat on either end while Lea napped between them. Jonas sat cross-legged on the grass behind them, gnawing on a piece of bread.

"Yes, we have to leave here, but no, we're not going to Odessa," Tomas said,

"Fine. I'll go by myself."

"You will not."

"Watch me."

"Malka, do you have any idea how far away Odessa is? Do you even know where Odessa is?"

"It doesn't matter."

"We'd have to go back through Przemyśl."

"I'll just stay on the train."

"Here is peace, there is war. Russia is imploding. They're all insane. You're insane."

"Maybe."

"I spent years there. I'm not going back."

"Then I will be heartbroken, and I'll miss you."

"Goddamn it!" Tomas leapt to his feet and stormed off, circling the Piazza before returning to the bench. They sat in silence, save the occasional truck passing by on its way to or from the port. "Malka?"

"Tomas?"

She looked up at him, her face more perfect than any French postcard. "I must really love you."

Malka began to laugh. "Yes, you must." She was joined by Lea, who was all too happy to emulate her mother.

Tomas joined in, "I do or I must?"

Jonas joined the family, laughing. Two women pedestrians passed them, shaking their heads, mumbling disapprovals.

Malka grabbed Tomas's coat and pulled him toward her, planting a long, wet kiss on his lips. "You do love me and you must love me, Tomas Lenard."

They left Trieste the next morning.

Ten

Paris • 3rd of Adar, 5679 – Monday, February 3, 1919

It was dark for the afternoon; the clouds were ominously low and occasionally spit a cold mixture of rain and sleet. They walked briskly with Elia in the middle holding Rivka's hand while escorting Zipre with his other arm.

"The poster said that the exhibition is attached to a gallery that also features Negro arts, Nubian masks I think, as well as a showing of photographic art."

"I'm excited too," Elia said, squeezing Rivka's hand as they crossed Boulevard Haussman at the place where Rue du Havre becomes Rue Tronchet. "My dreams never recovered from the first time I saw Picasso's works."

When they stopped to let a motor car clear the intersection, Rivka let go of Elia's hand and turned to Zipre. "Guillaume is brilliant. It's pure genius to juxtapose the primitive with the modern abstractions of Matisse and Picasso."

They crossed the alley and made their way toward the square. "Yes, yes, it is. I agree," Zipre said, ogling the vermillion *crêpe de chine* dress hanging in a shop window.

They picked up their pace as the precipitation turned to

rain and became heavier.

"The church is so beautiful," Rivka said, walking with her head to the monument. "So perfect, so... Greek. I love the columns." She paused, trying to identify them.

"Doric, I think. Yes, Doric," Elia said.

"They're Corinth—" Zipre bit her lip. "I would have thought you two would be more enamored with the work of Arp or perhaps Tzara—the anti-artists." The street again changed names, this time to Rue Royale.

"I'm not all that conversant in that genre," Rivka said.

"Anti-art is just what it sounds like. Duchamp put an old urinal on display and called it art"

"Oh, please. That's not—"

"There it is," Elia said, pointing down the street, across the boulevard. "Galerie Druet."

There was a small but boisterous crowd in front of the Gallery. He jogged off to investigate.

"A commode is not art," Rivka said to Zipre.

"Right, it's anti-art. Your reaction is exactly Duchamp's point. He's challenging the very definition of art, or what the masses believe is art."

Rivka laughed mockingly. "What they'd call challenge I'd call contempt. These anti-artists have an awfully low opinion of the masses."

"You have them figured out, Rivka!"

"I'm just anti-anti-art!"

They laughed until Elia returned.

"All I can see is two men, or an older man and a boy arguing in front of a painting, or rather a photograph of a painting," Elia reported.

Zipre pushed into the crowd to try to pick up the French.

"It is an abomination, and it certainly is not art!" a man in a fine top coat and hat said firmly, backed by lukewarm support from half of the crowd.

"To a philistine, anything beyond the ken of his own eye is

an abomination," a boy of fifteen years or so said. "How can you judge that which you so obviously do not understand?" Several onlookers voiced their support while others laughed.

"*Arlequin*? Are we to believe this to be, what, a portrait? Did the Spaniard hate this Arlequin? Wish to humiliate him?"

Promenading in front of the crowd, the boy, dressed in a brown suit with a wool topcoat commanded the audience like a master thespian. Articulate and dashing, with bushy brows and slightly droopy eyes, he looked like the teenage version of the Frenchmen he was sparring with. A well dressed middle-aged woman stood to his side, likewise contemplating the photograph.

"Sir, good sir," the boy began, not looking at his adversary, "Is a photograph of a beautiful woman superior to a rendering of the feminine form by a Rubens or a Raphael?" He spun to the Frenchman, raising his voice, "Of course not!"

Zipre reported to Elia and Rivka, "Aesthetic debate."

"The French: to war over art," Rivka observed.

"It's the boy from the train. From Nice. And his mother."

Once the bystanders lost interest, the argument quickly petered out and Zipre led Rivka and Elia toward the boy and his mother. "The train, from Nice, yes?" Zipre asked her in French.

"Why yes, of course."

"Zipporah Weiss, from Cracow."

The woman reached for her hand and shook it. "Rosa, Rosa Pike."

"And these are my friends, Rivka and Elia, Galicians too."

"Of course everyone in the arrondissement has had the pleasure of hearing my son, Theodore." Zipre and the boy smiled as Rivka and Elia moved closer. Turning to the couple, Rosa switched to German, "It is a pleasure to meet you. I am Rosa and this is my son Teddy. We come from, well, it's a long story."

Teddy shook hands with Elia and Rivka before lifting Zipre's hand to his lips, never allowing his gaze to wander from her blushing face. "*Enchanté, mademoiselle.*" Teddy gestured at the exhibition door, extending his elbow grandly. "Shall we?"

The five formed into language groups as they scrutinized the galleries of works by the two rising stars of the Paris art scene. Rivka, Elia and Rosa formed the German speaking contingent while Zipre and Theodore were delighted to exercise their wit and cultivation in the local tongue.

"Picasso is so clearly the master," Zipre said taking in *Homme Assis*.

Theodore scratched his chin, "I would agree, but with a caveat. Clearly, his top works are sublime, but I find much of his oeuvre to be dreadfully tedious."

"True genius can only be gauged by the artist's top works."

"Really? Is there a poor Chopin nocturne? A particularly flawed Michelangelo statue? Which ones? I thought I knew them all."

"Such chutzpah! Back home, we'd say a fellow like you *hoks a chainik*."

"I don't think I talk nonsense, at least not about art. I'm actually quite well versed in aesthetics, a real *maven* if you will."

"Yiddish? Theodore Pike, a Jew?"

"One-half Jew, one-hundred percent boulevardier, and—"

"Quite the know-it-all."

"Why thank you, Miss Weiss."

"*MONTELBAUN*," ELIA READ from the card. "As much as I admire what Picasso is trying to say, on balance I think I'd rather have this Matisse over my mantle."

"Mister Reifer," Rosa said, "It's an exhibition, not the Galleries Lafayette."

He shrugged and then smiled. "So Rosa, now that we

have some time, can you tell us the long story of where the Pikes are from?" Elia asked her while they studied Matisse's *Nude's Back*.

Rosa took a deep breath and exhaled through closed lips, making a sound like a small motor starting. "I was born Rosa Kravtzoff in Odessa. And yes, we are Jews."

"Really?" Elia said.

"My sister's husband was transferred to the east, to Shanghai. In oh-two I took a trip to Shanghai to see her and from there we traveled the Orient."

"Amazing. That must have been quite a train ride," Rivka said as they moved to the next painting, *Interior With A Violin Case.*

"Weeks to Vladivostok then a boat to China. In any case, I fell ill in Nippon, in a place called Nagasaki. Nearly died. In fact, I would have died had not a former American Naval doctor taken up residence there. He nursed me back to health. One thing led to another and I became Missus Doctor Robert Ignatius Pike in oh-three."

Rosa took a break to study the painting close-up with a small magnifying glass she kept in her purse.

"Theodore was born two years later. We lived a rich and exciting life in the sizable ex-patriot community in Nagasaki until Robert died suddenly, when Teddy was six."

"I'm so sorry," Rivka and Elia said.

"But life must go on, so we packed up and journeyed across the sea, then across Russia back to Odessa. Unfortunately, our town wasn't what it once was, especially for Jews, and I'd seen all the Russian winters I needed for two lifetimes. Robert left us with the wherewithal to go almost anywhere so we set our sights on southern France and moved to Nice."

"Which brings us to this sojourn."

"Nice was wonderful. Teddy thrived in the culture and academics. He made his old mother proud. But I knew that even as Nice was ideal for a child, soon little Teddy would grow into Theodore and need more challenge, more opportunity. America's the future, and besides, my late husband has three brothers in San Francisco, so that's where we're headed. We sail twenty-six April on La Savoie."

"From Le Havre?" Rivka asked.

"Of course."

"You are not going to believe this."

They moved to the last painting in the Matisse salon, the *Coup de Soleil.* "So that's my tale," Rosa said. "How about you?"

Elia and Rivka glanced at each other. "It's a long story," Rivka said.

Southern Ukraine • 28th of Nisan, 5679 – Monday, April 28, 1919

THE WHEEL'S BRAKE locked, sending a shriek through the boxcar the Lenard family had called home for three weeks. Tomas woke, pulled unceremoniously from the middle of a dream in which figured, incongruously, a lecture on partial differential equations, mounds of chocolate, and anonymous intercourse with a woman who might have been a maid at the Hotel back in Vienna. The train stopped with a characteristic lurch which the rest of the family slept through as they lay on top of straw and under a wool army blanket. Malka was on one end with Lea against her chest, one arm reaching over her daughter to cover Jonas. Tomas lay at the other end.

While diplomats from the victorious nations divided up the carcass of the Central Powers in Paris, the East, for years the quiet front, had reignited in war. Not so much a war pitting well-drilled troops across clearly defined fire lines and trenches, but a truly civil war in which every ethnic spite, every petty jealousy, and even every neighborly feud would be settled with violence. In order to pass through Przemyśl unnoticed, Babek had arranged for the Lenards to join with a group of several dozen Russian families—taken hostage by the Austrians early on in the war—on their rail trip back to the motherland. Conditions were abysmal, with most of their trip from Vienna to L'vov spent huddling for warmth in open cars previously used to transport horses and cattle. The Austrian guards assigned to deliver the hostages back to Russia either deserted or were put off the train by the time it reached Cracow, leaving the mostly aristocratic hostages alone to face repeated searches, shake-downs and robberies. By the time the train crossed the San nearly everyone on it was cold, hungry and had been stripped of anything valuable. By the time they reached L'vov, they had been threatened and set upon by Poles, Ukrainians, Bolsheviks and Whites, none of whom were in any way distinguishable from the innumerable gangs of common criminals prowling every station and viaduct from the Alps to the Urals. At Zhmerynka junction, halfway between L'vov and Odessa, the Lenards transferred to a much roomier Odessa-bound freighter, which would have allowed them luxury of spreading out had the temperature ever broken minus twenty.

After several unsuccessful attempts at rejoining his dream, Tomas got up just as the train again began moving. Bracing himself against the rough-hewn wooden sidewall with one arm, he struggled to keep his urine flowing through the hole in the floor. A hard bump over a bad segment of track caused him to foul the floorboard before he could redirect his stream back onto the passing ties. He smiled. As difficult as it was to navigate with the train moving, he was thankful for the forward progress of the last few days. Besides, they seemed to have left most of the more intense fighting behind them and while stops and delays were still frequent, they hadn't had a wait of more than a day since leaving Zhmerynka. Besides, the gash over his eye seemed to be healing without infection, a souvenir from a rag-tag detachment of soldiers,

Petlura's men, one of their fellow travelers thought he heard them say, who didn't appreciate his accented Ukrainian. It was cold and finding sufficient food was always a problem, but Odessa was finally within reach.

As twilight began to light a crack in the roof vent, Tomas unbuttoned his trousers, pulling them off as he slipped beneath the blanket next to Malka. Encircling her with his arms, his front to her backside, their bodies generated pleasing warmth. Tomas nibbled on the side of her neck, pausing just long enough to savor her unique aroma before working his way up to her earlobe so she would hear him whispering, "Good morning, sweetheart." Her hand found his and guided it under her blouse to her breast. "We'll be in Odessa tomorrow, then on the boat; in Palestine by Shavuot." He massaged her nipple playfully between his fingers. "I love having—" He pulled her night-dress up and began rubbing his penis along the cleavage of her rear-end, "optimism."

"Tomas?"

"She wakes."

Malka yawned. "Do you really love me?"

"Of course I do."

She moved her hips in rhythmic orbits, massaging his now erect member. "More than anything else?"

"More than a feather bed." He ran his tongue up the back of her neck, lingering on the fine wisps just below the hairline.

"Then bring me coffee. A full pot."

"With a basket of blintz?"

Malka reached behind and guided Tomas into her. "With sugar."

They made love, and then fell back into a dreamless sleep as the sun rose and the train rumbled toward the Black Sea.

North Atlantic • 28th of Nisan, 5679 – Monday, April 28, 1919

"THE OYSTERS WERE divine. Too bad you missed them," Zipre said as Theodore returned to his seat.

"The maitre d' said the Huntingtons and the Ingersolls are dining with the captain," Teddy said, gesturing toward the large round table at the far end of the dining room. "Oh, and I abhor oysters."

"Ingersoll? Like the pocket watch? Must be rolling in it," Rivka said, trying not to stare.

A small detachment of waiters descended on the table. While one held a tray next to Rivka, another lifted the immaculately polished silver half dome. "*Mademoiselle, vous voulez du saumon Mousseline?*"

"*Oui, merci,*" she answered, tightly focused on articulation. "*Et un verre de l'eau, s'il vous plait.*" For weeks now Teddy and Rosa had been tutoring her and Elia in French and English. She was pleased beyond words when the plate was delivered, followed a second later by a tall glass of water. The other women were similarly served.

"Ingersoll's a piker, no pun intended, next to Huntington, or so I'm told. His father built railroads across America. Say," Teddy asked with his usual enthusiasm, "What did your father build, Rivka?"

"Teddy!" Rosa snapped. "Manners!"

Elia responded to another waiter, shaking his head to make his selection known. Zipre looked up at Teddy.

"I'm so sorry, Rivka. I forgot," the boy said with sincerity.

"It's all right, really it is. Actually I'm happy to talk about daddy; it might just do me some good." She put her fork down and used the white linen napkin to dab her lips. "My daddy was named Tanchem and he was the finest furniture maker in Przemyśl. If you asked him, he would have told you he was the finest in all of Austria."

Waiters engulfed the table briefly, leaving fresh breads, pats of butter and filled wine glasses.

"Growing up, all of our finest furniture pieces were made by the Arm Factory," Zipre said. "Well not all, but most. His armoires were magnificent."

"He was a wonderful man. I worked for him for several years. Tough but fair. He was a soldier earlier in life, but always with the soul of an artisan," Elia said, solemnly.

"Thank you, sweetheart," Rivka said, taking his hand under the table.

Teddy lifted his wine glass and sipped at the straw-colored liquid, then nodded his head with reverence, "To Tanchem." They all drank.

"And Izac, her brother," Elia added. "Tanchem was the artist, but it was Izac who actually supervised the building."

"Here, here." Again, everyone drank. Rivka and Elia entwined their fingers.

"Zipporah, care to divulge?" Teddy asked, setting his wineglass on the linen.

"Father would be at ease at our table or at theirs," she gestured toward the far end of the dining room. "I think that's what I love the most about him. He's a chess player, and a good one at that. He can be sweet, he can be ruthless, he can lay in wait, he usually wins, but he always knows when he's beaten."

"Like when he tangles with his little girl, no doubt," Teddy added.

"And what of you, Theodore?" Rivka asked. "What kind of man is father to a son of your obvious...style?"

"I don't really remember him other than that he was a doctor and had a big bushy handlebar—"

"Teddy," Rosa cut in, "not every mustachioed American doctor was your father. Amazing how life's serendipity moves people around and brings them together."

The waiters cleared the plates and delivered fresh ones,

each laden with filet mignon *lili,* sauté of chicken *lyonnaise* and vegetable marrow *farci* as well as fresh crystal and a decanter of claret.

"During the war a school chum and I used to cliff dive at the far end of the quay in Nice. On my third dive, I must have hit something because my leg ripped open from knee to thigh. I passed out and woke up in the hospital, conveniently located, I might add, not more than a hundred meters from our flat on Rue Dubouchage. I was treated by an American naval doctor. We spoke about America for hours and hours. He loved President Wilson and the Saint Louis Cardinals."

"From then on, Teddy never stopped talking about America," Rosa said, "So here we are, on the way to San Francisco. Besides, Robert has family there."

"I can drink to that," Teddy said.

Affirmations were echoed by the others.

Teddy lifted his glass. "To new friends, to America!" Everyone drank.

"So delicious," Elia sighed. "Ted, what is this wine?"

Teddy held his glass aloft and made a slow circle with his arm, swirling the wine in the crystal. "Fifteen, Bonnes Mares, Vial."

"Sounds like wartime Marconi code."

He set the glass down on the table and reached to the center of the table for the wine bottle. "This is from the Bourgogne of France and is rouge, so the grape is almost always the Pinot Noir. The vintage refers to the year that the grapes were picked. This is important because the quality of the finished wine is heavily influenced by the vagaries of the weather where the vines are grown."

"Sounds like something my aunt would excel at."

"Ideal is rain in the spring then single downpours weekly through the growing season, followed by a bone dry, hot and sunny summer through harvest-time. Even a five-minute drenching before harvest can cause ruin the vintage."

Elia studied the label, "Because the grapes suck up water, diluting the flavor and thinning the wine."

"Exactly, Bonnes Mares is the vineyard, the plot of earth that the grapes grow on. In this case, it's a wonderful little plot of dirt which, over time, has produced such good grapes that it has been designated as Grand Cru, the top dirt in France and, therefore, in the world. In addition to fine soil, usually Grand Cru means the plot is well sloped, for good drainage, and faces southwest, for maximal sun."

"And Vial?" Elia asked while everyone worked on the sumptuous array of food on their plates.

"Vial is the house who made the wine, the craftsman if you will." Teddy and Elia picked up and clinked glasses while Rivka poked at her dinner with a fork. "Just remember, this is only for Bourgogne. In Bordeaux or Province or Loire, it's all different."

"To nineteen-fifteen, a great year in Bourgogne," Elia said.

Rivka dropped her fork and stood up as the sound of silver on porcelain spread across the first class dining room, briefly turning more than a few heads. "I feel sick. I need some air." She threw her napkin on the chair and headed out through the etched, smoked glass doors of the dining room, past the grand stair case, then out of the teak swing doors onto the foredeck.

Elia saw her about ten meters away, leaning against the railing, looking over the edge into the blackness of the North Atlantic. After draping his coat over her shoulders he joined her on the rail. "You all right?"

"So delicious." Her delivery was slow; mocking.

"It was."

She turned her head and a wisp of her hair whipped his face. "Nineteen-fifteen, a great year for Bourgogne?"

"Rivka, we're here. Why not enjoy?" Elia reached around her and into the exterior pocket of his coat, retrieving his cigarette case and the bullet-shaped trench lighter he had picked up in Paris.

"How desperate you are to be accepted by the bourgeoisie! Do you think they don't see through you? We wear the same clothes every day, speak the same fractured French each night, and, gasp, use the wrong fork with our salad. You talk a good game, Elia Reifer, but when it really comes down to it, you're a fraud."

"That's unfair, Rivka." He tried to light a cigarette but the wind kept blowing out the flame.

"No, what's unfair is you and I stuffing our faces with enough food to feed Przemyśl for a week and washing it down with drink made on hectares of otherwise good farmland but available only to the elites. That's unfair. We luxuriate under silk sheets on feather beds while ten floors below the proletariat sleep on wooden cots and eat oatmeal. That's unfair." Rivka pointed her finger at Elia. "What's wrong is how easily the most sacred tenets of our being are bought and sold by Weiss's money."

"I don't deserve this," he said while walking to the other side of the deck to light his cigarette. After a few good draws he was back next to Rivka, "Without Meyer, I'd be swinging from a rope and only God knows what would have become of you."

"There you go, compromising again when it suits you."

"We eat where we are, we drink what they serve, sleep where they house us."

"You like it just a little too much, don't you."

He lowered his voice, making it barely audible against the sea breeze. "We've done this together every step of the way. What I've done, you've done." Elia pointed his finger at Rivka, angrily. "May I have no pleasures other than you? That's it, isn't it?"

"No. And don't you point that finger at me!"

Elia took a step back to get a deep drag on his cigarette before continuing in a more conciliatory tone, "Why are you doing this to me, Rivka?"

She looked at him, eyes moist but not crying. "Elia, I don't want to fight with you. But I have to."

"Then why are you? Why are you picking a fight with me?"

"Because." She fought back tears. "Because I am you and you are me. Because—" tears streamed down her cheek, "Because, you're all I've got."

They came together, Rivka's arms around his waist, Elia's over her shoulders resting on the railing. Wisps of her hair swirled around both of them. Eventually the doors leading to the grand stairs swung open and they joined their fellow first-class passengers for a post-dinner promenade around the deck.

"Rivka?"

"What."

"I'm sorry."

"I am too, Elia."

"Sweetheart?"

"Yes."

"Let's make a pact."

"How so?"

"Two points."

"Only two?"

"From the moment we set foot in America, we are Socialists—revolutionaries—true to our class."

"I love you so much, Elia."

"We land Wednesday. Let's celebrate May Day as husband and wife."

"You're going to have to ask that question in a more direct manner, Mister Reifer."

"Thursday, in New York, will you marry me?"

Ellis Island • 30th of Nisan, 5679 – Wednesday, April 30, 1919

THE MORNING THE rain fell in sheets, the gray obscuring the ship's bow and rendering New York City all but invisible off La Savoie's starboard as the captain steered the ship into the wind and dropped anchor.

Over a light breakfast of coffee, cheese, fresh breads, and jam, the first class passengers filled in immigration papers. As soon as the second and third class passengers were safely aboard launches, steaming their way to the Ellis Island immigration facility, a uniformed officer appeared in the main dining room, ringing a small bell. With everyone's attention, he proceeded to apologize for interrupting breakfast, then respectfully requested that the American citizens line up at the door and directed the others to queue on the port side of the room for inspection of papers.

"See you in America," Teddy said, following his mother toward the door. Four more officials appeared and began perfunctory scans of American passports and the collection of travel papers for the citizens.

Rivka looked around at her fellow aliens, "I don't like how this looks."

"I don't think they give literacy tests to First Class passengers," Zipre said, tapping Elia to get his attention. "If they do, respond with confidence, even a bit of arrogance, and be sure to keep your answers as terse as possible."

Elia and Rivka nodded.

Teddy tugged at his mother's coat, "Look." He gestured to the alien line where an elderly woman was talking with great animation to an immigration officer, occasionally pointing at Elia, Rivka and Zipre.

The three heard the officer before they saw him. "Papers!" They froze. "Don't you peoples speak English? I want to see your travel documents and immigration papers, now." He was a large, tall man with puffy, rosy cheeks, freckles, and small, sharp eyes set a tad bit too close together. Pinned to his uniform, which looked to be a size or two too small, was a badge and above that, a name tag that read, "Meehan."

Zipre composed herself then answered, using her finest Queen's English. "My good Sir, there is no cause to raise your voice. We are fully fluent in the American tongue. French, German and Polish as well."

"Well I don't care so much for Frenchies. And I hate Krauts." He took her papers. "Weiss, eh? Says here race is Polish. None a youse look Polish. Look more like Hebrews ta me."

"Polish by nation, Hebrew by faith," Rivka said.

He looked at her and cocked his head, "Don't sound like Poles neither. Sound like Jews. And if you's Jews, then you need to put Hebrew down as your race."

Zipre crossed out "Polish" and neatly printed "Hebrew" on each of the three immigration forms. "Satisfied?"

He turned to Elia, grabbing his papers, scanning them twice, from top to bottom before looking up at him, perplexed. "Where the hell is Pressmill?"

"Austria," Elia said in remarkably good English.

"Poland," Zipre corrected, speaking before Elia finished talking.

The immigration officer bore down; his reddening face now only inches from Elia's. "Filthy kike bastard. I lost half my mates fighting your ilk at the Marne. Saw my own cousin take one of your bullets in the hip; watched his flesh turned from purple to black, rotted like bad meat; died like a dog. Now you have the gall to—"

"Sir," Zipre interrupted, "We are not people without means. Surely there is an accommodation that can be made."

"You tryin' to bribe me, Jewess?"

"Of course not, I'm just trying to..."

He turned and yelled at a group of uniformed men milling

about the door, "Reilly, Connor, over here!" Meehan turned to his compatriots, "Take these three to the island. Failed literacy test."

Teddy turned in time to see the authorities leading Rivka, Zipre, and Elia away. He took a step toward them but stopped when his mother's hand landed on his shoulder.

"But Mama,"

"Leave it be."

"We need to help them!"

"Nothing to be done here. We're more help from the other side."

"FOUR AND A half hours waiting like cattle. My legs are killing me," Rivka said, plopping down heavily on the wooden bench in the waiting room just past the great hall. "And I feel like throwing up."

"Six days in First Class and you've gone soft," Zipre said, dropping her valise on the ground and joining Rivka on the bench. "At least we have the stamp." She showed off her papers with the coveted "Admitted" stamped across the front in red. They searched the vast hall for Elia, Zipre eventually spotting him on aisle seven.

"Zu-ca-ro," Elia read from the name tag before the officer instructed him to put his valise on the table at the final examination station. Picking up the inspector's accent, Elia tried a few words of Italian which seemed to soften the uniformed man's steely cold demeanor.

"Italiano?" Zucaro asked, looking almost welcoming until he scanned to the part of Elia's papers that listed his ethnicity. He unlatched the case and flipped it open.

"I have an Italiano friend in America. Living in Pildefa," Elia said while the inspector fished through his bag.

Without looking up, he corrected, "Philadelphia. It's pronounced Philadelphia."

"That's what I meant, Phil-a-del-phi-a."

Seemingly satisfied, Zucaro inked his stamp on a soaked sponge sitting in a shallow metal tray before smacking Elia's papers, "Admitted."

While Rivka and Zipre readied to collect Elia in anticipation of making the next launch to the Battery, Elia tried to close his satchel, but was unable to get the latch to engage cleanly. He tried again, forcing the two sides of the valise together to no avail until the immigration officer handed Elia his admission papers. Forced to take a break and stow his documents in his jacket, Zucaro interceded, opening the case and probing the perimeter until he came to the source of the blockage—brown wax paper around a small book.

Elia grabbed for the book but the inspector moved it out of his reach. He'd been carrying the book ever since Malka declined to take it, never considering how in these exactly wrong circumstances it could ruin his life, like an incoming shell missing the field and landing in a meter-wide trench.

Zucaro unwrapped the package and opened the book; the text was nothing but scribbles to him. "Hebrew?"

"No, Yiddish."

"What is it?"

Elia's stomach knotted and his throat felt like it was coated with dirt. "It's a religious book."

The officer leafed through it, spinning the pages by in reverse order before stopping at the title page. In the middle of the page was an engraved portrait of two older men. One was balding, while the other with thick black hair. Both of them sported full, bushy grey beards and moustaches. But it wasn't the two profiles that caught the officer's eye, it was the fact that in a book of smudged black on dull white, the two men were rendered in that most nefarious of primary colors, red. "Stern!" he yelled to the man inspecting on aisle nine. "Come here."

"What's going on?" Rivka asked, concerned. "What are

they doing? Who is that?"

Zipre climbed up on the bench to get a better view. "God, please no!"

"What! What is it?"

"The book, it's the book."

Zucaro turned to Stern, "Says it's religious."

Stern opened the book to the title page and scanned the text. He looked up at the officer, then at Elia, then turned toward a small group of uniformed men near the doors, "Guards!"

From behind the inspection table, Elia yelled, "Rivka!"

Rivka tried to run toward him but was blocked by the luggage of a large group of newly admitted immigrants.

Zipre leapt off the bench and caught her, wrapping her arms around her waist.

"Rivka!" Elia cried again as he was escorted away by four guards, disappearing through a reinforced door just past aisle ten.

Rivka began to shout his name, but Zipre put her hand over the mouth before talking calmly into her ear, "No, Riv." Rivka struggled briefly. "Not here. We're no good to him in jail. We'll get him in." Rivka began to shake. "Quickly, let's get out of here." Zipre dragged her toward the pier and the Battery Park launch, stopping briefly to allow Rivka to vomit on the grass flanking the cobblestone walk.

"YEAH, THE MARITIME'S a nice building. Should be, it's the first place everyone sees commin' into New York," Julia said, pointing to the leaded patterned-glass laylight on the ceiling.

"'Cepting Ellis," Milton added.

"Stamped zinc, rolled iron, plaster, glass, steel, and, of course, the harbor view," Teddy said with enthusiasm. "The architecture speaks of—"

"Money," Julia said, finishing his sentence.

"Nothing more quintessential than that!"

Rosa noted the puzzled look on Julia's face and discreetly whispered to her, "Nothing more American."

Julia smiled broadly at the boy. "There is only one thing more American than money, and that's baseball. Tomorrow's opening day for the Giants, but it's also May Day so Milty and I got some work to do. Some of my tenants will be, how can I put this?"

"Moved out," Milton said hoarsely.

"Yes, out. But it doesn't really matter anyway 'cause they'll probably postpone the game on account of the rain."

"Please, mother, let's stay through the weekend," Theodore implored.

"Teddy, we have a train..."

He seized his mother's hand and with an arm around her waist, pulled her into a gentle waltz and sang in an exaggerated upward arpeggio. Spinning her around three-quarters of a turn, he sang, "There's a fine ship to San Francisco, sailing mid-month."

"It's only the Phillies, but it's supposed to clear up and be nice by Sunday," Julia continued. "Game's a historical event, the first ever Giant game on Sunday. Hell, it's the first Sunday baseball game in New York, ever, I think. And I can get hold of six tickets in the boxes. And if that's not enough, the oil magnate's back, and he's probably pitching. Teddy abruptly stopped dancing but didn't let go of his mother. He sang, "Oil magnate?" in his best operatic flair, lengthening the final syllable and bringing it to his highest register, then re-engaging the waltz.

"Pol Perritt won eighteen games last year for McGraw. Anyhow, off season he went home to Louisiana and struck oil, and now he's a millionaire. Probably moved to a spiffy place up by the Park; showed up at the field in a chauffeured car. Great arm and a million easy dollars. Luckiest bastard on earth if you ask me."

"How quintessentially American, again!"

"All right, all right all ready!" Rosa said, pulling away from her twirling son.

"It's settled then," Teddy said. "We're going to the Polo grounds. Can you think of a better way to spend our first weekend in the States?"

"Theodore," Rosa said, patting her son's cheek, "You know I can't resist a waltz."

"They're getting off," Milton said, pointing toward the quay.

The travelers disembarked from two gangplanks, slowed by many joyous reunions as they first set foot on Manhattan Island. "I don't see 'em," Julia said.

"There!" Teddy yelled, pointing at the aft debarkation point, "Zipporah and Rivka."

Julia pushed past Milton to be next to Teddy, "In the grey dress with the white shawl?"

"That's Zipre. Zipporah Weiss."

Julia squinted. "Next to her is Rivka."

"Yep."

Julia walked into the rain, toward the dock. "So then where the hell is Elia?" A minute later, after hugs, handshakes, and kisses in the rain, they all huddled back under the eaves while Zipre recounted what happened in the hall. Julia shook her head and spoke, sounding like Der Captain from the Katzenjammer Kids, "*Oy, vere sunk.*"

"What say we get on that there boat and just go get him?" Milton suggested.

"Milty," Julia said, resting her arm on his shoulder, "They think my Elia's a Red. They'll have him surrounded by a hundred guards." She turned to Rivka. "You had the same ashen look on your face last time we met. You probably don't remember. What were you, eight? You lost your dolly."

Rivka reached out and hugged Julia.

"Listen to me, everything will be all right. We'll have this red nonsense cleared up in time for the opening pitch. Beer,

Cracker Jack, and pop—"

"Julia?"

"Yes, Rivka."

"He is one."

"One what?"

"Elia's a Red, a socialist. And so am I."

Ellis Island • 1st of Iyyar, 5679 – Thursday, May 1, 1919

THERE WERE SEVERAL hundred men in the prison, little more than a dormitory with bars on the windows and a lock on the door. While some had been jailed for months waiting for a hearing date and others had just spent their first night, the common thread between nearly all of them was the "Red" label, the vast and finely articulated spectrum of political flavors represented being lost on the authorities. The detainees naturally sorted themselves, first by language, then by political affiliation, and finally by nationality. Within an hour of his arrival, Elia had been introduced to a dozen or so Yiddish speaking Bundists from what had been Austrian Galicia. While not the Savoie, Elia found that the accommodations far outclassed anything he had become accustomed to during the war years.

They unlocked the doors at six in the morning, allowing the Reds into the mess hall. Elia sat on a long wooden bench swapping war stories with David, a Jew from Łodz, and John, a Pole from Brody. It wasn't easy to talk amidst two hundred men rattling tableware and arguing politics with full vigor in nearly a dozen tongues.

"They're deporting us all," John said nearly yelling at Elia. "They're calling the ship 'The Red Ark'. No hearings, no appeals. Palmer's out for blood."

Elia felt like his heart hit an iceberg. "Who? Where to?"

"Russia—" David said.

"Palmer's some kind of legal General making war on the Reds, mostly the Wobblies," John added. "Hoover's his muscle."

Elia pushed his gruel aside and put his hands on his face and his head on the table. "Rivka's having coffee just across the bay." He had a knot in his stomach and a growing headache. A shiver ran down his spine.

"There, there, comrade, every man here looks across the harbor the same way," David said.

Elia lifted his head and saw that the men at his table were all looking to the far wall where a short, portly older man was climbing up on top of one of the tables. The man raised his arms and the din in the room dropped to where a strong orator would have had a chance to he heard.

"Comrades!" his voice boomed in German-inflected English. Few in the hall could believe such volume had come from a man of such small stature. "Welcome to America!" The room exploded with laughter, clapping, and cat-calls. "This morning, we celebrate May Day!" The room again went wild. "We will sing 'The International' but in a special way. We will sing the verses in English. The chorus we shall do in all the languages of the revolution. The people's choir!" The room let out a collective murmur, and quieted as he repeated his instructions in French and German.

He began to sing, his voice dominating the room even as everyone stood and scores and scores of men joined in the tune. Feeling a bit dizzy, Elia nonetheless stood and mouthed along with the English.

*Arise ye pris'ners of starvation, Arise ye wretched of the earth...*In English, the chorus! *'Tis the final conflict, Let each stand in his place The International Union, shall be the human race.* Verse two! *We want no condescending saviors, to rule us from their judgment hall...* En Français! *C'est la lutte finale, Groupons-nous, et demain...* And three! *The law* *oppresses us and tricks us, the wage slave system drains our blood... Völker hört die Signale, auf zum letzten Gefecht... Behold them seated in their glory, The kings of mine and rail and soil...* Sing any language! *We toilers from all fields united, Join hand in hand with all who work...*

Elia felt the room began to spin as cheers and slogans filled the air at the end of the song. A lightning bolt ran from the small of his back up the length of his spine hitting him in the base of his skull, reverberating like a hammer hitting a frozen anvil. The lights went out.

"Reifer? You all right? He's burning up. And bleeding."

"Hit his head on the way down."

"You, you, come and help. Let's get him back to the dormitory."

North Atlantic • 6th of Iyyar, 5679 – Tuesday, May 6, 1919

IT TOOK SEVERAL wipes of a handkerchief for Elia to clean the crystallized yellow crust from his lashes so that he could pry his eyes open. Vision blurred and head pounding, there was a sharp pain in his temples with each beat of his heart. A hand to his eyebrow noted bandage; slight pressure confirmed the wound was stitched. Elia closed his eyes, abandoning his attempt to sit up and tried instead to focus on the low rumble coursing through his body.

"*Buenos días, el sol,*" a male voice said. Elia sat up, straining to focus. There were small, round windows spaced about five meters apart over about twenty cots, three-quarters occupied by men in varying stages of illness. Some were sleeping, a few puking into tin pails, and a handful sitting up or sitting on a cot with their feet on the deck. An orderly and a nurse milled about them. It wasn't until he felt the unmistakable sensation of being lifted by a swell that it all began to make sense.

"*Buenos días, Señor.*"

The man turned to the nurse and her orderly who had walked over to Elia's bed, "*¡El vive! ¡El habla! El...*"

"*Por favor, yo no hablo español,*" Elia offered. "*Deutsch*? English? *Parlez Français*?"

The man laughed. "What do I look like, Nimrod?"

"You speak English?"

"You've been sleeping for too long, my boy."

"I'm sorry, I must have passed out."

"*Señor, por favor,*" the nurse interrupted, putting one hand on Elia's forehead and the other on his wrist, searching for a pulse. She turned to the tall, obese orderly and peeled off a string of words while the orderly scribbled mightily on his clipboard before abruptly moving to the next cot.

"You are, apparently, fully recovered," the man said, thrusting his hand across the void between the cots. "I am *Señor* Miguel Salgado Ochoa."

"Elia Reifer."

"Pleasure to meet you, *Señor* Reifer."

Elia rubbed his eyes vigorously. "Please, call me Elia. Say, you wouldn't happen to have a cig would you?"

"I wish. I'm trying to quit."

Elia yawned. "So Miguel, what happened?"

"You and I missed the boat."

"What day is it?"

"*Lunes*. Monday."

"What boat?"

"The Ark." The man reached into his shirt pocket and pulled out a package of gum, "Spearmint?" Elia accepted without hesitation. "So you were detained too?"

"*Si, si.* I was arrested at the Worker's Hall over on East Fifteenth, in the March raid; punched in the mouth by Detective Geren himself. You? Elia?" he was concerned, You all right?"

The room spun; images of death and gore knifed through his consciousness.

"Elia?"

"Sorry. My mind was wandering."

Miguel unwrapped a stick and popped it I his mouth, "Is all right. The ague will do that."

"We're not heading for Russia, are we?"

He laughed, "No, no, not yet comrade. Depending on how you want to look at it, we both got either lucky or unlucky, you with the ague, me with the flu. Too sick to deport. We missed the Russia boat so they tossed us on the next one leaving. Short ride for us. Make port by three tomorrow afternoon."

"Where?"

"*Habana.*"

"Cuba?"

"*Si comrade amigo.*"

"Oy." He covered his face with his hands and eased his head back to the pillow and reconstructed the past few days for Miguel. "We arrived on La Savoie on Wednesday. We, oh, I came from Przemyśl, in Austria via Paris. With my fiancée and friends."

"I've heard of Przemyśl. Big fight there early in the war."

"Bloody battles. Like everywhere."

"I managed to miss almost all the fun. I made shoes in Barcelona. You?"

"Wood, furniture maker. Rivka, my fiancée, is, um, was, a baker."

"Picture?"

Elia removed his hands from his face, sat up and swung his legs to the ruddy, irregularly varnished mahogany floorboards. Reaching under the cot, he located his valise and brought it up to the bed. "Looks like a few things have gone missing. The money for starters. All of it," he said after fishing for a while.

"Borrowed by some Mick, no doubt."

Elia pulled a postal card from his valise and looked at it. Tears forced their way out of his eyes as he fell back on the cot, his hands on his head, the card resting on his stomach. Once again, the room began to rotate.

"*Amigo*?"

Elia clutched the card, mumbling, "Two months ago we had three sepias made by a photographer in Paris. At the shop, I selected an open-air Renault as the backdrop but Rivka thought that an automobile was too bourgeois a setting for true socialists to be memorialized in so she led everyone on a five minute march across Rue Saint Michel that ended in brilliant sunshine on a gravel path in the Jardin du Luxembourg where we were framed by budding rose bushes and jonquils. A few days later we returned to *rive gauche* to pick up the cards, this time in a cold light rain. Over coffee, tea, and a pack of cigarettes at the Café Modern, Rivka and I wrote on the back of one of the cards and posted it to my aunt in Poland." Elia stared blankly at the ceiling, thinking about the rest of that day in Paris. *The long walk back to the hotel in the cold drizzle. Running up three flights with Rivka to the room, disrobing, entangling under the quilt, making love, napping, and then making love again. Bathing that night face to face with Rivka's legs wrapped around me. Laughing, caressing, and sharing a cigarette.*

"*Amigo*. You all right?"

"Damn this world. Damn it to hell."

Miguel took the card. "She is beautiful. Life is unfair."

"Five years, five meters," he said, between gulps for air.

"*¿Qué?*"

"We were apart for five years." He rubbed his eyes, "I was five meters from her, five lousy meters from Rivka, from a normal life. It's not fair. Not after what we've been through." He sat up. "Now I know there is no God. I'm sure of it, there is no—"

"Don't say it, comrade. Please."

Elia exhaled loudly.

"Elia, Elia my son." He looked down at the photograph, "Look at this. Such magnificence. How can you look into her eyes and believe this to be a mere accident of nature? Can't you see God's handiwork in her face?"

Elia looked at the card, "We are quite the couple, yes?"

"She looks... Spanish."

Elia laughed. "She'd be flattered to hear your estimation."

They each chewed another stick of gum.

"So Elia, tell me, how did you come to be here?"

"We were pulled from the first class line and ferried to—"

"First class?" the Spaniard whistled.

"Rivka and I are not bourgeois. We're dedicated socialists and proud to be of the working class. The passage was, was..." He searched for words. "We had problems getting out of Galicia. We hated the crossing but had no choice. It was—"

"Elia," Miguel interrupted, "You don't owe anyone any excuses so don't apologize. In the world we live in, just getting by is a major accomplishment. No one has the luxury of staying pure to their ideals." He paused, eyes cast down to the deck, "Not you and certainly not me." There was a long pause.

"They found the *Manifesto* Manes gave to me. He was my friend, my comrade; he fell in the war."

"And off to detention."

"I remember the dormitory at Ellis on May Day."

Miguel began singing, "*Agrupémonos todos, en la lucha final. El género humano es la internacional.*"

"That was something, wasn't it?" Elia said

"A magnificent moment to be sure."

"I felt it coming on. I must have collapsed."

"That would explain the bandage. What else?"

Elia racked his brain but could find no other memories.

"That's it until I woke up, not five minutes ago."

"Well, my friend, we are on the Esperanza, pride of the New York & Cuba Mail Steam Ship Company. One might say we have been posted from New York to Havana. One way."

"Damn!"

"What?"

"She won't know where I am, will she?"

"Rivka? Unless they fixed the deportation list at the last moment, all of America thinks you're on the way to Petrograd." Elia again covered his face and fell back into the pillow. "*Señor* Reifer, you know what means Esperanza?"

Through his fingers Elia mumbled, "Experience? Excitement?"

"No and no. But you know what?" He inched closer to Elia, lowering his voice, "This is a mail ship. They dump us with the mail at Havana tonight, then turn around and steam back to New York. A few hours in port, at most. One of the stevedores is a comrade; many of us are sending word to loved ones in a letter to my wife. If you have an address, she'll see that your note is delivered."

"So—"

"Rivka will know where you are by Thursday, at the latest." Miguel reached into his leather bag for a pen and a sheet of onion skin.

Elia looked at Miguel and smiled, "*Gracias, mi amigo.*"

"*Viva la revolución*, comrade Reifer. Now write. I'll be back in an hour." Miguel turned and began to walk away.

"Miguel!" The man from Barcelona stopped and looked at Elia. "*Señor* Salgado, you never told me what Esperanza means."

He began to laugh. A chuckle at first, then a hardy howl as he turned his back on Elia and began to walk away. As Miguel reached the bulkhead, he stopped, and with a pump of his right fist, shouted, "Hope!"

Eleven

New York • 14th of Iyyar, 5679 – Wednesday, May 14, 1919

ZIPRE AND RIVKA shared one of twenty-eight apartments at 109 Ridge Street. While the building had a separate mailing address, it was connected to 111 Ridge by short hallways on the odd numbered floors—like Siamese twins. Their room was ample, about ten by ten and well appointed by neighborhood standards: two beds, a plush chair with an ottoman, a small desk with a stool, and a four-drawer dresser.

"Where are you going?" Zipre asked.

"Out," Rivka said, reaching for her coat. "Did you see that?" She gestured toward the parlor, not more than twenty feet away through the hallway door. "This place is disgusting."

"It may well be, but it's putting food on the table and a roof over our heads."

"She kissed that *kurva* on the lips. And for a long time."

"So?"

"So? All you can say is so? Open your eyes!"

"My eyes are working fine. Perhaps you should—"

"And it wasn't the first time I've seen them embrace like that. If that tramp didn't spread her legs for anyone with a silver dollar, why I'd think she was some kind of, some kind of..." When Rivka was angry her voice tended to grow softer and more articulated. *"Lesbierin,"* she sputtered.

Zipre and Rivka stood facing each other in the center of the room, about an arm's length apart. Rivka was tight-faced and intense; Zipre cracked a thin smile before uttering, "No, you don't say?"

"Don't mock me!" Rivka shot back.

"I hear that Rivka Reifer is a—" She took a step forward and whispered, "Socialist."

"I said, don't—"

"Shut up and listen to me!" Zipre put her hand on Rivka's shoulder and steered her toward the chair. "Julia prefers to have relations with members of her own sex. It is simply the way she is. Just as you adore tea and abhor beer."

"Please," Rivka said, stretching the word out as she sunk into the chair. "It's not like that at all. I just find it, well, I find it sort of—"

"You find it sort of what? Who gave you the right to find offense in what another grown person chooses to like and dislike?"

"I'm sorry, but I find it disturbing and odd, that's all."

"Forcing your tastes on another person—you of all people—it's so very bourgeois. You Reds want freedom and justice for everyone unless they happen to have different personal desires than what your precious masses deem normal?"

"That is not fair and you know it!"

"Oh yes it is. Julia is a warm, feeling woman who loves you unconditionally because her brother loves you. She took the lot of us in, without passing judgment. She loves me in the same unconditional way merely because I am friends with you two."

"I love Julia, too."

"She didn't first ask me if I like coffee, what God I pray to or if I prefer to have sexual relations with men, women, or both. It insults me that you care who she sleeps with."

"Both?" Rivka asked, looking confused.

"God in heaven, Rivka Arm, you can be so provincial!"

"Provincial? At least I'm not the one in love with a teenage boy."

"And I'm not the one in love with an inmate."

"A political prisoner, held for his—for our—beliefs. Beliefs. You should try them sometime."

"Oh, that's right, I forgot. You and Elia get to do as you please because you are the leaders of the unwashed masses. You're just so superior, the vanguard, right?"

"At least my daddy wasn't a usurer. We couldn't afford to go to fancy schools in Cracow and Berlin and Paris. I make no apology for who and what we are."

"It's like Julia's business; you look down at it, but you don't hesitate when it comes to using the fruits of her labor. A dollar here a dollar there is just fine. You know this flat we're in? Did you ever stop and wonder how it became free just as we arrived? Did you?"

"Well, I, um..."

"Did you?"

"No."

"Julia had Milton toss the tenants out. On May Day. May Day! Men, women and children, booted out onto the street to make way for you, the vanguard of proletariat. But you sleep just fine here, don't you!"

"Stop it!"

"Because you Reds are all the same, all talk until it comes time to pay the bills. I cannot believe you dare to criticize Meyer. You wouldn't even be here if not for my father."

"And if not for me and my aunt, you'd be saddled with a five year old bastard instead of just being a plain old spinster."

All color drained from Zipre's face. She stepped toward Rivka and slapped her hard across the face.

Rivka stood stunned for an instant, and then dropped her

head in tears as Zipre grabbed her shawl and stormed out of the apartment via the hallway door.

THE TWO WOMEN walked briskly arm-in-arm, scarf-covered heads tilted down partly to navigate around the bevy of foul organic obstacles that littered the pedestrian routes of the Lower East Side, but mostly to avoid eye contact with those walking, those sitting on stoops, or those congregating in front of taverns along the way. One of them knew the fastest route to Ridge Street by heart, passing by it by six days a week walking from her home on Willett Street to the bottle factory she worked in at Avenue B and Third.

The block was typical. One side of the street was a solid row of six-story flats with a zigzag of black-iron fire escapes tacked to the brick and limestone façade. The other side was the same, save the two buildings in the middle that the women headed for which had airshafts on either side. One of the women read the street number etched into the keystone over the doorway, "*Ciento once—esto es.*"

The front door flew open and a well-dressed man with his top hat pulled low over his forehead bolted out before racing off in a motor car a bit too fancy for this neighborhood.

One of the women gestured toward the red stained-glass lamp behind a heavily barred garden level window, "*Ellos son putas.*"

"*Putas Judías,*" the other one answered, knocking on the door.

At first it was a typical brothel, part of the burgeoning supply of houses catering to anyone with a few dollars—subject to the brutal supply and demand economics that operated at the lower levels of prostitution. Like most houses of prostitution, the pressure for volume, fed by a river of soldiers passing through, drove the common denominator lower and lower, bringing with it the fights and credit problems commensurate with the clientele. The problem, in Julia's parlance, was that "Bad clients mean bad girls. Bad clients can't pay for good girls. Good clients won't pay for bad girls. So we need to get good girls and good clients all at the same time."

Marta was in charge of the house. Room by room, she transformed the building into a replica of a Fifth Avenue luxury apartment, not that any likely client would actually know what that was supposed to be like. The main floor had a fancy mahogany bar stocked with French cognac and cigars from Cuba. Most importantly, the lounging and greeting areas were segmented by walls and thick tapestries, all designed to offer the clientele strict anonymity.

Julia booked the men, who all liked and respected her or they were not invited back. It was Julia's idea to transform the business from one where men chose from a line up to one where all but the least experienced girls were available by appointment only. Volume dropped and prices skyrocketed. She had a saying that encapsulated what would quickly become one of the most successful houses in all of Manhattan: "Men have no appetite for a dish you have made too much of, but men have an unlimited appetite for a dish they think you're out of." Within two years Marta was recruiting a wide range of beauties to become "ladies in residence" for stints limited to three months at a time. A popular girl could make in a week what a seamstress or a baker would earn in a year. Milton was in charge of enforcing the strict conduct codes for both the girls and their clients. As the business grew, Julia's reputation for quality and discretion spread throughout the southern part of the island. Her encyclopedic knowledge of baseball, horseracing, boxing, and the movies also made her fine company for the civic officials and up-and-coming businessmen of lower Manhattan.

The iron plate on the door opened, revealing a masculine pair of blue-gray eyes.

"We are looking for Hullia—"

"Get lost. We don't need no girls." Milton slammed closed the plate.

"Excuse me, Christopher," Julia said rising from a love seat by the door to address Milton. "Who was it?"

"Coupl'a girls lookin' fer work. Look like gypsies." Another knock. Milton looked perturbed. "Don't worry ma'am, I'll send 'em packin.'"

"I'll take it, Milton." Julia turned back to the sergeant, "Chris, give me a minute, wont you? Have a drink." She walked to the door and opened the slide. "Two? Never come here in pairs. What the hell am I supposed to do when one is homely and one is a knockout? You sisters?"

The pretty one spoke, "Hullia. We look for Hullia."

"Julia?"

"*Si, si, Hulia Harmon.*" She held up the onionskin with her name and address. Julia shut the slide and pulled the deadbolt.

"Oh my God, I'm so sorry. I am Julia Harmon. Please, come in . *¿El español? Entre.* Thank you, *gracias. Entre.*"

Neither budged from the stoop. "*No, gracias.*"

Milton poked out from behind Julia, "Everything okay, ma'am?"

"Yes, yes. Go."

The older woman spoke in fractured English, "I am Frieda Saldago. My husband and your brother were expelled together. This is Isabella, my sister. Five letters come to her flat yesterday. We deliver." She nodded at her sister and she handed the letter to Julia. "Now we leave."

They turned and descended the three stone treads to the sidewalk. Julia stared at the return address written on the letter: Elia Reifer c/o Casa de Unión de Trabajadores, Obispo 20, La Habana, Cuba. "Please, come in. Allow me to thank you!" Julia called.

The two women stopped and turned. "May God forgive you," the older woman said as she crossed herself. As Julia closed the house door, the younger woman spit on the corner of her building.

Havana • 15th of Iyyar, 5679 – Thursday, May 15, 1919

ELIA AND MIGUEL turned the corner and passed under the *Paifang* into *El Barrio Chino*, picking up a sea breeze, bringing much needed relief from the heat and the flies. "This is my favorite part of Havana," Miguel said with a hint of pride.

"Why's that?" Elia asked as he tossed his cigarette into a rain-filled pothole.

"Look around; no one stands out. The rich in silk, the poor in rags. Artisans, sailors, priests and whores; no questions asked."

They turned onto a dead-end when Miguel stopped walking, "You're sure you want to go through with it?"

Elia exhaled heavily. "The bastards ripped our lives apart over a book." He put his hand on Miguel's shoulder and drew him close. "A book. A bunch of words keeps us from our loved ones."

"To the capitalists, these are not just words."

"We both are on the list. You heard what they said at the Union Hall; we have no chance. None, forever. Check and mate."

"Nonsense, my friend, there is always hope. In Havana, forever has a habit of becoming tomorrow."

"Fine, but today, the capitalists must pay." Miguel shrugged as Elia continued. "They jail me for my thoughts, for my beliefs; for being a revolutionary. So now a revolutionary I will be."

"You're a thinker, not a fighter, Elia."

"I'm done thinking. To them, the punishment for words is the same as the consequence of actions."

"Just—"

"I am what I am, Miguel. Besides, Rivka and I have a pact."

"Just be careful. These are very serious people."

"So am I."

The Spaniard pointed to the *cervezaria* across the street, "There. Through the door, in back. Keep your head down and don't look at anybody on the way in. And remember to knock three times."

"What gets me in with them?"

"Just be yourself, Elia. Answer the questions. The Mexican just needs to know you're not an amateur."

Elia dodged a horse-wagon, walked in and hustled through the dark to a door in the back. He knocked three times. Nothing. A bead of sweat ran down his forehead into his eye, stinging. The door cracked open just enough for a man to be seen head to toe. Younger and taller than Elia, with an aggressive posture and a complex face, he had a flattened nose, a cinnamon complexion, and a squared-off jaw under deep, almond-shaped eyes set at an angle that gave away a trace of Eastern origin. He flashed a grin that sent chills down Elia's spine before disappearing back into the room.

A dim electric bulb dangled from the ceiling, casting eerie shadows on the walls.

"Bolt it and sit," said the man at the far end of a large square table that took up nearly the whole room. He was a dark, fat, older man, his badly yellowed teeth crushing the end of a cigar that he puffed on intermittently through a fixed grin. To his right was a man in a stylish but ill-pressed light-hued suit, looking like a waiter from one of the better *cantinas* down by the wharf.

"Smoke? Drink?" said the man to Elia's left, as he pushed a wooden tray toward him.

Elia snapped up a cigarette, studying the three mute men, silently practicing the soliloquies he would use to pass the test.

"Speak."

Elia sat up in the chair, looking across the table, "I am Elia R—"

The order-giver interrupted him, "We don't care."

Elia lit up as the man across the table continued.

"Perhaps where you are from it is allowed to be openly revolutionary? Perhaps there are no secret police to hang you upside-down and beat your man-parts with rubber hoses? Maybe they don't murder your brothers and rape your sisters when they find out who you are? But in Cuba they do. So you will know only this cell by code name. Only I know the next cell. This way, if you are taken, you can give up only four."

"I would never betray—"

"So we organize with stealth and guile to survive; no one has a name, no one has a family to betray." The man patted his chest. "They call me El Quintana or just Quino. This is Taíno and our comrade in the fine attire is Milo."

Elia extended his hand. No one took it. "History!" Quintana barked at Elia.

"You want to know about me?" The leader nodded. "I am a worker from Galicia. I was taken from the island in New York and deported for being a socialist. They found my *Manifesto*. I wish to, to continue the struggle. I was a Bundist before the war, before I was taken into the army. The Austrian army, for years. During the war I embraced bolshevism. Now I want to extend the work of Lenin around the globe."

"Army? Capitalist tool," Milo dismissed.

"Ten million pressed into to war. They cannot all be tools," Taíno retorted.

"Armed and trained yet they did their master's bidding instead of defending their class. We don't need a sheep."

"Sheep? While you were sipping cool tea under the palms, he was in the trenches, learning the arts of war." Taíno turned to Milo. "Ever put a bullet between someone's eyes?

Ever killed a man? Well?" Milo shook his head. "Who's the sheep then?" Taíno pointed his finger at Elia. "You. You ever kill anyone?" He snickered. "Of course you have. You were a soldier in the war." He laughed. "How many? One? Ten? Fifty? Taíno's face turned dead serious. "Galicia's no sheep; he's a wolf, and we could use a trained killer."

Elia's hand had a slight tremble as he drew on his cigarette. Everyone else turned to the older man awaiting his judgment. "Bundists are thinkers but they are all talk and no action. We are not about talk. We are not about debate. We are not about politics. We are about revolution." Elia nodded. "So I have three questions for you. First, are you about talk or are you about revolution?"

"I am a revolutionary," Elia said, looking the Mexican in the eyes.

"Good. Second, are you willing to do anything for the revolution?"

"Yes."

"Excellent. The third is much easier. What shall you be known as?"

Elia wandered back in time to the Fort. "Hirko. Call me Hirko."

Everyone shook hands while Milo poured four shots of rum and distributed them. "El Hirko," Taíno said, lifting his glass. Everyone emptied their drinks then looked at Taíno. "Hirko, meet me Saturday, in front of the station at nine." Elia cocked his head as a wicked grin oozed from the edges of Taíno's mouth. "Initiation."

New York • 16th of Iyyar, 5679 – Friday, May 16, 1919

ON ARRIVAL, EVERYONE agreed that the Oak Room at the Algonquin Hotel was the perfect locale for a farewell dinner.

For Rosa and Teddy, it was an elevator ride away, for Rivka it was a return to the First Class dining room on La Savoie. For Milton it was a great steak, for Julia, a place to see and be seen, and for Zipre, it was one last chance to be with Theodore.

The sommelier expertly sliced off the lead capsule and twisted the screw into the cork, removing it with a dramatic pull and a muted pop. Checking the neckline of the bottle for remnant he nodded his approval and sniffed at the cork, similarly impressed. "Chateau Latour, o-four." His eyes raced around the table, lingering on Teddy before settling on Milton, pouring a taste into his glass. Julia immediately reached across the table and seized the goblet.

Draining it, she glanced over at the sommelier, "It'll do."

"Ma'am." He nodded, then filled all but Teddy's glass before departing, leaving the bottle next to Julia.

"Dinner's on Sir Barton tonight," Julia said. "None for six as a two year old. Ran the Derby as a rabbit for Billy Kelly. Led wire to wire. Two-ten on a heavy track."

"That's a lot of numbers," Teddy said.

"The only numbers you need to care about is thirty to one." She picked up the Latour and emptied it into Teddy's glass. "Odds."

Teddy lifted, "To Sir Barton."

"Here, here!" They each sipped.

Teddy swirled the wine around the inside of his mouth before swallowing it. He smacked his lips before speaking. "Julia, I read how everyone ate horses in Przemyśl during the war. Better to bet them then to eat them, yes?"

"Absolutely, my boy."

Teddy set his glass down and spoke to the group with a scholarly look. "So the siege of Przemyśl reminds one of the siege of Troy, but with this difference; that at Troy the men sat in horses, whereas at Przemyśl the horses were sitting in the men![8]"

Rivka burst into laughter. Zipre, who was sipping water from a glass, had to cover her mouth to avoid spraying the other diners. Rosa leaned over and whispered in Julia's ear, soon causing her to join in the revelry. They continued to exchange bon mots and laugh over two courses of starters. After lemon coconut sorbet, Zipre excused herself for the powder room. A few moments later, Rivka also excused herself.

Rivka pushed the smoked glass swing door to the Oak Room's ladies room open and walked in, confronted by a crystal chandelier, two pedestal sinks in front of floor to ceiling mirrors framed in ornate etching and marble privy stalls, all resting on a granite inlayed floor spelling out a graceful script "A." Rivka walked to one of the sinks and began to wash her hands.

A flush and the sound of a bolt sliding proceeded Zipre's appearance at the sink next to Rivka. The women rubbed their hands together vigorous under streams of warm water, their eyes fixed on the brass drains at the bottom of their respective porcelain basins.

"Zipporah, this is insane."

Zipre turned the ivory stopcock to the off position.

"After all we've been through. I can't stand to lose you."

Zipre took a towel from the small pile on the ledge beneath the sink.

"Please, accept my apology. We can't fight, not now. I need you."

Zipre dried her hands and tossed the towel into the wicker basket between the sinks as she turned to face Rivka.

Their eyes met in a stare that quickly softened. "Goddamn it, Zipre, I'm sorry," Rivka said, lips pursed, shaking.

Zipre let out a sigh. "I need you too, Riv. I really do."

"Then you—"

Zipre cut her off. "Forgive you. Yes, I forgive you. But only if you forgive me too."

"For what?" Rivka queried.

"For being so damn condescending. For judging you."

"I'm sure I earned it," Rivka said, extending her arms. As they embraced, Zipre began to cry. "I was stupid. We're like sisters. Sisters should not compare the favors they do for each other."

Zipre pushed back, their eyes met. "What makes everyone so goddamn sure they did me a favor?" She wiped her cheek dry.

Rivka recoiled, "What?"

"I was raped, it was awful and I will never fully recover from it. But what about the baby? What did it do wrong? Tell me, what did my baby do wrong?"

"But is wasn't a—"

"Listen, I was seventeen and I told you and Gitla to do it. It was my decision and I blame no one but myself. But make no mistake, it was no great gift. How do you think I feel every single time I see a five-year-old girl tugging at her mother's dress? Or a boy throwing a ball in the park?"

"I had no idea."

"Remember how Gitla said it was a raisin?"

Rivka nodded.

"She lied."

"Oh God, I never saw it that way. I just assumed, I just thought, I guess I just didn't think about it."

"I know. No one did. Not even me, until later." She extended her arms. "Friends?"

Rivka hesitated. "Look Rivka, I'm not mad or anything. It is what it is. I just needed you to understand how I feel about this. You're my best friend. It's part of who I am."

Rivka started to shiver. "It's not that, Zipre. There's something I have to tell you and it may hurt."

"What?"

"Promise you won't hate me. Promise."

"What is it?"

"I'm pregnant."

A smile spread across Zipre's face. "I've known since we landed. I wasn't born yesterday."

Again they embraced tightly.

Rivka stepped back, consternation on her face, "We best get back before they think we're lesbians."

Zipre slapped her playfully on the thigh, "You are such a bad, bad girl, Rivka Arm."

Fueled by Latour and the rapprochement of Rivka and Zipre, the mood over the main course was markedly improved. The girls chatted like gossiping schoolgirls all the way through dessert. As the waiters cleared the last of the dishes, there was a lull in conversation. Rosa seized the moment, leaning in over the table, raising both arms to bring the attention of everyone to her. "So, friends, what's the plan for Elia?"

Everyone looked at Julia. "I made some enquiries." She lowered her voice to just above a whisper. "He has a file in a room on the island with a red stamp on it. Pull that record and he's just a Jew from Cuba."

"What about transit papers?" Rosa asked.

"He'll need to get those in Havana."

"From what I hear, you can buy anything in Havana," Zipre said.

"How are we going to get to his file?" Rivka asked.

"I know an alderman. He knows a cop. The cop has a buddy who..."

"Four degrees removed?"

Julia wagged her finger at Rivka. "Listen missy, it's the way it works here. Everything that happens starts with knowing someone who knows someone. And I end up with a name—a name of a clerk on the island with access to our precious records. From there, it's up to us."

"Up to us to find the right mix of the twin oils that lubricate business the City: bribes and threats," Teddy said.

Everyone chuckled nervously except Julia who tapped her

temple with her finger and said, "Yiddisher Kop."

Zipre took the floor. "So the plan is as follows, someone will have to go to Havana to find Elia and secure transit papers for him. Back here, we will need to apply," she smiled at Teddy, "oil to this clerk, known only by name."

"I'll go to Cuba," Rivka said. "With Zipre."

The waiters brought coffee and a plate of cookies forcing the plotters to hold their tongues.

"I guess that leaves me with the threats and bribes," Julia said.

Rosa stirred a teaspoon of sugar into her coffee. "With all respect, Rivka, I'm afraid yours is an extraordinarily poor idea. First of all, you two girls cannot leave the country—not citizens—too risky. Besides, then you need three new sets of transit papers for Cuba instead of just one. Most importantly, Julia needs to be the one to grease the wheels of justice for Elia's return to Ellis—none of us here has anything even close to her *savoir faire* in such realms." She sipped her coffee.

"Then who goes to Havana to get Elia?" Zipre asked.

Teddy blurted, "We're on a ship—"

Rosa lifted her index finger. "My son has always wanted to see the great canal. As his term at Berkeley does not start until September, I was able to book us on the Ventura to San Francisco via Acapulco, Panama City, Veracruz," she said, reaching for a chocolate-covered shortbread cookie. "And Havana."

"We sail Monday; parcels and mail at nine, anchors up at noon," Teddy added.

Havana • 17th of Iyyar, 5679 – Saturday, May 17, 1919

IGNORING THE INCREASINGLY vocal come-ons from the prostitutes working the entrance of the station, Elia headed toward the darkened alcoves in front of a row of tightly shuttered shops at the far end of Calle Arsenal. Out of the reach of the many arc-lamps illuminating the train plaza in garish yellow, Elia smoked a cigarette while trying to spot his contact amidst the churning swell of pedestrians. As he crossed Calle Egido they made eye contact and a tilt of Taíno's head had them heading toward Curazao, a diagonal that led into the heart of La Habana Vieja, where the city's details faded quickly to undifferentiated gray.

They walked wordlessly through a series of quick turns: across boulevards, down small streets, and up narrow alleys until Taíno pulled Elia into a doorway. After unlocking the door and pushing Elia through it, Taíno stuck his head out for one last peek around the corner. Confident they hadn't been followed, he joined Elia, bolting the door behind him.

The room was pitch-black and smelled of solvents. There was a loud metallic crash, then another.

"Goddamn it!" Elia heard him say from the dark before a low-watt light clicked on, illuminating Taíno's reptilian grin.

Taíno pointed to a large glass jug near the wall. "I'll hold the carboy, you tip the barrel."

"What's the plan?" Elia asked, tipping the surprisingly light barrel onto its rim.

"His name is Villavicencio. Capitalist and monopolist."

Elia braced himself and lowered the edge of the barrel until the petrol trickled out into the jug.

"Raised sugar prices. The biggest crop in Cuban history and they raised the price. How many starved? And he fired the workers who complained."

"Pig. How many?"

"He fires us, we fire him back, yes comrade?" As they finished, some gasoline spilled on Taíno's hands and pants.

After the Cuban stuffed a large cork into the top of the bottle, Elia hoisted it onto his shoulder, securing it with one arm. They hiked through the old city and down the Prado Marti, which was packed with strolling merrymakers and scandalously dressed whores. The carboy on Elia's shoulder went unnoticed, thought to be beer, rum, or some other fuel for another night of debauchery.

Taíno pointed across and down the alley. "There it is."

"You sure?"

"That's one of his factories. Let's teach the bastard a lesson, yes?"

"Tell me again what he did."

Taíno checked for onlookers then headed for the back of the factory. Elia followed.

"Let's go, army-man. Time for some revolution," he said with, eyes afire while a dog barked in the distance.

The small crowbar that the Cuban had brought just barely moved the hasp so Elia set the jug down to try his hand. While he was tugging, Taíno fished through the garbage bins in the alley, retrieving a length of metal pipe. The longer lever did the trick, ripping the four screws along with a sizable chunk of wood from the door-frame with a loud groan. Both men froze when the dog barked again before quiet settled again on the alley.

"Quickly!" the Cuban urged. Both men rushed inside.

"Tell me, what, exactly, did Villavicencio do?" Elia lifted the carboy and Taíno pulled the cork and then supervised the spreading of petrol through the nearly dark establishment.

"Get back to the door, Hirko! We're both soaked. Let's not go up with the building." As they made for the door, Taíno wiped his hands on his shirt then struck a match, illuminating him, bringing every curve on his smirking face into perfect focus as he tossed the flame into the store. "Run!"

Elia stared motionless into the business, now fully illuminated by the fast moving conflagration. "You idiot! It's not a factory, it's a store!" he screamed. "The wrong place, goddamn it!"

"Yes, a store. He gouged the neighborhood."

"But you said—" Something exploded in the store.

"Run!"

They dashed back through a different series of quick turns: across boulevards, down small streets and up narrow alleys until they were back in the garage and the door was bolted behind them.

"So army-man, we start the revolution!"

Elia ignored him, focusing instead on the steel-chain block-and-tackle hanging from the ceiling with a gigantic, soot-covered motor dangling beneath it.

"Be proud, comrade."

"Don't comrade me, you bastard! What the hell did we just do?"

"We burned down a capitalist's store."

"You told me he was a sugar baron, not the corner grocer."

"What's the difference?"

Elia wiped sweat and petrol from his brow with his shirttail.

"Come on, killer, it was the time for action."

Elia looked him in the eyes, stone-faced. "Do not call me killer. Do you understand? Never."

Taíno briefly lost his smirk. "What are you going to do? What?" He flashed his evil smile again. "Kill me?"

Elia looked at the wall of specialized tools, particularly at the crowbars. "I'm warning you."

They glared at each other until Taíno eased into a smile and began to nod his head. "You misread me, comrade. I mean it not as a slight, but as the highest of complements. You are a hero."

Elia finally exhaled. "Hero? Hardly."

"I'm serious. As a man, I've been in my share of fights.

Some I've won others I've been beaten within an inch of my life. But fights change only relations between men. It is war that alters the dynamics of nations. I've scared a few capitalist swine; you've moved mountains. The army is the way to revolution. Lenin may have inspired with his oration, but without armed, disciplined troops, he'd have been just another raving hot-head." He glanced around the shop, then at Elia. "In fact, I am thinking about joining the army in the next year."

"It's not what you think it is."

"Tell me what it's like."

"What are you, insane? There's no glory. If mountains move, it's a shovelful at a time. It's hell."

"Tell me about open combat."

"Since you're so impressed with me, why don't I just tell you about the first man I shot? About your hero's first kill."

"That would be—"

"He was a capitalist. A Bolshevik. An anarchist. No, he wasn't anything; he was just a target. No one in war is anything but a target. And you know where your hero shot him?" Elia poked his finger at Taíno. "In the heart? In the head? No, I shot him in the back. He was running away and I shot him in the back. Quite a hero, eh?"

"Still, I—"

"Then there was my friend, my brother, my comrade, Manes. A hero if ever there was one. Ten times the man either of us will ever be. One second we're sharing a cigarette, the next moment he's dead. Gone. Cold. Forever. Who killed him? British? Italian? Why? In war, the shell doesn't care about politics. The shrapnel couldn't care less if it tears through a goat or a hero."

"So?"

"And finally, in a coup de grace, the hero lights up a sugar baron's factory—or is it a gouger's business—or did he just torch some poor family's grocery store?"

“We did what we were told to do. What we had to do. Like you did in the war.”

“Whatever meaning you need to draw from this, by all means, draw. Just don’t smile when you call me killer and don’t ever call me a hero or I swear you’ll—”

“May I remind you who’s in charge here? You’re upset. Don’t say anything you’ll regret in the morning.”

“Morning? Are you joking? I’ve done things I’ll regret every hour of every single day of the rest of my life. And who the hell are you to tell—”

“Easy, Hirko.”

“Fuck Hirko. My name’s Elia. From Medyka.”

“And I’m Fulgencio. From Banes.”

Elia stared at the Cuban with his lips held firmly together, eyes tightened and skin flushed. Fulgencio stared back with equal ferocity before the left side of his mouth began to lift and tremble, contorting his face into a crooked, unconvincing grin.

Fulgencio extended his hand, “Comrade. We’ve had a tense night; we’re both wound a bit too tight. Why don’t we forget all this and go have a drink, as friends.”

Elia looked at his hand, “Get your filthy hand out of my face.” He backed away slowly, toward the door.

“*Bastardo.*” Fulgencio pulled his hand back. “No one leaves the cell.”

Elia turned and ripped the door open.

“And no one refuses the hand of Fulgencio Batista! No one!”

Elia ran out into the street.

“You’re a dead man, Elia!” Batista yelled. “If I ever see you again, you’re a dead man!”

Elia ran to past the edge of town. After scrubbing his body with sand in the ocean, he fell asleep behind a stand of yucca on the beach.

Odessa • 18th of Iyyar, 5679 – Sunday, May 18, 1919

JONAS TAPPED TOMAS'S right fist, which he opened, revealing a pawn. He held it up to his son. "Black. Say black, son." Jonas smiled, then took the pawn and began to set up the board sitting between them on the cot.

Malka dressed while Lea played at her feet. "I know what you think, but I'm going back to the factory. We really don't have any other choice. Eighty rubles is eighty rubles," she added.

Tomas and Jonas played speed chess, each move taking no more than five seconds. "And a loaf of bread is what, five-hundred? It's as hopeless as it is insane," Tomas replied. "We need to head back to Italy."

Malka picked up Lea and her Steiff elephant doll that she hadn't let go of since Vienna, and dropped her on Tomas's lap. "No, and I will not have that kind of talk around the children. The *Hashomir* and the Rabbis are in talks directly with Denikin—right to the top—no intermediaries to bribe. I know they'll let our boat go this time."

"Let's hope the third time's a charm." Tomas pushed a pawn. "Sending our Reds to ask for favors from a White General was not this rabble's finest political maneuver."

"*Poalei Zion* isn't exactly Reds, more like—" Malka shrieked, then jumped on the cot, scattering the chessmen.

"What? What's wrong?"

"Rat!"

Tomas rolled his eyes as Lea scurried into her mother's lap.

"Please, kill it," she begged.

Tomas swung his legs to the deck and slipped into his shoes. As he reached for the cracked engine rod that he kept propped in the corner by the bed, the rat scurried under the canvas curtain that divided the steerage hall into family cabins. "Some other Zionist's problem now."

Malka brushed Lea's hair. "Don't worry sweetheart, it'll all be fine when we get to Jaffa. There aren't any rats in Palestine, only camels."

Tomas let the rod hit the floor loudly. "We're not going to Jaffa. Not on this garbage scow and not from here."

"Oh yes we are."

"Listen Malka, I love you and I love the kids, but enough's enough. I'm tired of boxcars, I'm tired of Odessa, and I'm tired of this stinking boat. I've been shot at for five years. Five years! So don't tell me that everything will be rosy tomorrow. I'm sick to death of tomorrow."

"We're here, aren't we? Alive, I do believe."

"Dumb luck; the rock-stupid mathematics of war. That a bullet didn't find us, a germ didn't infect us, or plain old starvation didn't take us, is just—"

"God."

"A statistical anomaly."

"No, it's fate. We're going to get to—"

"Enough! To hell with fate. Was it God's will that the Reds and Whites should trade off occupying Odessa—not once but four times—just when we arrive? God may have a plan for you, but he sure as hell doesn't seem to have one for the rest of us." Tomas exhaled loudly. "I'm sick and tired of God."

Jonas began setting up the chess pieces while Malka began to brush Lea's hair, trying to keep her from crying. "That is so sad, Tomas."

"You've known how I feel about it."

"To think that we four find ourselves on the Roslan in Odessa harbor as the result of statistics is... sad. To think that Jonas was brought back to you by some equation is lunacy." Jonas banged a pawn on the board. "It's one thing to not believe in God but it's wholly different to have no faith, to believe that there is no purpose. That is truly sad."

"I'm not a sad person, I'm a logical person. I can look

at a set of facts and make educated conjectures about the future."

"Without faith, without believing, there is no happiness. If life is just a big machine with each part acting precisely in accordance with the laws of nature, then what is love? Is it just another statistical anomaly? Of course not."

Tomas exhaled toward the ceiling before chuckling. "You're quite the optimist, Malka. I wish, I really do wish, I could see the world like you do. It might actually make more sense."

"I will always love you, Mister Lenard, but you need to understand that we are leaving Odessa on this boat. We will get to Palestine and make it to Ein Gev. We are going to build happy and fulfilling lives for ourselves and for the children."

"And I love you too, Malka, but you need to understand that—"

"Father, your move."

"Jonas?" They swiveled toward the boy. The chess board had been reset exactly as it was before Malka had upended it and Jonas was contemplating the board with the same flat affect his parents had become accustomed to since he came to them in Vienna. Tomas and Malka tackled the boy, and along with Lea, everyone took turns hugging and kissing each other as the chess pieces again scattered.

New York • 19th of Iyyar, 5679 – Monday, May 19, 1919

"HOW YOU FEELING, Rivka?"

She patted her stomach, "Tired."

"Good. Let's take Broadway, I need to pick up a German paper."

"Sure Zipre."

"It's Sarah, S-A-R-A-H."

"All right already, Sarah Weiss, baker's assistant." They

walked arm in arm at a fast clip south on the grand boulevard.

"My back is shot, and I don't think I can even feel my hands. I need a hot bath in the worst way. Wiltz is such a putz; a slave driver."

"Poor Sarah!"

"And a lecher. He should be arrested."

"Oh, how I wish I could bottle this moment of enlightenment for all times," Rivka said grandly. Only ten hours kneading dough and the golden child of the bourgeoisie embraces worker's solidarity; calls for revolution."

"I must admit, labor does focus one's attention on the darker dynamics of capitalism."

"Say it loud, sister-comrade!"

"Not so fast, comrade Arm.

"The capitalist pedigree is strong in her!"

"I think that we can agree on one thing—after tasting Wiltz's breads the Vienna Model Bakery wouldn't make it ten minutes in Vienna."

"Or Przemyśl, for that matter. Say, any word on your accounts?" Rivka asked.

"That's just too hysterical, sister-comrade!" Sarah said in her own grand voice. "Oh, how I wish I could bottle this moment of enlightenment for all times. Only ten hours kneading dough and the vanguard of the proletariat embraces a bourgeois' bank account."

Rivka raised one bushy eyebrow. "Touché, S-A-R-A-H Weiss. Touché."

"Oh, I'm just pulling on your leg. Anyway, all the bank would say is that the account has been frozen. I cabled father on Monday. No word yet."

"I'm sure it's just some spanner in the works."

"Probably. But things are not all that good back home. Poles and Ruthians are at it."

"Again."

"Currency all over the continent is becoming worthless."

"The system collapses under its own weight."

"I'm worried about Meyer." They turned east on Houston, stopping at Max's News and Candy, a sliver of a storefront on the corner of Lafayette. Sarah went in and re-emerged with a newspaper and a bag of popcorn.

"What's the news from *das Vaterland*?"

Sarah read silently.

"What?" protested Rivka.

She continued to read, opening the paper to continue an article. "They still won't trade Marks until the surrender agreements are signed. Only the neutral countries are making a market. In Switzerland, it's down over seventy per cent. If you do the mathematics, a Mark here would be worth…" they crossed the Bowery. "Seven cents."

"Oh my God."

"And dropping fast."

"Don't worry; your dad's the shrewdest banker in Galicia."

"Which would be fine if there still were a Galicia."

"Good point."

"Listen, I've still got a few hundred dollars and we both have steady jobs. No worries!"

"You disobeyed you father and ran off to America. I'm pregnant and my husband's in Cuba, a deported undesirable. No worries."

"Rosa and Teddy are on their way to Havana."

"And Julia goes to see the clerk next week."

"Perhaps we'll have a good Shabbat."

"Perhaps."

They walked in silence, munching on popcorn. After crossing Houston they saw two paddy wagons heading up Ridge and could see that there was one more being loaded with girls by policemen in front of the stoop at Number 111. "Damn," Rivka said, recognizing a Captain from his previous visits to the house. "Cross and keep walking," Sarah said under her breath.

They spent the next two nights on the couch of a co-worker over on Stanton, a few blocks away, before agreeing to a seven month sub-lease for a small but private single at the end of a five-story climb in their friend's building.

Twelve

Havana • 21st of Iyyar, 5679 – Wednesday, May 21, 1919

"*VEINTE CALLE DE Obispo, por favor*," Rosa said to the driver as they climbed into the old Ford, her spirits lifted by the change in aroma from ocean detritus to smoldering tobacco. While the driver looked and dressed nothing like her late husband, the sweet cigar aroma brought back memories of the Officer's Club in Nagasaki. No matter how hot and humid it was Robert would always be bathed, moustache trimmed, sporting a clean white shirt, a tie and a coat while working. She smiled, and then turned to her son, "It lacks the drama of the ravines, but with the ocean smells, the port complex, and especially the stifling heat and humidity, it reminds me a little of Nagasaki."

Five city blocks later the taxi turned off the Avenue Del Puerto, putting the harbor behind them, heading into La Habana Vieja, coming to a stop a few intersections later. The driver parked in the shade and pointed two doors up the street. Rosa paid him three American dollars, more than twice the usual fare. "Teddy, tell him to wait. And stay with him."

"But mama—"

She raised her finger.

Rosa walked into the Casa de Unión de Trabajadores' reception hall either completely unnoticed or thoroughly ignored. She stood in the hall, taking in the frenetic scene around her. An artist was painting a wall as men argued in six languages next to a table with a small printing press manned by three dark women. There were children everywhere.

Wielding a photograph of Elia from the previous autumn, she circulated through the building. Most of the adults, suspicious of well-dressed people, tried to avoid her or refused even to look at the photo. The few who would look either said they didn't recognize him or simply shook their heads and walked away, even after she rattled the coins in her dress pocket. Discouraged after ten minutes, she headed down the concrete steps to the sidewalk.

Just before Rosa got back to the taxicab she became aware of footsteps following her. She spun around. "Are you following me? Who are you?"

The man looked back at the entrance to the Casa then quickly scanned up and down the street before pointing to the archway of the apartment building they were standing in front of. Rosa signaled to Teddy that she was all right before joining the man under the arch.

"Missus Reifer?"

"I am a friend. Do you know where he is?"

"Why are you here?"

"I'm here to help him."

"What's his woman's name?"

"Rivka."

The man smiled, relieved. "I am Miguel. We were on the boat together."

"Rosa Pike." She gestured toward the car. "And my son, Theodore. We crossed the Atlantic with Elia and Rivka."

"I know."

They shook hands. "Pleasure," she said. "I hate to be rude, but we sail in a few hours. I have to find him and arrange for papers."

"Papers? That takes weeks."

"I have some connections."

Miguel raised his eyebrows.

"So, where is he?"

"There was..."

"What?"

"Trouble. He became involved with some bad people, *Pistoleros*"

"Is he hurt?"

"He'll be all right."

"Where?"

"There is much new building being done to the west. Many men hired for construction."

Rosa pulled a small roll of bills from her pocket, peeled off an American ten. She offered what was a small fortune to Miguel.

"I don't want your money."

"No, take it. Please."

"I don't know why you're helping Elia, but I can only assume that it's because you are a caring person. Yes? So allow me to put my terms it terms that you will appreciate. Elia has his Rivka, I have my Frieda."

Soon Rosa and Miguel were back in the taxi with Teddy, heading out of town to the west, along the coastal road.

"There, at the sign. Pull in," Miguel said, pointing.

Teddy read, "*Nuevo Club Náutico de Miramar.*"

The ocean stretched across more than half their field of vision behind the nearly finished club. It was a cream-colored stucco structure, laid out with two wings off a main building, set at obtuse angles to follow the arc of the cove on which it sat. Where each of the two wings met the main building, stylized lighthouses soared five stories into the air.

The top of each of the three structures were covered with workers and small piles of masonry.

Miguel told the driver to turn off the engine and wait before pointing to a well-trodden path that led into the scrub-covered rise to the right of the development. A hundred meters later they came to clearing; a garbage dump, littered with broken crates, empty petrol drums, and assorted construction debris. Their noisy approach had the half-dozen or so people who lived in the dump scurrying for cover, like roaches fleeing a kitchen light.

"He's here," Miguel said.

"A socialist hiding at a yacht club. Now that's irony for you," Teddy said, dryly.

THE WAITER BROUGHT Rosa a pot of tea and poured it into a tall glass over ice with fresh mint and sugar. Teddy and Elia ate black beans with ham, washed down with carbonated lime water. Miguel drank beer while he wasn't working on a bowl of steamed clams. They talked, each bringing the other up to date on the circumstances that led to their having lunch at a café on the waterfront at Playa Baracoa.

"Rosa, I can't accept this," Elia pleaded.

"The last time someone turned down money I pushed at them," Rosa mused, looking at Miguel, then back to Elia, "he ended up blackmailing me."

"It was not blackmail. I would have told her where you were," Mig protested. "You know me."

Rosa patted him on the shoulder. "You're what we call a *mensch*, Miguel. How about we just call it emotional blackmail?"

Everyone had a good chuckle before Elia turned serious. "Rosa, I mean it, I can't accept this money. It violates everything I believe in, everything that is me," Elia protested, sliding the wad of bills back across the table at Rosa. "Don't worry, I'll be fine."

With surprising speed Rosa pushed the bills back toward him then held his wrist in place, sandwiching the twenty dollar bills between Elia's palm and the table. She wagged a free finger at him, "Mister Reifer—"

Teddy sat back into his wicker chair.

"You're stranded in Cuba, flat broke, gangsters are out to kill you, and you've slept for a week in a pile of garbage." Rosa's finger made exclamation points in the air with each phrase she spoke. "'I'll be fine' just doesn't cut it."

"I've been through worse, Missus Pike."

"Don't be wise with me, Elia Reifer," she said, her tone turning distinctly authoritarian. "You may have seen war and you might have been through hardship, but you've never been responsible for your own child and until you do, you don't really know accountability."

"All right, but for now, it's just me. Me and Rivka. And we'll get by, we've got morals and we've got pride. And revolution is our life."

"If there is one thing I can speak to you about with great authority, it is that life does not always follow the script you write. I didn't plan to get sick in Japan and I didn't expect to marry the doctor that nursed me to health. And I certainly didn't expect him to pass on so soon, leaving me at the far corner of the earth with a little boy. It would have been easy to quit, bobbing up and down in the river of life, pushed only by the current, but that is not how a responsible adult acts, not one with the responsibility of a child."

"I understand it. You have children so you understand responsibility. What you don't seem to understand is just how far I'm—we're—willing to go to build a new world."

She knocked on her head with her fist. "I don't know why we're even here, why I even bothered coming to Cuba. Maybe I misjudged you, Elia Reifer."

Elia exhaled while looking up at the sky. "Rosa, please,

I'm sorry." He looked back to her, "Everything came apart for us at home. We are dead to our roots. We can never return. We'd lost everything except each other. Then there was Paris and Savoie, like a dream, a fairy tale of taste and art, of romance and friendship. Then from the highest of highs, it all comes crashing down again." He put his free hand on top of hers. "You've been the closest thing I've had to a mother since we escaped, since Gitla. And I don't really know why you do it. I'm not sure that we're worthy."

Rosa looked sternly at Elia, "Buck up and listen to me, Mister Reifer." Her finger pointed to within inches of his forehead. "The Pikes do not take people under their wings casually. But when we do, we have a few principals that must be adhered to. First, there is nothing wrong with charity. Second, we do not want to be paid back. Rather, if the circumstance ever arises, help out a worthy stranger. Third, we don't keep an account of deeds, God does that for us." She let go of his wrist, "Are you with me?"

"Yes ma'am. And I thank you."

"I don't know what they did to you, and I don't want to know. I just need you to grow up; stop being so selfish."

"I'm trying to, Missus Pike. Life doesn't always cooperate."

"If you're half the man I know you are, you'll put your happiness, your pride, even your beliefs aside and put the needs of your children first. There must be no limit to what you are willing to endure for the good of your issue, now and forever after. Get it?"

"Um, yes."

"So do you see now why you must take the money?"

"Yes, but I don't—"

"Givalt! Men can be such idiots."

"You sound just like my aunt."

She shook her finger at Elia, "For heaven sakes, Rivka is carrying your baby."

His fist closed around the money; the lull in conversation

filled by the sounds of breaking surf and foraging gulls.

Teddy glanced at his watch. "If we leave now, the embassy should be open by the time we get back to town."

ICED TEA, COFFEE, and cookies were served by two stern-faced men in crisply pressed uniforms on the embassy's palm-shaded veranda.

Rosa poured cream into her coffee. "Thank you for seeing me on such short notice, Commander McGerr. We're only here until seventeen-hundred."

"Once a navy wife, always a navy wife."

"Thank you, I appreciate your hospitality." She sipped her coffee. "I feel very much at home here."

"The pleasure's all mine. I can't tell you how delighted I am to finally meet you in person, Missus Pike." He stirred his iced tea. "As you know, I fancy myself something of a historian."

"Of course, but Havana is such an important post for our Navy. Perhaps the single most strategic port anywhere. Where do you find the time?"

"Naval attaché is my vocation, but history is my passion. Well, history and opera. In any case, I'm writing a book about Perry's first anchorage at Edo Harbor—the Black Ships, the opening of Nippon—that sort of thing."

"I still have the *katana* he brought back."

"Amazing. I have so many questions for you about Lieutenant Pike, and letters can never take the place of an in-person interview."

"You know, Commander, that I never met my father-in-law in person."

"Please, call me Michael."

By the time she was done talking, McGerr had taken nearly a dozen pages of notes, and had promised Rosa a prominent spot on the acknowledgements page of his book.

As the waiters cleared the service, an ensign delivered two sets of steamer tickets to New York, along with travel papers embossed with the official seal of the United States Navy.

New York • 22nd of Iyyar, 5679 – Thursday, May 22, 1919

THURSDAY AFTERNOON MILTON dropped off a large envelope for Rivka Arm in care of the Vienna Model Bakery, 788 Broadway. Sarah by her side, she opened it as soon as the quit-whistle went off. Inside were two letters, one addressed to each woman in Julia's barely legible script. Rivka opened hers first.

WESTERN UNION
HAVANA CUBA 22 MAY 1919
JULIA HARMON 111 RIDGE STREET NYC USA

NEED PAPERS MIGUEL SALGADO AND E
ARR MONTSERRAT 26 MAY
LOVE R AND T

Scribbled on the cable was:

See Hutchinson. Say you know Mickelson. –JH

"Thank God," Rivka whispered.

Sarah flipped open *The Times* to page thirteen and scanned the Shipping and Mails in the last column. "Leviathan from Brest... El Norte from Galveston... Caronia from Liverpool... here it is, Montserrat from Havana. Due Monday. You know we're going to have to go see Hutchinson tomorrow."

"I know."

Sarah opened the much thicker letter. She liked seeing

her American name in print, even if in penmanship it resembled that of a six year old. Inside were several legal looking documents. "The deeds to the buildings, and this, I think—yes, it's called, what—yes, here, 'Power of Attorney.'"

Przemyśl • 22nd of Iyyar, 5679 – Thursday, May 22, 1919

"PAWN TO QUEEN'S four."

"Pawn to queen's four."

Jurek pushed his white queen's bishop pawn forward, undefended into the teeth of Meyer's defenses. "Any word from your daughter?"

"Queen's gambit?" Meyer queried, contemplating the board as if it were a fancy desert with a big fuzzy-green mold on it.

"I'll take that as no."

"*Putz.*"

Jurek smiled and drew deeply on his cigar. Tapping the ash from the smoldering tip into the ash tray, he exhaled then addressed his friend, "You know, Meyer, in thirty years you've never once failed to complain about an opening. There's no pleasing some people."

Meyer leaned back in his chair and repeated the cigar ritual. "Every decision, every move early in the game leads to trouble."

"Oh, please."

"There is no right move. I take, you have an open file, I decline, and you hold a sword over my head."

"Meyer," the Pole said, leaning in toward the Jew. "You can win either way. In chess, in life, one move in the opening does not a game make."

"Unless it's a blunder."

"Players like us do not blunder, at least not in the opening." Jurek caught the eye of the waiter and signaled him with a wave of his index finger.

Meyer reached across the board, "Pawn takes Pawn."

"Accepted; excellent. You know, Meyer, openings, to players of our caliber, are a bore. Every gambit, every variation already played a million times, analyzed and documented. Quite one dimensional, really."

"Agreed. You know the same could be said about the end. It's more subtle for sure, but ultimately, at least for strong players, nothing but mechanics and tempo."

"The middle's the real game: gambits, sacrifices, and attacks."

Meyer stared, transfixed, as reflected light danced off the deeply etched surface of his empty glass. "She calls herself Sarah."

"Who?"

"My Zipporah is now Sarah. She's in America, in New York." The waiter arrived with vodka. Positioning a small glass in front of each man he poured each three-quarter full from a decanter before scurrying off to take orders from a group of military men who had just arrived.

"I know, with that couple." Jurek winked. "It's a fine place for her. With Europe in ruins and Russia with the Reds, America is in perfect position for the future. All of the opening variations are done."

Meyer picked up his glass, emptied it in a single swallow then eased back into his red velvet chair. "Then I guess it's time for the real part of the game to start."

New York • 23rd of Iyyar, 5679 – Friday, May 23, 1919

THE GROWING NUMBER of detainees on the island made the authorities nervous, so they banned anyone who didn't have a good excuse from riding the ferry. If the Red sympathizers were going to make scenes and foment protests, better it happen at the Battery than on Ellis Island. Nevertheless, "We have an appointment with Mister Hutchinson," was ample for Rivka and Sarah to secure the twenty-minute passage. The ride was choppy and Rivka vomited just after landing.

They walked toward the Great Hall, reviewing the plan. "Remember, we have less than three hundred so we need to start much lower," Sarah cautioned.

"What if he says no?"

"Calm down. The more agitated we appear, the higher the price."

"Worse still, what if he has us arrested?"

Sarah put her arm on Rivka's shoulder and stopped, each turning to face each other. "Rivka, we already know he's on the take. Julia doesn't know anyone who isn't on the take. We just won't let him say no. Okay?"

"Thanks."

"You ready?"

"Let's go."

The door has a panel on it with the words "Mr. P. Hutchinson, Asst. Mgr. Records" etched onto the smoked glass insert. After what seemed like eternity, it opened and a man said, "Please, come in." It was a private office, barely big enough to fit a desk, a metal file cabinet and a single chair in front of the desk that had to be angled just so in order for the door to be freely opened and closed. A bulb hung at the end of a cord over the desk. Rivka took the chair, Sarah stood beside her. Hutchinson rearranged the mess on his desk with an air of supreme importance. Abruptly stopping, but not in any sense finished, he looked up. "So, what can I do for you?"

He was a slight, balding man wearing a grey flannel suit that appeared to be a size too large. It was hard to tell if he was closer to twenty five or fifty.

Sarah composed herself, determined to choose each

word carefully before speaking, “We are friends of Mister Mickelson.” No reaction to the name, none. “He suggested we speak with you; that perhaps you might be able to offer us assistance.”

“And who might we be?”

“Pardon my manners. I am Miss Weiss and this is my cousin, Missus Reifer.”

“Citizens?”

“We are legally admitted, working aliens, looking forward to becoming American citizens.”

“I see. And what kind of assistance are you seeking?”

“My husband, Mister Elia Reifer, arrived last month—”

“First class, on La Savoie,” Sarah interjected, thinking that Rivka’s accented English wouldn’t help. “It seems, somehow, that between the liner and this island, some anarchist, possibly a Bolshevik, stashed one of his vile diatribes in her husband’s valise. It was discovered on inspection and he was denied entry.”

“Go on.”

“I have known this couple for quite some time and I can attest to you that they are not anarchists.”

“Then why doesn’t your cousin’s husband file an appeal?”

“Oh we would. Yes, of that there can be no doubt. But, unfortunately, time does not permit us to work through the appropriate legal channels. Rivka, Missus Reifer here,” Sarah lowered her voice to just above a whisper, “she’s with child.”

He nodded his head. “Yes, I see. So what can I do?”

“Well, if, perhaps, his record were to go missing...”

He glanced at the photograph on his desk, his wife and two young children Sarah assumed, then back at her. “Do go on.”

“Most of our funds are still in transit from the continent. We can offer you one hundred dollars in gratuity if you can facilitate his re-landing.”

"Wait here." He rose from his desk and was out the door.

"Is he going for the guards?" Rivka asked Sarah.

"He's going to check the files."

Hutchinson returned surprisingly quickly. After securing the lock on the door he sat on the edge of the desk, one foot on the floor, the other dangling next to Rivka. In his hand he clutched a manila folder.

Rivka spoke, "I see you've found his—"

"Let's cut the BS, shall we?"

"I was just—"

Sarah put her arm on Rivka and squeezed gently. "Yes, let's get down to business Mister Hutchinson."

He dropped the folder into Rivka's lap. "First of all, your husband, or whoever he is, is as Red as a tomato in September. So don't offend me by sayin' he ain't. Okay?" He waited. "I said, okay?"

"Okay," both women replied.

"Good. Now yes, his records can be misplaced, but this is particularly hard to do as he was caught with the goods out and out, open and shut. So understand that one hundred isn't even close to the number needed to fix a problem like this. In fact, it's a bit insulting."

"But it's all we have," Sarah said.

"I see."

"Really!"

"You think I'm an idiot?"

"No sir."

"Then you expect me to believe that a bunch of kikes come over here first class on a ship like Savoie and all you brought with you is a lousy hundred bucks? Please." He stood and walked around to his chair. "I wasn't born yesterday, you know."

Sarah fumed at herself for having impulsively shown her hand, thinking of how her father would have scolded her relentlessly for committing such an obvious blunder.

"How much?"

"Five hundred."

Sarah thought through the possible moves, taking into account her precarious financial condition, running through the permutations in her head, quickly settling on the best possible gambit. "Rivka, will you please excuse us for a moment?"

"What?"

Sarah lifted at her arm, pulling her from the chair. "Please excuse us." She moved her friend toward the door.

"No, I'm—"

"Rivka, please! Don't argue with me."

"But—"

The door closed behind Sarah and she moved to where she was facing the assistant manager across the desk. She stared at him and he returned the gaze.

"So, Miss Weiss?"

With a hand she reached for and released the clasp holding her hair fast on her head. "Call me Sarah." She shook her head gently back and forth and her tresses cascaded down her neck and over her shoulders. She unbuttoned the top clasp on her blouse, parting the fabric along with a few stray hairs, inhaling deeply to accentuate the depth of her ivory cleavage. "Two hundred."

"Ma'am, please." Hutchinson tugged nervously at his collar.

Sarah put a hand on the table and began to walk around to where the clerk was seated, dragging her hand across his desk as she moved. His stare moved from her chest to the hand. As it approached him, he recoiled, pressing himself hard against his chair back, avoiding her hand as if it were attached to some sort of monster. "Mister Hutchinson," she cooed. When she reached him she let her hand slide off the table, on to his thigh where it wandered purposefully.

He was trapped in the chair up against the wall. To one

side he could see his wife and children, staring at him, their smiles now shouting in disgust and outrage. To the other side, inches from his nose, were two shockingly exposed, sickeningly alluring breasts. "Please. Please. I think I'm going to be ill."

Sarah moved the crevice between her breasts to within an inch of his nose, "Two hundred, Mister Hutchinson. Do we have a deal?"

He sprung out of the chair, interposing the table between them.

"Well?" She moved around the table toward him.

He moved, keeping her a full desk away. "All right, fine, whatever. Please, just button up."

She put her hands on her top button. "Then we have a deal?"

"Yes."

"There is one more little item," Sarah said, tugging at the neckline of her blouse. "I think he was a sick deportee. Healthy now. A Mister Miguel Salgado—"

"I'll do what I can, now please, leave!"

Sarah turned away from him and secured her buttons before opening her handbag.

"Not here," Hutchinson said in a loud whisper, wiping his forehead with a handkerchief.

"Where?"

"Meet me… Meet me at the corner of Pearl and Fulton. Six fifteen. Know where it is?"

"I'll find it. You just bring the files. Two files."

"It's right by the Brooklyn Bridge."

"Convenient to your home then," Sarah said, flashing a very brief smile.

"How? Listen, I don't ever want to see you as much as set foot in Brooklyn. If you do, I swear I'll—"

"Once this is done, this never happened; we never met, Mister Hutchinson." She made for the door.

"TWO HUNDRED. EXCHANGE this afternoon."

"Thank God. Can we trust him after we pay him?"

"You know what Rivka? That's exactly what he's thinking about us right now."

How'd you do it?"

"I reasoned with him."

"Why alone? What did you tell him?"

"Like Teddy said, bribes and threats."

"You didn't tell him about Milton, did you?"

"There are things that some men are more scared of than thugs."

"Like what?"

She cupped her breasts in her hands, "These."

"No!"

"Oh, yes. Only took one button. I was willing to go to two."

Rivka laughed before abruptly stopping. She thought for a moment before continuing, "So what the hell were you going to do if he took you up on it? If he wanted a sample of the goods?"

"Oh, I knew he wouldn't. Look at him, such a—"

"You had no plan, did you? My God, Zipre, were you planning to let him have his way with you?"

"I took a risk. A calculated gamble."

"You didn't answer my question."

"This is serious stuff, Rivka. Lives are at stake. We don't always get to choose between black and white, sometimes, we have to go with gray."

Rivka raised her voice. "Answer me. Would you have slept with him?"

"I don't know."

Eastern Mediterranean • 25th of Iyyar, 5679 – Sunday, May 25, 1919

"WE TOOK THE Bari from Trieste."

"Did you say Trieste?"

"Why, yes, I did."

"You came by boat from Trieste?"

"Yes."

The color drained from Tomas's face and he lost focus on the slightly older man with whom he'd struck up a conversation.

"What's wrong?" the stranger asked.

Tomas turned his head aft, following the ship's wake back to the rapidly shrinking port of Limassol. "I don't know if I should laugh…" He leaned heavily on the ship's railing. "Or cry."

A hand gently squeezed Lenard's shoulder. "In my life as a scholar, a physician, and a Jew, it has always been quite obvious that when you have a choice between laugh and cry you are invariably better off selecting the laughing route."

Tomas stood upright and offered his hand. "Tomas Lenard."

They shook. "Martin Scherzer." Somewhat portly with a full but well-groomed beard, which, like his hair, was pitch black, he wore his spectacles at the very end of his rather large nose, peering over the top of them for any object more than an arm's length away.

"The walk of a drunken sailor," Lenard mumbled before laughing out loud.

"What's so funny, Mister Lenard?"

"It's just that we were in Trieste five months ago. There were no ships, so we had to find an alternate port. We traveled all the way to Odessa by train."

"Ah, yes. The drunken sailor of Brownian motion. I get it now."

"I'm sorry; I don't mean to be rude."

"Of course not. Ugly time to be touring Russia, though."

"When we arrived, Odessa was no, what is it, Berlin? Frankfurt?"

"Tübingen. I was a doctor, a surgeon, actually, during the war; before that I lectured at University. Trieste was merely our port of embarkation."

"Ours too, or at least that was the plan."

"Our train, our boat to Limassol, our transfer to the Roslan, all smooth as a baby's bottom."

"Of course." Tomas smiled while exhaling and shaking his head back and forth. "Ours was as smooth as a wood rasp."

"I'm sorry."

"No need to apologize, we're fine now. It's just mathematics, I guess."

"Hard trip but you still have your humor. That's a blessing." Martin pulled a leather pouch from his jacket and began preparing a pipe. After several failed attempts at ignition, Tomas moved close to him, cupping his hands around the match until the tobacco glowed bright red in the rapidly ebbing twilight. After several puffs, Martin was satisfied with the effort and nodded his head. "Mathematician?"

"Prisoner and mechanic is probably the most apt description, but I digress. Professor of Physics and Mathematics, Budapest and Szeged. Retired."

"Tillie, my wife, has family in the Crimea." He massaged the bowl of his pipe. "Actually, her father. She's heard nothing for months other than what horrors we read of in the newspapers."

"A Jew?" Tomas asked.

"Yes. Her father is, or was, a surgeon in the Imperial German Navy. Last we heard his ship made port at Sevastopol. Almost exactly one year ago."

Tomas exhaled loudly, shaking his head.

They both leaned on the railing and looked out to sea. The slice of moon had become obscured by clouds as full darkness descended on the eastern Mediterranean. The two men stood in silence for several minutes.

"Children?" Martin asked.

"Jonas and Lea. Fourteen and three. You?"

"Two." He went silent for a moment. "One. Harold. I'm joining him at Rothschild Hospital in Jerusalem."

Tomas looked out toward the dark ocher glow a few degrees above the horizon. "We're headed for Ein Gev, a cooperative in the north. She read about it in a Zionist publication then fell in love with a photograph of the Kinneret."

"Interesting way to choose a life."

"That's my Malka."

"So you're to be farmers?"

"I suppose so."

"Know anything about the agricultural arts?"

"No, but I'm sure we will figure it out."

"How?"

"Reason." There was a break in the clouds overhead; Tomas gazed at the stars in the Pleiades. "And faith."

New York • 26th of Iyyar, 5679 – Monday, May 26, 1919

IT PROVED MUCH easier for Sarah to post the bond required to get Julia out of jail than to explain to her exactly what a second mortgage was. Harder still was the argument over what to do with the house, which was like a running gun battle that started as soon as Julia was sprung and continued all the way to Battery Park.

Sarah was adamant, "Between what you pay the girls and buying off the police, from the beat cops up to their captain, you make *bubkis*. And what happens when a precinct comes under scrutiny from City Hall? I'll tell you what. They toss your behind in jail."

"So how do you want to put bread on the table, open a bakery?"

"You're not listening! Two things are going on. The bankers in this town are aching to lend money on the cheap and everyone wants a nicer apartment. We took five thousand out of Ridge Street after a five minute meeting with the bank."

"Yes, but if the rents aren't paid, we lose the building!"

"That depends."

"How?"

"You paid ten thousand for Ridge, right?"

"Five in cash and borrowed five."

"Right. But I just took five out, so how much do you have in the place now?"

"Nothin', I guess."

"But we still own it."

"How?"

"Because the value of the place went way up."

"So what happens if the value keeps going up and you sell it?"

"We pay off the bank..."

"And keep the rest as profit."

"And if the value goes down?"

"We give it back to the bank. Walk away."

Julia smiled. "No risk."

THREE BLASTS FROM the Montserrat's foghorn pulled Elia from sleep. He sat up in his cot, trying desperately to focus the images from his dream which were disappearing like constellations at dawn. As he slipped into his shoes, a fully formed, if not highly abstract, vision of Rivka splayed on the bed of the hotel in Paris filled his senses. A moment later it was replaced by an inspector yelling for guards in the hall on Ellis Island. Elia's stomach ached; he fumbled for his cigarettes before heading upstairs to the promenade.

The fresh air and sunshine cleared Elia's head as he found a viewing spot along the railing.

"*Buenos días, Elia,*" a voice said over his shoulder.

Elia turned to see Miguel surveying the panorama. "*Buenos días, Miguel.*"

The two men embraced tightly as a pair of gulls hovered high over the deck before peeling off toward the shore.

"Good luck, Elia," the Spaniard whispered.

"And to you, comrade."

"Let's hope our women were convincing."

"Otherwise..." Elia started humming *The International.* After the first few bars, Miguel joined him. The two men stayed embraced on the deck of the ship until the song ended.

Elia leaned his elbows on the gritty railing, one foot on his small valise, the other braced against a row of silver-dollar sized rivets lining on a piece of steel ribbing that protruded from the deck. Neither man spoke as the city's skyline grew on the horizon by the minute, details of its shining towers and belching smokestacks emerging through damp eyes barely held open against a fresh offshore breeze.

"Elia?"

"Sorry, I was drifting."

"Thinking about a name?"

"Kind of... I need to have a cigarette. There's something I need to do; to decide on. Alone, I'm afraid."

Miguel nodded.

Elia picked up his bag and made for the stern of the ship, largely deserted as the better view of the Statue, Coney Island and the Manhattan skyline was off the bow. He found a spot against the lee bulkhead and lit a cigarette.

"We need to talk, Manes." Smoke rushed over his shoulder as he exhaled. "My friend, my comrade, my brother, my dear, dear Manes, I know you're here with me and I know you'll know what I should do." Elia knelt, opened his valise, and wrapped his hands around Manes's book. Clutching it to his chest, he inched his way to the gunwale.

"Maybe you know that Rivka carries my child—maybe from where you are you see everything. Doesn't this mean I have to toss it? You're a father too so you have to see that nothing—not happiness, not belief, not even principal—comes before your own flesh and blood." Elia leaned out over the railing; oil-soaked trash bobbed in the water as medicinal odors wafted in over Staten Island from the densely packed factories on the New Jersey shoreline. "But I have never felt as connected to the working class and have never been more committed to the revolution then I am at this moment. And if I am willing to jettison all I believe in so easily, what kind of father could I possibly be?" Elia brought the book to his lips then balanced it on the boat's gently arched gunwale. He filled his lungs with a long deep pull, exhaling as he spoke, "So what do I do Manes? What shall I become, a principled deserter or a responsible coward?"

A gust flipped open the leather cover and turned the pages one by one before the *Manifesto* fell from the railing, As the ship's foghorn cut through the rumble of the boat's turbines, Elia laughed triumphantly into the wind then flicked his cigarette into the foaming black waters of New York Harbor.

Afterword

If it is axiomatic that you only experience your grandparents in their senior years, then how can you know who and what they were in their youth? For those with great family continuity, taking stock of them in their early years is comparatively easy – just look at your parents or your own early life and extrapolate back in time. But what could I do? My grandparents were immigrants from a place with strange traditions, different languages, and an opaque history. Comparisons rang hollow and my experience was worthless because there just wasn't anything analogous between my youth in Vietnam-era America and Belle Epoch Imperial Austrian Galicia where they spent their formative years.

Luckily, a few months before my grandmother died, I flew down to Miami to spend the weekend with my Bubbie Fannie before heading to the beach with my college friends. Over the course of two late nights she told me her life story - not the familiar, middle-aged one that I knew by heart that started with my mother's birth, but another one. It was a story about her when she was *my* age.

It was a story of war, of siege, of cannons and marauding Cossacks. It was set in some unpronounceable town in a nation that no longer exists in a time before radios and airlines. A beautiful place with rivers, castles, forts, forests and parks; a place where people stayed up late, drinking and smoking in cafés and beer halls or taking in theater and cinema. There was joy and love, but there was also hardship, heartbreak, and death; the highs seemed higher, the lows, definitely lower. This wasn't the gray, drab shtetl I'd imagined; it was dangerous, dynamic, edgy, and dare I say, *fun*. To my utter astonishment, Grandma and Grandpa were, once upon a time, *cool*.

"11th of Av" is a work of fiction. Nonetheless, the inspiration for much of the plot and many of the personalities are drawn from the memory of that weekend some thirty years ago.

Elia and Rivka were inspired by my mother's parents, Emanuel Silberman and Fannie Metzger. Both grew up in Przemyśl and were there for the Great War and the siege. Emanuel (or Manny as I knew him) really did work in a furniture factory and was a dedicated socialist, at least until the Nazi-Soviet pact of 1939. He served in the Polish Army and saw action at Caporetto on the Austrian side of the Italian front where he contracted malaria. To the best of my knowledge, Fannie never killed anything other than the occasional piece of *flanken.*

Fannie immigrated to the Lower East Side of New York in 1925. Manny was detained at Ellis Island as an "anarchist," denied entry into America, and deported to Havana where he worked as a waiter and joined a "cell" that included Fulgencio Batista. He made at least one attempt to sneak into America as a stowaway, spending four months in jail at Ellis Island in 1928 before again being deported. Family lore has it that Fannie bribed an immigration clerk into allowing Manny to enter the U.S. in 1931. A garment union organizer for the International Worker's Order after immigrating to America, and a pressman back when the presses were made of asbestos, Manny was also a life-long smoker of unfiltered Chesterfields. He died of lung cancer way too young.

Teddy and Rosa are Theodore Bowie and Rosa Muriechowski Bowie, my wife's father and grandmother. She was from Odessa and really did marry a U.S. Naval doctor in Japan. If you happen to be in Nagasaki, you can visit Dr. Robert Bowie's grave in the Sakamoto Foreigner's Cemetery. Theodore Bowie grew up in Nice, France and was, if anything, smarter, wittier and even more cultured in real life than I was able to portray in this story.

Isidore Besser, the baker, is the name of my father's

grandfather. In real life his daughter Rose married Morris Semmel, my grandfather. Rose and Morris were the owner-proprietors of the Ansonia Bakery in Brooklyn from the mid-'20s through the depression. I believe that they made *semmel* rolls.

Most of the other characters stem from very small slivers of family lore. An aunt mentioning a second cousin who "left her husband and came to America because he was a drunk," was the inspiration for Jette. My great-great grandmother Blima Malz was a well-known Przemysl midwife. She morphed into Gitla.

In the twenty-plus years since the last of my grandparents passed away, I've come to see that not only were they "cool," they were also driven, courageous, loving people replete with all the warts and flaws we all share as human beings. Were they Elia and Rivka? No, they were real people with infinitely complex, interwoven lives that we can only minimally access and crudely recreate.

They were not Elia and Rivka, but they could have been.

Acknowledgments

There are so many people I'd like to thank for helping me to finally bring this novel to print. Forgive me if I've forgotten someone: my parents Dorothy and Melvyn Semmel, my sister Lisa Sharp, aunt and family matriarch Evelyn Blustein, dear friends Mark and Marcie Achler, Lee Rosenberg, and Alanna Clare, readers Randall Marks and Roma Baran, editors Rebecca Peters-Golden and Kathleen Connors, map maker Martin Bordovsky Horne, graphic artist Lesa Petersen, design and technology whiz Robert Wadholm, Jewish Przemyśl experts Dr. John Hartman and Lukasz Biedka, and Yiddish maven Professor Jeffrey Veidlinger.

Several sources were used in researching this novel. First and foremost, there is the Przemysl Memorial Book, Sefer Przemysl, published in Israel by Irgun Yotzei Przemysl, 1964 in Hebrew and Yiddish, translations from the JewishGen Yizkor Book Project website at: http://www.jewishgen.org/yizkor/przemysl/przemysl.html I'd also like to thank the Austro-Hungarian Land Forces 1848-1918 website at http://www.austro-hungarian-army.co.uk/index.htm for an excellent history lesson.

Finally, there is my muse, my uber-editor, and the love of my life, my wife, Jocelyn Bowie. Exacting, demanding, yet unwaveringly supportive, Jocelyn talked me through each plot turn and re-united all my infinitives while keeping me focused on the character's motivation, personality, and soul. Without her, this novel would just be a pile of words. Thank you, sweetheart.

Historical Characters

Béla Guttmann: Hungarian-Jewish football star and coach
Vladimir Medem: Russian Bund leader
Jozef Pilsudski: Polish Nationalist Leader
Generalmajor Unschuld von Melasfeld: Commander 47th Infantry Brigade
Hermann Kusmanek von Burgneustätten: Austrian Commander of Przemyśl
Field-Marshal-Lt. von Tamassy: Hungarian second in command, Przemyśl
General Artamonoff: Russian Commander of Przemyśl, 1915
Ruben Fulgencio Batista Zaldívar: Cuban dictator 1930s-50s

Notes

1 Excerpts from Bund and Zionism A. Merezhin, July, 1918
2 Quote of Archduke Franz Ferdinand
3 In 1914 Colonel Unschuld was in command of the 71st regiment.
4 German: *Kaiserlich und königlich.* Imperial and Royal. Refers to the Dual Monarchy of Austria-Hungary.
5 Kusmanek speech quoted from The Great War part 48, July 17, 1915 Edited by H. Wilson.
6 From The War of the Nations Edgar Wallace, CHAPTER LXII
7 From the Communist Manifesto K. Marx and F. Engels.
8 New York Times article, "Przemysl and its defenders" March 25, 1915. Un-attributed quote.